D1547791

HEAVEN GOT A GHETTO

Renta

Lock Down Publications and Ca$h
Presents
HEAVEN GOT A GHETTO
A Novel by *Renta*

Renta

Lock Down Publications
P.O. Box 944
Stockbridge, Ga 30281

Visit our website @
www.lockdownpublications.com

Copyright 2021 Renta
HEAVEN GOT A GHETTO

First Edition April 2021
Printed in the United States of America

Lock Down Publications
Like our page on Facebook: Lock Down Publications @
www.facebook.com/lockdownpublications.ldp
Cover design and layout by: **Dynasty Cover Me**
Book interior design by: **Shawn Walker**
Edited by: **Tamira Butler**

4

Stay Connected with Us!

Text **LOCKDOWN** to 22828 to stay up-to-date with new releases, sneak peaks, contests and more...

Thank you.

Submission Guideline.

Submit the first three chapters of your completed manuscript to ldpsubmissions@gmail.com, subject line: Your book's title. The manuscript must be in a .doc file and sent as an attachment. Document should be in Times New Roman, double spaced and in size 12 font. Also, provide your synopsis and full contact information. If sending multiple submissions, they must each be in a separate email.

Have a story but no way to send it electronically? You can still submit to LDP/Ca$h Presents. Send in the first three chapters, written or typed, of your completed manuscript to:

LDP: Submissions Dept
P.O. Box 944
Stockbridge, Ga 30281

DO NOT send original manuscript. Must be a duplicate.

Provide your synopsis and a cover letter containing your full contact information.

Thanks for considering LDP and Ca$h Presents.

Acknowledgements

Have you ever wondered if there's really a God? Wondered why He allows certain shit to happen? I wrote this tale for all the ones that have. Y'all ride with me through the what ifs...the whys, and **real-isms** of my mental. This tale is a little different than my usual, but I vow to create a masterpiece out of this piece of my imagination. I've always been big on the spiritual aspects of life, and now I'm stepping out on the ledge of the shit I've always wondered.

I really didn't plan to write any acknowledgements, but shid, I owe it to so many! Y'all already know how I'm comin', so, I'll start with my fans, those of y'all that rock with me no matter the weather, I love y'all... My fam, loves y'all... and I told y'all we would run it up on 'em! I salute you! Drea, what's the business, lady? You love me? Promise? For you, I'll try it all! You're forever my super woman, mama, and before I turn sour, they can bury me alive and set my casket on fire.

Mama Helen? Mama Leah? You ladies! I love both of y'all with the soul of me. If it wasn't for y'all, I wouldn't even be trying my hand at this author shit. Real spit. Cash, wud up, Big Homie? What you think? I told you, nigga! I truly appreciate the pointers you gave me, my dude. I'm tryna shut the show down!

LDP, we're at their heads! To my niggas... My brothers? Lil' Nukkey, you ain't my daddy, fam! Lol! I love you though, bruh. You keep the boy focused. Dunte, them hoes gonna cut them chains off you soon. We can't afford to lose in the fourth quarter, bro. Nigga, you're my twin, right now, it's all of you. I'm livin' through you, fam. A love too deep.

Papa, Too Black, Waco Shawn Tillis, LeLe, Thugga, TRU, Keylo D, Vino, Katta the boss, Yap, Tee Ashford, E-Man, Ken D, Dino, Joe, White boy AD, Green Eyes, Beta, Fifth Ward Tracy, and all you boys I ain't name, I love you boys and I'm proud to call y'all family. At the end of the day, if a nigga can't trust the ones at the table with 'em, he has to cut off their hands. If you can't trust the ones you claim to love, you may as well put a gun to your chest and blow out your own heart, we all we got! Last but not least, if you're locked behind these walls and want to send your loved ones a gift of any sort, if there is any particular flix you desire, or just need help getting something done beyond those walls, hit us up at B.I.T.S, P.O. Box 2387, Baytown, TX 77521.

For the lowest prices, we can get it done. Hit us and ask for our services, it's official! No bullshit! It's beauty in the struggle, fam, you just have to find it. *B.I.T.S,* Beauty in the struggle, it's more than a business, it's a culture! Y'all get out and vote...

You count... Your vote matters! Come on, fam, Medgar Evers was killed for this! M.L. King's 1963 March on Washington was just for this! There was a time when we couldn't vote... it wasn't legal! Now that our people's blood has paved the way for us, why wouldn't you honor their reasons for dying? We can't fold now! Vote!

Dedication

This book is dedicated to the ones that we've lost, but will never forget. George Floyd, Breonna Taylor, Eric Garner, Sandra Bland, Douglas Lewis, Tamir Rice, Freddy Gray, Trayvon Martin, and the many others that lost their lives due to the color of their skin. Through us, you'll live on, and if there's a ghetto up there, y'all save me a spot. It's beauty in our struggle.

Glossary of Terms

Flesh - a member of RNO's body/of one body, but different DNA.

R.N.O. - Real niggas only/Real niggas official.

Fruits - Knowledge, Raw game, or Truth!

B.L.O.W. - Acronym for boss live niggas owning the world, or brothers loyalty over whatever!

The Table - Answer to a greeting or spoken in reference to everyone at the table with you./The people that's eating with you.

Two-Twenty one - The second and twenty-first letters of the alphabet. B - for business, and the U - for understood.

12:30 - Matthew 12:30 in the Bible.

R.B.O. - Real Bitches only, the female sect of RNO.

NuBians - Spoken in reference to the females of RNO.

Civilian - Outsiders, one that's not at the table with you.

Bless You - A reminder to members of RNO to not speak family business in the presence of civilians or may the Lord bless you during the consequences.

Stick/Pipe - Automatic assault rifle/pole.

Round - Term of endearment between homies from Louisiana. Potna, friend, or bullet.

Diamonds - Tears.
Stepped on - Murdered/spanked.

Renta

In the Beginning
-Heaven-

I stared down at the card for the fifth time that night, hoping it would change, but no matter how much I yearned to tamper with providence, the future couldn't be derailed. I stared at the image of the hooded figure that held a scythe gripped in his left hand—*The reaper!* It was the card of death, and it was the last card I'd drawn in my father's reading. I'd shuffled and redealt the cards over and over again, only to obtain the exact same outcome—*Death!*

"What does it mean, Heaven, why ju looking like that?" my sister, Catrina, asked. I merely glanced up at my father. The black silk Versace shirt was opened at his neck, allowing the gold and diamond necklace to peek out in a teasing shine. The black slacks he wore were tailored to perfection and allowed just a glimpse of his ankles, and I loved the burgundy, Italian loafers he stepped in as he spun my mother around before pulling her in so close to his chest that they seemed to merge as one.

Dalvian Domingo was a boss personified, and he was one of the biggest Dominican drug exporters on this side of the Western hemisphere to ever flood the streets of KKK USA. To many, that qualified him as a monster—a low-down, dirty ma'fucka—but to me, my sister, Catrina, and our mother, Ismerelda Domingo, he was a God. We loved my father *not* merely because he spoiled us rotten, but because he took boss care of his family, and the man was a nurturer at heart. He was everything I wanted my husband to be when that time came. "Heaven, come dance with an old man, Mami, let me show ju a ting or two." He smiled bright with the proposal. Catrina nudged me in encouragement, and with a quick glance, I was forced to smile at the untamed giggles that ensued from her.

Catrina was my beautiful opposite. Whereas I had taken on my father's rich, dark complexion, she'd inherited our mother's high-yellow hue, and though both of our heads were filled with a mass of wavy curls due to our Dominican and Afro American genetics, I usually kept mine in braids or cascading to the back in a waterfall of wet waves. I slid from the couch and made my way over to him, my mother's hazel eyes drowning me within their amber gaze as she smiled at me. She stepped to the side as I took my handsome father's hands in mine and allowed him to choreograph our steps.

At that moment, nothing else mattered outside of that dance with my old man. He had an aura about himself that just made a girl feel like a lady. Johnny Gill's "My, My, My" played softly as we danced. "What have the cards been saying, anything interesting?" He was curious. He'd always found my gift of card reading amusing, but his mother read the cards of providence, and he knew the truth of the spiritual eye. I glanced up at him before resting my head against his chest.

"They're blurry, Papi. They speak of death. I'm scared," I whispered, but my father merely chuckled before kissing the top of my head.

"Nada, Hija, nada. No te preocupes, Mami." He told me not to worry. I smiled.

"Ju tink ju slick, huh, Papi?" I asked him with a mischievous smirk.

"Huh, wha ju speaking of, Princess? I'm jus' having a dance with my baby girl." His Dominican accent was thick as he smiled down at me. I twisted my lips up at him in that *nigga, palease!* kinda way before nodding my head in understanding. At times, I felt as if I knew him better than anyone, including my mother. I think he knew it as well. I always knew when he was preparing to leave out on one of his famous, two-week *business* trips. He smiled down at me. He could see it in my eyes that I was onto him, but rather than verbalize what we both knew, I merely rested my head against his chest and enjoyed the moment. My mother would give him all the grief he could stomach. I just prayed that the reaper wouldn't come for him for a hundred more years.

***

-Ghetto-

Deep in the woods of Opelousas, Louisiana, the moon was full and glared like an evil eye in the black sky. The night was absolute as a giant alligator slipped into the inky blackness of the mossy swamp. The sounds of nature made the night come to life as an ink-black panther stalked through the high brush. It paused to gaze up at a thick, black snake that coiled around a thick branch of a withering tree. The serpent's black tongue flickered at a rapid pace as it paused, sensing another predator. The two predators analyzed each other to see if the other was fit for a meal, until the panther lost interest and slipped into the brush. Deeper into the marsh, a lone shack house slightly sagged from the weight of age, and up its rickety porch steps, deep inside its womb, a beautiful Creole woman chanted in a strange tongue. Her face was illuminated by small flames as she lit the last black candle in a circle of dark energy she'd created in the center of her basement floor.

She'd used goat's blood and snake venom to create a huge, blood-red hexagram, and at each point of the six-point star, a big black candle was aflame. Genevieve Bousard's smooth skin contradicted her sixty-five years of living, and since she rarely left the shelter of the swamp, the folks of Opelousas created wild stories that spoke of a hundred-year-old ugly woman that practiced black magic in that old house in the woods. The stories were only partially true, but as she made her way over to the baby's crib she'd created out of a weed called devil's root and pieces of old oak wood, she gazed down at the sleeping child that made the rumors irrelevant. The only thing that mattered was him. He was the only person in the cold world that loved her, and Genevieve never wanted to share that love.

She remembered the day she walked out to feed the gators and found the newborn lying slightly submerged within the muddy muck of the swamp, inches away from Shelly, a giant gator she'd fed and raised from a hatchling. She figured if Shelly could find peace with the child, so could she. From that day forward, Genevieve nurtured the boy like her own and had grown to love him just as deeply. She reached down and took the infant into her wrinkled hands, and as soon as he was snatched from his sleep, the boy's cries permeated the room.

"Hush now, child, love ja no hurt, yea." Her Cajun dialect was as thick as the mud of the swamp. Yet, her voice was a lullaby that soothed the cries of the child. He became silent as he fixated his big eyes on her. Her dark gaze seemed to tickle him, and the sweet sounds of his laughter filled the room. Genevieve carried him over to the center of the hexagram and placed him in the center of its body. The black candles cast flickering shadows around the room, and as soon as the woman turned to walk away, the boy cried from the absence of her touch. Genevieve laughed.

"Jah heart's weak, but de soul knows not de love of de body, but the existence of survival," she spoke as if he could understand her. Genevieve made her way over to a stone slab she'd converted into a shrine and gazed down at her supplies. There was a blood-spotted butcher's knife she'd used for years, a belladonna, a poisonous perennial herb that was natural to Eurasia and North Africa, a goat's head, and a tin bucket. The pet she'd trapped inside the bucket was aggressive, but the old woman captured it behind its neck and held it tight as she extracted it from its captivity.

The long water moccasin's mouth opened wide. As it writhed and coiled itself around her arm, Genevieve used her free hand to grab the blood-stained knife and very carefully, she positioned the head of the serpent on the cold slab—hiss!

The snake hissed as it bared its teeth, but the old Creole woman smiled wickedly. She'd been handling the slithering reptiles since she'd been passed the art of dark magic earlier on in her life. She raised the blade high above her head while chanting a rapid song in an old Latin tongue, and with a cry of finality, she brought the sharp blade down on the reptile's neck. Dark blood shot forth as the severed head rolled away from the body, but the still active nerves allowed the slick body to hold tight to its perch. The old woman reached for a tin cup that she'd filled to the brim with white rose petals and lifted it under the faucet of blood. She watched as the dark liquid stained the petals of the flower, and once she was *satisfied, she tossed the then limp body of the serpent onto the table and made her way back to her bundle of joy.*

Sensing her presence, the child quieted as if he knew something out of the ordinary was about to take place. With each step, Genevieve's strange tongue became more pronounced—more intense. The temperature seemed to drop as dark shadows played frantically over the walls, and as soon as she reached the circumference of the hexagram, one of the candles blew out, and dark smoke snaked from its wick. The old woman's piercing eyes drifted to it, and as if relit by some dark force, the burnt wick ignited into a burning flame. Genevieve went to her knees and smiled down at the curious eyes of the infant. His love was a possession she called on a dark existence to keep as her own.

She bargained that if he was to ever love or fall in love with another woman, she asked for her soul to be snatched from her body. As she prayed, her fingers became saturated with blood. As she plucked one of the soft petals from the dark substance, Genevieve leaned over the boy and began to bathe him red as she bargained with her soul. She redipped the wet petal before creating a strange sign of blood across his small chest. Her body began to tremble violently as she chanted—shadows began moving over the walls, seemingly from nowhere. The flames of the candles began to drift sideways, and as she placed the cup on the floor, she retrieved the sharp blade. Her eyes were pools of darkness that reflected the dancing flames as she placed it to the palm of her hand.

Genevieve cried out in bliss as its tip pierced her flesh and slid across, creating a burgundy river. The old woman reached out and placed her bloodied palm inches above the infant's forehead. Her body jerked in an unorthodox dance as she bargained, and once her hand made contact with the child's flesh, the air was sucked from her lungs as each of the six candles blew out one at a time!

"Huuuugh!" I exploded up from the mattress, my eyes wild as I tried to gather my sense of reality.

"Damn, Ghetto, what's wrong wit' ya crazy ass, Jea?" Myiesha snapped as she fought her way from underneath the sheets where she'd been swallowing my nature while I was asleep. As soon as

17

my eyes fell to lil' one's pretty face, flashes of our wild night attempted to override the remnants of the recurring dream I'd been having for the past few months. I exhaled a long whoosh of breath before falling back against the pillow.

"Damn, that shit was spooky!" I chuckled. Myiesha slid up beside me and pulled the blanket up midway, her high-yella complexion aglow against the darkness of the room, causing her erect chocolate nipples to salute me like a soljah in the presence of his superior. Lady swiped a curly strand of hair away from her face before attempting the unthinkable. She leaned down to kiss me, and I damn near knocked her lips to the back of her head. Instead, I kept it playa rather than allowing that beast in me to surface. I big faced shawty wit' a gentle shove of the face. "Watch out, Round, you bein' disrespectful, huh." I frowned as I slid from the bed.

"Wha? Nigga, ya spazzin', Jea. It's ya own dick a bitch suckin', and ya actin' like ya shit ain't clean!" Myiesha snaked her neck with that quick attitude that only women from the south had mastered. That sexy way of bein' ugly typa shit, nah mean. My dick was still on strong when I slid my boxers on. I could feel Lady's glare boiling me like a hot pot of crawfish. Me and lil' one had been rockin' since the sandbox, and it seemed like Lady only grew freakier with age. I was on the level wit' piping lil' baby. I'd learned earlier on in my eighteen years of thuggin' that a nigga couldn't be getting to a real bag if he spent all his time between a bitch's thighs.

"That don't mean *I* wanna taste it, feel me?" I laughed at the way she scrunched her nose at me. "Dig, lil' baby, you gotta mash before my memaw wake up, but I'mma bounce wit' ya later though." Myiesha wasn't feelin' my gangsterisms. *Nigga, you got me fucked up!* was what her eyes said before she rolled 'em and got outta bed.

"Ya down bad, ya heard me. Ya think ya gone just keep jumping up and down in this wet, wet and doin' me raw, huh, ya dead wrong, Jea." She pouted as she got dressed. Lil' one was real jazzy, though, Creole descent, 'bout five-five with catlike green eyes. Her stare found mine as the moonlight shone through the window. I momentarily allowed my dick head to think for me, but my pockets defeated the urge of wanting to bury myself inside that pussy. I pulled on a pair of black Levi's before pulling my black and purple LSU hoodie over my head. I reached between the mattress and the box spring to retrieve my bankroll and the triple-black MP I'd stashed. After extracting the thirty to ensure the clip was full, I nodded at the golden slugs that gleamed under the kiss of the moon. Pushin' the clip back into place, I stuffed the burna in the pocket of the hoodie before peeling four hunnid from the knot. I tossed it to her side of the bed just to see if the bitch would have a lil' bit of dignity, but as I watched the smirk spread across Myiesha's face, I knew I could never let a bitch like her be my main gal. A bitch that only saw the money would lead the enemy to her own nigga for the right price.

"Awww, thank you, boo, you know I love ya stank ass, ya just be on ya otha shit, Jea." Her attitude did a three sixty as she snatched the bread up and stuffed it in her bra.

"No doubt, no doubt, but let's dip. I got shit to do, Round."

I ignored her profession of love. Love had never been my motive, and since the only form of love I'd ever believed to be solid was the type that was often built off conditions, I kept my heart in my pocket to remind myself that outside my memaw, Genevieve, the only thang that it should beat for was the love of money. Myiesha's eyes turned to slits.

"Shit to do? So, you'd rather be out in them triflin' ass streets than to be up in dis pussy, Ghetto?" She looked up at me in disgust. The vibrations of my horn saved the lady from a stiff checkin'. I was tired of the good-for-nothin' ass bitch.

Gang Gang on deck, Flesh, wud up! the text read. Myiesha stormed around the bed until she stood before me.

"Let me see ya phone, Ghetto. I know ya not flexin' on me and lettin' ya hoes hit ya jack in the A.M., nah? Ya down bad, Round, and if I was to give one ah these otha niggas this pussy, ya'd be Louisiana hot, so let-me-see-this-mu'fuckin-phone!" She punctuated each word with a poke to my forehead. I chuckled and swept my long dreads out my face before lettin' that gangsta shit peek out *just a little.* As fast as a pit viper, my hand was around her slim neck. I applied enough pressure to scare her, but not enough to kill.

"Bitch, I'm tired of ya ass anyway, ya stay on the dumb shit, Jea! *If* you gave that pussy to anotha nigga?" I laughed.

"Bitch, you don't think I know ya fuckin' Slim from cross Canal, huh? I just don't give a fuck 'bout ya pussy, yea, I'm a boss. Look, I don't wanna see you in the woods no mo', hear me? We ova!" My gangsterisms were absolute. Lady nodded her head in agreement. She knew I was wit' the shit and wouldn't hesitate to dirt sommin. Little did either of us know, that would be our last encounter.

***

- Heaven-

Hours later

"Heaven, Heaven, wake up!" I could hear Catrina's voice from afar. Subconsciously, I could feel her shaking me. "Heaven!" she whispered urgently.

"What! What's up, Catrina, why you ain't sleep, damn?" I hissed as my eyes cracked open and found the clock—*3:30 A.M.*

Oh, hell naw! I thought as I rolled over onto my side and prepared to drift back to sleep. "Catrina, get you some sleep. I'll talk to you manana, aiight."

"But, Heaven, something's wrong with Mama and Papa!" she cried while pulling my shoulder. My eyes popped back open—I was wide awake.

"What!" I was swimming in the waters of confusion. I didn't even remember falling asleep. The last thing I remembered was logging into Facebook and then waking up to my sister's cries. I sat up and wiped the sleep from my eyes.

"What ju talking about, Catrina, aclarar! You're talking in—"

I was saying when the sound of shouting ensued followed by the sound of shattering glass. I shot out the bed and ran over to my dresser. Flinging the bottom drawer open, I frantically searched for the small twenty-five my father had given me for my sixteenth birthday. It was stuffed under my many colors of panties, and as my fingers wrapped around its handle, I had one thing on my mind—*Nobody fucks with my family!* With Catrina on my heels, we snuck out to the long hallway and paused to listen.

"My dude, you must think this a game or summin. I won't ask you again, my G, where the work at?" an unfamiliar voice growled.

"I done told ju, Papi, I don't keep anything here at my—"

Pissshhh! The sound of flesh against flesh brought my father's words to a screeching halt. We lived in a two-story mini-mansion, so the lavish hallways were long. Catrina and I moved like thieves in the night, but the thoughts of our mother and father being harmed sped our footsteps. My heart beat against my small chest like the laws demanding entry. My sister and I crept to the banister that overlooked our spacious living room, and as soon as my eyes captured the scene below, my heart despised the view.

I instinctively pulled Catrina down to the floor, and lying on our bellies, out of sight, we peered down at a nightmare that would brand itself in the collage of my memory bank from that faithful night until the day I took my last breath. My mother and father were bound at the wrists, both bloodied from the hate of the three men that stood over them, holding them at gunpoint. All three wore masks, but it was the one that appeared to be in charge that was on the bullshit. Catrina and I watched in horror as he arched the hand clutching the pistol and brought it down onto the bridge of my mother's nose—*Crack!* The sound of the bone snapping was resounding.

"Ahhh!" she cried as a spray of blood exploded from it.

"Nigga, I'mma break a different part of this hoe's face until you come on wit' it, homie. Don't get yo' peeps spanked ova some shit you can get back!" the leader demanded. His face was concealed by a clown's mask, and it reminded me of *It*.

"Just tell blem, Bralvian, gib 'em wha they want." My mother's words came out in a wheeze due to the destruction of her face. I could feel Catrina crying beside me as our young eyes witnessed

God forsake us. My mother's fear was feeding the evil in the room, and even at that age, I could understand how sour life could become. I knew those savages didn't plan on leaving nothin' breathin' when they left up outta there, even before the words spoken sealed the deal. I guess that same realization became clear to my father when—

"Man, Bos, let's just do what we came to do and get the fuck up outta here! Big Vino's orders were to whack everything movin' and leave everythang else! You—"

"Brah, fuck Vino!" Clown face cut his boy off. The clown's dark eyes shifted to his potna. "That boy done bird fed us for the last time, folk. That nigga ain't out here in these trenches gettin' his hands bloody—*we* is!" he spat before his vision returned to my father, and even from my perch, I could tell that the name of the man who'd sent the hit squad meant something.

No sixteen-year-old girl should see in her father's eyes what I'd witnessed that night. The resolution of a man that *knows* it's over a conflicting peace that can't be placed into words. It's a tug of war of not wanting to let go but knowing that your hands are too slippery to hold onto whatever you're tryin' to hold sacred.

In an instant, things took on a slow-motion effect when, bound, my father lunged for the man with the clown mask. He rammed him with his shoulder. "Vamos a mirar el diablo!" he shouted as he and the man crumbled to the floor.

Let's meet the devil? His words played in my mind. The other two men seemed shocked into place as they watched the clown mask pop off their fallen comrade's head as he wrestled himself on top of my father. Hovering above him, the stranger gazed down at the man I adored more than life and smiled.

"Damn, OG, you shoulda just came up off that bankroll. I woulda at least made this shit quick and painless, but now you 'bout to go to sleep knowin' yo' bitch had to pay for ya sins. We may even see what that pussy talm 'bout before we leave the hoe stankin'," he hissed the evil with a smirk.

"Pinc`he joto tu` die!"

Boom! The lead silenced my father's last words. The sound of the explosion echoed throughout the big house as Catrina's cries became violent. As I pulled her into me to muffle the sound, I watched as one of the other two men disappeared from my view, no doubt on his way to plunder our home for anything of value. My mother's screams crushed my soul. "Nooo, please, God, not my Dalvian. Nooo!" she cried, and before I could stop her, my sister's pain clawed its way up and out her lips.

"Mamaaa, no Mommie, hellllp!" she shouted. In horror, my eyes shot down to the surprised stares of the devil. Two sets of eyes stared, wide eyed, up at where we laid, and once our cover was blown, I did the only sensible thing a child at my age could do. I rushed to my feet and pulled a hysterical Catrina up with me. I'd never shot a gun before, but it didn't take a genius to know that those two niggas didn't give a damn about my experience. Without thinking, I aimed the small pistol down at them, and with my eyes squeezed shut, I pulled the trigger. *Boca! Boca!* The shots scared me so bad, I dropped the gun. My eyes opened to see one of the men racing toward the spiral staircase, and the one that had killed my father gazing up at me with a predatory glare. I snatched Catrina by the hand and tried to flee, but she was so crazed over the events she fought against me.

"Nooo, Heaven, Mamma needs us!" she cried.

"Heaven, run!" our mother demanded. Catrina was still out of it, but I'd lost my patience. I slapped the shit out of her. She calmed and stared at me through wet eyes.

"Catrina, you heard Mama, remember what Papa told us! We have to get to the room!" I shouted as the man ran up the stairs. I pulled her arm. "Come on!" I demanded, and to my relief, her common sense returned by the time the man was a few steps away from the landing. We ran for our lives. "Come onnn, Catrina!" I urged as I heard the footfalls of our pursuer.

Our father was a thinker and had a knack for planning ahead. He must've known that when a man played poker with the game, it was only a matter of time before he was dealt a losing hand. He'd had a safe room built into our house, and the only way to open the bulletproof door was by hand recognition. We made it a few feet away from our safe haven when the hands of fate gave us the middle finger.

"Ahhhhah!" Catrina cried as her foot caught and she crashed to the floor. I slammed my hand into the digital handprint on the wall and glanced back in time to see the masked man round the corner. He was all business as he aimed the pistol and pulled the trigger. *Boom!*

The gun jumped in his hand. The impact of the bullet knocked me back against the door at the same time that the dark hand imprint glowed green.

"Heaven!" I could hear Catrina scream my name, but I'd never felt a pain as excruciating as the shit I was feeling. At that moment, all I wanted to do was die! I watched through blurring eyes as the heartless cock sucker aimed to finish me off, and as the door behind me blew open with a soft decompression, all I could remember was the screams of my baby sister intermingling with the deep growl and barks of Trouble, our ninety-pound pitbull.

"What the fuck!" I could hear the surprised exclamation of one of the men that had stalked into my and my family's fairytale and in one night, stolen our belief in magic.

"Get up, Heaven, we have to get in the room. Get uuppp!" Catrina cried as she banged her hands against my shoulders. I didn't remember crawling into the room, nor the blessing of the door hissing closed to ensure our safety. What I did remember was the cries of the thief that had robbed my family of our peace. I smiled at the snarling attack of our dog as he fought the good fight before a bullet closed his eyes eternally, but what I'd never forget was the second explosion of a gunshot. It was too distant to have come from the man that glared down at us.

It wasn't even the sudden ear-splitting, hysterical screams that ensued from my thirteen-year-old sister that drowned out every other sound, but my heart cracked because that last bullet couldn't have been destined for any other recipient but one person—*my mother!*

***

One Month Later
- No love-

-Heaven-

"Shiiiish, be quiet, nigga, before you wake my lil' cousin up!" I heard Poetry whisper from the other side of the room. They say when it rained it poured, so I guess any sane person would expect a flood, *if* that analogy was even partially correct. It had been a month since it rained inside our home, and even though things could've been worse, I just couldn't bring myself to thank God for small blessings. That night had ended with me being hospitalized for the bullet that pierced me right above where my heart resided, and I didn't know if it was just a strategy the doctors used to scare folks or if thousands of gunshot victims escaped death by inches, but I was told that if the lead would've entered just four inches lower, I wouldn't have been here to tell my story.

My mother? Ismerelda Domingo hadn't escaped death, at least not in the mental or spiritual sense. My queen had taken a bullet to the eye and been left for dead, but God—or maybe the devil—kept air in her lungs so that she could not only live with the loss of her husband, but so that she could admire her blemished reflection. Yet, as I'd observed her those past few weeks, I wondered if she'd been better off dying beside the man she loved. My father never opened his eyes again, and life hadn't been the same for either of us. The feds had been there, plotting to take my father down *that* night! They'd been parked a block away, listening to it all. They'd sat back and watched the three men enter our home but did nothing!

They had to have heard the shots fired—and they did nothing! The only thing those crooked mu'fuckas did was let niggas do their job for them and kill our own people. Two of those men got away that night, but one was caught attempting to burn the getaway car. Our lives? Me and my family? We were kept women. My mother had never worked a day in her life, and sadly, neither of us knew if my father kept a stash. So, when the feds came and put us out on our asses, when our accounts were frozen and the assets seized, *all our asses* were forced out into a world we'd never known existed, with nothin' but the clothes on our backs. My mother and her mother had been at odds ever since my queen left the hood for my dad. My grandmother had warned her of the outcome, but love did to my mother what it had done to every other young woman that thought she knew what she was doing when trading home for love.

Now she'd *earned* the jewel that her mother had been trying to give her for free. We were stuck with my grandmother; in some ratchet ass apartments the natives dubbed the third gate. Village Creek was a molten pot of drama in the murderous streets of Fort Worth, Texas, and that's where Catrina, my mama, and I found ourselves—smack dab in the middle of the bullshit!

"Hisses, slow down, Lil' Truman, we can't make too mu-much noise!" Poetry's soft voice was tinged with pleasurable pain. I was a sixteen-year-old virgin, and though I wasn't lame to the act of sex, I'd never been that close to the art of fuckin'. The headboard knocked as dude drove himself into her, and after a while, Poetry's cries of protest surrendered to the wild thrusts of Lil' Truman's dick. I covered my head with the pillow, but that shit was useless. My eighteen-year-old cousin had no shame. They went at it for hours before dude got his rocks off and slipped back out the window he'd entered through. Shit had changed drastically in my life and little did I know, small blessings could get smaller.

***

-Ghetto-

I pulled the mask down my face before checking the banana on the Draco. All thirty-five seven-point sixty-twos were stuffed down into the clip, and the second one I'd duct taped upside down to it was just as pregnant.

"Look, Flesh, we only got twenty-five minutes to get in this bitch and get out before shit gets ugly. No mo', nothin' less. We goin' in this bitch together and comin' up out this mu'fucka the same way!" My blow, Keist, laid the law down.

We were five deep in the stolen Yukon, Kiest, me, Thugga, and our flesh, Lil' Nukkey. Four official RNO niggas, and the fifth wheel was a civilian I knew as Chucky D, who I'd *neva* fucked with like that. He was one of them niggas that just wanted to be down, but neva took into consideration the cost of ballin'. The clown was a bozo, and the only things he was missin' were the big red nose and the big floppy shoes. Everyone nodded as we locked and loaded, and the only reason I didn't down the clown right then and there was, because not only was it the wrong place and time, but he was also my flesh Keist's relative.

"We doin' for the table, Flesh, no greedy shit!" I added. My blow, Thugga, slid the ape mask down over his face after flicking the butt of a sherm stick out the cracked window.

"Two, twenty-one!" we all spoke in unison, but since you had to be RNO to know the lingo, Chucky D was lost in the sauce. As he and Kiest dapped each other, I gritted on that boy. I didn't trust the bottom feedin' ass nigga, and *he* knew it. Kiest's eyes found me, and after I made sure the nigga Chucky D saw that gangsta shit in my stare, I allowed my vision to lock up with my flesh. No words needed to be exchanged. *Real Niggas Only* was more than a clique and motto, and I really *lived* that shit. My blow nodded his understanding before sliding his gorilla mask down over his face and pushin' his door open. *Show time!* I thought as my eyes went to Lil' Nukkey, who was behind the wheel and our getaway driver.

The little nigga was one of my favorite niggas in this life, and as our eyes locked in the rearview, neither one of our lips needed to move for me to know what Flesh's eyes conveyed. *Any time can be a nigga's last, the love is thick, Blow, just in case.* I nodded before jumpin' out that truck with the squad. We were piped up and 'bout that action as we filed out the stolo. My eyes swept the deserted streets of the small country town. Kiest was the first one to enter the bank, but I could still sense the panic in the air.

"Ohhh my god, please don't hurt anyone, we'll give you the money!" the country ass teller at the first counter declared as she threw her hands in the air.

"You mu'fuckas be easy. Don't fuck around and have to die ova Trump's money. That cracka don't give a damn 'bout nothin' but international connections anyway!" I heard Kiest shout as he rushed over to the first two tellers and waved the stick back and forth between them. "You beautiful bitches come on from back there and keep ya knees and hands still. We don't want nobody to *accidently* hit that button down there," he demanded before nodding at the counters.

"Naw, naw, Grandpaw, don't be a *typical* white person and try and be a hero, come on with it!" Thugga warned while rushing the old security guard who stood frozen with his hand on the butt of his service pistol. The old man's hands shot up before his country ass spat a thick glob of chewing tobacco juice onto the floor. Thugga snatched the .357 out the man's holster and tossed it to me before ruffly snatching dude by the back of his neck and forcing him to the floor. My eyes diverted to the fourth counter where Chucky D was unnecessarily handling a defenseless middle-aged woman. I stuffed the extra burna down into my waist and blocked everything else out. My eyes swept the fear-contorted faces of the crowd. We'd been sitting on that bank for a month straight, and I knew *everythang* about that hoe. *Peeka boooo!* I thought as I spotted my target. I almost burst into laughter at the audacity of the fat fuck that called himself hiding behind a small office chair. Jerry Benedict was the VP of the bank and was one pompous dick sucka. I made my way over to dude and got straight to the bidness.

"Huh, wait, what's going on?" he cried.

"Get ya fat ass up, Jea. Fuck made you think you could hide ya fat ass behind this *skinny* ass chair!" I spat as I struggled to pull dude to his feet, and as soon as he bared witnessed to that gangsta shit in my eyes, old buddy's knees began to knock in fear. The angry gorilla mask was a trademark of RNO's we used when it was time to play with the pipes and banana clips.

"I bet when ya fuck ass woke up this morning all cuddled up wit' ya wife, *Jenny*, you didn't think today could be ya last day, Jea? Now, you can beat the hands of death and lead the ape to my food or prove that the reaper can't be cheated." I proposed my demands. I'd purposely used his wife's name to show 'em how deep the gorilla had ventured into his personal so we could skip all the play time. Old Benedict's face was as red as a stop sign. I could tell he was thinking of a way to prevent from comin' up off Uncle Sam's loot. "Nigga, you betta move ya feet. You have three minutes to give me what I came for, and I already know you only have six seconds between each number before a silent alarm is triggered, so don't play wit' ya life, Jea. Move, bitch!" I shouted. I could hear my blows emptying the counters as Benedict led me to the back, and right around the corner was one of the most majestic sights I'd ever set eyes on.

The vault was the size of a cave's mouth, and I knew there had to be some big security measures on that bitch. I pushed fat boy forward at the same time that the sound of hurried footsteps caused us to glance back in curiosity. The gorilla mask concealed his facial, but I knew the nigga was merely a pussycat in an ape's clothing. I glanced down at my watch. I'd set the timer, and time didn't give a fuck about friendship—when it was up, it was up. We'd entered the bank at three p.m. sharp, and eight minutes had passed.

"Fuck you doin', Round? You 'pose to be holdin' bro nem down in the front!" I spazzed on the fuck boy. Chucky D's eyes turned to slits behind the mask.

"Nigga, you ain't my mu'fuckin' daddy. While you wastin' time, the *clock* tickin'!" His response snapped me back to the bidness, and my vision returned to the bank manager.

"Open this mu'fucka up, and don't be on no sneaky shit, white boy!" I urged him. Benedict perspired so badly that sweat dripped from the sides of his chubby cheeks and saturated the collar of his pressed shirt. He pulled a card from his pocket and pushed it into a scanner slot that brought the small screen to life. It requested a numerical confirmation code, and as Benedict raised his hand to enter it, I noticed that it shook. I held my breath as he punched in the code, and to my surprise, the screen flashed red with three skulls that read *incorrect passcode*! I watched in horror as the screen began a slow countdown—*Ten, nine...* And before it reached eight, I'd snatched a fistful of the man's slicked-back, gelled hair and rammed his face into the thick steel door *twice!*

"Fuck! Oh god, please," he cried as blood shot from his nose and mouth. *Eight... Seven ... Six ...* The timer ticked away.

"God ain't got shit to do wit' this shit. You got five seconds before ya stupidity gets ya cerebellum splashed all ova this mu'fuckin' door, Jea!" I gritted.

"Hurry the fuck up, hurry! Aww, mane, we goin' to jail!" Chucky D panicked as Benedict's fingers glided across the sensor, and just as he entered the last number—*Two... One... Click!* The screen glowed green as the vault clicked open. By that time, even *I* was sweating like a fat man in a sauna. My heart pounded against my rib cage like a wild animal that'd been trapped in a cage.

"Dumb, Benedict, very dumb!" I slapped him in the back of the head.

"It's in ya policy to come off the bread when handed a *note* demandin' it, so what's the procedure when a *banga* to ya shit?" I spat as I pushed his fat ass aside. I pulled the heavy door open and damn near busted a nut. I was in jack boy's heaven! Rows and rows of Ulysses Grants, Andrew Jacksons, and Benjamin Franklins. There was even some weird shit with salmon chase on 'em, but I knew that typa bread would cause too much attention, so I tossed the duffle to Chucky D's sucka ass and nodded. "Brah, fill that hoe up with all big faces."

I paused to glance down at my watch—*3:15.*

"We ain't got much time, my dude, don't worry 'bout the small shit. We ain't here to let our stomachs override our survival." I schooled lil' daddy. The clown rolled his eyes like a lil' bitch before mumbling, no doubt, some fag shit. He got to the bidness as I held the leaking banker at bay. Dude's mouth, chin, and the front of his shirt were soaked with the shit his veins pumped.

"Tof broked my nofse!" he wheezed, causing me to laugh.

"You lucky I ain't break ya brain!" I hissed. Glancing down at the watch, it read *3:19.* "Hurry the fuck up, Blow, we damn near on flat line!" I shouted. Chucky D had moved behind me, and the intensity of the clock running out on us had me on edge. Out of nowhere, a peculiar expression fell over Benedict's face, and curiously, my vision followed his. My heart filled with disgust at the sight. Chucky D was so busy stuffing bread down his pants that not only didn't he notice us watchin' his snake ass, but he had the bag only partially full.

"Chucky D, what kinda lunatic shit you on, bruh? Fill the bag up, we only got two minutes left!" I lied. Dude chuckled at the instance of getting caught, the boy had no shame. Chucky D shrugged his shoulders in indifference.

"I'm hungry, brah." He chuckled after the admission, as if it made shit cool. Dude began to sweep loot into the bag with no regard for dye packs or trackers. I glanced down at my watch—*3:23!*

"Fuck it!" I hissed more to myself than to either of them.

"Dead that shit, Round, time's up, let's vanish," I demanded. Chucky D looked as if he wanted to argue as his eyes bounced back and forth between me and the rows of dead presidents, but the look I gave him was odious and warned of any more stupidity. The clown snatched up the heavy bag and strode past, mumbling under his breath. He never noticed me inching the tool off my waist. *Bocaaaa!* The .357's explosion was offensive in the closed quarters, but the clock had ran out on me. At that moment, it was two minutes left and it was show time. Chucky D's body had pitched forward when the bullet had caved the back of his cranium in, and I had to wrestle the heavy bag off his shoulder.

"Nooo!" Benedict pleaded when I turned on him with the tool at the ready. I shrugged.

"I don't like when niggas steal food from the table."

Boca! Boca! I hit dude with two to the chest, and he crumbled to the floor. I didn't waste time wonderin' if he had checked out. I ran over and stood over him.

Boca! Boca! I gave it to 'em for reassurance. We both had ran out of time.

***

-Heaven-

"Heaven, Uncle JJ is nasty." Catrina's words caught me off guard. Words are a powerful river that can either drown you or be used as a form of detergency, and in my case, I was forced down and submerged in the current. We were walking home from school when she said it. Though my heart pounded against my chest, I wanted to live within the bliss of ignorance, if only for the little bit of faith I still had in the almighty, but it was said that the devil came to steal, kill, and destroy, and at that moment, the mu'fucka did all three!

"What ju talkin' about, Catrina, how would *you* know how nasty our uncle is?" I asked with a roll of my eyes. I never broke my stride. The third gate was right behind Dunbar High School, and all one had to do was walk through the football field and slip through the gate to enter the run-down apartments. We were half-way to our destination when two things transpired that ruined my mu'fuckin' day.

"'Cause, he be comin' into my room and doin'—"

"What's up now, bitch, you think yo' prissy ass was gonna get away from this ass whoopin'!" The hateful voice cut my sister's revelation off. I stopped walking. Though I didn't turn around, I knew who the hatin' ass bitch was, 'cause she'd cried sour grapes ever since I'd enrolled at that ghetto ass school. If it wasn't about the wavy texture of my hair, the bitch wanted smoke about my clothes being more expensive. If it wasn't that, the girl wanted smoke behind her dude eye fuckin' me. I'd avoided her and her thirsty ass homegirls as much as I could, but after Catrina's confession, coupled with Mr. Hightower, my teacher, giving me a *D* on my history assignment for *not wanting to stay after school and let him tutor me on shit I already knew*, I wasn't havin' it!

I spun on my heels and faced off with the four ratchet ass girls, but it was the chubby, dark-skinned bitch with the bad weave that I set my sights on.

"Heaven, let's just goooo!" Catrina huffed, but even in her fear, I knew she wouldn't desert me. I shrugged her off.

"Why you always hatin'? I don't even know you. It's a shame that you wanna tear down anotha black woman because you feel inferior. It ain't my fault that ju mama made you ugly! Fealdad, que' opinas, Catrina?" I was so green back then, and even lamer when I pulled my sister into the bullshit by asking her if she agreed that ole girl was ugly.

"Estoy de acuerdo con usted," she agreed with me, which only fed the flames. In actuality, Lala was one of those pretty girls that had a nice ass, but her love for food kept the baby fat on. I'd never understood what anotha bitch had, that could create envy in a woman. *All* women were born with a pussy between their legs, ass shots had changed the game for *all* women, and cosmetics were an invisible mask that could make *any* woman attractive. The only things that the next bitch could have over me were a hatin' ass heart and envious tendencies, and that's because I was broke in that department.

"Ugly bitch, ya dopefiend ass mama ugly, hoe!" Lala shouted. I dropped my book bag before pulling the diamond studs out my ears. I'd never had an actual fight in my life, but *every* woman had to have a limit.

"Oh yeaaa, I'm 'bout to beat that ass, hoe!" LaLa nodded with a menacing glare. She bent down to tie her shoes, and that's when I tore into her ass! I rushed her, and before she could upright herself, I kicked her in the face. Her head snapped back, and I went to work. All the techniques my father had taught me, I used.

"Unun, get that hoe, LaLa, you bet not let that prissy bitch whoop you!" one of her friends shouted as I worked LaLa's ass like I'd been born to squabble. I eased up, thinking the girl had learned her lesson, but that was my biggest mistake.

"RRRRuugh!" LaLa growled as she charged me. I tried to side-step her, but the girl had it on her mind. She tackled me to the sun-dried grass, her big ass landing on top of me and damn near crushing my soul out my body.

"Whoop that hoe, LaLa, show her how us eastside bitches get down!" a bitch from the sideline encouraged. It amazed me how when shit popped off, no one was around, but somehow, when you gettin' yo' ass kicked, the entire hood wound up there. LaLa reached down and grabbed a handful of my long hair and began punching me in the face. I swung wildly, just tryin' to land a punch *anywhere!* Somehow, I caught the collar of her shirt and, without thinking, I ripped that mu'fucka right down the middle. Toilet paper sprang forth from her bra. Somehow, her titties swung free, causing the soft paper to fall. An explosion of laughter ensued from the spectators.

"Aww, shit, LaLa be stuffin' her bra, mane. I knew that hoe's titties wasn't that fluffy!" someone shouted. LaLa's embarrassment ran deep, and it was all she could do to cover her breasts. She climbed off me, and I didn't know if she was 'bout to stomp me or run-in shame, but I wasn't taking any chances. I reared back and kicked her ass in the stomach as hard as I could. She doubled over, saggy titties flying loose as I scrambled to my feet. I returned the favor and grabbed a handful of her nappy ass hair and tried to yank the fucked-up weave out her head. Then, *bam!* Someone blindsided me, and before I knew it, I was being jumped! Catrina jumped in and got her ass tore up right along with me, but just over the punches, kicks, and the *yea hoe's,* and *take that bitch,* a savior intervened.

"Ununn, you hoes ain't gonna do no clickin'!" a boy I knew as Preston shouted as he went to work. He tried his best, but pretty soon, he was getting his ass kicked right along with me and my sister.

***

"Let's go, Flesh, fuck took you niggas so long? Let's go!" Kiest shouted as I made it back to the front where they had everyone faced down with their hands tied. "Say, Blow, where Chucky D?" Kiest asked, but it was time to burn.

"Shit got stupid, Flesh. Dude we was holdin' down tried to strong arm our dude and while they wrestled for the banga, homie took one to the heart. Blow DOA, fam." The deception crushed me, but the truth woulda held us up. Kiest studied me, but I never looked him in the eyes, as if, *if* I didn't, he would never be able to say I looked him in the windows to his soul and lied to his face. I made my way to the door and as soon as I pushed it open, my life flashed before my eyes. I pulled back suddenly, causing Kiest to run into my back.

"Nigga, what the fuck you—" His words died in his throat when he spotted the BRPD patrol parked at the curb. The officer was speaking on his radio as we glanced at each other, both our eyes relaying the same message: *I ain't goin' to nobody's jail!*

"Say, Flesh, why you boys playin'? we gotta get the fuck outta here!" Thugga shouted as he stormed over with two bags of money on both shoulders. As soon as his eyes followed ours, he tensed before verbalizing the conclusion any true street nigga would come to if they *couldn't* picture themselves spending the rest of their lives caged up on some Willie Lynch plantation.

"Awww, man, Blow, we gotta take 'em down before his backup gets here. That's our *only* way out, Flesh." His words were the fruits. I glanced back at the people we'd laid down as I thought of the two dead cats I'd left stankin' back in the vault. That alone had made the crime punishable by death. I turned back to the window, and that's when I noticed the missing piece to our puzzle. Kiest must've noticed the Yukon was absent from the picture as well, 'cause he spat on the ground in spite.

"Pussy ass nigga left us! He gotta—"

"Tame ya tongue, Blow, that's *our* Flesh you speakin' blaspheme of. *We* raised Lil' Nukkey, he built to last, Flesh, that lil' nigga ain't eva let us down." I tapped brah's chest as I fed him the fruits of our creed. It was a bylaw of RNO that anyone *of our flesh* deserved the benefit of the doubt. In order for any man or woman to be embraced by the body, it had to be done by either a blood tie or the *full vote of the table.* A nigga came in knowin' that *any* mortal sin—*fuckin' one of your flesh's bitches on some snake shit, theft of anyone of the body of RNO, any fuck shit that stained the name of our sect*—any of that kinda shit was automatically closed curtains, so I had faith in Nukkey.

"Two twenty-one, Flesh, you feedin' the fruits, but damn!" Kiest relented.

"Fuck all that, we need to get busy before shit gets too sour for us to digest." Thugga spoke his mental, but as soon as the words slipped from between his lips, a second patrol car was added to the equation. If that wasn't enough to rob a nigga of his hopes of ballin', the hysterical cries of one of our hostages pervaded the room and were loud enough to get the attention of the first patrolman. He spun toward the bank and unholstered his weapon before radioing it in. It was official, it was either court wit' a system that didn't give a fuck 'bout rehabilitation but would gladly hide a nigga for the rest of his existence or holdin' court in the street where a nigga had the chance to either get one up on the system or at least make the news by dyin' a real nigga. Either or, we needed to make a choice—*quickly.* I already knew how *I* was goin' out, and just as I pushed the door open and leveled the chop stick—

Vroommm, skurrr! The LS1 motor in the stolen Yukon growled as the truck jumped the curb and skidded to a stop *right at the doors of the bank.* The shit caught us all by surprise, but Lil' Nukkey leaning over and pushing the door open brought us out of our daze.

"Fuck wrong wit' you niggas? Ya betta act like ya wanna stay free, ya heard me!" he shouted.

Boca! Boca! Boca!
Boom! Boom!

Gunshots merged into a symphony of danger. Thugga dove in the back after tossing the bags of money in, and I turned to follow when I heard the tell-tale song of that stick talk. *Ttttah! Ttttahh!* The pipe let off volleys of lead. Kiest was givin' it to 'em. AK bullets didn't spit out like regular slugs, 7.62s *flipped* when they made their exit from the barrel, and as they made contact with the patrol cars, they tore chunks out the metal. The first cop dove over his car, but the second patrolman wasn't as quick to get cover. A spray of 7.62s *tumbled* into his chest, through his Kevlar, and turned him a half-flip when it ate through his chest. He was on his way to the pearly gates before his body fell back to the ground.

"Fuck you on, Flesh, you done split ya marbles, Jea!" Thugga shouted from the back seat. "Let's get the fuck outta here!" he demanded as he pounded his fist against the head rest, as if just moments ago, he wasn't promoting violence. Yet, I agreed with the blow. It was time to mash.

I yanked brah's arm. "Let's flip, Kiest."

My nigga spat on the ground before turning to jump in the truck, but Johnny law didn't take their spankins lying down. *Boca! Boca! Boca! Boca!* Shots sang out. I felt Kiest's body jerk at the same time a burning sensation exploded into my right shoulder.

"Awww, shit, I'm hit, Flesh, I'm hit!" Kiest cried as he fell against the side of the truck. Thugga pulled him the rest of the way in and slammed the door shut. I was leaking as I hopped in the passenger's seat, but nothin' was gonna stop me from pulling that bag of money in—*nothin'!* Before I could get it all the way in, Lil' Nukkey mashed the gas and I barely pulled the bag to safety before he left rubber on the street. The sudden sound of rushing air caused me to glance back in time to see Thugga slide out onto the windowsill and trade fire with the remaining officer. The windshield of the patrol car exploded as the Yukon blew past, but a real street nigga knew not to relish in a moment of time when there was too much time left on the clock for the op to score. In seconds, it seemed as if the entire BRPD law enforcement was on our asses. My eyes fell to the army fatigue-colored duffle bag that was filled with dead faces and speckled with another man's blood. *Finally made it, and gotta die over the same bread we killed for!* My mind was a torrent of dark thoughts. "Fuuuck! Roll sommin, Round, roll sommin!"

Kiest's cries snatched my attention. I clutched my shoulder as I gritted my teeth against the pain, glancing back at bro bro. Thugga had pulled our flesh's head into his lap and was already dipping a pre-rolled blunt into a streak of embalming fluid. The truck jerked, snatching my attention back toward the windshield, and I damn near freaked. Lil' Nukkey was going against traffic as he swerved to avoid an eighteen-wheeler.

"Watch out, fam!" I panicked as the big truck swerved one way and Nukkey the other, causing the eighteen wheeler's trailer to fishtail directly in front of us. The trailer was filled with fresh-cut lumber, and though we all knew Lil' Nukkey had been stealing and driving cars since the sandbox, I didn't think either of us expected to survive what happened next. The trailer skidded sideways, tilting onto the left side on six wheels. "Oh shit, ohh shit!" I shouted as I slapped my hand against the dashboard repeatedly, as if that would prevent the collision. Lil' Nukkey was all in as he swung the wheel to the left in a hard turn and maneuvered the truck toward the concrete guard rail. The boy didn't even flinch as the ends of the trailer jackknifed across the driver's side of the truck. *Skissssss!*

It sounded like nails scratching against a chalkboard. For a moment, we were sandwiched, ping ponging back and forth between the guard rail and the trailer's end, until lil' Nukkey jerked the wheel to the right and the Yukon clipped the tail end of the trailer before spinning into a full three sixty. The crunching of metal and the sounds of shattering glass surrounded us as cars slammed into each other. We'd turnt I-10 into a crash course, but as the windshield exploded from the impact of someone slamming into the side of the SUV, we ended up earning one for the bad guys. The truck spun before coming out of its dizzying spin and stopping in a clear path going in the correct direction.

Lil' Nukkey didn't waste time. Mashing the gas, he got us the fuck out of there, and while motorists were getting out to check the damage, lil' Nukkey used the pile up as a means to ride the shoulder and make our escape.

***

-Heaven-
3:20 A.M.

The day had wound down and my ass was sore, scratched up, and dog tired. After the smoke had cleared, Catrina, the boy Preston, and I had gotten our asses beat, but them hoes now knew that if it was smoke, I wasn't runnin'. Yet, as I laid there on that stained mattress, watching shadows dance across the moonlit window, my mind was miles away from the events of the day. *Heaven, Uncle JJ is nasty! He be comin' in my room and doin'*—Catrina's words played in my head. As I laid there listening to the light snores of my cousin, Poetry, I wondered how she could sleep so peacefully in poverty. I understood the analogy of the rich person going broke and not knowing how to handle it, versus the poor person coming into money, losing it, but not trippin' because they're already accustomed to the reality, but *how* would *anyone* become accustomed to being broke? I didn't understand, and as pretty as Poetry was, she could've been a model, but she chose the life frequently traveled. I rolled over onto my side and stared at the dingy wall. I knew I couldn't allow myself or my family to live like that. *Something* had to change.

That was exactly my thought as my eyes began to drift shut, but the soft footsteps descending down the hall toward the bathroom caused them to snap back open. The sound of a door clicking shut could be heard in the distance, and as I listened and waited, I knew if I had to, I was gonna commit murder that night. I was as scared as a child that believed monsters were underneath the bed as I laid there, clutching the small twenty-five between my legs.

Seconds passed before a second sound of footfalls eased past the door, followed by the opening and closing of a door. I eased from the warmth of my bed, silently praying, scared. I made my way to the door and slipped out into the dark hallway, glancing around until I spotted the slit of light that emitted from the bottom of the bathroom door. My heart pounded in my chest as I tip-toed toward it, and as soon as I got close—*Why though? Why Catrina, my sister?* I wondered as I stood outside that door, listening to Catrina.

"No, Uncle JJ, you nasty!" Catrina's voice sounded strained. There was a sound of someone being slapped before a reply.

"You, lil' bitch, you gonna give me—"

That's as far as he made it before I saw red, and right there, in that dark hallway of my grandma's clustered apartment, my life changed forever. I pushed the door open and caught them by surprise, yet I didn't give the nigga a chance to recapture his composure, nor did I allow myself to consider what I was doing. I raised the small pistol and—*Boca! Boca!* The first two bullets met in his chest area, but to my surprise, things didn't happen like in the movies where the person falls to the ground dead. Instead, my uncle JJ stumbled toward me with a menacing glare in his stare. *Boca! Boca! Boca!* I squeezed the trigger. *Boca! Click! Click! Click!*

My eyes widened at the sound of the tool clicking empty. I stared at it curiously, scared, but the feeling was unwarranted. One of the bullets had struck him in the jaw, whereas another had entered through his neck. My uncle's hands shot to this throat before his lifeless body made an awkward descent to the floor, but I'd retreated to a dark island in my mind where the squeeze of the trigger seemed to be a beautiful stress reliever. *Click! Click! Click! Click!* With each pull of the trigger, I was back at that house where my father had taken his last breath, but this time I'd reacted differently. Each time I saw that clown's face, I squeezed the trigger again. *Click! Click! Click! Click!*

In that bathroom, where my uncle lay dead at my feet, and my sister's screams woke the dead, I became a different kinda bitch, and that kinda bitch would no doubt find herself in a whirlwind of fucked-up situations.

***

-Ghetto-

We'd gotten the ups on them people, but we were a long way from freedom. Nukkey got us off the interstate in one piece and pulled into a McDonald's right off the exit right as the Yukon began smokin' like a broken stove. He'd jumped out and took off in search of some new wheels, and as we sat there wit' our stolen treasures, I did something I'd never done.

"Say, Flesh, let me hit that shit." I turned to Thugga. The request caught him by surprise. He knew I didn't do drugs, but as both of our eyes fell to our flesh, he knew there would be stranger shit to happen in life.

"Fuck you niggas lookin' at me like I'm already dead fa, Round?" Kiest mumbled as I accepted the sherm. I smiled as I took a shallow pull from the dead man's chemicals. Its bitter taste caused me to frown as I exhaled.

"You gone make it, Blow, you a soljah, Jea. We swamp niggas, we built different." I gave 'em my truths. I glanced in the rearview and my heart sank. Not even a football field away, the colorful lights that had nothin' to do with Christmas stretched out along the street for as far as the eyes could see. My vision found Thugga's in the glass. He merely smiled with our flesh's blood smeared on the side of his face. He'd noticed our doom as well. They say that before the ending of a nigga's story, he felt nothin'... Just this unexplainable peace, but I knew whichever weenie ass nigga came up wit' that bullshit *must've* never sat in the backseat of a police car. My heart was knockin' like six eighteens in the trunk of an old school Fleetwood, and just when I pushed the door open, Nukkey fishtailed around the corner in a blue neon. He skidded to a stop beside us.

"Come on, Round, we ain't got no time left!" He spoke the obvious as he glanced back at the rapidly approaching convoy. Thugga hopped out with two bags of dirty money and ran to the smaller car.

"Hurry up, Flesh, hurry, hurry. Them folks are—"

"Shut the fuck up, Jea!" I cut Nukkey's rants off before turning to look at Kiest. "Can you walk, Blow? We gotta mash." The look my dude gave me was strange as he winced and sat up.

"Arrrugh!" he growled. I hopped out and snatched up the bag of loot, handing it to Thug. I turned back to my blow, but to my surprise, he'd climbed over the front seat and hopped behind the wheel.

"Blow, what the fuck are—"

"Get the fuck outta here, Flesh, ain't no time left!" he shouted as he tried to crank the truck. It wouldn't turn over the first few times, but finally, the devil smiled up at my flesh's crooked intentions. *Vroom!* The truck chugged to life in a growl of puffy smoke.

"Bruh, ya lost ya thinkin' cap? Nigga, get the fuck—"

"Flesh, get-the-fuck-on!" my blow shouted while throwing the gear into drive and turning to smile at me. I stumbled back in surprise, not from the beast's growl in his tone, but because my flesh stared back at me wit' somethin' staining his face that I didn't think he'd eva reveal to me. Tears ran red down his face as they intermingled with the smears of blood on his cheeks. "It's just not in the cards for me, Flesh. *Every* nigga can't ball, *someone* has to be the sacrifice." He shrugged before mashin' the gas. The truck jerked forward with all four doors open.

"Blow, if you don't come on, Flesh's sacrifice gonna be in vain." Lil' Nukkey shook his head in awe as we watched the Yukon pick up speed and smash into the first police car coming into the lot. I wanted to let my diamonds fall, but I'd been bred that gangstas don't cry—we let the doves do it for us.

***

Part 1
3 years later

What's love if it's momentary? Why invest so much of yourself into a moment in time, just to turn your back on the investment? That's not love—love is the endurance of the shit that threatens to drive you crazy. More so, it's the patience of taking the time to find the beauty in one's struggle.

-Renta-

Chapter 1
RNO Official

-Heaven-

"Ms. Domingo, Ms. Domingo, if you would please?" The sound of Professor Kennedy's voice penetrated my nap before Empress kicked my foot. My eyes shot open in alarm.

"Huh, yea-yea, I understand," I stammered as I wiped drool from the side of my mouth. I'd drifted to sleep in the middle of one of his lectures, and the suppressed snickers of my classmates told me I'd been caught in the act.

"And what do you understand, Ms. Domingo? Please, enlighten us. It's such a pleasure to have you join us here in this fare little class, by the way." He put me on the spot, but Empress saved the day.

"Well, *I* think that the history books left out a lot! Like in the year of eighteen hundred and eight when legislators outlawed slave importing, but it continued for fifty-two years after the law was passed! Some two hundred and fifty thousand people were *illegally* imported as slaves during that time!" She snapped her fingers.

Though I knew my bestie was smart, I doubted that her revelation had anything to do with the topic. Professor Kennedy's pale skin turned beet red, and it gave his all-white hair a comical contrast as he pointed his lecture stick at the smart board that projected the notes of the lecture. On the life of my dead father, I had to literally bite my tongue to keep from laughing at my girl.

"And what does *that* have to do with the Emancipation Proclamation, Ms. Lockhart?" the professor inquired with a snide expression. There was a gentle laughter that circulated around the room. Empress shrugged with a smirk on her face that I'd grown to relate to as her sneaky smile.

"It correlates, Professor, that's all." She giggled before leaning back in her seat and crossing her arms over her C cups. Ever since she'd intervened when those hoes jumped me, Empress and I had become like sisters. We were both smart and had plans of college, so it was destined for us to link up after graduation. We did it all together, hustled, lied, and played on niggas, so it was only logical that we leave the hood and go half on a cute little duplex in East Arlington. My girls and I were getting to a bag, but we played it smart.

"Well, it just may correlate, my dear, but rather than focusing on the sins of the many misguided souls of the past, why not acknowledge the *few* that had a grandeur effect of change for African American people?" Professor Kennedy's question caused my friend to raise a questioning brow, as if the *only* white folks she'd heard of were the ones that were proslavery.

"Well, what about Harriet Beecher Stowe?" The man was persistent. Empress's shoulders rose and fell in her conceit of naivety. The professor chuckled before aiming his stick at her.

"Mrs. Stowe was a Caucasian woman whose antislavery novel, *Uncle Tom's Cabin*, she inscribed in eighteen fifty-two had had a powerful influence and pushed the act of abolition," he spoke proudly. "Yet, tonight's assignment doesn't cover the life of Mrs. Stowe, I'm afraid." He paused to address the class. I exhaled a sigh of relief that he'd eased up off me and my girl before I gave her an appreciative glance.

"Tonight's study will be of the Civil War. There will be a quiz on the subject Thursday morning, so happy hunting, ladies and gents. Class dismissed," he announced. Empress rolled her eyes as she gathered her books. Out of every class we took at the University of Texas in Arlington, Government and History were the ones she detested the most.

"I can't wait to be through with this shit, girl, I'm thinking about skipping next semester." She huffed as we made our way toward the door.

"Look out, lil' one, ya left this back there in the seat, ya heard me." The soft voice washed over me like a warm wave of heat on a winter's night. I paused before turning to see who was speaking, and as soon as my eyes penetrated the Cartier glasses and connected with his, my pussy became a river. He stood at a clean six three with long dreads that were twisted back into an intricate design. Even through the clear lenses, I could see that his big almond-shaped eyes were complemented by some of the longest lashes I'd ever seen possessed by a man. I discreetly took inventory of the fit he wore and damn near came on myself. The black Fendi pants slightly sagged off his waist, and the matching Fendi hoodie he wore spoke of his thug appeal. When my eyes fell to the black and royal blue Fendi kicks, I knew playboy had passed the inspection.

Boss! I thought of his drip. Yet, none of that was more intriguing to his pretty boy aura than the small Draco with the letters *RNO* shaped in the form of a banana clip he'd had tattooed underneath his left eye. I was speechless!

"Look, Queen, you want this shit or what? I'm pressed for time." His demand reminded me of who I was—*A boss bitch.*

"Excuse me?" were the first words my lips seemed capable of forming as that bitch in me rose to the surface. I damn near spazzed on dude, but I was way too bossy to allow *any* nigga to control my emotions. I gave pretty boy a forced smile that didn't match the threat in my eyes. I knew Empress was merely waiting for me to make the first move and the smoke would've been up. The baby nine I'd stashed in my Birkin bag was calling to me, but the call was long distance 'cause I'd left the bag in my car. Without much more verbal, I snatched my phone from his extended hand and turned on the heels of my red bottoms, but I didn't miss the arrogant smirk on the nigga's face. *I've murked niggas for less, lil' daddy. You're cute, but don't become a handsome corpse!*

My thoughts were turbulent. Empress and I made our way out the door.

"What was all that about, Ms. Heaven?" Empress was up in my mix as soon as our feet exited the building. Curiosity had always been more powerful than not caring. I slid a pair of YSL sunglasses over my eyes as we made our way over to my new baby. It was a smoke-gray 2018 Aston Martin Vanquish, and once I made it to the driver's side, I paused.

"What? Dude was just returning my phone, damn, bitch!" I laughed at *the eyes* she was giving me. My girl was one of them high-yella queens that had a bunch of ass but a lil' bit of titties. Empress was a stallion that stood five ten with a layered bob hair cut that she wore long in the front, hiding one eye like Aaliyah, and tapered in the back. The small Marilyn Monroe mole just above her juicy lips just added to her appeal and highlighted the diamond stud in her bottom lip. Her only flaw *to me* were her addictions. She loved poppin' molly and eating pussy, but her worst trait was her jealousy! She hated for *any* man to get close to me.

"Yea, but what 'bout all the eye fuckin' and loss for words? You almost got that boy smashed right there in that classroom." She giggled with the words while forming a gun with her fingers and mockingly pulling the trigger. I deactivated the alarm before checking my best friend.

"It was nothin' special, lil' daddy just caught me off guard, aiiight?" I eased her apprehensions. "Besides, I saw how yo' freak ass was recklessly eye ballin' dude. You was salivating over him like he was a giant dick that you couldn't wait to suck." I pulled my door open and tilted the designers down the bridge of my nose. "Stop playin' me so close, Empress. I'm your sister, not ya bitch. You know how I get when I feel crowded." I kept it gully with her, but just as I anticipated, Empress had to get the last word. She slid on her own pair of designer glasses before staring at me through the transitional lenses that were darkening by the second.

"No need to remind me, *sis*, but don't fault me for remembering how sweet my *sister's* pussy tastes." She smiled while putting emphasis on the titles. I watched as she slid into the passenger's seat, and just before I slid into the car, my eyes drifted to the passing hammerhead silver Maserati. It was as sleek as a panther, and whatever he had in the truck sounded as if it was desperate to get out. The bass shook the ground as the twenty-six-inch, *retro* button rims reflected off the pavement, and though he had the *stay out my business* tints on the windows, the glow of the TVs he'd had installed allowed me to catch a teasing glimpse of Mr. RNO. *What the fuck is RNO?* I wondered as I slid behind the wheel. What I did know, if a nigga could drip the way dude was *and* push a foreign, he *had* to be deep in his bag, and that made him food to me and my ladies.

***

-Ghetto-

"Yea, I'm pullin' up now. I'll thug wit' you when I get in," I spoke into the phone before disconnecting the call. I was valeted outside the bando, allowing the vibrations of the bass to massage my back. Lil' Baby had just dropped anotha banga, and I was fuckin' wit' everything lil' buddy dropped. I killed the ignition and slid from the machine wit' a quick sweep of my surroundings. One could never be too safe, especially in my profession. I adjusted the burna on my waist before makin' my way to the door of the spot I'd copped on the west side of Arlington, Texas, nowhere by the slums. As soon as the door opened, I was greeted by a loud blast of smoke that almost made me cough.

I allowed my eyes to take in the empty two-story, gray brick Victorian I'd purchased as a stash for me and my flesh. It was empty of all furnishings outside of the Italian marble counters and the shit that was built in it. If anyone was to tour the spot, they'd wonder why a nigga would spend a check on such a sight of beauty and not spend one night within its splendor, but only real boss niggas knew the play of the stash. I chuckled as my thoughts carried me back to the Pocahontas that had gotten put on blast in class earlier. Lil' baby was as jazzy as a saxophone and as thick as gumbo, but there was somming mysterious 'bout lil' one that had me thinkin' she'd mastered the art of secrets. I was still allowin' Queen to burglarize my mental when I made it to the two-car garage and was greeted by six youngins that me and the table were 'bout to induct into RNO.

Everyone *besides* my flesh Stick Talk was new to the fold, but Reaper, Big Hurk, Daddyo, Fats, and Twitcha Lee were all certified head bussas, and I'd personally chosen each of 'em to thug beside me. I'd been in the Lone Star State for the past two and a half years, and wit' the aid of my blow, Stick Talk, RNO was a hunnid and ninety niggas strong in the metroplex. Lil' Nukkey had added to the numbers in Florida, and Thug to the *H.* Altogether, we'd turned RNO into a juggernaut.

"What's blessings, Flesh?" Stick Talk greeted properly. We shook up as I allowed my eyes to digest the group of wolves that I'd no doubt put my life on the line for, and finally, my vision swallowed the boy they'd bound to a chair as naked as a newborn. He'd been beaten to sleep, face disfigured to the point that if he was to have a funeral at that moment, he'd have to have a closed casket.

"The table eatin' and there's no snakes in the garden, Blow." I finally returned bruh's greeting. He nodded as his eyes took in the piece of shit nigga that had violated the laws of RNO.

"Two twenty-one, Flesh, two twenty-one," he acknowledged as he nodded at Insane as blood leaked from his nose.

"What's the bidness wit' this fuck nigga, Flesh?" His question caused me to look at him as if he'd asked one of the strangest questions I'd ever heard. I pulled my horn off my hip and brought the screen to life, and after clicking into Facebook messenger, I started the conference call. Nukkey and Thug's faces appeared on the screen.

"What's blessings, Flesh?" they both spoke in union.

"The table," I responded in kind, but Nukkey was ready to get to it. He was always 'bout the bidness.

"Say, Blow, where that snake at?" he inquired.

"Hold this for me, my G." I handed Stick Talk the phone and waited until he focused the camera on the room. I walked over to Insane's bitch ass and slapped the shit out of 'em.

"Ahhh, wait, huh!" He came to, disoriented. I turned to the lil' niggas in the room.

"Today is the day of forever for you niggas! Each one of you have been handpicked by *one*, one of the heads of *the table*." I allowed my words to marinate before continuing. "RNO is a *family*! Not a gang, not a clique, not a hood, we're a family of men and *queens to be* that stand on righteousness. There's a creed to this shit that can't and won't be violated." I paused to up the Glock 17. "There's one thang that all men and women must understand when fuckin' with others, Flesh, and that's the truth. That truth is this, every nigga, every bitch, every man, and every woman sins! We're gonna fuck up no matter how solid we are as a people. Yet—" I paced before the men that I would view as my brothas from that day forward.

"Ghetto, Blow, I don't know what's—" Insane began.

Smiish! The butt of the tool cut a red river down the side of his face. "Ahhhh!" His cry was deep as he rocked back and forth so hard that the chair threatened to tip over.

"Shut yo' bitch ass up when real niggas talkin', nigga. You ain't my blow, you a low-down, dirty nigga that can't control ya dick, Jea," I spat. All eyes went to the clown. The only ones privy to dude's sin were Stick Talk and the two men on the conference call. "RNO is exactly that, *Real! Niggas! Only!*" I shouted. My eyes found the other five men in the room. Outside of curiosity, neither man showed fear in the presence of my gangsterisms. "There's sins and then there's *unforgivable* transgressions that a nigga just can't wash off or turn his attention away from, and in RNO, there's five sins that will get you took down by the same niggas you crawl through the mud wit'. Rattin', fuckin a wife or bitch of ya flesh, switchin' sides, detrimental deceit, and taintin' the body of this family."

I turned my attention back to the violator of the shit we all vowed to stand on. He was done for and didn't even know why. Insane tried to crack his eyes open, but his energy was gone.

"Why?" was the only word he could muster before his chin fell back to his chest. That's when I reached into the front pocket of my hoodie and pulled out a stack of pictures and handed them to Twitcha Lee.

"What, nigga, you thought you was gonna get away wit' dippin' off with the flesh's bitch, huh? Oh, you thought just 'cause y'all committed the sin outside the city we wouldn't find out? Nigga, we like WiFi, we everywhere!" I spat as I jacked one in the chamber. "Oh, and don't trip, my dude, you won't be takin' this nap alone. That hoe already at the gates waitin' to be reunited wit' you!" I chuckled before raising the tool.

"Noooo—" *Boom!* The first slug pushed his scalp back and silenced his plea. His soul was long gone by the time I turned to my brethren.

"Tonight, you boys sign ya life into RNO wit' a blood tie. This *till death*! Neva cross ya bro. If you thug wit' a nigga, it ain't no reason for snake shit, 'cause real niggas know how to control their minds, dick, and stomach. Never forget this shit, Flesh, a nigga wit' no limitations will do *anythang!*" I jeweled before passing my burna to Reaper. I turned and retrieved my horn before walking out with Stick Talk on my heels. Lookin' down at the screen, my heart ached for the missing piece of our body. Kiest had went down with the ship and kept it RNO wit' us, and for his realism, those crackas sentenced him to death.

I could tell from the expressions on my blows' faces that our mentals were of one body, we all missed the bro. As I made my way to the Masi, I gazed up to the heavens. *Boom! Boom! Boom! Boom! Boom!* I heard the five shots that had no doubt penetrated the skull and body of the dead man. He didn't die because of the bitch, he died 'cause rather than pulling his potna's coat to the fact that his gal being a snake bitch, he chose to run dick in the slut and keep it secret. That made him just as serpentine as the bitch, and that typa shit should neva be in the script of a solid nigga's vibrations.

"So, what's the bidness, Flesh, what's good for the night?" Stick Talk asked before pulling the passenger's door open. I slid behind the wheel and glanced around before replying.

"Gather the body, we steppin' out to celebrate the newest members of the flesh."

*

Chapter 2
So We Meet Again

-Heaven-

Stiletto's was lit that Saturday night, and as I sat at the vanity mirror in the club's dressing room, I could tell that the freaks really came out at night. Every hoe in there was turnt up and practicing her twerk in the mirror. As I applied my eyeliner, I watched Empress from the reflection of the mirror. She'd just popped something in her mouth before turning a plastic cup filled with liquor up to her lips to wash it down. I shook my head in pity. *Molly!*

"Sup, Heaven, baby, I know you 'bout to kill 'em tonight. I'm feelin' ya get-up too, gurl!" Egypt was too much. She was the fourth link in our four-girl clique. She, Catrina, Empress, and I were as thick as thieves and had all the other bitches on our clits. Most envied us, but kept that shit hidden behind false lashes and friendly smiles, and others had learned the hard way that bitches got gangsta too. I slid from my seat and admired myself in the mirror before leaning over and using the glittery eyeliner pencil to create a sharp angle at the corner of my eyes. I smiled appreciatively at the Egyptian effect I'd created.

Smack! Egypt slapped me on the ass before nodding down at the last piece of my ensemble. I smiled as I freed it from its case. It was a rose gold and ruby-studded face mask that only covered the bottom portion of my face.

"Let me do the honors, sis. Lil' Boosie and that nigga Mo3 gonna throw their entire sack at you tonight!" she exclaimed while talking the mask from my hands. I giggled as I let her pull the mask around my nose and mouth and fastened it behind my head. That night, I was a goddess. My entire body was oiled and kissed with thousands of little gold flakes that brought more attention to the gold G-string I wore than to my exotic, Dominican skin tone. With a mischievous smirk on my face, I took the small panties by their thin sides and pulled them up, causing my lower lips to pout as the golden material revealed the imprint. It was a girl thing, and since as long as I could remember, men had yet to learn how to resist the power of the *P!* It just took a boss bitch to prey on that weakness, and even back then, young and ambitious, I knew that the key to seduction was *the mystery* of how good the pussy was, versus actually allowing a nigga between my thighs.

"Yea, I heard Badass and his lil' friends was up there payin' a bitch's rent." I giggled while strutting my size seven Olympia peep-toe, high-heeled boots toward the door.

"Hopefully, the nigga let's all this ass and titties talk to his dickhead, if so…" I paused before slipping out the door. Empress stepped beside Egypt, both awaiting what we all knew would happen if Lil' Boosie fell victim to my sex appeal. "Well, let's just say that insulin won't be the worst of his problems." I brought a smile to their faces before slapping my own ass and letting them watch it jiggle as I headed to shut that bitch down.

***

-Ghetto-

Lil' mama dropped to the splits in completion of her act, and niggas went berserk. I glanced up in time to see Boosie and his entourage makin' it rain on lil' one like she was trapped underneath a storm cloud. I smirked at my fellow swamp nigga when he glanced over at the wild youngins wit' me that were tryin' to make their forecast. I wasn't really into shawty, but a pretty face that was connected to a body with a fat ass would never suffer from the lack of attention from *one* nigga, so lil' baby still received her fill of affections. I glanced back down at the screen of my jack and read the newest text. *I can accommodate you on all the school supplies you need, but our business must be on me and my associate's terms.*

I nodded as if the sender could see my consent before giving my reply. *Where * when**

A few moments passed before my phone vibrated with his entry. *Louisiana. Friday. You'll get exact location.*

As soon as I read the text, my attention was kidnapped by the sound of police sirens as the overhead lights began to flash red and blue like the top of a patrol car. My hand instinctively drifted toward the FN on my waist as my mental boomeranged me back two and a half years before that moment.

I burst through the door of my memaw's house, bloodied and out of breath as I lugged the bag of money behind me. Me and the squad had split up, and if fate said the same, we'd reunite and split our stolen treasures. As I stumbled through the living room, exhausted, in pain, and prayin' for a blessin', adrenaline betrayed me. I fell to my knees and succumbed to darkness. Subconsciously, I could hear my memaw speaking in rapid French as she found me slumped in my own blood, but as she tore the bloodied shirt and inspected the bullet wound, the last thing I remembered her saying was, "Ya always into shit, boy. Let's get you fixed up and hid before the sheriff comes."

Then, I snapped back to the present to the familiar feel of the glizzy clutched in my palm. I glanced down. Sometime while lost within the reverie of the past, I'd slipped the tool from my waist and had it clutched so tight that if I'd applied an iota more of pressure, I would've blown my thigh off.

I shivered before resting the burna in my lap. *Chill, lil' daddy, they ain't comin' for you just yet!* I calmed myself. I tossed the iPhone onto the table before reaching for one of the bottles of Ace and taking it to the head. I got two good gulps before one of the most exotic visions I'd ever beheld caused me to choke on the expensive drink. The lights blinked off, bathing the club in a darkness that was absolute before blaring back to life briefly in a soft golden spotlight. Nicki Minaj's "Anaconda" began to blare from the club's boisterous sound system at the same time that two golden canisters rolled onto the stage's surface. The anticipation was thick as all that had eyes stared curiously at the stage.

"Uhohoooo, you mu'fuckas done fucked up now! Get ya ones, fifties, and hunnids out and let's make it rain on her thick ass. It's a bad bitch, y'all. Show some love for my favorite ass shaka, Heavenly!" the DJ announced over the music. At that moment, both canisters exploded into nostrils of escalating smoke, and there, crawling through the dense mist, was a dark feline with skin that seemed to shimmer under the glow of the golden light. Queen's skin was exotic, foreign. It was a mixture of caramel Egyptian hue and as richly dark as an African Goddess that slept on a cloud and used the sun as a pillow. The canisters emptied, but the fog remained for a moment as it fanned out around the room and evaporated into the air.

By the time it cleared completely, Queen had turned her ass toward the crowd, the toes of the golden-heeled boots hanging over the edge of the stage. She'd placed her elbows on the surface before cupping the sides of her face in the palms of her hands, and when that ass began to percolate, the crowd went stupid. As she gave us a vulgar round of applause, I got a collage of peeks of the golden string of her G-string in the moments of those thick ass cheeks opening and closing in their rapid dance. The brief interlude of quick peeks of lady's asshole was one of the most erotic games of peeka boo I'd ever bared witness to, and the downpour of raining George Washingtons was a testament of each man *and* woman's mutual agreement. I wiped my lips before taking the bottle to the head once more, my eyes never leaving the stage, but somehow, Queen had removed her top without me noticing.

Her body was serpentine as she made her way toward the pole in the center of the stage, and midway, lady got on some acrobatic shit and flipped herself onto her hands. She held herself upside down, the heels of her boots suspended in the air, and all that ass and titties balanced on two manicured hands. My mental fought a lustful war against my dickhead as the liquor swam through my veins. I watched in awe as lady walked on her hands the rest of the way to the pole and hooked it behind the crease of her left leg. With her back to the crowd and her right leg extended toward the heavens, lil' baby leaned back until the pole sunk between her ample ass cheeks. Somehow, she began to flex her cheeks, causing her dark backside to appear to be gnawing on the metal pole.

"You see this bitch, mane? She need to be in one of my videos, brah!" Lil' Boosie was turnt up as he popped a bottle and laughed as the champaign shot out in a bubbly explosion. Queen was bringing her act to a close when I glanced down at the ten blue-banded blocks of ones in front of me. I'd intended to shower the club, but the playa in me had *never* allowed me to play the role of a trick, and that night wouldn't be any different. I was so in tune with the loot that I didn't notice her slip into my heaven.

"So, did you enjoy my show?" The feminine, soft voice shook me. My eyes found hers, and though the half-mask would make love to any man's imagination, her eyes gave birth to a moment of déjà vu, a vague familiarity. I'd never forget the chinky tightness of those eyes, and as I explored her geography, her skin seemed to glow. I couldn't tell if she'd bathed herself in some sort of golden flakes or if her act merely had her skin aglow with sweat, but the strange effect had my dick on salute. Lady's vision fell to the blocks of hundreds on the table until a moment of craziness stole our attention. *Spow!*

The sound of flesh against flesh caused both our eyes to fly to the man that had just slapped her ass, and though I relented to the demand of laughter, Queen's eyes turned to homicidal slits as she glared at my main man.

"I *had* to see if that shit was official, mama, and damn…" Stick Talk's words trailed off as both of our eyes fell to all that ass. I knew my flesh was wondering if lady was intentionally tryin' to entice us or if her ass was *still jiggling* on its own.

"Damn, Blow, you's a lucky nigga, fam!" Bruh exclaimed before walking off with an amazed shake of his head. Baby girl's glare followed Flesh until he disappeared into the crowd, and only then did she fix me with her stare. She placed a hand on her waist, causing my vision to follow the act, and that's when I noticed the *slight* stretch marks that ran *sexily* at her waist. Some complemented her bulging thighs and blended into the thickness, as if her skin had to fight to hold all that sexiness in. Lil' baby was bossy.

"So, that's how you and yours give it up?" she sassed with a roll of her eyes. Queen was as hot as boiling water when she turnt on her heels to exit my universe, and though I surprised even myself when I did it, I slid from the seat in hot pursuit. *Fuck it!* I gave in to

55

that boss shit within me that had always made me mash for the shit I felt was mine to conquer. I caught mama by her hand and impulsively, she attempted to pull away, but what typa nigga would let go of a bag of money in a club filled with hungry niggas? Ms. Lady spun to confront me, and as soon as she did, I violated her comfort zone.

"I ain't *eva* known the Earth to run from God, Queen, and all I'm askin' for is a real nigga's chance to build and destroy the illusion you got of niggas like me. I'm worth that much, huh?" I asked before releasing her hand and standin' tall under her penetrating observation. *Any* real woman could recognize the difference between a wolf and a fox, just as only a god could differentiate the virtue between a *bad* bitch and a *boss* bitch. I allowed Queen to see into my gangsterisms before turning and allowing my Mark Jellous shoes to carry me back to my throwin'.

***

-Heaven-

He stood so close that if I'd puckered my lips, we'd be kissing. His Givenchy cologne played with my sense of smell as our eyes danced, but it was his word play, the strange lingo he used that toyed with my curiosity. Dude had a bitch's heart on rapid. *Is this nigga 'bout to kiss me? Why can't I move?* My mind became my enemy, but before I could calm the confliction of my heart, playboy turnt and drifted back toward his seat. I watched him until he got comfortable before I made my move. I knew I was a bossy bitch, so it had me off balance that the nigga felt as if he could leave me standing in the middle of the club like some random.

I was seasoned enough to know that I was dealing with a different kinda animal, but what he didn't know was, me and my girls hungered for niggas like him. The entire time I'd danced, I observed him and his squad as they turnt up, and though I knew killas when I saw 'em, I knew that this *proclaimed* God and the boy that had slapped my ass would be the ones to speak the loudest pipe talk out of their team. As I sashayed my way toward him, our eyes spoke a different typa language. King was surely a boss, and I was gonna truly hate getting his blood on my hands, but a girl had to eat.

My ass cheeks jiggled with each step as I put a lil' extra to my strut. As soon as I made it to his table, all eyes shot to my five-foot stature. Two other strippers I knew as Coco and Plush were doing their thang, and as soon as Coco's hatin' ass set eyes on me, she sucked her teeth. I paid the envious hoe no never mind. I had one thing on my mind, and I wouldn't be deterred. The black bandanna he'd worn around his forehead kept the long dreads from hanging over his face and for the first time, I noticed how evil his pretty eyes were.

"You gonna let me earn some of that or what?" I purred with a nod toward the stacks of ones. I estimated a clean five bandos, and when mystery man shrugged his indifference, I knew I'd be walking away with *at least* a stack of that. To his surprise, I straddled him like he was a show horse, and as the DJ announced Empress for her set, he played the perfect song for my seduction.

I throw that ass back to see if he gone catch it/ I ain't athletic but it's tennis for the necklace/ Aye, where that cash at, I stack it like Tetris/Real gutta bitch, real plug and connections.

I began to make that ass bounce before taking his hands and placing them on my jiggling cheeks. I grinded against his nature until I felt him come to life underneath me, and just when I felt I had his complete attention, I removed his hands and stood up. Playboy's eyes may have been as dark as night, but I was a predator that had mastered the art of seeing the weakness in my prey. Turning so he could be up close and personal with the roaring lioness head I'd had tattooed over my left ass cheek; I bent all the way over until my manicured hands were touching the floor, and without bending my knees, I made that ass do tricks I knew no respectful lady would attempt. I could feel hundreds of eyes molesting my curves, but it was only one nigga's attention that I craved for that night, so I looked back at it just to see what he was seeing.

The DJ was turnt that Saturday as he began to intermingle Foxy's old school hit into the mix. *Ooouuu, baby, gotta get you home with me tonight/Ooouuu, baby.* I bent at the knee as I rolled my hips, my eyes captured his as I stood upright. We both could hear Boosie and his squad bidding for my attention, but I wasn't no ditzy bitch. I knew it would be much harder to take Lil' Boosie down than it would be to stick to the young hood nigga that was running a checkup. The most a bitch would get outta Boosie was some jewelery and a few hundred. At least when we stuck the dread for his bag, we had a lesser threat of jail. I straddled him for the second time before wrapping my arms around his neck and freaking him.

His hands instinctively found my ass as I leaned forward and sang along with Foxy Brown. *I'm 'bout to say peace to my mans for you/when it's all said and done, I got plans for you.* I smiled behind the mask at the irony of that line. I sat up and glanced down at him as I grinded against all that dick.

"Does God have a name?" I whispered. Though I was the seductress, my lower lips were directly on top of his masculinity, and as I grinded, I discreetly worked myself into a pool of stickiness.

"Ghetto." His response brought an instant frown to my face. *Ghetto!* I studied dude as if he'd spat in my face, until it dawned on me that he spoke in reference of his name rather than disrespecting my character. I smiled behind the mask and he must have seen it in my eyes, because he chuckled. Without warning, he reached up and behind my head to find the clasp to my mask, and as soon as he found it, he looked up into my vision for consent. I didn't concede, nor did I reject, and just as God usually did in life when one was indecisive, he took it upon himself to make the decision for me. Ghetto removed my mask and as soon as it fell away, he smiled a gold-fanged smile. "You never gave me a name, *sleepy head.*" He caused me to blush with the reminder of my little nap in class.

Yet, that wasn't the reason I slid from his lap and prepared to make my exit. I knew that seduction had to be given in doses or it would be viewed as normal. I wanted to leave Mr. Ghetto with nothin' but hard dick and curiosity. I reached over and separated two blue-banded blocks from the stacks of money on the table before smiling down at him.

"God knows all things. He's omniscient and knows without the presence of my name. He has nowhere to rule from." I turnt to allow him to lose himself in the sway of my hips but paused to look back over my shoulder. "If you want it bad enough, you'll figure it out." I smiled before strutting away. Lil' Boosie attempted to stop me, but I paid him no mind. *Not tonight, Badass. You're lucky, 'cause I sure wouldn't mind fuckin' ya crazy ass before leavin' yo' brains on the pillow.* I giggled at the thought.

Renta

Chapter 3
Strapped Up...Seatbelts

-Ghetto-
Friday, 4 pm

Dressed identically in black-over-black Fendi attire, accessorized with oversized, dark designer shades, me, Thugga, and Stick Talk were just three young niggas, new to the ways of boss shit. Me and Thugga stood at the front of the flat-bottom boat, staring longingly out at the muddy waters we'd had to forsake in the name of survival. That saturated land was home to us, and I knew my flesh missed the home of jazz and Mardi Gras just as much as I did. The wind blew my dreads wild as the airboat glided over the murky waters as smoothly as a shark's fin cutting through the surface of the ocean. The country ass white man that piloted the watercraft chewed on a thick plug of chewing tobacco as he navigated us through the thick, woody plants and congealed algae like he'd been doin' it his entire life. My eyes drifted to the flesh, Stick Talk. Brah was lost in wonder as he stared out at the many gators that broke the surface of the water.

My eyes followed his transfixed gaze, until I spotted the twelve-point buck that had just bent his head to sip from the tainted waters. The deer was so lost within its moment of hydration that it never noticed nature turning its back on him. Life slowed down as a vicious alligator exploded from the dark water in a splash of evil intent. The big deer's eyes grew wide as he attempted to retreat, but the massive gator was unmerciful in his pursuit, and as soon as its powerful jaws snapped shut, it was murder she wrote. The big buck fought for a second chance at life, but the slick reptile drug him in the water and flipped him under. As the gator drowned the beautiful animal, another of its kin drifted over and bit down on the rear of the deer.

"Damn, Flesh, that was crazy!" Stick Talk shouted over the roar of the giant fan that propelled the watercraft. I nodded before turning my eyes forward. I frowned in confusion at the hanging mass of trees before us. It seemed as if the crazy ass dude was heading straight for 'em. Thug stiffened beside me. He looked as if he was 'bout to dive into the dark waters.

"Where you say you met these folks at again?" he shouted. I was on the verge of answering him when the flat-bottom boat seemed to lift out the water and float in mid-air for seconds of eternity before skidding back down and curving around the drooping trees with merely a few inches between them and the boat. My heart pounded against my chest, but as my glaring eyes found the hillbilly, I knew he'd done the weak ass shit purposely to shake us up. He spat a brown glob into the waters.

"Yeeeaah! Hell, yea! Ya boys hol' on ta ya jimmies, we got anotha ruff turn up ahead, yea." His Cajun was thick in each word. Stick Talk wanted to jump on that dumb shit, I could see it in his stare, but I rejected it with a quick nod.

"Say, Playboy, warn us next time, ya heard me." I kept the peace as me and the white's eyes sized each other up. He nodded, but as I turnt my back to him, I could've sworn I heard him whisper, *nigger!*

***

-Heaven-

It seemed to me that niggas could suck pussy, fuck pussy, and play pussy, but no matter how in tuned with pussy they were, they just didn't learn to respect the power of the *P*! To weak niggas, and even with a few strong-willed brothas, pussy was the strongest force on earth and would *forever* be the weakness that boss bitches like me and my sisters could use to turn their pockets inside out. The doorbell rang for the third time before it was heard over the loud music.

"Yea, wud up?" I could hear him as he opened the door.

"Oh, shit, you must be one of the stripper hoes we ordered." The sucka was so disrespectful. "Where the rest of the hoes at? We asked for three."

He glanced around. Even without seeing her, I knew Empress was smiling as she placed a manicured hand on her small waist.

"Yea, but who the hell yo' *fine* ass think in this big ass cardboard cake, nigga, the tooth fairy? This cake is filled with all kinds of surprises!" she seduced, and I could tell she had that *sneaky* smile that suggested more than she'd revealed. I pictured dude allowing his eyes to travel over all Empress's barely clothed curves before looking to the giant cake I was concealed in. I knew he wondered how many girls could fit inside the false container, because Empress giggled.

"There's only the surprise girl in there, but our homegirl coming right behind us, she's just running a lil' late." She eased his apprehensions. "Look, you gone let us in or what, lil' daddy? Time is money, and I'm sure ya folks wouldn't be feelin' you keepin' all this ass out here on stand still. What, *you* ain't tryin' to see how pretty this pussy is, nigga?" Empress always knew how to lure a sucka into her web. Playboy must've moved aside, 'cause the false cake began to move. *Thank God, this hoe must be tryin' to suffocate me in here!* I thought.

"That bitch in there bet not pop out lookin' mo' like Megan *NO* good than Megan Good, either. I'mma put all you hoes out this mu'fucka." Homeboy chuckled. The loud smack was a tell-tale sign that he'd slapped Empress's ass.

"That ass juicy ain't it, daddy?" She giggled. I could picture her pausing in her strut to smile back at lil' daddy.

"And wait till you see my girl in here." She paused to slap the side of the cake. "That pussy will *catch* you by surprise with the power of her nut, if the money right."

***

-Ghetto-

The house was made of old wood that was weather beaten but made stronger by the climate of the marsh. Moss Bluff, Louisiana was a small piece of the state that was more swamp than land but was a good hideaway for a fugitive like Caveman. The rickety steps leading up to the cabin-like house were supported by bricks to prevent a nigga from falling through the brittle wood, and when I glanced over at Stick Talk, the frown on his face told me that he was questioning my judgement. The Cavalli duffle bag I carried bounced against my leg as I stepped onto the porch. *Shid, I hope this boy Caveman ain't all cap and got me lookin' like no clown. If he is, my bros might wig out and—*

The thought was incomplete due to the door opening to reveal a Wrestlemania swole ass white dude that stared at me and my fleshes as if we were the scum of the earth. I allowed my vision to relay my sentiments. *Punk ass cracka!*

The man was covered head to waist with tattoos, and each one of them was a jailhouse depiction of Nazi propaganda. The damn fool even had hail Hitler inked across his forehead, but it was the massive *AR* he aimed at us that froze my blood. It was stocked with a giant drum that promised a body if he let that hoe breathe.

"At ease, Tank, be easy, Bubba, dat ole boy out yonder did me a wagon of good when we was locked in ole Angola," the familiar voice rasped. Tank sneered, but he lowered the stick and stepped out our way. I looked him up and down with that gangsta shit in my stare.

"Ghetto, get ya crazy ass on in here, boy, and let me see ya!" Caveman's gruff voice was filled with mirth. I pushed on from the muscled sucka, and as soon as I spotted him, I smiled at the obese white man. The small living room was bathed in shadows and caused Caveman to look like a big ole fluffy polar bear. The man was a six-six giant with three hundred pounds of *good livin'* weighin' him down. Caveman used to be a body builder that was addicted to food, steroids, and weights, but over the years, though the love of food remained, he'd traded the latter two euphorias for the love of crawfish, white hoes with big titties, and smugglin' illegal shit through the black market. My mans was a boulder of hardened fat, and as I studied fam, I smiled. With his long blonde hair tied to the back and the fullness of his Santa Claus beard, the man truly lived up to his moniker. I watched in amusement as he dabbed at his mouth with a white cloth as a topless snow bunny extended a steaming spoon toward his lips. The aroma of the etouffee wafted throughout the old house as the big man pushed the spoon away, but the Carmen Electra lookin' bitch seemed adamant to add a few extra pounds to the heavy weighter.

Smack!

The spoon flew across the room when Cavemen slapped it out her hand, causing some of the Cajun stew to spill onto the lady's surgically enhanced triple D's.

"Goddammit, Caveman, ya crazy motherfucker, ya tryin' to boil my tits!" she cried as she leaped from the sunken couch. I smirked at the fact that those silicon-filled titties didn't budge in the least as she began to blow and wipe at the spot the hot stew landed on.

"Well, I told ya, you ditzy broad, I got company, ya hear. Now get lost, Barbara," Caveman demanded. The woman gave him an evil glare before giving him the finger and storming off.

"And don't ya be in dere doin' up all my dope, whore!" Caveman's words followed her out the room.

"Fuck you, Caveman, just fuck yourself!" she spat.

I laughed when the fat man leaned forward from the shadows and fixed me with a dark stare of amusement. I felt Thugga stiffen beside me as he and Stick Talk bared witness to the work of art the fat man had done to his face. The letters *ABT* were scrawled across his right cheek in big block letters. My mans was one of the five generals of the Aryan Brotherhood of Texas, but due to his infamy and being wanted down in the Lone Star State for organized crime, he'd relocated to the boot to get lost in the backwood swamps. Me and the man had met when I'd had to do a lil' skid bid at the big house. Those dirty mu'fuckas had tossed me in the cell with the mammoth white man expecting me to be dead by morning. Yet, killas respect killas, and though our racial differences were as real as those iron bars that held us captive, we got on our grown man shit and found a colorless common ground that allowed us to learn from the misology of our inherited dogmas. One day, I'd come to our cell to find Caveman hemmed up by a group of gangstas that wasn't feelin' that white power shit, and since I'd never fucked wit' bullies like that, I handled that. Since then, the white supremacist had kept it more gully with me than most of the men of my same ethnic group.

"Hope the ride through that dere bayou wasn't too troublesome. I know dem dere gators are as ornery as a pregnant bitch searching for a place to have her pups." Caveman's wordplay was evidence of how he'd become one with his environment. He chuckled as his eyes swept over Thugga and Stick Talk. "I don't think I've met ya kin, Ghetto, and I don't think I like that one too much." He nodded at Stick Talk. The tension shot up a few degrees as the big man reached for the golden cane that I'd just noticed leaning against the couch. The big man rocked forward in an attempt at getting to his feet. I impulsively moved beside the older man to assist him in his pursuit, but he waved me off. "I've been gettin' around on my own since ya was just a squirt of water in ya pappy's nut sack, son, let me be." His pride was strong as he wobbled forward and made it halfway to his feet, but gravity whooped weight's ass as it pulled Caveman's big ass back down to the couch.

Poof! He fell onto it while knocking the left leg off the bottom of the furniture. Caveman muttered curses as he glanced back up at me, ever stubborn, but relenting. "Well, the old legs may not be as sturdy as they were back then, either, eh." We shared a laugh as I helped him to his feet. The big man retrieved his golden cane before making his way over to my blows. He and Stick Talk eye wrestled for a moment before Stick Talk gave in to that "G" shit.

"Mane, I don't give a fuck who you like, white—"

"But"—the big man cut his gangsterisms in half—"any friend of Ghetto's is a friend of mine. I trust dis here boy with my life!" He smiled a tobacco-stained smile before slapping Stick Talk on the back so hard that the man's knees buckled.

"Now, let's talk business," Caveman spoke as he walked toward the back of the house. Me and my blows locked eyes. Both men seemed speechless as I moved to follow the big man. I chuckled as Stick Talk rubbed his shoulder.

"You niggas be easy. Ain't too many young niggas bossin' up like we 'bout to, *tttttah*!" I made a mock Draco with my hands and pretended to spray the room with bullets.

***

-Heaven-

"Heeyyyy, party over here!" I could hear Egypt shout drunkenly. I perspired slightly as I awaited Empress to give me the cue to pop out the cake and show my ass. I still couldn't believe them niggas was so lame that they'd invite a bunch of bitches they didn't know to the bando. They didn't know if we were the type of women that set niggas up or not, and that's why most niggas weren't fit to sit on the throne. *How the hell can a man rule an empire, protect his queen, and secure a bag, if he can't even control his own dick!* I thought as I waited.

"Say, lil' bitch, what's up wit' the cake girl, when she gone let a nigga see that pussy?" I could hear one of them disrespectful niggas shouting. We hadn't been there but for a few minutes, so that told me that they'd started to turn up way before the pussy arrived. I smiled, nothin' took niggas off their game like liquor, pussy, or impatience, and me and my ladies encouraged all three. "Naw, on God! Tell that hoe to come on up out that mu'fucka, and she bet not be ugly, tryin' to pop out the cake like she a bad bitch, but is really a nightmare. Don't worry 'bout it, I'm 'bout to get her ass up outta there. What you niggas wanna bet this hoe the lil' sista that's bigger than the big sista!" I could hear the voice approaching. I had to suppress a giggle, but—

"I bet this bitch hop out wit' a fat ass, some long feet like LeBron, and some ashy ass elbows!" Dude's potnas fed in and caused me to lose the war with my laughter. The room became silent. The only sound being the loud music they were playing. "See, even *she* knows a nigga ain't lyin'!" The voice was upon me. The room burst into laughter as I smiled. *BOOM!* The first bullet tore through the cardboard cake in a flaming ball. The paper sparked but died out when the gun jumped in my hands. The slug found home in his abdomen, folding him over. "What the fuck!" he cried as a long river of blood slid from the corner of his mouth. The surprise was deep as I exploded from the top of the cake and with no time to waste, I gripped the pink baby nine with both hands. *BOOM!*

The second ball of lead closed his curtains and knocked a squirt of his blood across my mouth and chin. "Surprise!" I shouted before running my tongue over my bloody lips. I aimed the tool at the eight or so men in the room. Egypt rushed over. "Bitch, give me my heat so we can get this party poppin' in boss bitch fashion!" she shouted before I handed her Empress's and her tools. Egypt had shown up only minutes earlier, and her short, thick ass had mesmerized the room. She tossed the gun and as soon as her fingers closed around that steel, Empress became *she woman!*

"Aiiight, you niggas act like y'all know and get dick—I mean, get face down, y'all know what's up!" she demanded with a giggle as I freed myself from the *still* smoking cake. I shook my head, *so shame!* The girl was too extra. "Uh uh, everybody, but *you*, you're the lucky man tonight, playboy, what—" She stormed over and snatched a light-skinned cat up by the thick necklace he flossed with. She put the .380 to the man's temple as she pulled the diamond-filled pendant close to her eyes for inspection. Empress sucked her teeth in disgust. "Frontin' ass nigga, this shit is just as fraudulent as the nigga that's wearin' these cloudy ass diamonds!" she spat as she forced him in front of her.

"Hol' up, mane, what kinda shit you hoes on!" he shouted as Empress *squeezed* his ass. She giggled before digging the barrel into the back of his head.

"We ain't gone be too many more of yo' bitches and hoes, bitch! What, you thought you was gonna get a free feel? Nigga, *please*, this ass expensive! Now, tell me where that Fetti at before I put ya face all ova this floor for slapping it earlier." The crazy bitch kissed the back of dude's neck as if they were sharing an intimate moment.

"They killed Tweet, Mane, hell naw, they smoked my dog!" one of the cats Egypt had face down cried. I smirked. It was a rule of ours to kill one, or even two, to set the bar in every lick we hit. There was nothin' a man respected more than a bitch that was about her check, especially when she had a fat ass and a pistol she wasn't afraid to bust. Empress giggled as she pushed dude forward. "I told you my girl's pussy would *surprise* you if that money right. Surprise, nigga!" She slapped him on the ass as they headed down the hallway. "You're cute, I might have to put this pussy on ya lips before I kill you. You eva ate pussy at gunpoint?" I shook my head as me and Egypt glanced at each other.

"Empress, don't be on ya *extra* shit, just secure the bag and let's get the hell outta here!" I rolled my eyes with the demand.

"Bitch, quit crying, I won't be long. *I know* you seen the lips on this boy!" Her voice came from down the hallway. I frowned, but the shit must've really tickled Egypt, 'cause my girl giggled so hard she could barely hold the pistol straight. *Crazy bitches!* I shook my head.

***

-Ghetto-

We were surrounded by trees and swamp land as we watched Caveman dig into a big bucket and pull out a bloody pig's head. The man tossed it out into the large yard and as soon as it touched his tongue, the big alligator's jaws clamped shut on the raw piece of meat before it scrambled backwards as if someone would try to steal its food. The expression on Thugga's face was evident. *White folks!* We were in the back yard where we'd been introduced to three other hill billies, but it was the man in the center of the madness that had my attention. He was a mere five foot ten inches, a no-nonsense white boy that wore one of those high and tight buzz cuts that high-ranking military white men sported. He was shirtless, but the army fatigue pants and some extra laced up shiny boots told a tale all in its own.

"This here boy is my brother, Bobby, he's special ops and a damned good thief," Caveman made the intros. The man looked as if his name should've been Butch or GI Joe or some shit like that, but who was I to argue. The other two men were also armed forces and obviously lower in rank. My eyes kept falling to the five wooden crates that resembled coffins without all the gloss and interior decorating. Each were stamped with big, bold, red codes, like *G66AOL*. Though I knew it was some kinda military propaganda, I was still curious as to what the fuck it meant.

"So, my brother tells me that you did him a good service up there in Angola." Bobby's first words were stained by his exhale of a long stream of nicotinic smoke. I nodded as my eyes went to the pal-mal cigarette he was taking deep pulls from. I wasn't sure if he'd somehow saw through the dark lenses of my aviators or if his senses were just that acute, but pimp took another pull from the cancer stick before tossing it to the moist ground and smashing it with his foot.

"Sorry, bad habits die hard." He chuckled as his eyes took me in before falling over Thugga and Stick Talk in a studious gaze. Coming to some sort of conclusion, the man nodded his head to his two subordinates. The men came to life at his command and took crowbars to two of the crates. We watched as the tops popped off and the mute men went back to standing at attention. Thugga whistled at the dangerous sight, but it was Stick Talk that almost busted a nut.

"Yea, that's what the fuck I'm talm 'bout!" he exclaimed before reaching down and pulling one of the .223s from the stockpile. The assault rifle looked like some sort of gadget, and noticing my intrigue, buzz cut felt the need to enlighten me.

"That there beauty is a .223 with a sighting scope that's two times bigger than a man's mouth. The magnification can see an eyelash that's falling from a man's eyelids. It comes with a see-through cartridge that will allow you to see each round you fire." He smiled before making his way to the second crate. "These beauties are

M110s. They fire rounds seconds within a volley. These here drums is what we call *partners in crime* because they're two in one!" He smiled as I nodded at the drums the streets knew as monkey nuts.

"What's this gonna run me, my dude?" I spoke the question we all anticipated. Bobby pulled a short-bodied rifle from the crate and tossed it to me. Our eyes danced before he spoke.

"It's thirty-six high-powered work here, some with extra clips and others equipped with sound suppressors," he baited for his play. I gave him a crooked smirk to let him know I was on to him.

"Let's say thirty grand."

I raised the pipe and admired it. It resembled a Draco, but with more edge and definition. "Twenty-seven and we can lock it in," I bargained. The silence was thick as the man and his peoples communicated with their eyes before Ole Bobby's gaze found his brother. He and Caveman smiled.

"Well, looks like we're in business." Bobby sealed the deal while extending his hand. We shook as Stick Talk aimed the empty gun out at the woods and took a peek through the scope.

"Saaaayy, mane, homie wasn't lyin'!" he shouted. Me and Thugga gave him a puzzled expression until he elaborated.

"Fam, I just saw two mosquitos fuckin' in mid-air, Flesh, on God!" he declared. We all burst into laughter. I knew my flesh was gonna have fun with his new toy.

Renta

Chapter 4
Gangstas...Intelligence...and Intrigue

-Heaven-

Days later

I knew I looked like shit. I'd spent half the night arguing with my ex, and the nigga just couldn't seem to get it through his thick ass head that it was over. Pap had come over, and just because I'd let him Netflix and chill, he thought my diplomacy rectified the relationship. The night had also been long at the club. Yo Gotti and his squad had made it thunderstorm, and though I'd raked up my share of ones, my ass was wore down and only God knew how bitchy I was that morning. I clutched my books and assignments to my chest as I returned Empress's text, and as soon as I turned the corner leading to the Lincoln's building—*Bam!*

The collision was so powerful that my books crashed to the ground and I fell on my ass right beside 'em. My temperature rose as I stared up at him. Ghetto was just as stunned as I was and gritted on me just as tough. "Say, fam, watch where..." His words trailed off and his eyes softened when he recognized me. I didn't know if it was more of the fact of me being a woman or it being *me* that caused the transformation, but dude reached his hand out.

"My fault, Ms. Lady, it's all on me." I pushed his gesture away with a roll of my eyes before climbing to my feet and dusting myself off.

"Well, you need to watch where the hell you're going, clumsy ass nigga," I fumed, though I knew it was me that wasn't paying attention to where I was going. Ghetto ignored me and gathered my things while I stood there pouting. I crossed my arms over my breasts impatiently as he dusted my things off.

"I think this is yours, ma." He handed me my written assignment along with my government book but felt the need to get in my business. "What you know 'bout *Life Among the Lowly?*" he inquired with a humorous chuckle. My blood began to boil. I never

73

understood why people shunned knowledge. After so many years of the Caucasians forbidding us the right of education in an attempt at keeping black people inferior. After so much of this miseducation? I just didn't understand *why* a people would *willingly* choose to mentally handicap themselves. It's as if after so many years of forced ignorance, the trait had become a choice. I snatched the book out dude's hand with a roll of my eyes. Ever since Professor Kennedy had spoken of the woman Harriet Beecher Stowe and her influential novel, *Uncle Tom's Cabin*, I'd been intrigued with the daring white woman who at a time that one could be hung for siding with black people, inscribed a book that not only caused white people to see our struggle, but the book was also a main contributor to the abolition of slavery.

"I wouldn't expect a bird-brained ass dude like you to know. You probably barely completed school and think selling drugs your entire life is a life's career! Boy, move!" I spazzed as dude jumped in front of me with a smile on his face. I was so *not* in the mood for the kid games, but Ghetto seemed to either not notice or he just didn't give a damn. Every time I attempted to pass, he'd move in front of me.

"So, you're not feelin' me? Dig this, Queen, I don't know you and you don't know me, but that's part of the cliché of *perfect* strangers," he jazzed before walking backwards up the building's steps. With a roll of my eyes and a pitying shake of my head, I *had* to follow the clown—we were heading to the same lecture hall. "So, you're the little woman who wrote the book that made this great war." Ghetto's nerve-wrecking ass called himself spitting some kinda game. It was *lame*! I paused in humor as I looked up at him.

"What? I know you can come better than that, that was—"

"Abraham Lincoln." He cut me off with a mischievous smirk.

"Excuse me?" I was dumbfounded.

"That *shit* you speak of was what Abraham Lincoln said to Harriet Stowe when he met her in 1862." He burst into laughter. "When the slave mother, Lucy, drowned herself after her seed was stolen and sold, that shit fucked wit' my heart. Shid, that book is where slaves coined the term *Uncle Tom*. That humbled slave was really just too scared and chose submission over gettin' his ass whooped, but that dick sucka Simon Legree still whacked Uncle Tom's humble ass." His humor at the shocked expression on my face echoed down the hall as Ghetto turned and left me in awe!

***

-Ghetto-

I sat slouched down in my seat, halfway sleep as the pink ass white man praised a corrupted history. My memaw had been reading to me since I was a lil' nigga, and as soon as I was old enough to understand, the woman force fed me history, and the knowledge of the gods and Earths. She made sure that I didn't believe in a spook in the sky or pray to a white man with blonde hair and blue eyes. As I reflected on my queen, my horn vibrated on my hip, causing me to jump in surprise. I pulled it from its clip and brought the screen to life.

This pussy wet, when you comin' for a swim? The text made me smile. Kasha was a supa freak I'd been pipin' for a few weeks, and the hoe had a pussy that gripped that dick like it neva wanted to let go. *School, I'll pull up on you, show that work after I tend to my B-I.* I returned the text.

I, nor she, can't wait, daddy. It's been waaayyy too long! :(I smiled until the devil interrupted my vibe.

"I'm not too sure, Professor, but I'm sure that he can enlighten us." The girl whose name I still hadn't learned caught my attention.

"Could he now, and why don't you, Mr. Bousard, *without* the assistance of Google, may I add." My eyes shot up at the request of the professor. All eyes diverted to me as I slid the phone back into its holder and set my vision on the woman who'd just put me on blast. The lady sat a few rows down from me with a smug expression on her face.

"Huh? I mean, can you repeat the question, Mr. Kennedy? It was important that I respond to that," I lied with a nod at my phone. The man gave me a knowing smile but didn't push it.

"We were just speaking on how the great Abraham Lincoln fought so courageously for the freedom of the slaves against the confederate," the man spoke before pointing up at the smart board where a blown-up picture of the Emancipation Proclamation was on display. I sat up in my seat on the verge of playing naive, but as my eyes fell back to Ms. Lady, her earlier disrespect played within the walls of my mental. *"I wouldn't expect a bird-brained ass nigga like you to know. You probably barely completed school and think selling drugs your entire life is a life's career! Boy, move!"* Her assumption was the same one that society as a whole used to pass judgement on brothas that didn't fit their opinion of trustworthy. Merely because a nigga had gold teeth, wore urban wear, and came from the slums, mu'fuckas held the misconception that he was ignorant. I smiled at lil' baby before facin' off with the white man that undoubtedly had preached that warped and twisted history to thousands of black students before me.

"Professor, Abraham was a smart strategist, but dude didn't free the slaves." My announcement caused a stir in the room.

"Ungrateful, motherfuckers!" a freckled faced white cat a few seats down from me spat with a shake of his head. I could feel Ms. Lady studying me, curiosity intermingling with surprise in her gaze.

"And why might you speak such nonsense of the forefather that made it possible for you and your great people to be free from bondage?" The professor seemed intrigued, but more so disrespected. I chuckled, I knew his word play had an underlying meaning, *you and your not so great people*, but his nuts weren't big enough to speak his truths. I leaned forward and rested my elbows on the back of the chair in front of me.

"Dig this, out the gate of the war, free blacks tried to volunteer to rock wit' the Union Army, but Lincoln and his folks wasn't feelin' putting negroes in uniform. In fact," I paused to make quotations with my fingers, "Ole Lincoln stated in the spring of 1862 that to arm Negroes would turn fifty thousand bayonets from the loyal border states against us that were for us." I laughed at the blood that rushed to Professor Kennedy's face, but they'd asked for my input, so I wasn't gonna sugarcoat shit. I spread my arms wide

like the wings of that bald eagle the United States used as their insignia and gave it to 'em.

"It took months until Abraham came up with the perfect plan to aid in that war. On September twenty-second, he issued the Emancipation Proclamation sayin' that on the first of January of 1863, all slaves in areas of rebellion against the United States were free. The man even defended the proclamation by claiming that the emancipation was a military necessity and absolutely *essential to the preservation of the Union!* To top that off, Abraham Lincoln even argued a point—*we must free the slaves or be ourselves subdued!*" I leaned back in my seat and allowed my words to be digested. The silence was thick until Professor cleared his throat.

"You must understand, Mr. Bousard, that Mr. Lincoln was under great pressure from not only southerners, but the white northerners who didn't want blacks to—"

"Naw, naw, OG, that shit didn't matter, because dude didn't free *any* slaves. That emancipation only applied to the slaves in confederate territories where Lincoln *didn't have jurisdiction,* but the white boy tried to keep slaves under *his* control—*the Union's* control. Even the secretary of state, William Seward, knew the play. *That's* why he said, *where he could, he didn't. Where he did, he couldn't.*" I silenced the older man. He cut the power on the smart board before pulling the thick reading glasses from his face. I smiled before glancing down at the stunned woman who'd earlier spat on the Godism.

Checkmate, I thought.

***

-Heaven-

"Say, hol' up, lil' mama, let me holla at you real quick!" someone shouted from behind me. I turned with attitude to find a cute muscular brother approaching. I paused and let him catch up.

"Damn, gorgeous, where's the fire?" He smiled with some of the world's deepest dimples. His smile was contagious.

"Well, that depends on what type of fire you're referring to, the wild or tamed one?" I gave a suggestive glance down at my bulging *lower* lips. I had fun watching brotha man fumble for a reply. I knew I'd caught him off guard. He chuckled away his surprise.

"Was there somethin' you wanted? I'm kinda pressed." I kept it bossy with cutie. He freed something from a stack and extended it to me. Confusion was evident on my face as I skeptically accepted it. Glancing down at the card, I smiled.

Omega Psi Phi's *putting on for this year's graduates, come turn up with us and*—I stopped reading as I found his hopeful gaze.

"And why would I wanna go to this little party and be entertained by a bunch of drunk men?" I smirked.

"I was just wondering if-if maybe you, umm..." he stuttered, fearful of rejection.

"Maybe I'll what, be your trophy date or somethin'?" I teased.

"Yea—I mean no, mann, look, I'm just trying to vibe with you, Black woman. I'm in your class and I'm feelin' what I see."

Dude was as bashful as an eighth grader asking an attractive girl to the school dance. It was cute though.

"What's your name, dimples?" I reached up and pinched his cheek.

"DeJun, and yours?"

"Catrina." I gave him my sister's name. Turning and hitting the automatic locks on the Aston caused baby boy to finally take notice of the pretty bitch.

"Man, tell me that's not the Vanquish, hell naw!" His bopping was a cute turn off, but I understood. That car was *almost* as bossy as me. I slid behind the wheel and hit the push-button start before closing my door on him.

I'd rather be ya B.I.T.C.H, 'cause that's what you gone call me when I'm trippin' anyway. Megan Thee Stallion spoke the gospel before I muted her and let the window down.

"I may or may not come, you're too cute for me to just diss you, but I'm too bossy to make promises I can't keep. We'll see, Papi." I smiled before easing out the parking space, careful not to run over

the Retro's he was rocking. Lil' daddy was still standing there gazing awestruck at the taillights of the Aston Martin as I pulled out the lot, and just when I was about to let Megan talk that real shit— "What the fuck!" I shouted as I stomped down on the brake. The vibrations from the trunk of his Masi were earth shaking as Lil' Baby's "Something to Prove" roared from the speakers.

***

-Ghetto-

Though it wasn't intentional, I'd caught lil' baby at the perfect time. I'd watched her exchange wit' lil' daddy and gauging from the way he stood back in the parking lot, mouth agape and lookin' like a bonafide weenie, she either rejected him or put playboy on pause. I contemplated it for a lil' bit before tossing caution to the wind, and that's why I'd cut her off and blocked her exit before sliding from the driver's seat. She'd had her fun in class, it was my turn.

"What the fuck you think you're doing, dude? You can't just cut people off in the middle of traffic like this," she spazzed before glancing in her rearview at the line of cars behind her.

Beeeeep! Beeeeeep! Someone laid on their horn. I ignored their impatience as I gave shawty the once over with my gaze. "I neva got a name, mama, and I find that's real disrespectful being as though I blessed you with mine."

"Well, that's *your* problem, not mine! Look, I don't have time for the games. You need to move your car so I can—what the fuck!" Lil' one was caught off guard as I reached down into her lap and freed the promotional card from off her thigh.

"Omega Psi Phi, huh? I didn't take you for the schoolboy type." Lil' mama rolled her eyes before swiping her curly hair out her face.

"And how the fuck would you know my type, *Einstein*? You don't know shit about me!"

"I know enough about you to know you strip for a *past time*, 'cause there's no way you're puttin' on like this"—I nodded down at the foreign—"on no stripper's salary. I know enough about ya to know that you hidin' a bunch of hurt behind all that designer bullshit you wear to make a nigga focus more on ya ass and titties than the cracks in yo' heart." I stood erect and flickered the card back inside the car, and as it fluttered to the floor on the passenger's side, I hit Queen with a fatality of the verbal realm.

"Most of all, I know enough about you to know that you've been hurt so much by the faith you've placed into a slave-given God that you've lost faith in *God* altogether. *That's* why you can't recognize God in his *physical,* because the shit you was taught to believe will rescue you from the pain, lead you to feel as if you're talking to yourself when you pray, huh?"

I turned to mash off, but stopped to put the nail in her coffin, yet she was ever stubborn. "You through? Can I go now?" she asked, but I was a wolf, I sensed her weakness. I'd knocked a crack through that weak ass facade she hid her heart behind. I smiled.

"Naw, I'm not. Not until I got your attention, and maybe even just a *small* piece of what I want."

"And what is it you want from me, Mr. Ghetto?"

I turned to face her, smile absent, and straight to the bidness. "You can hide ya heart behind a million bricks, barricade it behind all the designer clothes you can find, but know this, ma, I'm comin' in and *takin'* what I want. By the way…" I spoke over my shoulder as I made my way toward my slab. I hopped behind the wheel and muted the music for merely seconds before speaking to her from the enclosure of woodgrain. "I'm a god you can believe in, mama, and I promise you'll never feel as if you're talking to yourself."

I gave it to Lady before unmuting Lil' Baby's "Something to Prove," and doing an injustice to the twenty-six-inch big heads as I left burnt rubber and gold reflections on the asphalt. *Beeeeep! Beeeeep!* I could hear the congested traffic mashing on their horns, demanding Queen to move out the way. I smirked when I looked up into the rearview. She was still on pause as I blended into traffic, and the crazy part was, *I still didn't know Lady's name.*

Chapter 5
Finally... A Proper Introduction...Then... Death

-Heaven-
Later that night

The sounds of the barking were loud. We heard the call before we saw them. It sounded as if an army was marching toward us, but when the line of black brothas entered the room, they may not have been an army, but they did show up in raw fashion. The first man was shirtless and his six pack was on fleek as he drummed his hands against his chest like it was a congo drum. His feet moved at a rapid pace as if they were at war with his hands, a vicious battle of seeing who could move the quickest. "Q dawwwg! Woof! If you ain't a Q dawg you ain't shit!" the other eight brothers chanted as they stomped and clapped their hands between their legs in sync.

"Ohooo, bitch, look at 'em!" Egypt was excited. My eyes scanned the room of the frat house. It wasn't our usual hype, but it felt good not to be on the lurk for a nigga. Even my sis, Catrina, was enjoying herself, and she didn't even like men. My baby girl had never been the same after the shit with our uncle, and though she'd taken on the qualities of a man, the girl was just too pretty to make it work for her. She tried, though, and I loved her regardless, but as my eyes found Empress's party popping ass, I impulsively sucked my teeth. She always found a way to try and kill my vibe.

"Man, this shit whack. I could be at the club, at least I'd be able to get paid for my attention," she huffed before pulling out her phone. Egypt and I rolled our eyes simultaneously. *This bitch!* I bet her thoughts were a mutual sentiment of mine. My girl must've felt my disgust 'cause she glanced up from the screen and rolled her eyes.

"The fuck? What *you* need to worry 'bout is pretty boy that you *act* like you not feelin'." She snaked her neck. I didn't understand, but it was the sly smile that caused me to follow her gaze. I turned to see what she was speaking of, and my heart did this funny trick in my chest. *This nigga just don't quit! What is he doing here?* I wondered as my eyes devoured him. *Delicious!*

***

-Ghetto-

I knew me and Stick Talk stuck out like skinny hoes wit' a fat ass. The black thermal shirt I wore wasn't a smart idea for that night, 'cause though it was a perfect match for the black Dior pants I wore, the .40 was ever noticeable. The only splash of color I wore was the red alligator Dior belt that complemented the candy red Dior shoes on my feet. The thick Cuban link sat pretty around my neck as it glistened against the darkness of the thermal shirt. My dreads were twisted back into two thick braids, and as I glanced down at the *AP* on my wrist, I almost laughed. The stones in that bitch were so watery, it was hard to tell what time it was. My blow Stick Talk was on his designer shit, Chanel *everythang*! The drip was too hard, from the tie-dyed silk shirt to the black Mark Jellous' that did it to 'em. They were high fashion with golden spikes glistening all over them. "Flesh, tell me again why we here?" My youngin's eyes revealed his distaste as his hand grazed the *thirty* I'd requested him not to bring. I chuckled. Stick Talk was a seventeen-year-old dope fiend's son that didn't give a fuck 'bout life. At times, I wondered if lil' bro *lived* to *step on sommin'!*

"Chill, Flesh, never be afraid to experience new shit, feel me?" I responded. Bro didn't respond, and when my eye drifted to him to see the bidness, I followed his gaze. As soon as me and Queen's eyes met, I realized that gangstas needed love too. Subconsciously, I knew that I wanted to be loved by *a real woman*, but consciously I knew that I *couldn't,* didn't know how to reciprocate that love. I frowned in frustration, but *why?* I wondered. I *wanted* to! Shit in the streets was so crazy that the relations between a man and woman had become disrespectful. Niggas was so in tune with what was between a woman's legs that they didn't give a fuck about her virtue, and that's what had niggas wakin' up with bangas in their face... Set

82

up by the same bitch they fell asleep next to. Women had lost so much of their self-worth that they'd trade virtue for the sake of some good dick or the pleasure of getting their pussy sucked.

As I watched Ms. Lady pull all that wavy ass hair over her left shoulder, and smile at something her homegirl said, I knew *I* needed more. Lil' baby was surrounded by a group of bad bitches, one of which had captured Stick Talk's attention. "Damn, Blow, who dat?" he inquired, tryin' to keep it playa and appear as if he wasn't sweatin' lil' mama, but I was making it official that *I* was on the hunt.

I willed my eyes to reveal to her that I was a special kinda nigga. I was the sun and needed an earth to revolve around me that I could fertilize with my godism. Queen tilted her head to the side as she ran her fingers through her long hair and *pretended* not to notice the god watching her. I smiled as she was interrupted by playboy that had invited her there, and before she even gave him the *extra* smile she gave him, I knew she was 'bout to put on just to see my reaction. I chuckled at her play. As I observed lil' baby, I fell in love with the *idea* of ballin' and blowin' bags wit' her. I could see that lady carried herself differently than the norm, but I'd learned earlier on that the eyes had a way of playin' tricks on the mind, and by the time a mu'fucka figured out they'd been robbed, their heart was stolen by a thief that would never be able to appreciate the shit they'd pocketed.

***

-Heaven-

"Glad you made it, boo, how're you enjoying yourself?" DeJun smiled that dimpled smile that was enough to make a girl melt in her panties.

"Oh, I think I'm a lil' parched, y'all excuse me. Aren't y'all thirsty?" Egypt felt the need to excuse herself. She and Catrina smiled a knowing smile as they departed, but Empress's crazy ass was in raw form.

"Naw, I ain't thirsty," she replied, even though they couldn't hear her. Her yellow ass turned a crooked smirk on the college man.

"What's ya name, birthday, and license plate number? I heard about you frat boys. Y'all like to get a girl drunk and do all kinds of—"

"Empress!" I cut her off with a roll of my eyes, but the bitch was just *her!*

"What?" She gave me that *sneaky* smirk. "*He* knows I ain't lyin'!" She giggled. I could tell that DeJun wasn't used to women like my girl, and I was sure he'd never been that up close and personal with bitches as bad as us. He didn't know how to respond, but the stack of cards I'd begun to shuffle rescued him from his discomfort.

"Is those what I think they are?" He beamed.

"Lame, lame, be quiet," Empress muttered. I elbowed her for being ghetto.

"That depends on what you think they are?" I made my way over to the dining room table and took a seat. Shuffling the cards, I gave him a suggestive smile. "Yea, they're cards of fate. People with *the gift* usually use them." He sat down across from me. I splayed the cards out before me, and from that moment on, I charged thirty dollars a head for a reading.

***

-Ghetto-

"Can I get my future read, or are gangstas not allowed?" I asked as I walked up to the table.

"Say, brah, wait ya turn," the cornball that sat across from her fumed. Queen gave me a quick glance before returning her gaze back to the cards. She looked up at her customer and smiled as she flipped over another card.

"This says you're gonna come into a lot of money, it's the sign of prosperity." She nodded down to the depiction of a golden cup that was so full that what I assumed to be wine, ran over the lip of it.

"You're persistent, I give you that." She giggled, and I knew her words were meant for me.

84

"Say, playboy, excuse us real quick, let me convo wit' the lady for a second." I tried my hand at addressing the sucka wit' tact, but just as I assessed, lil' daddy didn't respect playerism.

"Brah, I paid thirty bucks for this shit, back up off me," he spat as he glared up at me as if he was lookin' for some smoke. I chuckled, mentally taming that *action* in me. It took all I had not to up the tool and put dude's next thoughts all over that table. I dug in my pocket and pulled three hundred from the dope boy knot.

"Peace, sun, look, you paid thirty punk dollas for this shit, here's three hundred to disappear," I reasoned.

"Ghetto, let the man—"

"Two kings versin', Queen, ain't no room for your inputs. I'll get to you in a minute." I decapitated Lady's interruption and laid the law down. She sat back in her seat and pouted.

"Say, homie, you ain't gotta talk to her like—"

"Mane, let me see this shit, Flesh, you *see* diplomacy ain't workin'!" Stick Talk growled before snatching *one* of the bills out my hand and pullin' up on playboy on that gangsta shit. Before I could stop him, Stick had the FN in his clutch and pressed against dude's thinkin' cap.

"Open your mouth, nigga. Open it before I shoot you in it!" he demanded. The party came to a screeching halt as the room filled with fearful anticipation. Dude must've known that my flesh was wit' the shit, 'cause he cracked his mouth open. Stick Talk gripped homie by the jaws, causing his lips to pucker before stuffing the barrel down his throat.

"Nigga, I don't know what you heard, but this *RNO* shit official! Now you gonna take this hundo and get yo' *stomp the yard* ass up out this seat, so my flesh can do what he do, right?" he growled. Dude's eyes watered as he trembled in fear, yet he nodded his head feverishly in consent. Stick Talk pulled the tool free of its baptism, homies saliva dripping from the barrel, and shoved the money into dude's shirt. With the burna still trained on him, my *Blow* put on for this RNO shit.

"Now, apologize to RNO, nigga!" I gritted.

"I apologize, my bad, man."

"Bitch, don't play silly games wit' a grown man. I said apologize to *RNO!*" Stick Talk was beastin'.

"I apologize to RNO, I apologize, man, *please* don't kill me. I'm just a college kid tryin' to get my MBA!" Dude had lost the spunk he'd had only moments ago. Stick Talk used the man's UTA hoodie to clean the spit off the gun before gritting on him.

"Fuck outta here, corn ball ass nigga!"

Playboy didn't waste time scurrying from his seat, and as he bolted past, Stick Talk placed a spiked foot right in the crack of his ass. I laughed as bro tucked the banga and glared at the stunned faces in the room.

"Fuck y'all starin' at me for? I only fuck wit' *Real Niggas Only*, and that chump ain't fit the description."

***

-Heaven-

I sat with my arms crossed over my chest, staring as his arrogant ass plopped down in the chair across from me. My eyes fell to the Cuban link around his neck before falling to the matching Audemars that was embellished with diamonds that was as clear as purified water. Though I wasn't feelin' the way he'd handled me, the ocean my pussy had melted into gave a contradicting argument.

"So?" he asked as if he hadn't just strong armed a man for that seat and paid him *ten* times the fee.

"So?" I reflected his inquiry before lifting my left hand to observe the fresh French tips I'd just gotten done that day. Whoever *the extra* in Ghetto's movie was, burst into laughter at our stand-off, but before he could compose himself, he ran into a challenge of his own.

"*Damn*, nigga, I know what I'm 'bout to say ain't lady like, but only a grown woman can speak her mind without concern of other's opinions." Empress's voice greeted him before he turned his eyes upon her. She sashayed our way, being *extra* with the sway of her hips. She gave dude that *scandalous* ass smile before being *soooo*

Empress. "That shit you just did made this pussy wetttt!" she purred as she nodded down at the bulge that imprinted the one-piece cat suit she wore. I glanced over to see if Ghetto was doggish enough to *sneak* him a peek, but to my surprise, his eyes were trained on me, as if he was attempting to memorize *every* detail of my face.

"Yea, I usually have that effect on women, it's just my RNO aroma." Ghetto's sidekick smirked arrogantly. That's when it dawned on me. *This the nigga that slapped my ass at the club!* My eyes turned to slits as I contemplated going for the baby Ruger I had strapped to my ankle, but luckily—

"RNO aroma? You lost me, lil' daddy." Empress was confused as she placed her manicured hands on her shapely hips. The girl had mastered this pigeon-toed stance that drove niggas crazy, and dude was no different. He shook his head, lust drunk from Empress's seduction.

"It's that unique shit you smell on real niggas only. It's a lifestyle, lil' baby, but only a real bitch can smell it. We'll get to that in a minute. What's ya name, Lady?" the crazy man asked as he stepped into my girl's space. Empress didn't back down, and as lion and lioness faced off, I wondered the outcome.

"Yella, my name is Yella Girl." She gave him *the* smile and as soon as she gave him the false identity, I knew my best friend had marked dude—he was *food!* Our eyes met briefly before she took the man's hand.

"And what they call yo' sexy ass? I know you *have* to have a *gangsta* name to fit that crazy ass persona," she asked as she pulled him toward a far corner of the room.

"Stick Talk." He smirked as his hand subconsciously grazed the butt of his burna. "Stick Talk? What's all that about?" Empress smiled, her quick eyes noting the move.

"Stick Talk, you know, as in, when it's smoke, that's the *only* language I speak," Stick Talk introduced himself. There was something in my gut that old me that his proclamation was more than merely a punch line to impress her. I truly believed dude was 'bout that action.

"Hey, you have a full movie in front of you, why you settling for the commercial?" Ghetto was on his cocky shit. My eyes diverted until they were captured by his.

"I find commercials more informative, and I'm honestly not into gangsta movies where the bad boy makes a million promises to the girl that falls for him, only to trade those exact vows for some streets that can never love him," I prophesied. Ghetto leaned forward on his elbows, studying me intently. It was something different about him that I couldn't seem to put my finger on. *Real Niggas Only?* I remembered what Stick Talk said the acronym meant as I studied the tattoo underneath his eye.

"Maybe you're just watching the wrong gangsta movies, if that's the only conclusion you've seen. See, the thang about cinerama is that the director and the characters *want* you to see the belittlement of a man that's had to get it out the mud. It's a message in that shit that's forged by mu'fuckas that's never had to borrow hot water from their neighbor or steal cable. It's just how people that's never been in the streets view street niggas, but I wouldn't expect *you* to understand," Ghetto shot with a smirk. I smiled coyly before shuffling the cards. It never ceased to amaze me how people saw a pretty face, a black woman that had found *her* emancipation from the slavery of other's opinions, and just figured that she hadn't been through shit. I knew when Ghetto looked at me, all he saw was the beauty, all this ass, and titties, but I wondered if he'd still be so persistent in his pursuit if he knew the ugliness behind what he found so beautiful.

I spread the cards out before us as dude gave me his realisms. "The difference between reality and the movies is in a movie, life is fabricated, you already know the bad guy's life will end *tragically*, but in real life, ma, there's no actors." Ghetto tapped his chest with an open palm before pointing at me. "Only me and you can determine our destiny." His words, the verbal foreplay, caused me to glance up at him. We sat there lost within the silence of our stare for a moment of forever before I smiled in amazement and allowed my eyes to fall back to the cards of fate.

"Sometimes, it's not the bad guy that's the villain," I whispered. I could feel Ghetto's stare branding me as if he were attempting to trespass into portions of my mind that were forbidden to the world. "Heaven," I finally relented.

"Heaven?" Ghetto repeated in confusion. I'd caught him off guard. My lips betrayed me in a surrendering smile.

"Yes, Heaven, my name is Heaven." My eyes lifted to find that cocky smirk of his. I didn't know what made me tell him my government, but it felt right. Ghetto nodded before the smile slipped from his face, and he studied me as if he were trying to gauge if I was serious or not. Out of nowhere, he burst into laughter, but the confusion on my face must've told him that I'd rather be a part of the laughter than the butt of the joke. Ghetto raised his hands in surrender when my look of confusion converted into an expression of suppressed anger.

"Whoa, whoooaaa." He composed himself. "Heaven and Ghetto, get it?" He'd lost me with the correlation of our names. He realized he'd left me on the side of a road where I had to hitch hike for an understanding, and luckily for him, he turned around to retrieve me.

"Heaven Gotta Ghetto!" he declared as if he'd spoken one of the world's most profound eurekas. Once I realized his play on our names, I rolled my eyes. I could tell his pride was touched, but I had a low tolerance for lames. "Are you ready?" I asked with a hand on the first card of the five-card spread. His eyes fell to the cards before returning to me with a humorous glint in his stare. He lacked faith in the cards of providence. *Let's see what the future holds for you, Mr. Ghetto!* I thought as I flipped the first card. Our eyes fell to the card. *The card of dirty money!* It was the depiction of a serpent coiling around a bag of money.

"This card shows that you will come into a lot of money by *ill* means." Our eyes touched. Though I could see surprise hidden just beyond the surface, Ghetto held tight to the indifferent expression. I reached down and flipped the second card, it showed a man with a traveler's bag tied to a stick. The man was shown staring out at a long road that snaked out beyond what the eyes could see. I reached up and played with the long braid of my hair that I'd pulled to rest over my shoulder.

"This is the card of searching, it says that you've been searching for something that's been elusive, something that you'll find *soon*." My hands began to sweat. What I didn't tell him was that, that *something* was love! I glanced up at him and to my surprise, he wasn't so cocky anymore. The smile had even melted into an expression of curiosity. I wanted so badly to laugh in his face, but I settled for flipping the third card. *The conflicting heart!* The picture showed a heart with a dagger through it. Black on one side and red on the other, I studied the heart as if it was my first time seeing it.

"This is the card of conflicted hearts, it says that your heart has been broken by someone close to you, *but* you're gonna meet someone that overpowers the pain." I didn't look up to see how he'd taken my revelation. I didn't have to, I could *feel* his energy. Flipping the fourth card, a look of bewilderment fell over my face. The picture depicted a man in a dark room, *praying* to a dark spirit. I glanced up into Ghetto's dark eyes. I'd never read such a reading before. Wiping my hands on my Moschino jeans, I took a deep breath. "This one says you're gonna have a deeply spirited encounter." My words seemed distant even to me.

"Ma, you're live at this shit! I mean, where'd you learn the theatrics, the monotone, the looks?" He laughed at the foresight of the spirits, and I wondered if that's why the hands of fate grinned back. I ignored his sarcasm and flipped the fifth and last card, and as soon as my eyes fell upon the hands of death, the same card that had robbed my father of his life, I bolted up from my seat. The chair fell to the floor as I backed away from the table and the strange man. Our eyes danced as my heartbeat pounded against my chest.

"Sup, Queen, you good?" he inquired as his eyes fell to the card. There, face up and as real as the breaths I took, was the face of the gate keeper.

"I-I have to go." I almost cried as I turned and ran from what I knew no human could escape—*Fate!*

Chapter 6
Just One Week... If I Don't Win Your Heart,
I'll ?
-Heaven-

Ohhh fuck! You-you're—Baby, you gonna make me-me, cum in, your...moooooouth!" I cried as he licked, kissed, hissss, and... shit, sucked my pussy. Ghetto suckled my clit as if it were the sweetest peach he'd ever partaken of, and he was determined to suck all the juices out of it. My back arched and my toes curled. "Ghett-oooo!" I cried as passion surged through me like a speeding train. Ghetto held me tight with his arms gripped around my thighs, forcing my legs to stay open as he held my clit captive and used his lips and tongue as an erotic jail cell.

"And baby it's youuuuuu/The way you walk... The way you talk/The wayyyy you say my name/The way you move." Jessie Powell's sweet melody serenaded the room as the flickering flame of the candle cast dancing silhouettes around the room, and just when I thought I'd drowned within the waters of intimacy, the man slid his thumb inside my ass, introducing me to a hidden door of euphoria. My face was contorted in a multitude of fuck faces when I lifted my head up to glare down at him, and with one hand grasping the sheets, I used the other one to reach down and grasp a handful of his wild dreads. I fought to close my legs while at the same time, bucking my hips, grinding my oasis into his face. "I'm—you—Babyyyy!" I lost the war, over and over. "Ohhh!"

My eyes popped open at the same time that the dam broke between my legs. I squeezed my thighs closed as I tried to gather my senses while burying my face into the pillow and muffling the cry of ecstasy that frantically fought its way up my throat. By the time I realized something was off, I'd damned near suffocated her.

"Mmmmh, what the hell, bitch!" Empress shouted in surprise. Shaking the sluggishness of sleep away, my eyes became slits. I swear to the Lord almighty that if it wasn't for the Egyptian sheets I'd just bought earlier that week, I'd have snatched the baby Nina Ross from underneath my pillow and put her face on the wall. I

91

glanced down at how my hardened nipples swelled under the baby tee before my vision dropped to the saturated thong that she'd pulled to the side in her quest of robbing me for my pussy.

This bitch just don't quit! I thought as my eyes slowly lifted to find her wiping my juices away from her lips. "Bitch, what the fuck is your problem, what's up?" I growled before snatching the pistol from under the pillow and scrambling out the bed on some real gangstress shit. As soon as we were woman to woman, I put the ratchet to Empress's forehead. "You that thirsty, hoe, huh!" My free hand found its way around her neck as I let her see that boss bitch that reflected from deep in my glare.

"I ain't gonna tell you 'bout this dyke shit, I'm just gonna tell you *one* more time, *sis*. I don't bump pussies, that's your hype and that's cool. We slipped up and did that shit *once*, Empress, curiosity was satiated, and we'll *never* go down that path again—ever!" I spat as we faced off, lioness versus lioness. Empress's face morphed into a mask of drama.

"Truth or dare, Heaven?" the silly bitch proposed. My eyes were searching as I attempted to figure out her meaning. Empress never broke our stare down as she slowly pushed the gun away from her face. My hand slipped away from her neck as I exhaled my frustrations. I loved Empress like a sister, but love would *never* be enough for me to accept disrespect from *anyone*, let alone *someone I'd kill for*. At that moment, I realized that some people weren't meant to live with. No matter how much you loved them, no matter how close y'all may be, you never truly knew a person until y'all stayed under the same roof.

"What the hell does that mean, Empress?" I asked while righting the crotch of my thong. The sticky material disgusted me, and reality became as real as that steel I clutched in my hand. I was gonna begin looking for another place to rest my head. Empress must've noticed the resolution. She rolled her eyes.

"It means the truth is, you're fallin' for that nigga! The entire time I was sucking your pussy, you called out *his* name. You're fallin' for a nigga we're about to rob and possibly *kill*!" I knew she could see it in my eyes, so I held my tongue. My best friend rolled her eyes and sucked her teeth. "You know the rules, Heaven, we don't put niggas ova our money. You better get your head out ya ass and check ya feelings at the door, 'cause that nigga Stick Talk taking me out, and pretty soon, I'll know all we need to know about these boys," she spoke before heading for the door.

"Stay out my room, Empress, that shit you just pulled while I was sleep was foul, and if you play me like that again, we're gonna tear this bitch up," I vowed before tossing the tool on my bed and pulling the wet thong down my thighs and off completely. I peeled the baby tee over my head. I *had* to get to that shower, I felt violated. Truth was, the dream I'd had of Ghetto seemed so real! I shivered in bliss at the thoughts of him. *Am I falling for this nigga?* I wondered.

"Empress?" I stopped her as she was making her exit. She turned and as soon as she beheld my nudity, the freaky bitch's eyes filled with expectation. "Dare?" I needed understanding. Seeing that curiosity was miles away from her desires, Empress sucked her teeth.

"Yea, I dare you to deny your feelings for that fool!" she proposed before crossing her arms over her breasts and studying me. I *wanted* to lie and denounce her claims, but I was way too real to have to lie to *anyone*! So, I did what any real bitch would've done. I shrugged my shoulders indifferently.

"And if I am? He can *still* get it, my *attraction* will never get in the way of my paper route. I know how to tame my pussy, Empress, unlike the weak bitches that use theirs as a *thinking mechanism*." I stared her up and down before making my way to the door where I kept my silk robe hung up. I slipped the soft material on and tied the sash before standing before the woman that knew more about me than my own mother. I leaned in and hugged her tight. Empress seemed surprised by the act but reluctantly reciprocated the love. I kissed her on the cheek before breaking the embrace, but before she could turn and make her exit, I placed my hands on her shoulders so we could be eye to eye, gangsta bitch to gangsta bitch.

"Empress, I love you, Queen, you know the motto. It's sistas ova niggas, and when the time comes, I'll be ready to quiet my heart and turn those niggas' pockets inside out, *but*"—I paused to run a finger down her pretty face—"if you touch me again, if you *ever* disrespect my space again, I'm gonna disregard sisterhood and treat you like a random. Let's not take it there. I'm all *woman*, sis, and a real bitch *has* to have values that she won't violate for *nobody*!" I allowed my eyes to trail from hers, down to her pedicured toes, and right back up to the windows of her soul. Without another word, I opened the door for her to make her exit, and although I shook my head in disappointment, Empress was the last thing on my mind as I made my way to the shower. *I'm about to play with this kitty cat while I think about you, Mr. Ghetto. I wonder what you're doing?* I thought with a mischievous smile on my face.

***

-Stick Talk-
-Hours Later-

I was naked from the waist down. She'd pulled me to the edge of the couch, so much so that I was in a reclining position and my ass cheeks were the only thing that kept me on that mu'fucka. The spot was empty, save for me and the thick bitch that was swallowing me whole as if my thick dick wasn't shit. I gripped the back of her head and fucked her mouth. The bitch was a savage at tongue and lip service, and I can't lie, I wanted to scream her name as if it was my favorite mantra. Instead, I took it like a "G" and pumped that dick down her throat, but—S*mop!* Empress pulled back and her lips popped when releasing my dick head.

"Is it good to you, daddy, huh? You like the way mama suck—*muah*—this dick?" She'd kissed it as she talked that freak shit. Empress stroked me at a feverish pace before dipping her head and gargling my nuts. Her soft hands massaged my lower head, and the combination of her tongue bathing my balls and jacking my length at the same time caused my toes to curl up in my Ovo Jordan 12s. I was just a young, wild nigga from the slums of Stop Six projects, hungry and willing to do it all to get that bag. Empress was five years older and prolly had been fucking niggas her daddy's age since she was wearing Wonder Woman panties. It was written that the bitch would introduce me to taboos I'd never known existed, so when I felt her tongue descend lower, dancing on that small island that separated my nuts from my asshole, I didn't know how to react.

My face slowly eased into a frown of confusion and before I could check her, the freak bitch did the unthinkable! I wanted to slap the hoe's lips off, but in that exact moment of feeling violated, just beyond my pride, *pleasure* rose it's pretty little head. Empress licked my ass as she stroked that dick, and though I didn't intend to be enjoying that shit, my left leg rose to give her easier access. As her tongue went back and forth between my balls and exit wound, her hands milked me.

"Goddd damn, bitchhhh!" I cried as her hand massaged the head of my dick in a soft, wet circle. My toes pointed toward the heavens, and it felt as if I'd fall off the couch as my subconscious told me I was in a compromising position that no man should be in, but that nut was swirlin' through me like an *angry* snake. "I'm 'bout to-to—shitttt!" I growled as that demon shot from me and coated her hand as she continued to stroke me at a feverish pace. Empress seemed to have her entire face buried in my ass, and that's exactly how my flesh found me—in violation of a playa's code.

"Saaaayyy, Flesh, what kinda games you playin'? Bitch, get ya face out my nigga's ass! Now!" Hurk spat in surprise.

***

-Heaven-

My father had always loved water, and my mother told me that he'd once told her that when he died, he wanted to be cremated and spread out across the Caribbean Sea, but since we'd been one step away from homeless, we'd had him turned to ashes and spread out over the closest body of water we could find. Arlington Lake was a body of water shared by two cities, Arlington and Fort Worth, Texas, and as I sat on the moist sand, I watched the waves of murky water clash against one another. The sun was high in the sky and a strong wind was a humid kiss upon my skin as I inhaled a deep breath.

"Daddy, I know it's been a long time since I came to visit you, but things haven't been so good for us. I know you've been looking down on me, and may be disappointed in the life I live, but, Dad"— I paused to dig my fingers into the soggy sand—"I've never judged you, so I only ask that you don't judge me, Pa. I'm just living my life and-and…" I was at a loss for words as I squeezed my hand closed on the sand and watched it squish through my fingers. I missed him. My father had been stolen from us too early. Regardless of what people thought, a girl needed a *man* to teach her about men.

A mother could invest in her daughter the concept of womanhood, but she could only teach *her* experience with a man. *What if* that particular mother's only experiences with the opposite sex were through nothin' ass niggas? That would mean the only things she'd be able to pass down were her *misconceptions* of a man's nature based solely off of the actions of a nigga that was more dog than he was man. That type of knowledge could only be *destructive* and turn a girl so against men that she'd seek refuge in the embrace of one of the same sex, an abnormal love that was fed by an abnormal teaching. I stared out at the dark water as I allowed the dirt to fall from my hand before continuing my conversation with the man that had contributed to creating me.

"Papi, there's so much that I need your advice on. Catrina is ok, but she's becoming more distant with time, and Mom?" I allowed the question to linger on the wind before continuing. "Your queen is lost without you, Papi. Drugs have stolen her dignity and I-I don't know *how* to help her." I became choked up at the thought of my mother. All she knew was my father, he'd sheltered her, and without him, *life* had become a harsh enemy that she couldn't contend against. I smiled, though my smile didn't quite meet my eyes. "Well, I do have *some* good news, Pa." My words seemed sheepish. I pulled my knees in close to my chest before wrapping my arms around them and gazing out at the reflection of the sun that played over the dirty water.

"I've met this man, Papa, I like him. He's witty, intellectual, and I'm not too sure if he's a thug or not, but he reminds me *soooo* much of you, Papi. And-and…"

"And to top all that off, I think I'm fallin' for you." His voice startled me. I spun while hurriedly climbing to my feet. Only few knew of that secluded spot I'd unlawfully claimed as my own, so for Ghetto to have found me there, it had to mean that he—

"What are you doing here? Are you stalking me or something?" I shot off question after question while marching straight for him. Once we were merely separated by only a foot of air and space, I crossed my arms over my chest and glared up at him. His cocky ass fed my frustrations with a *cute* smile.

"One question at a time, Queen. See, you either prefer a bitch over a man, or you've contracted that disease that the majority of black women have contracted. Either or is a sin against what's natural, and if what I crave from you ain't organic, I'd rather leave you within the triple stages of darkness." His word play was over my head, but I was a woman who loved to learn, so when he turned to excuse himself, I reached out and grabbed his arm.

"Wait, listen, I apologize for spazzing on you, but nobody really knows about this place. Now, I don't know what the hell the triple stages of darkness are, nor have I contracted whateva kinda disease you speak on, and unless you were being disrespectful, I think you need to not only enlighten me, but also give me a *good* reason of why the hell you're so fixed on pursuing me." I cast caution to the gods and caused lil' daddy to stand before me naked. *Figuratively speaking!* Ghetto turned to face me, and that's when I noticed it. There was a silent storm that raged deep in the man's eyes that was so powerful that if I hadn't looked away, I would've been swept into its dark pain.

He's hurting inside, I thought as he made his way over to me and took my hand. Without having to be told, I led him to the place I'd just been sitting but paused when I noticed he'd adorned the type of attire that wasn't meant to be worn while sitting in dirt.

"I didn't bring a towel, and those Louie V pants don't look as if you should be—"

"You're a mu'fucka, Ms. Lady," Ghetto cut me off before taking a seat on the moist earth with his legs spread. He patted the ground in front of him, and once I claimed my seat, he wrapped his arms around me and pulled my back against his chest. "A lot of women have given themselves to so many niggas that didn't know how to appreciate them. They've loved and been fucked over so much to where they *subconsciously* become the distributor of the fucking that they were once a recipient of."

The man surprised as well as intrigued me with his perspective, so I held my silence and allowed him to open my eyes. "After being accustomed to a particular feelin' and culture for so long, it becomes your—*our* culture, and *anything* that affects the system of our thinking abnormally *or* negatively is a disease. When the word disease is broken down, the word *dis* is a prefix that means *disrespect!* The word dis means *the opposite* of the word it comes before, so if *ease* comes behind that prefix, that means you *can't* be at peace." Ghetto's lips were right by my right ear, and I didn't know which he was feeding more, my mind or my arousal. I glided my fingers over his arms before turning my head just enough that I could see his face out my peripheral.

"I understand, Papi, but how do *I* have this *dis*ease as you say?" I was curious. Ghetto chuckled before placing his head in the crook of my neck.

"Your defense, the assumptions of my breed of nigga. Not only you, but many women have contracted the disease that a fuck nigga infects you with. This disease is broken trust, a cracked heart, and all the other poisons that come along with rockin' wit' a man that knows *not* how to cultivate a real woman. Dealing wit' that kind of man for so long, will blindfold you to the ways of a real nigga, because the disease will cause you to reflect on the last cat that loved you through his dick while you loved him through yo' heart. Feel me?" he asked before kissing the back of my neck and stealing my breath. I nodded my understanding.

"Now, I found out 'bout this place 'cause yo' homegirl Egypt was at the club when I went lookin' for you. The woman seems to think I can save you from a lifetime of singleness. She's so wit' us lockin' in that she not only told me 'bout this place, but she also showed me where you rest ya head at." Ghetto's revelation created an instant fire in my stomach. I was gonna beat Egypt's ass!

"Now, who were you speaking to before I rudely interrupted your vibe?" He was digging too deep. I shifted in his embrace, unsure as to how I should answer him. I contemplated lying, but that quality had never complemented my attitude.

"How much did you hear?" I attempted to avoid the question. Ghetto must've felt I would try to deceive him.

"You're avoiding the question, ma, so dig. Benjamin Franklin once said that the only way to keep a secret between three people, *two* of 'em has to be dead, so if I have to die to keep your secrets, Heaven, that's the hand good or evil will deal me. Yet don't *ever* attempt to deceive me, lil' baby, only snake mu'fuckas lie. Perspective is thirty percent of a relationship, but it's the *actions* of a person that's the seventy percent of realism needed to be successful in the building of the castle," he jeweled me. I reached down and pulled his arms free. I could feel the wet earth soaking into the purple boy shorts I wore, and as I turned and pushed Ghetto backwards, I climbed on top of him in the manner of a famished lioness stalking her prey. I saw his eyes drop to the imprint of my nipples against the white fabric of my muscle shirt. I hovered above him on all fours as our eyes tangoed.

"I was talking to my father. He was killed in a robbery when I was sixteen. They killed my old man and left me and my family for dead." I peeled the scab from a wound that left me as vulnerable as Samson was after Delilah had his head shaved. Even through the pain in his eyes, I could see that loss was nothin' new to him, and before I could catch it, a tear tumbled from my eye and splashed against his face.

***

-Ghetto-

The tear was like a bucketful of water being thrown into my face. It was unexpected, and as Queen opened her heart to me, she painted a picture that had the power to turn the purest of hearts black. As my eyes digested Queen, I learned that Black women carried the burden of their men because down through history, *that's* what they were taught to do. I reached up and used my thumbs to clear the forming rivers from her eyes. I knew that it took a lot for a woman like Heaven to cry, and even more so in the presence of a man.

"Why do you gotta act so tough, ma, who told you that the epitome of a woman is found within how much resistance you have?" I gave her my verbal. Heaven smiled a strange smile before rolling away from me and climbing to her feet. She had to pull the shorts that had somehow bunched up between her legs and backside.

"It was cool to vibe with you, Ghetto, but I have to go."

"Spend a week with me, just a week," I responded. Her facial contorted into an expression of curiosity, but with a hint of confusion.

"What? I'm not sure I heard you correctly." I rushed to my feet. I knew she'd heard me, but if she got off on mental foreplay, I was willing to strap her to the bed of her mind and make love to her every thought. I stepped into her breathing room and got up close and personal.

"Look, I can tell that you're the kinda bitch that's used to seducin' niggas with your beauty and the subtle hints of how good that pussy is, but *I'm* not moved by appearances. From this day forward, I need you to leave yo' pussy at the house and step to me with nothin' but ya mind and heart, 'cause that's what I'm playin' for. *I know* you're scared of me. You know just as well as I know that your heart wants to belong to me, but it's that disease I'm tellin' you 'bout that makes you fight against what's natural." I pulled Queen against me and leaned forward until our lips were inches apart. I could see that *want* in Lady's vision, she wanted me to kiss her pain away. I watched her lick her lips as if they were dry, before I smiled.

"I ain't askin' for much, just a week with me, and if I don't win your heart in that time, I'll keep my distance. *One* week, ma." I cast my dare. Heaven's eyes studied me—a mixture of *willing* my lips to hers and trying to figure my addition. The thing was, I didn't have any subtraction in my manifestation, I honestly just had a jones for Queen that no other drug could quench, and I knew my sleep would be elusive until the sun in me was balanced by the moon in her. Heaven kissed my nose before freeing herself from my galaxy.

"I'll think about it. Thank you for the company, Ghetto." She smiled before allowing the Gucci slippers to carry her away from my presence. I watched that ass jiggle with each step, but my mental was set aflame by an entirely different kidnapper of attention. The imprint of the tool she'd had stuffed down the back of her booty shorts was barely visible, but I had a sharp eye for armed people. *Now, why would a pretty woman that's going to school for criminal justice need a tool? There's a lot of you, Ms. Heaven Domingo, that got ya boy curious*, I thought with a shake of my head. I squatted down and used my finger to inscribe something into the moist sand—*Heaven gotta Ghetto.*

Renta

Chapter 7
Game Over

-Ghetto-

Next day

"Big bruh, I'm telling you, dude, I'mma be aiiight, quit sweating me man!" Jamal sucked his teeth at Stick Talk. The park behind the MLK was packed on that Saturday, and Stick wasn't feeling his younger brotha goin' out on that chipped and uneven court with the rest of the young boys from the ghetto. He knew the hate of men and didn't trust those boys to play fair. I laughed at the irony. Jamal had grown up playing on that same court, but since everybody around *the world* knew the young boy was a prodigy with the rock, and it was already known that he'd be the number one pick in the draft that year, Stick Talk wasn't taking any chances. He and their granmoms had put all they had into keeping youngin' out the streets, and it had finally paid off. Lil' bro had decided to get his one year of higher learning at Duke University, and jump right into the pros. I was proud of sun. I saluted every man that had a vision, *any* man that found a way out the slums for him and his people.

"Yea, but accidents happen, lil' nigga. Me and Big Mama ain't waste all this time and money to get you where you're at just to see you fuck it off on the *same* court we sent you to all those summer camps to avoid." Stick Talk was stomp down with his decision. Jamal glanced over at me with pleading eyes.

"Come on, Ghetto, help a brotha out, mane. I'll be careful *and* I'll assist more than steal these boys' shine!" he pleaded.

"What's up, Jamal, we tryin' to run this game. These south side niggas need to be taught a lesson!" one of his boys shouted from the court. Jamal glanced back before returning his eyes to us. I was merely a friend of the family, so I would never impose my views over my man's. I twisted the kush stick I'd just filled and sparked a flame to dry it.

"Bruh, that lil' nigga *can't* forget where he came from. It's these same niggas out the gutta that came up with him and helped him manifest his skills. Plus"—I paused to glance at Jamal—"I don't think he's dumb enough to blow the money, especially when he's so close to being the first nigga out *the six* to carry not only the fam, but the entire hood on his back." My vision returned to Stick. "But it's on *you.*" I chuckled at the appreciative look lil' bro gave me before looking to the man he'd looked up to his entire life.

"Come on, dawg, I ain't no kid no mo', Stick. Watch me shine and stop tryin' to baby me, fool!" He got his grown man on.

"Mannnnn, dawg, you better play as—"

"*That's* what I'm talm 'bout, fam, watch me put on for the East!" Jamal exclaimed before taking off for the court. Stick Talk's expression was comical, mouth ajar in surprise.

"Fam, dude ain't even let me finish my spiel!" he spoke before bursting into a fit of laughter. I lit the gas at the same time that—

"Sup, Stick Talk, Ghetto? You boys tryin' to do a lil' light weight gambling? Y'all *know* the East ain't *everrrrr* had nothin' on the crippin' south!" a dark-skinned, chubby cat we knew as Pumpkin challenged. I took a deep pull from the good as my eyes rolled over playboy. He was *clued up* from his shoes up, and I knew he was a respected OG out the south. I glanced over at the rowdy clique of southside niggas that he was mobbing with and smirked over a lungful of exotic smoke. He knew just as well as I did that if he'd been caught on the East a few years ago, murda would've been the language of the people, but times had changed in *the funk*, and it was a *good* thang the natives were making a positive elevation away from the reasons the city had once been dubbed the murda capital of the world. *Money changes shit, fam!* I thought as I caught the vision of Stick Talk digging in his pocket. He freed a thick bankroll and peeled eight hundreds away from it.

"What you talkin', Big Money? You niggas *know* what it is ova here. We roguish *every day*, neva trustin' authorities, and now I gotta get a sack!"

My flesh was always on his *RNO* campaign. Pumpkin wasn't moved, he liberated an even larger knot and peeled twenty-five hundred from it. "You know we talk big and blow big money on my side, cuzz." He smirked. Stick Talk shrugged indifferently before matching the bet. They both handed me the bread before Pumpkin saluted us and made his way back over to his wolves. I laughed at the sight of some of the *thots* them boys had on their arms. Though *the murda* had some jazzy queens, one could *always* tell a southside bitch from the rest. It was all in their demeanor! Some of those girls had more golds in their mouths than the niggas they'd come with. Stick Talk took a seat beside me on the top of the picnic table and tuned his attention on the court.

"This boy ain't ever lied to me." Stick Talk's voice seemed skeptical. For some reason, I knew he was 'bout to add to the proclamation. I glanced over at him curiously. "I just hope he has a change of heart and his *assist* game is really his *all-star playoffs* game!" He caused me to choke on the weed smoke. I laughed hard as a mu'fucka before passing him the blunt. He took a deep intake while staring down at the red tip of the stick. I guess people felt that the harder they hit the dope, the redder the cherry would burn. I smirked at fam when that *Cali* attacked his lungs. He coughed so hard I thought he'd throw up, but my dude reclaimed his "G" as he held the blunt out and stared at it as if he were attempting to figure out the shit that made the cannabis-filled cigar so potent. Still, Blow wiped the tears from his eyes and *respectfully* became one with the dope. He exhaled before passing me the blunt back.

"Flesh, let me ask you sommin'," he spoke as Jamal stole the ball from the opposing team and drove it back to the goal with a *freaky* dunk. The crowd went wild, but the entire time his brother glided through the air for that slam, I could feel my flesh's intake of breath until the boy made it back safely to the ground. I glanced over at Pumpkin, and he chuckled before nodding his appreciation. "What's the b-I, Blow, you know you can ask me *whateva*." I opened the door for my flesh's inquisition. I allowed Mary Jane to make love to my senses as I let some of the kush smoke escape from my lips and be captured by my nostrils.

"You believe in God, Ghetto?" Stick Talk caught me off guard. My vision found my brethren for a quick second before I gazed out at the court. One of the southside players had just pulled up for a *gliding* three that swooshed through the chainmail basketball net.

"Up by six!" someone shouted, and without having to look his way, I knew Pumpkin was gloating. I exhaled in a slow breath.

"My nigga, if there is a God, he don't give a fuck 'bout niggas like us. God *gotta* be a white boy just like all dem pictures be depictin', my dude, and that white boy don't like niggas too much."

"So, you don't believe in heaven or hell?" Bro asked at the same time my phone vibrated. I pulled it off my hip and glanced at the screen. *Daddyyyyy, I miss you, what happened?* the text read. I replaced the phone without a response. I'd forgotten all about Kasha. When a nigga's mental was on that sack, pussy was the last thing on his mind.

"Flesh, when we die, ain't no movin' on to no mansion in the sky wit' golden streets! Ain't no big ass fire waitin' for the big bad wolf, Stick Talk. When you dead, it's ova! Closed curtains! We livin' in hell *now*, homie. When a nigga gotta watch his people starve 'cause the price of livin' is up? When them crackas sentencin' mu'fuckas to life on some plantation for doing shit to prevent the fam from starvin'? Watching ya mama suckin' dick for her next hit." I paused to hit the blunt and wave my hand out at the park. Young brothas as young as eleven were out exchanging vice for the rent money. Young girls as young as twelve were out with their ass cheeks out, hoping to capture the attention of one of the hustlas, merely for the smallest of hopes he could make shit better for 'em. "*This* is hell, my nigga." I chuckled as the opposing team went up three more points. Stick Talk flinched as the tall, lanky cat sank the shot, and both of our eyes shot to Pumpkin as he *C walked* in his Chucks.

"Yea! Go get my fetti, cuz!" he encouraged. Stick Talk spat on the ground as his hand grazed the butt of the *FN* on his waist. I noticed the move and knew that lil' bro had no intention of comin' up off that loot in the events of takin' that *L. No honor amongst thieves, fam, no honor*, I thought with a crooked grin. "So, you don't fuck wit' Jesus either, huh?" he asked while accepting the end of the blunt clip. I nodded with that, *come on, my nigga*, expression on my face.

"My guy, Jesus wants us to suffer *now*! Take ass whoopins and turn the other cheek. Jesus wants a nigga to let life shit on 'em *right now* and get the riches and bad bitches when we die and go to heaven! The devil offers money, foreign cars, and bad bitches *right now!*" I shrugged as if it was a no brainer. "Shid, I'd rather fuck with the nigga that's offering me a bankroll while I'm struggling than wait till I'm dead to bless me, feel me, Flesh?" I was as high as Mars when I fixed him with my gaze. Blow was nodding his understanding. I knew if nobody else felt my third eye, Stick Talk would. He tossed the stub of the blunt to the ground.

"I see you skipped the part 'bout what the devil gives you when you die." He laughed as if he'd cracked the funniest joke in the world. I stood up from the bench and stretched.

"Shid, 'cause that part don't matter. If I can't feel my soul *now*, while I'm livin', why the fuck would I be able to when I'm *DOA?*" I glanced out at the court just in time to see Jamal cross the man guarding him and punch the ball into the goal.

"Yea, nigga, stop six in this bitch, down three!" he capped.

I smirked. "Fuck my soul, let that bitch burn in fire and brimstone. It ain't did shit to help me anyway. Heaven may be the place where streets are paved in gold, but all our niggas in hell, it's gonna be a family reunion." I laughed at the same time that Jamal AI'd a nigga and watched him fall on his ass before pulling up for the three.

Swish! The ball slipped through the chains with ease. I handed Flesh his money as the park exploded in hysterics. The last I looked, Pumpkin was as hot as fish grease. *Game ova!*

Renta

Part 2

When the looting starts, the shooting starts.

-Donald Trump

Renta

Chapter 8
I Wondered

-Ghetto-

The small cooler I held bounced against my leg as I walked and stared out at the vast expanse of land. When I'd made the move from the boot to the Lone Star State, I'd sought out a place of seclusion, so the two-story, ash brick, ranch house sitting in the middle of fifteen acres of *nowhere* was a perfect hideaway for an imperfect man. The lush green grass seemed to stretch on forever, and the cultivated woods and vegetation that marked the separation of me and my neighbors' properties were manicured to complement the view of the Brazos River that ran diagonally through the natural grounds. It didn't hurt that my neighbors were *almost* a mile up the road and desired just as much privacy as I did. Weatherford, Texas was a nice duckoff, *the country,* and as I strolled through my property, gazing out at the horizon, I became transfixed with the heavens.

The sky began at a dark purple and descended into a collage of yellow and dark pinks. The sun seemed to be at war with the night, not wanting the moon to take its place, and as I stared up at the pink ball of fire, I wondered how many black folk lost their lives that day? How many of my people had gotten slain by the same people that had taken an oath to protect and serve their community? My heart went out to Ahmaud Arbery, to George Floyd, Tamir, Breonna, Tatianna, and every other person of color that had been killed in police brutality. The worst part about it all was, when it came to a man killing for his family, they threw the book at him, but when it came to the injustice of a public servant, the judicial system seemed to tie a blindfold around the eyes of Lady Justice and contradict the purpose of that lying, copper bitch in New York.

What's liberty at gunpoint? I wondered how many women would wake up to an empty bed, but still whisper *I love you* to the spot their incarcerated men had left vacant, but overall, I wondered why such ugliness took place underneath the canopy of something so beautiful?

"Dre Dre, Kiesha, come!" I demanded. Out of the brush came my two *massive*, all-black K9s. Both dogs were police-trained guard dogs that I'd inherited from an ex-officer that owed me a few favors. Both were females, and those bitches were as vicious as those alligators I'd grown up playing wit' back in those swamps. The two dogs looked more like *she wolves* than domestic animals, and as Dre Dre trotted beside me, occasionally brushing up against me, she gazed up at me with her long tongue hanging out over her sharp teeth. I laughed, she was more of a daddy's girl than Kiesha, who tended to get in her feelings when I didn't give her *all* my attention, but both K9s would kill at my command.

When I finally made it to one of my favorite retreats in the world, I smiled. The secluded area was the place I'd escape to when I sought a peace undisturbed. My eyes digested the beauty of the man-made pond that was more like a baby lake. The house had come with the beautiful amenity, but the blanket of flowers surrounding the bench that was a mere few feet away from the water was an added feature for my vision of relaxation. The garden surrounding the bench was filled with begonias, bearded iris, and a variety of different species of plant life, but it was the red and white roses that always captured my vision. My eyes drifted up to the giant oak that provided shade for the bench, and I had to appreciate the beauty of nature.

Taking my seat, I sat the cooler on the ground before popping it open. I smiled down at the only addictions I'd adopted outside of gettin' to that bag. I extracted the Styrofoam cup of crushed ice before freeing the two liter of Sprite, three pre-rolled blunts of *grandaddy*, and the pint of *lean* I'd brought along for the occasion. I knew I'd need all three to numb the pain I was sure to feel after digesting the words of a nigga I loved as deeply as if we'd been conceived from the same pussy. Breaking the seal on the bottle of oil, I stared out a Dre Dre and Kiesha as they growled at something they'd spotted in the water. I chuckled before cracking the top on the two liter. *It's a shame, a man has to place more trust in two animals than he would in a creation from his own rib.* I shook my head in shame. I wondered what had changed such a beautiful culture of women so drastically that black women led the race in the *ethnic ground of women* to leave their black kings lost in captivity?

I wondered when us as black men had begun to depreciate our black queens so much so that they'd begun to find more love and confidence in lesbian relations than in the masculinity of a king that could create a tribe with them. Pouring a sip of the Sprite on the ground, I replaced it with an eighth of drank, and as soon as the purple medicine clouded the clarity of the soda, the combination caused a foamy gush. The soda rushed up like a volcanic eruption, and I placed my mouth over the top of it, swallowing until the pressure subsided.

I twisted the top back onto the bottle before sparking one of the sweets. I wanted that drank to settle in before I poured up. Taking a deep pull from the gas, I had to fight the urge to cough the powerful smoke back up. I held the breath captive for as long as I could before my lungs lost the war and I was forced to exhale in a slow swirl of smoke. That's when my eyes fell to the reason I'd come to that spot in the first place, but before I got to it, I swirled the bottle of drank, turned it upside down, and shook it slightly, before uprighting it and twisting the cap off.

As I poured up, I watched as the purple medicine stained the ice chips and submerged them in a muddy ocean. *This shit gone kill me one day!* I thought as I wondered why I and so many other people consciously flirted with death, merely for the sake of a momentary escape from the shit that was unavoidable. Still, I tilted the chilled cup to my lips and allowed the cold codeine to numb the stress of the day, before sitting the cup down on the bench. I retrieved the letter.

Kiest Osborne # 1824142
Angola State Prison

I read the inscription on the surface of the envelope. I could *feel* my flesh's presence, and as I tore the paper open, I sucked the soul from the blunt, mentally rationalizing that if his words stole my soul, at least I'd be able to fill the void with the spirit of weed smoke. The missive was two pages long, a letter and a decision.

The state of Louisiana vs. Kiest Osborne. In the cause of case number 0634219, and the appellants motion for exhaustion of remedies, the board has reviewed the request and finds it acceptable in the manner of human rights. Your request has been accepted and will go into effect as soon as the day of—

My vision blurred as the paper slipped from my grip and drifted on the wind. I fought the pain and cleared my eyes just in time to see the evidence of my nigga's death date land on the surface of the pond. I watched as it absorbed the water until they became one, and it drifted out like a bottled message. I attempted to tame that portion of self that I'd never been in touch with. That portion of every street runner that made him vulnerable. As I exhaled a long whoosh of tainted smoke, Kiesha trotted over to me and stared with her head cocked to the side before she timidly nuzzled my knee with her nose. I guess she could feel the power of my pain. I scratched behind her ear. "It's gucci, baby girl, it don't make a man weak to hurt. Real niggas cry too."

I didn't know if I was speaking more to her or to myself. I had to force myself to pick up the second page and digest my dude's truths, and as I did, I realized that money had never been the root of all evil, *poverty* was! Poverty was the reason niggas steal, kill, and destroy loyalty over the almighty dollar. Being broke was the worst reality in the world, and *that's* what brought the evil out of people, *that's* what had my flesh caged up on death row, preparing for his last meal.

Ghetto,

What's the fruits, Flesh? I hope the table is prosperous and you boys holdin' the torch righteously for this lil' thang of ours. Brah, since I've been held against my will here in the belly of this tarantula, I've come to understand that the only separation between life and death is found in the shit a man is livin' for versus the reasons he'll die for. Both are decisions, yet, when a nigga livin', he thinks he'll ball forever, but not really thinkin' 'bout the "purpose" he's here on earth. Most times, a man meets the reaper and gets his life snatched for shit that's really meaningless! He leaves behind "all" the reasons he "should've" lived for, never knowing he's leaving behind a chapter to a story that his sons or a tribe of young brothas will read and follow in its wake. "Self" genocide, Flesh. The reaper is that reminder that what a nigga does, no matter how much money he has, and no matter how many bad bitches he pipes, the clock doesn't stop ticking. A man has to live for somethin' or he's gone die for the shit he didn't give a damn bout! Foolish!

Blow, you remember when we use to fantasize of ballin'? Zap cars and play bingo when fly whips flew by? That was the same dream and fantasy of "every" other nigga that's ever known what it was like to wake up with no electricity, nothin' in the fridge but some rotten potatoes, an Arm and Hammer box and a half pitcher of Kool-Aid. Guess what I'm tryin' to say is, I traded my life to give you and every other nigga that is or becomes RNO the chance to not only ball, but to live for the same shit you will die for. Purpose! Here on death row, there's hundreds of men that's lost their minds because the regrets become too big for their sanity.

Me? Shid, I don't regret a second of thuggin' wit' my dudes. I'm dying the same way I lived...For a cause.. As a real nigga! Let no man destroy what we've created, Flesh, don't "ever" allow your lust for a bad bitch or the hunger pains of ya stomach cause you to defile your morale. Everybody screams this real shit, but only few will die, trade their freedom, family, or riches for the consequences of "self-choice." They'd rather trade the shit they claimed to love for another chance at doin' the same shit! The streets dead, Ghetto, but I'm not here to preach to you. I just want you and the body of RNO to know that there's sacrifices that come wit' ballin', and sometimes the sacrifice is self! Keep suckas away from you, Flesh, surround ya self wit' "real niggas only" and they'll either kill with you, for you, or y'all will die together! They stick the needle in my arm in a week. My last request is that you live and die a real nigga. Get out the streets, Ghetto, they don't love nobody!

From the cradle to the grave ... RNO Kiest.

As I concluded the letter, a lone tear dropped from my left eye. Kiest had *asked* to forfeit his remaining appeals, he'd sped up his execution! Before I could form a counter thought, I'd snatched the burna off my waist and—

"Fuck you, nigga, you don't give a fuck 'bout us, nigga, you ain't real! You can't be!" I cried as I stared up and took aim at the heavens.

Boca! Boca! Boca! Boca! Boca! Boca! Boca!

"Fuck you, God, you hear me, nigga, huh!" I growled as the pain of every street nigga that had rolled the dice with life and lost rolled down my face. I knew gangstas was 'pose to let the doves cry for us. I was taught that stiff men wasn't pose to cry, but since there wasn't any doves around to do it for me, and my heart rotted right there in that moment, I did the only logical that I could think of. I aimed at the sky and fed it the twenty-three remaining slugs in the clip.

Boca! Boca! Boca! Boca! Boca! Boca! Boca! Boca!

"Fuck you, my nigga!" I shouted as shells jumped out the side of the tool. *Boca! Boca! Boca! Boca! Boca! Boca!*

***

-Jamal-

The day had ended well. The scouts had shown up to our last game, and I'd shown my ass! To top that off, I'd capped it off with cutting Tammy, a fine ass mixed breed that I'd been tryin' to get up with all year! It was crazy how just the mention of the boy going pro had given me a black card of free sex! Every girl from the hood *and* their mamas wanted a part of me, but I tried not to let it go to my head—my granma Sharon had raised me to be humble. *You are the same man when you're broke as you should be when you're rich, boy, don't ever let money change ya!* I could hear her telling me. As I walked home, I fantasized about what they'd say when I made it to the pros. "Jamal Jackson runs down the court, *ohhh* he shakes LeBron, and ohhh yeaaah, monster dunk to win the game for the

Mavericks!" I dribbled the ball I carried through my legs as I mock shot in the air.

Squeakkk! The tell-tale signs of trouble caused me to pause in my stride and turn to see who'd pulled behind me. The night was early and as the patrol car eased beside me, I gave the officer my best smile. I'd grown accustomed to officers pullin' up on me and congratulating me on my talents, but this pale man didn't seem too friendly, not in the mood for bullshit.

"Would you mind using the sidewalk, boy, rather than using the middle of the street for your personal basketball court?" he requested before nodding at the basketball I held between my arm and rib cage.

"Yes, sir, my bad," I hurriedly responded before making my way to the sidewalk. I exhaled as the policeman eased his car forward, but when he pulled the car to the curb only a few feet ahead, my heartbeat sounded like a trapped gorilla trying to get free from a steel box. I'd never been in the streets, nor had any run-ins with the law, so I didn't understand the dilemma. I stopped short and stood as still as a scarecrow in a corn field on a windless day. As the white man stepped out the car, his hand automatically fell to the butt of his gun, though I was merely standing there with my basketball.

"Aren't you that boy that Dunbar High School claims as some sort of boy wonder?" he asked with a peculiar expression on his face. I nodded but didn't reply. I wasn't feelin' dude callin' me *boy*. The way he pronounced it just sounded like he meant to say *nigger!*

"Boy, don't you hear me?" he asked as he stepped toward me. I could see people pausing to see what was going on, so I didn't worry *too much*.

"Look, man, I don't know *why* you're stoppin' me, I'm just on my way home from a friend's house." I gave in.

"Yea, that's you, my son was benched because those coaches up there at that school of yours want to give *you* all the exposure. You have some identification, boy?"

"I ain't yo' *boy*, sir, and what Coach does with *his* team ain't got nothin' to do with *me*," I replied. No matter what dude was

117

talkin' 'bout, I wasn't gonna reach for *anything*. He'd have to do it himself. That's exactly what he did too. The man aggressively grabbed my shoulder and forced me to turn around.

"Oh, you're a smart ass too, huh!" he growled. "Put ya hands behind your head, and you better not move!" he demanded. I stood there, shaking with anger as a man I'd never met, a man I'd never had a problem with, gave me his anger. I dropped the ball as that man I'd never tripped with, violated me for no apparent reason outside of the fact I had too much melanin on my skin. He patted me down before putting his knee behind mine. "Get on your knees. I don't want you kicking me when I pat you down," he demanded. I wasn't feelin' that shit and resisted.

"Hell naw, I ain't did nothin' and I ain't got nothin' for you to be doin' all this, man. My I.D. is in my left pocket," I instructed.

"Are you resisting arrest, boy?" The man's face had turned as red as a tomato. I was six four and about six inches taller than his weak ass, so I guess his inferior complex was getting the best of him.

"Leave him alone, that boy ain't did nothin' to you! I got ya ass on *live* too, everythang you doin' is bein' recorded!" I could hear a woman's attempt at keeping the man in pocket, but it only seemed to encourage him in his aggression. I decided to do all I could to keep a semblance of peace, so I went to my knees.

"Aiiight, man, I'm down, do what you have to do and let me go," I spat as dude held one hand on my shoulder while frisking me with the other. I looked to my left and there, about ten feet way, a boy around the age of six or seven stood staring wide eyed at the defamation of my character. I gave him a reassuring smile that he returned, but life had never been that forgiving. The officer must've noticed the crowd that was gathering and became fearful, 'cause for some reason, he began holdin' my wrists to the point that it hurt. In that instant, things spiraled out of control, I attempted to turn to voice myself.

"Say, dude, you're hurting my—"

"Stop resisting!" the public servant shouted while attempting to force me down onto my stomach. I fell forward and scraped my hands on the pavement when the officer wrestled me to the ground with brute force.

"You betta leave that boy alone, you're being recorded!" someone shouted.

"Y'all see this shit, huh? Look at this white boy, mane, this shit fucked up!" another spectator spoke out. By that time, I was flat on my face and the man's knee was on my neck.

"I-can't-breathe! Hel-p! I-I can't-can't-can't-bre-athe!" I cried, but the officer seemed to not give a fuck.

"He said he can't breathe, mu'fucka, get your knee off that boy's neck. You're gonna kill 'em!" another voice demanded. At that moment, I wondered why so many people just stood around *watching,* but not doing anything to help me. I wondered what good was *recording* my pain, but not moving to intervene? Was my death gonna be captured to show the abandonment of my people? To mock me? *Lord, help me!* My thoughts became spiritual, and in that moment, in the midst of the chaos, something deep transpired. Though I'd come to terms with the fact that I might die, I prayed that small moment in time would one day save another black man or woman's life. As my basketball, my ticket out the hood, rolled by my face, I looked up and into the eyes of that same young boy I'd just shared a smile with. We were now sharing our tears. As my eyes pled for him to grow into the type of man that would never allow that type of injustice to happen to another person of color, as a stream of salty tears ran down his dark cheeks, we both knew that would be the last day I shared a smile with another. I began to see spots, my lungs burned from deprivation of oxygen, and as my and the boy's eyes bore into each other's, I fought for my life until my last breath betrayed me.

"I-can't-bre-athe! Plea-*please*-I-can't...breathe!"

Renta

Chapter 9
Wrong House

-Ghetto-

I pulled the slab to the curb and jumped out without closing the door. Stick Talk had called me and busted my heart in my chest. *They killed Jamal, Flesh, Jamal's dead!* His words echoed through the alleyways of my mind like a tortured scream in an abandoned building. The crowd was thick, but it was the silence that struck me as off. It was the silence that only suppressed rage, a rage that only a community in pain could give birth to. I pushed my way through the throng of people, and the closer I got, the harder my heart pounded against my chest.

"Wake up, lil' bro, get up, we gotta go home. You goin' to the league, my nigga, wake up!" Stick Talk's pain tore through me like a sharp blade. I made it to the front of the crowd, and it was there I found my nigga on his knees on the asphalt, kneeling over his younger brother. It proved that gangstas shed tears as I watched my flesh lean over and do CPR on Jamal. He blew air into fam's body before pushing down on his chest.

"Come on, lil' bro, Granny waitin' on us to make it home. Quit playin' and get up, fam, *please.*" Bro attempted to encourage Jamal's spirit back from wherever it had relocated to, and as if he could feel my presence, Stick Talk looked straight up and into my eyes.

"Wake up, fam," he whispered, but I knew fam's words weren't meant for me. *Damn, lil' bruh, we was 'pose to be there for you. I'm sorry, bro.* I hoped Jamal could read the thoughts of a solid nigga. My eyes fell to his cold body before returning to the baptized gaze of Stick Talk.

"Why they take 'em, Flesh? He wasn't like us, Ghetto, why they take my lil' nigga like this, huh?" he cried while extending his arms out wide and tilting his head to the left as he awaited my answer. I was in the midst of tellin' him that I didn't know why fuck shit always seemed to happen to good people. I wanted to tell my dawg that I didn't know why the good always seemed to die young, but—

"Step away from the boy. Please, sir, we're trying to help and maybe we can save him." My eyes shot to my left and for the first time since arriving on the block, I noticed the group of FWPD. The speaker was an older black man, and *he* had his service pistol out and aimed toward my dude. I pondered going for the burna on my waist, but I tamed the urge. "Put the boy down, you're doing him more harm than good. Don't do this, son, there's been enough tragedy here," the police sergeant reasoned and caused my vision to return to Stick Talk. I shook my head at what I saw. A tainted river clouded my eyes, and my pain robbed me of my peace.

Stick Talk had scooped Jamal's limp body into his arms and held him like a man does his wife when carrying her over the threshold of their new home. Jamal's head tilted toward the ground as my flesh lost it. "You was right, my nigga. God ain't real, He can't be! Tell Jamal to wake up, bro, tell him! Help me wake 'em up, Flesh, he goin' to the pros." I dropped my head as raindrops dripped from my eyes, and when I looked to the right, the discarded basketball Jamal loved so much was proof that Jamal wouldn't be wakin' back up.

***

-Heaven-

Hours Later

The clap of thunder was so powerful that it shook the windowpane. The rain fell so hard that it seemed that *every* angel in heaven had to be crying along with God himself! I laid on my stomach as I typed away on my laptop. My essay was due in two days, and I didn't know a damn thang about James Maxwell, nor Edward Murphy, let alone the differences in their theories.

"Bitch, you think I should wear the gold one or the invisible one?" Egypt held up a gold thong with her left hand and extended her empty right. I frowned in confusion as I tried to figure out the catch. My girl rolled her eyes as if I was the ditziest broad on this side of the western hemisphere. "Girl, the *invisible one!* You know, the one you *don't* wear?" She giggled. When she saw my eyes lift toward the ceiling while shaking my head, as if to say *lame,* Egypt sucked her teeth. "I was just wondering if I should wear the gold panties or let my clit breathe and go panti*less,* but I see you're not feelin' my *swag!*"

She tossed the thong at me and stuck her tongue out in jest. She turned to her overnight bag to continue her search.

"Isn't it raining a little too hard for you to be taking your hot tail ass out on a date? Where'd you meet dude at anyway? You say he's from East Arlington?" I inquired. She gave me *that* look.

"Bitch, palease! You think bills stop needin' to be paid or shoppin' sprees stop existing just 'cause it's raining?" We both giggled when she tossed a golden bra at me. "Yes, he's from the East, and from the looks of it, lil' daddy *in his bag!*" she sang while doing a little dance. My sis pulled a sassy, yellow dress from the bag. "We'll see if Earl of East Arlington runnin' his check up, and if so, *you know* what time it is!" she declared before turning to look at me with a suspicious glint in her stare. Before she parted her lips, I knew what she'd say.

"Speaking of *time,* ain't it 'bout time you wrapped ole buddy up so we can see about him?" Egypt placed her hands on her hips in anticipation of my answer. I kept my eyes trained on the computer, fingers gliding over the smart board as if I was typing, but if she would've stepped around to look at the screen, she would've seen *AbbnnGtttttxxz23!* The evidence of my fingers feverishly tapping miscellaneous buttons in my attempt to buy time. Luckily, the ringing of my phone saved me from not only having to lie, but also explaining how I was falling for a nigga that was only meant as a lick. Egypt's eyes were mock evil slits as I rushed from the bed and over to the bureau where I'd left my phone. I frowned at the number. I'd seen it before and usually sent the unknowns to the VM, but something was telling me, *Bitch, answer it!* So, with Egypt's suspicious gaze on me, I did.

"Hello?" Silence! I could hear the rain in the background and *we were close friends, also lovers/did everythang for one another/ But now you're gone and I'm lost without you here and now/but I know I gotta live and make it somehow*, Aaliyah's "Missing You," played in the background. I lost patience.

"Hellooo!"

"I need you, come outside." The sound of his voice sent chills down my spine, but it was the lack of his usual arrogance that gave birth to my concern.

"Huh, *outside!* Boy, it's raining cats and dogs out there, as a matter of fact, how do you know where I..." My words trailed off as my eyes shot to Egypt's sneaky ass. *I found out 'bout this place 'cause yo' homegirl Egypt was at the club when I went lookin' for you. The woman seems to think I can save you from a lifetime of singleness.* His words played in my head as me and my partner in crime had a stare off. She threw her hands up.

"What's up?" she whispered. I rolled my eyes at her. *Bitch, you talk too much, that's what's up!* I thought.

"Look, I'm drownin', ma, internally. Come outside, I need you." Ghetto's request sounded more like a plea, but the disconnected call somehow converted it into a demand. My confused gaze drifted to the window, and lightning streaked across the glass before my vision returned to Egypt. She smiled knowingly as she began to comb her hair.

"The devil is a lie, gurl, the devil is a lie!" She laughed.

***

-Ghetto-

The night was humid as the heavens cried an unrelenting cry. As its tears soaked through my clothes, my tears became camouflage. The headlights of the Masi illuminated me as I knelt down in front of the car. I didn't know why I'd valeted the machine in the middle of the street, but at that moment, I didn't give a fuck. I just needed the rain to purge me, to baptize me and wash away the reality of how life could deal a nigga a crooked hand. Both my heart and mind were raging rivers that I couldn't seem to wade through, and every time I tried, I was pulled underneath the current of whys. *Why'd the good always die young? Why does people's hatred run so deep? Why are my people being murdered merely for the color of their skin?* The driver's side door was open and Aaliyah's "Missing You" beat low, but enough to make the car rumble. My dreads hung wild over my face, drenched in water as I held my head bowed. I felt like the world was on my shoulders, my nigga, and just when I felt it was gonna crush me—

"Oh my god, Ghetto, why are you out here like this?" Her voice bathed me more than the tears of heaven. My head lifted slowly and I gazed up at her through the jail cell my long hair captured my face within. I wondered if my tears blended in with the raindrops, but the look she was giving me told the tale. *She sees my pain*, I thought as I climbed to my feet and faced off with Queen. Heaven stood underneath the refuge of a giant umbrella, all that thickness sheltered by a thin pair of black tights and a sports bra. Without breaking eye contact, I stepped into her space, a foot apart. "I ain't ever been in love, ma, I never believed in it. I hail from the slums where life was a gamble, and my granmamma was my mother *and* father. A place where a controlled substance was really an *uncontrolled* substance that most of my niggas' mamas used to escape the madness. I fear believing in God 'cause if the mu'fucka was real, He'd be a hoe ass nigga for the shit He's allowed to happen down here!" That animal in me had risen to the surface as I stretched my arms out wide as if I could fly away.

I turned my face up to the downpour of rain and allowed it to intermingle with the mini rainstorm that fell from my eyes. Heaven's vision was studious as she took in the heartbroken melody of a real nigga.

"People say that everybody has a choice, but the people that say that shit, they ain't come up how me and my niggas did. I was bred by a beautiful culture turnt sour by the hate of other mu'fuckas. Heaven, what you know 'bout bein' crossed by a mu'fucka you'd kill for, huh? You know what it feels like to wanna love somebody, *anybody,* but you've been hurt so much that your heart just doesn't know how to no mo'?" I spat before allowing my vision to find her. Water dripped from my face as a scar of lightning cut across the sky.

"Ghetto, I understand your plight, daddy, I do."

Heaven's words were filled with understanding. Lady reached out and pulled me underneath the protection of the umbrella before putting a hand to the side of my face. "I may not come from where you come from, but my skin tone is the same color as yours, and choice may not be something that you were *born* with, *but* I can assure you that there was a moment in your life that you *could've* embraced change. Not only you, Papi, but *every* other black man that was bred by the culture of the streets has enslaved our culture to the things Willie Lynch, Jim Crow, and every other Caucasian slave master intended from the beginning." Our eyes danced as I tried to figure out her truths, but when her lips beat my mind to the punch, my soul felt it.

"Destruction, Pa, what you faced in these cold streets, the same bullshit you've witnessed, *you've* embraced. *You* passed those same ideologies down to our youth, your perspectives, you give them to our women of color and expect the type of women *you* help to create to be different from the last bitch that hurt you, but all you're doing is cultivating that exact breed of woman." Heaven reached up and pushed the wet dreads away from my face. "The woman will only reflect what her king instills in her, and she will pass those same traits to her son or daughter. So, no, Ghetto, it's not about what you've been through, it's about the things you do to change that culture." For a moment, I was as speechless as a mute. The rain splashed against the pavement, creating a river underneath our feet.

I smiled through my pain and as my eyes touched every portion of her features. I reached up and freed the umbrella from her hands. Queen flinched when I tossed the umbrella and the rain began to soak through the thin material she wore. Her curly hair fell down and began to stick to her face as her nipples imprinted the sports bra. I wrapped my arms around her waist, and maybe it was just the gangsta in me, but my hands instinctively fell down to cup all that ass. "I need two things from you, Queen," I proposed as Aaliyah sang about missin' the dude she'd fallen for. Heaven wiped the wet hair away from her eyes at the same time that thunder echoed across the Heavens and lightning flashed and illuminated our forms. She looked up at me, lifting an eyebrow in curiosity.

"Teach me how to love, Heaven. A king can't rule an empire by himself, he needs that feminine perspective that gives him sight when he ain't seeing straight. Sometimes I'mma need you to be more of my friend than just my gal, sometimes I'mma need you to be more of my bitch than merely my queen, but at *all times* I'll need you to be a *real woman*. I need a rida, ma, that won't fold on me when it's raining on my head," I spoke the crave of my heart. Heaven smiled up at me before sweeping my dreads away once more.

"That's one, what's the second one, slick?" She allowed my eyes to see the possibilities that reflected in her gaze.

"I'm 'bout to run away for three days. I gotta pack a bag, then we can mash out and cop whateva you need when we get where we're goin'. I just need you wit' a nigga. I don't even know where we'll end up, I just wanna thug wit' you, Heaven." I kept it thorough wit' mama. Heaven's eyes were searching as she attempted to figure out my play, and in that moment, I'd realized that a person could become so immune to fuckery, become so accustomed to deception that that's all they expect. Yet, as the umbrella rolled and tumbled mindlessly through the puddled streets, I took Queen by the hand and pulled her into the middle of the road. Her expression was stained in confusion as I wrapped my arms back around her waist. I'd never been the dancing type, but as Heaven allowed me to choreograph our steps, I danced with shawty as the song changed to my dude Rod Waves. *Girl of my dreams, I know you're not no good for me, but you look so good to me/I don't need another broken heart or sleepless night/God please guide me right/she looks like the girl of my dreams.* He sang, and I began to wonder if Heaven was my angel in high heels or the devil in high heels.

I could tell from the way Lady was staring at me that she'd neva rocked wit' a real nigga before, and as we danced in the rain, I'd come to realize that most men barricaded their hearts behind a wall of false perceptions and insecure realities, not only because they'd grown up engaging *and* seeing a love built on fucked-up foundations, but *more* because they'd never really experienced the love of *a real bitch.*

***

-Stick Talk-

The night was as black as a raven's feathers. As I sparked the end of the soaked rag, I watched the flames race up the kerosene-drenched material and just when the fire was midway up, I chunked the Molotov cocktail at the police car.

Pissshhh! The bottle shattered, *instantly* igniting into a roaring flame. I stared out at the chaos the streets of Fort Worth had become. The patrol car had been left unoccupied as the two officers that showed up in it attempted to bring a sense of peace to a moment of pandemonium.

"No more killing our people, we matter, Black lives matter!" someone shouted.

"Black lives matter! Black lives matter!" the angry mob of rioters chanted, as if the mantra would change the fucked-up reality we as a colored people faced.

"Get back, this is your last warning!" an officer shouted at an angry mother who held a tearful infant in her arms as she spoke out about the injustices inflicted on a race of people that had never harmed anyone! The metroplex of Dallas/Ft. Worth was ablaze and riots had sparked all over the nation. The sad part was, rather than hear our plight, the fag ass president chose to declare martial law. *Pissssss!* The sound caused my eyes to fly back to the mother and her child, and as soon as my eyes beheld the barbarity that was *forced* upon Queen, my hand drifted toward my waist.

"At ease, Flesh, that'll only make shit worse, and it's a war we can't win," my blow, Daddyo, rationalized. I gritted my teeth as Queen cried out.

"Ahhhh, I can't, my baby, somebody take my baby!" she cried as she fought against the tear gas she'd been sprayed with.

"Mamaaaa!" The child's cries cut through my spirit and made me reconsider letting bullets fly. A storefront window exploded, and when my eyes roved to the group of youngins that were causing the damage, my breath caught in my throat. There were five young brothas expressing their rage, but there in their midst, *Jamal* was standing, smiling at me as he dribbled his basketball. Lil' bro nodded what's up to me and before I knew it, I was heading for him.

"Jamal, lil' bro?" I whispered, but—

"Flesh, you good or what? Who you talkin' to?" Daddyo grabbed me by the arm and caused me to zone in on him. I was ready to up that burna and serve 'em for attempting to stand in the way of me and my lil' man's reunion. My eyes fell to his hand before they drifted back to where I'd spotted my lil' bro. I was just in time to capture the five young boys take off into the night and in that moment, Jamal dribbled the ball through his legs before he shot it at an invisible goal. We both watched the basketball fly into the air until there, out of thin air, a basketball goal appeared and— *Swisssh!*

The ball soared through the net. My eyes found my younger brother, the boy wonder whose only crime had been his dream of hoopin' to get us out the hood. His face was tear streaked when his eyes diverted to where the protesters faced off with *armed* soldiers, and when his attention returned to me, my heart escaped my chest. *Each* of his tears depicted a vision of a black man or woman being slain in hate and brutality. *Jamal Crawford, Fernando, Cornelius Brown, Terrence Franklin, Emmett Till, Sandra Bland, Betty Jones, Victor, Oscar, Tionna, and the many others that had been murdered for merely being a part of the minority.* They all had a tear—a tear that replayed their death. Jamal chunked me the deuce before turning and walking toward the mob of protesters. I watched until he disappeared into the crowd, and only then did I feel the wetness on my face. I frowned and gazed up at the sky.

Is it raining? I wondered, but when another soft drizzle fell from *my eyes*, I knew the storm had nothing to do with the heavens and everythang to do with that pain in me needing an escape. I wiped the salty water away before staring down at my fingertips.

My eyes fell back to the hold Daddyo had on my arm. "Get the fuck off me, bruh, it's them crackas you need to be holdin' back!" I spat before jerking my arm free from my flesh's grasp. Bro looked as if he wanted to get on that gangsta shit, but instead, his vision left mine and studied the mass of officers that were suited up in full riot gear, some *beating* defenseless protesters, and others standing, *watching* their comrades violate their duty. For some reason, his eyes drifted to the place Jamal had just stood.

"Homie, I was just tryin' to let you know it's a betta way. I heard you call your brotha's name, and then you..." His words died off and a peculiar expression eased onto his face. His shocked eyes found me. I assumed he'd realized I was on the verge of losin' my mu'fuckin' mind. Jamal's apparition was too real, and I still had a mind to go after him, but—

"Damn, I feel you, my 'G.' I know shit ugly for you, ain't nothin' wrong wit' cryin, fam." He nodded as if he could really feel that shit I was feelin'! That cracka had killed my lil' brother and his only punishment was suspension *with pay*! Fuck naw, not even God himself could understand some fuck shit like that, especially when there were seventy-five percent of black men locked in cages for lesser offenses. I spat on the ground.

"Nigga, I ain't cryin', it's sommin' in my eyes."

***

No Knock

They cuddled in the bed, just vibing. Brella lay curled up beside her man with a frustrated expression on her face.

"Boy, that's all you do, smoke, smoke, smoke! Bae, this 'pose to be *our* night, remember?" she whined with a cute pout to her face. *"Tonight, is all on you, baby, I swearrr!"* she mimicked with a roll of her eyes. Jamarius smirked down at her before placing the unlit cigar in his mouth. Their love was real, and as he began to tickle her, he knew he'd go to the grave rockin' with her. Brella laughed.

"I'm home, ain't I? You gonna stop being a big cry baby or what?" Jamarius asked as he kept his fingers moving over the spots he'd learned made her weak.

"Stoooop, boy, you're gonna make me pee!" she cried.

"Apologize, say you gone stop whining or I ain't gonna—"

"Ok, ok, I'm sorry, I ain't gonna cry no more!" She surrendered. Jamarius pulled back and made a funny face, a goofy threat in his facial features.

"Aiiight, Brella, don't be playin'. If you break ya word, it's goin' down!" he playfully threatened.

"What's up, we gonna watch *The Black Klansman*, or we can just check out some back episodes of *Thirteen Reasons Why?* What you in the mood for, boo?" he inquired while scrolling through his Netflix account. Brella rolled her eyes.

"Bae, we've seen *The Black Klansman* a million times, and *Thirteen Reasons Why* is—"

Boom! The blunt fell from his mouth as the sound of the front door crashing in cut her spiel short, but Jamarius didn't waste time. He snatched a registered Glock nine from underneath the bed and rushed toward the bedroom door. "Stay here, Brella, and call the police!" he shouted over his shoulder before disappearing into the hallway. As soon as he got midway to the living room, the group of black-clad men aimed their guns with *malicious* intent. A moment of insanity was born as Jamarius aimed, and at the same time, bullets spat from both directions. Within the melee, two things caused the black man to stand down.

"Police! Police! *No-knock warrant!*" He could hear the shouts between the exchange of fire. Confused, Jamarius lowered his weapon and attempted to gain understanding, but the situation was beyond reasoning. *Boca! Boca! Boca! Boom! Boom! Pow!* An orchestra of different guns sang out in evil synchrony.

"Fuuuccck!" Jamarius took one to the shoulder and crumbled to the ground. Adrenaline was an aid as he dropped the pistol and hurriedly army crawled his way back to the room. Chunks flew off the plastered walls as he made it into the room and kicked the door shut.

"Brella, Brella, get down, baby, get down!" he shouted as his eyes frantically searched for her. He spotted her hiding on the side of the bed, and as he made his way to shelter her from what no man was strong enough to digest too much of, his mind ran wild. *Fuck? No-knock warrant? Why would they need a warrant to come in our home! I thought these boys were tryin' to rob us, but it's the mu'fuckin' law, man!* His mental was so congested that he never noticed that the shooting had ceased until—

"Darnell Johnson, this is the police! Put your weapon down and come out with your hands up. I repeat—" the officer was saying when Jamarius frowned in confusion. *Who the fuck is Darnell Johnson?* he wondered, but the thought was short lived. He'd made it over to Brella and his heart began to hammer against his chest. His breath came in short breaths as his mind attempted to wrap around what he was seeing. "Brella, baby?" he whispered. Jamarius rolled her over onto her back and—

"W-hy?" Brella coughed up a spray of blood.

"Hellllp! Hellllp us! My girl needs hellllp, please!" the man cried as he watched his queen's eyes roll to the back of her head. His tears fell and splashed against Brella's face as he wiped blood away from the corners of her mouth. "Baby, hold on, just-just don't talk! It's gonna be ok! It's gonna be ok!" he soothed. Brella didn't have a chance. Her young life was being stolen by an injustice that would never be punished at the same degree of hate that stole Queen's legacy.

"Our-our day, ba-b-a-by!" the words came out, riding on the winds of her last breath. Her eyes focused on the man she was meant to spend her life, memories, and love with. Jamarius cried so hard that he couldn't see beyond the river that overflowed before his vision.

"No! No, you better not die, baby, *fight!*" he cried, but love wasn't strong enough to call back the spirit to a betraying body. Brella was gone. Jamarius buried his face in her bloodied chest, and at that moment—

"Freeze, get down! Nobody move!" The door burst open as officer after officer stormed the room with their weapons drawn. "Darnell Jackson, you're under arrest and you better—"

"Who the fuck is Darnell Johnson, you sons a bitches? *Whoever that man is doesn't live here!*" Jamarius exploded as he lifted his tear-streaked face. Brella's blood soaked his face, and as the stunned officers stared bewilderedly at the scene before them, Jamarius's voice seemed to echo around the room. *Whoever that man is, he doesn't live here. Whoever that man is, he doesn't live here!* The leading officer's face contorted in confusion when Jamarius's drowned eyes focused on him.

"My name is Jamarius Mophi, my gun is registered, and I thought y'all were robbers! There's no Darnell Johnson that has been here, nor stays here. You have the wrong house!"

Renta

Chapter 10
Comedy and Good Conversation

-Heaven-

Day one

"I'm tellin' y'all, skinny jeans wasn't meant for fat people. Seriously, though, what the hell is a fat mu'fucka doin' in skinny *anything!*" The comedian chuckled as he paced the stage. He paused and suddenly spun on his heels before pointing his finger out at a heavyset man in the audience. The big man had chosen the wrong table, and the skinny jeans and gray tee shirt he wore made him an easy target. The shirt was stretched over his stomach and had the words *where the money at, I'm ready to eat!* embossed across the front in gold cursive. All eyes diverted to the big man that was now a part of the man's act.

"Look at this nigga. Boy, you stittin' there lookin' like them tight ass pants cuttin' off ya circulation! I bet if you fart, the fumes will be trapped in them mu'fuckas so tight that yo' whole bottom half will become a nuclear bomb, and if yo' funky ass moves, you'll blow the top off this bitch! *You ready to eat!*" he spat with a shocked expression on his face before his eyes fell down to the man's stomach.

"Fat ass nigga, from the looks of it, you ate the whole buffet before you got here. Yo' big ass still hungry?" the comedian shouted before his eyes grew wide in shock. "Boy, *you know* you wrong! Nigga, you knew them jeans wasn't meant for you when you had to *jump* to put 'em on! *I know* yo' ass cheeks sweatin' in them baaaad mu'fuckas, ain't no air circulation through them shits!" The man had no mercy on the brotha, and though he laughed, I could tell the overweight brotha wasn't feeling being the butt of the man's jokes. Yet, I was tickled as the comedian began to huff and puff real extra like. "Them pants remind me of the pads on one of those hypertension machines the doctors use to check a mu'fucka's blood pressure. Y'all know what I'm talm 'bout!" the man commanded the stage.

He paused and squatted like he was riding a motorcycle. "Well, Mr. Thornton, it seems as if your blood pressure is unusually high, and if I didn't know any better, I'd think you're suffocating!" The comedian paused to unbuckle his belt and as soon as it was loosened, his pants fell to the floor. The brotha wore a black pair of *bikini* briefs.

"Whewww, Doc, it's the pants. I been holdin' my breath all day!" The crowd was hysterical with laughter as the man made his way to the middle of the stage, his pants still down at his ankles.

"Naw, for real, though, my grandpa used to tell me all sorts of crazy shit, y'all, and I neva paid the old mu'fucka no attention till I got older and realized that dem old mu'fuckas be knowin' what they talkin' 'bout, even when they drunk! Don't they!" He laughed over the *amens* and *riiiiights!* that ensued from the crowd. "Yea, my grandaddy was one of them old *southern* men that didn't have no teeth and always seemed to be suckin' his lips in and grindin' his gums together and shit. One day, while we were out fixin' his ole truck, the old nigga did that lil' thang he does with his lips." The goofy man sucked his lips in and grinded them together as his eyes grew wide and he held the microphone tight with both hands. "That old nigga say, Teddy, the three worse things a person can do is give a black man authority over his own people, give a Chinese man a restaurant, or give a Mexican a driver's license!" He paused his tale to raise his left eyebrow.

Damn, here this nigga go! His facial expression told the tale as he began to hit himself over the head with the mic before bringing it back to his lips.

"I'm thinkin', damn, I knew I shoulda *been* left before his ole ass went to talkin' shit and slobberin' *everywhere!* But I won't lie to y'all, the shit he laid on me made a lot of sense in the world! He say, son, if you give a black man authority, he'll turn his nose up and shit on his own people! You give that Chink a place to sell food, the mu'fucka will barbecue or sauté you a wild dog's leg and swear it's lamb chop with a honey sauce! You give tha Spanish speaking mu'fucka a right to drive, they're gonna run over whoever's in their path, and when the laws show up, they gonna act like they don't know English!"

The man turnt and gazed out at the crowd. "Bro, you ran that light and rear ended me!" he shouted before turning and facing the opposite direction.

"No, homes, tu was jus driving too slow and your rear end ran into me! The Mexican responds." The comedian was in raw form as he turned his back to the crowd.

"The officer walks up y'all. What's going on here, what happened here? *He asks the white man.* Y'all know ain't no nigga or ese got no chance wit' a white policeman. As soon as he sees the man of color, the police gonna go for his gun!"

The crowd was on their feet as he mimicked the white man. "This-this spic rear ended me when he ran the light! I can't wait until Trump kills all the niggers and builds that wall to stop these *swimmers* from having all those babies and buying up all our tortillas! *We* like tortillas toooo, man!" I was in tears when the comedian spun back to face the crowd. "The cop glares at the Mexican man, y'all. Whatchagot to say for yourself, padre?" The goofy man spread his arms out wide and bugged his eyes wide.

"Me no comprendé ingles, me no nada!"

The crowd went wild as I wiped the mirthful tears away. I slowly regained my composure as my eyes drifted to Ghetto, only to find his eyes glued, fixated on me as if he were reading my thoughts through my skull. He drank me in as if he wanted to become intoxicated off whatever he saw in me. I blushed for the first time in my life, and that stole a smile from him. The man was looking scrumptious in an ink-black Dior dress shirt. The top three buttons were undone to allow the diamond choker to peek out and play a trick of colors from the way the soft light touched the pave and VVS diamond necklace he loved so much. As I lifted my martini glass to my lips, my eyes fell in love with the way he had his dreads twisted into some thick curls. "So, what does *RNO* stand for again?"

I smiled before taking a ladylike sip from my glass.

***

-Ghetto-

I leaned back in my seat, shot glass of Remy halfway to my lips when she asked the question. I studied her—her wavy hair was pulled tight into a bun on top of her head. The woman was beautiful, no makeup needed, and as my vision fell to the ensemble she'd chosen for the night, my mental caught on fire. She'd chosen a see-through, silver cat suit that was highlighted with hundreds of rhinestones. Her see-through outfit allowed *a freak's peek* of her nakedness. She wore nothin' underneath, save for a white thong and two white pasties over her nipples, and as my eyes fell to the two heart-shaped stickers, I wondered the color of her areola. *Real bossy mama!* I mentally saluted her. "RNO is an acronym for *Real Niggas Only*, it's a *family affair*, Queen." I obliged her before taking a sip from the drink. "Real life business."

"Real niggas only, huh? So, what, it's your little gang? I wouldn't have taken you for the gang banging type, and what's this *fruits* mess I heard you speaking on the phone?" she asked with a raised brow and mischievous smirk on her face. Our chemistry wasn't a mystery, but I knew Queen still questioned my intent. I returned her smirk.

"Gang?" I chuckled before reaching behind my neck to un-clamp the choker. It slipped from around my neck with a dance of reflecting diamonds as I extended it to her. Heaven's eyes studied me before accepting the gesture. I watched as she studied the jeweled pendant, her eyes digesting every intricate detail. RNO's insignia was two Dracos facing each other with a single drum melding them together, and there, in the middle of the drum, two 7.62s formed the letter *N*.

"Let me guess, the two guns symbolize the *R's*, the drum is the *O*, and the bullets..." She smiled, knowing there was no need to voice the obvious. I nodded my confirmation.

"That still doesn't answer my question, Mr. Ghetto." She leaned forward and placed her elbows on the table, and when she cupped her face in her hands, I had the mind to lean over and kiss her sexy ass.

"I created RNO as a means of standing for something *more*, something different than what a gang represents. My family is successful men and women who come from corrupt environments but didn't allow that environment to make them a product of its conduct. RNO is a *family* of *real* people that won't tolerate fake shit, *Period!* Not in our midst at least." I came from the hip with her.

"And the fruits?" The smile slipped away and was replaced by a genuine curiosity.

The body of RNO means us as a whole. We have a lingo that make us kin, and only members of the body understand our language. *The fruits* means a topic we choose to build on for the day. It means enlighten me. If someone asks me, what's the fruits?"—I paused to sip from my drink before pointing at my head—"I'll give 'em a piece of my mental. The shit that will nourish their mind."

"Such as?" Heaven was persistent. I smiled.

"Ask me. Ask me what's the fruits," I challenged. Heaven seemed confused as she leaned back in her seat and crossed those sexy ass legs. She crossed her arms over her succulent titties and gave me a sly smirk that made me take notice of the coat of lip gloss she'd applied to her lips.

"What's the fruits, Ghetto, do tell?"

"The fruits for the day, love, is culture. It's the culture of the woman that tells a nigga what type of woman she is. The culture of the woman she was bred by, the culture she's embraced as a queen. If she builds her foundation off of the typa shit Megan Thee Stallion, Nicki, or the City Girls teach in their music, that's her culture! That's the kind of bitch she'll be. Yet, no matter which culture she embraces, the girls that admire her, the generation of younger women that learns from her, she'll pass down that culture to them and in return, with that same culture is how they'll teach the tribe of our brothas to treat and love them." I fed her the fruits of my mental garden. Heaven plucked the olive from her drink and slid it in her mouth as she studied me.

139

"What about the culture of the man? Doesn't that play a role in the talk of a culture? It's more of the men that can't control their dick, right?" She jumped on her feminist shit. I chuckled. *A typical black woman, always takin' offense or thinkin' a nigga on some machismo shit*, I thought before downing the rest of my drink and slipping from my seat. I carried my chair to her side of the table and sat beside her. Heaven watched me as I took her hand in mine and began to massage her ring finger.

"Who was the bright person that made it *law* that the ring should go on the left hand, on this finger?" I asked before releasing her and slipping my hand underneath the table and onto her thigh. Queen tensed and an instant frown eased onto her face.

"You're going a little too—"

"And who can say that pussy is any more powerful than dick when both have driven a multitude of each side of the sexes to do some of the most foolish shit behind them?" I knocked through her defense as my hand traveled higher up her thickness, and right as my finger grazed the inside of her thigh, that crevice that connected the thigh to the pelvis, I stopped.

"Ghetto, you better…" Her words trailed off as she squirmed under my touch. I freed Lady from the physical and allowed my vision to fall to her bouncing right leg, the action caused all that sexiness to jiggle. Queen smelt like…like, somethin' fruity, and it made me wonder how that pussy would taste, though I'd never partaken of the delicacy. I reached up and reclaimed her hand and starting at her thumb, I counted off as I opened her mental.

"You should give me a chance, you should give me a chance *not!*" Two fingers down and I had three more to go. "You should give me a chance, you should give me a chance *not!*" I smiled up at mama. "Last finger, you *should* give me a chance." She rolled her eyes with a girlish giggle before I started over, but this time using the play in the opposite direction.

"You should give me a chance *not;* you should give me a chance. You should give me a chance *not;* you should give me a chance." I paused at her pinkie, the last finger. Pulling it up to my lips, Heaven's and my eyes connected as I ran my tongue up it before placing a soft kiss against her pedicured nail. "You should give me a chance *not!* See, mama, it's never 'bout dick or pussy, man or woman. It's 'bout the beginning of a journey, how one starts. That day at the lake, you spoke about culture and gave it to me in a way that *I* could've *assumed* you were blaming men for the sins of a woman, but" I paused to run a finger down the side of her face, "truth is universal. Even if you add twenty percent of it to eighty percent of deception, it makes the lie the truth, ya dig."

"What do you want from me, Ghetto, like really?" The question caught me off guard, and as I studied Ms. Lady, she appeared as fragile as fine China, but before I could answer her—

"What's the business? I'm hungry, Flesh, what's the fruits?" Lil' Nukkey approached our table.

***

-Heaven-

The man had appeared out of nowhere, a butter pecan-colored handsome man with wavy long hair he wore to the back. The white three-piece suit he wore was set off by a pair of sky-blue gators that matched the sky-blue handkerchief that peeked from his breast pocket.

"Blessings, Flesh, the fruits for the day is paradox." Ghetto's response confused me, I thought the fruits were culture. I held my peace and soaked it all in.

"What's the build, Flesh? You know you can't offer me the fruits and not tell me how it can nourish me, what—" The man in the suit paused to smooth his *manicured* hands down over the front on his suit, even though there wasn't a single wrinkle in his attire. "You think I'm a cannibal or sommin', my "G"? you know our creed *G*, like at all times. *G*, as in gentleman, that is." He smirked, and for the first time, I noticed that the bottom row of his teeth were wrapped in rose gold and covered in soft pink diamonds. Ghetto stood to embrace the man.

"Paradox, as in, we as a family must be cautious of what we choose to create, 'cause a lot of times mu'fuckas create things that wind up turning on them in the end. Gangs were created to protect the hood, but ended up terrorizin' it, the police were meant to protect us, but wind up shootin' us. The power of power is too powerful for one man to not turn rotten because of it. Paradox, Flesh," he spoke as they embraced.

"Speakin' of power, Flesh, such beauty is too powerful for *any* one man to call as his own, but we still try. I'd be grateful for just the name of the queen that if this shit didn't cost a check and if I was the kinda cat that bowed to a woman, I'd gladly kneel before, yet, I'm afraid you'll have to settle for my gangsterisms." The stranger smiled before reaching for my hand. I was reluctant and knew that it showed all over my face when my eyes drifted to Ghetto. *Fuck do these dudes come from, and where they learn to converse at?* I wondered, taken aback by dude's approach.

I knew they took me looking for Ghetto's consent as some sort of macho, *look how I got my bitch*, type of thing, but I was bred to be ladylike and submissive to my man. In Ghetto's case, the man I was vibing with, so I fed the fire and gave the man that seemed to be running a marathon to capture my heart a seductive smile, and only after he nodded his consent did I extend my hand. Mr. Sweet Talker did something rare and rather than kiss my hand, he bent at the waist and touched my fingers to his forehead.

"A god's greeting for a nubian, I'm Nukkey, a piece of RNO's body, always a gentleman, the God brother of this lucky mu'fucka that I assume has captured your heart, or at least your attention," the man called Nukkey introduced.

"Why'd you do that, the head thing, I mean?" I was curious. Nukkey seemed appalled as his eyes flew to Ghetto.

"Nigga, you mean to tell me you've brought a woman to the table without jewelin' her?"

Ghetto chuckled before slipping my hand out of his brother's. "Nukkey, this is Heaven, my nubian in progress, and naw, I haven't birthed her yet, Flesh, but since you're dry talking table talk in front of a civilian, allow me to help you." He shook his head with a smirk. Ghetto looked to me.

"Heaven, Nubian is what we call a female of RBO, which means real bitches only, it's the feminine sect of this lil' thang of ours. My godbrother touched your hand to his forehead because it's against our laws to put our lips on another brother's lady, and so we touch the lady's hand to our head because the mind is the strongest portion of a man and the deepest thing he can give to a woman," he *jeweled* me.

"Two twenty-one, flesh, two twenty-one. Don't take so long next time, you *have* to jewel ya nubian so the next nigga doesn't. You know what they say about women and diamonds." Nukkey winked at me. I retrieved my glass and sipped the clear alcohol.

"Two twenty-one?" I wanted to know it all and Nukkey cured my curiosity.

"Two is the second letter of the alphabet and twenty-one is the *U, B-U* stands for business understood. Or *just I understand.* Enough about the politics of RNO, that's no way to welcome the *first* woman my godbrother has even brought to *the table.*" Nukkey glanced around until he made eye contact with a light-skinned chick with thick braids.

"Dominique, bring a bottle over of your best wine, I'm thinkin' like…" His words trailed as he glanced down at the floor. "Yeaaa, bring out the 1962." He smiled as his eyes rose to land on me. My eyes were still on the girl he'd called Dominique. She smiled, though I could see that she wasn't feelin' him.

Yea, he's fucking her, I concluded.

"Don't sweat, lil' baby, sis, all these hoes you see workin' for me are my exes. Either of 'em could've been my queen, but their actions revealed their traits of a peasant. So—" He finally revealed that *other* side of his mannerisms, and as I finished my apple martini, I wondered how I could implement him in me and my sisters' plans. *The more the merrier*, I thought as I returned Ghetto's smile.

Renta

Chapter 11
-Stick Talk-

Revenge

Draped up in all black, me and eight RNO goons blended in with the night. Ghetto had left me in command of the body of the squad and I planned to utilize it. Each one of us wore a gorilla mask to conceal our identities, and as I allowed my eyes to capture the apes that surrounded me, I nodded to give the signal to spread out, and like trained marines, they separated and took up their positions. Each figure clutched a pipe that was stocked with a drum, but I'd opted for an all-black baseball bat that was as solid as a tree and as fat as a wrestler's forearm. I'd had two long strips of razor wire wrapped around it from top to just before the handle. I stood in front of that house as still as the night, my only movement being the periodic pulls I took from the toon stick to the face.

The cigarillo of K2 had me as numb as Novocain as I glanced up at the moon. It was red tinged and full, and I didn't know if it was the effects of the dope or if what I was seeing was more than just a figment of my imagination. I watched the full moon melt in the sky before congealing and taking the form of the devil's face. I glared up at old Lucifer as he smiled down at me. I glared up at ole buddy like that type of shit was normal before nodding like, *What it do, my "G"?*

Homie gave me a wink before my gaze fell to the bat in my grip, my fingers tightened around it in my thirst for blood. I glanced back up at the heavens but instead of the devil, it was Jamal's face I found staring down at me. My heart cracked for my lil' nigga as tears dripped from his eyes. As he studied me, the tears dripped off and became stars in the night's sky. I hit the blunt before my vision fell to the red-brick colonial home. "This one for you, lil' bro. Rest well, fam," I whispered as I exhaled that evil smoke. It was time to let that song of revenge play.

***

-Heaven-

That old house was the most terrifying place I'd ever been. It seemed alive with dark power as if it was literally breathing. We'd arrived in the thick woods of Louisiana earlier that day, and from the first moment I'd set eyes on the landscape, I knew that for a person to have called that secluded house that was hidden deep in that rugged parish *home*, they had to have been as dark spirited as the vibe that place gave off. At first glance, Genevieve was a beautiful woman that didn't appear a day over forty, save for the few wrinkles at the corners of her eyes and mouth. Her skin was still as smooth as melted butter and as light as vanilla ice cream.

She'd smiled at me with a smile that revealed all thirty-two of her cloud-white teeth, but as soon as her grandson introduced me as the woman that had stolen his heart, *something* that I couldn't explain passed before her eyes. There was something off about that old hag, and every time Ghetto turned his back, I caught the bitch *glaring* at me as if I did her something. In spite of the lady's stank attitude, I'd really enjoyed learning about Ghetto's upbringing. The boy had really come from the slums, and though the way he fed those alligators was a bit too much for my taste, he'd taught me that there was a thin line between man and beast, and the only thing separating the two was the mere fact that *some* men had a moral conscience.

I had a lot on my mind, and that's exactly why I found myself up at two in the A.M., shuffling the cards of fate as I watched the leafless branches of a skeletal tree sway in the wind. I had my ear buds in listening to my MP4, Lauren Hill's "Ex Factor" had me feelin' some kinda way, and as my eyes fell to Ghetto's sleeping form, I smiled. He continued to surprise me with his ways of dealing with me. Any other man would've been trying to get into my panties, but not only had playboy kept things at the tempo I'd set, he also opted to sleep on the floor beside the bed rather than attempting the norm.

I keep lettin' you back in... How can I, explain myself /As painful as this thang has been/I just can't be...with no one else/see, I know what we gotta doooo/you let go, and I'll let go toooo/Kuz no one has hurt me more than youuuu, and no one ever will/no matter...

Lauren's lyrics had a way of playing with my heartstrings and before I realized it, my mind had taken me on a brief journey through my past. I reflected on past lovers that were really good men, but just not the men for me. I thought of every relationship that I thought would last forever—the ones *I wanted* to last forever— and in that reflection, I came to realize that most women may find the perfect man *for them*, but due to their *superficial* expectations, they'd leave him for a man that's more materialistic than attentive to the actual woman.

I remembered all the *I love yous* that were more verbal than an action. I was so lost in my reflections that I hadn't noticed when Ghetto had slipped from the pallet he'd made on the floor and made his way to the side of the bed, until he'd pulled the right earbud out my ear. I jumped in surprise.

"Boyyyy!" I hissed before slapping his arm. He chuckled as his dark eyes trailed over my barely clothed body.

"Scoot ova, mama, this floor is hard and cold as a polar bear's booty cheeks, Jea." He nodded toward to the other side of the mattress. I allowed the mischief in my eyes to tell him that I wasn't lame and I was up on the little games men played when in the bed with a half-naked woman. He smiled down at me with a suppressed freakiness peeking from behind the darkness of his stare. I shook my head in amusement before obliging him.

Spoke too soon, he's just like the rest, think he's gonna get some pussy just 'cause I'm in his bed. That's a nigga for you! I thought as he slid into the bed and turned on his side to face me.

"What's on ya mind, lil' baby, why you can't sleep?" His question echoed in my mind as I shuffled the cards. I saw his eyes drop to the deck as I pulled the first card free. *The card of searching*! I'd done his reading numerous times that night, and the sequence of the cards may have varied, but the conclusion never changed.

"Everything, pa, everything. These people are killing us and getting away with it! I mean, why, because they fear the color of

147

our skin? Then, *you*! I'm tired of trying to figure it out, so why don't you just tell me, Ghetto, what is it that you're searching for?" I paused to hold the card up so he could see it. Ghetto studied the depiction of the man with the traveler's bag, staring out at a long road. I allowed the card to flutter from my fingers and both our eyes watched it tumble to the mattress.

"What do you want from me?" My words were skeptical.

Ghetto turned onto his back, placed his hands behind his head, and stared up at the ceiling. I watched him as the shadows played across his features.

"You've never met a man that just wanted to fuck wit' you *for you*, Heaven? Just 'cause you're Heaven?" he asked before turning his head so he'd be able to see me. My mind ran wild in search of an answer to his question, 'cause in truth, I didn't know. I'd always believed that *everyone* had a motive, but at that moment, I wondered was it possible for a person, for *a man*, to pursue without intent? Ghetto chuckled at my silence before reaching down and retrieving the fallen card. He brought it close to his face and studied it by way of the moonlight.

"Is *want* the same thing as intent, ma? Why can't I just *want* you in my world because you balance the vibe? Why can't I just *wanna* thug with you? What if I'm just cool with us sitting and enjoying each other's company? If I just wanna sit in silence, or I just wanna see the world with you? What if I just want you 'cause you're a real bitch?" His realisms were different for me and caused me to cross my arms over my chest to conceal my hardened nipples. Yet, I held my silence.

"See, you can't answer my questions because you really don't believe that *everyone* doesn't come with the bullshit. Every nigga you've fucked with either intended to use you for your pussy or wanted to possess your beauty because a boss bitch is a trophy for a man that knows not what a true trophy is. So, when you ask what I want from you, what I'm searching for, *that's* my answer. The trophy." He confused me as he extended the card.

"The trophy? You want me to be your trophy! Nigga, you got me all the way fucked up!" I declared before scrambling from the bed and searching for my shoes. I could feel his eyes on my jiggling ass cheeks. The black satin boy shorts I wore were a poor excuse for clothing, but usually I slept naked, so they were suitable for the occasion. Ghetto slipped from the bed and made his way over to me as I slipped my feet into my Air Max '95s, and before I could make it to my overnight bag, he reached down and took my hand. I snatched away from him.

"Nigga, uh uh, don't touch ... me!" I glared at him and allowed him to see that gangstress in me. "I knew you wasn't no different from those other—"

"Sayyyy," Ghetto drug the word out as his eyes narrowed and he extended his hand to me. "I know you're not being disrespect-ful?" His eyes seemed to threaten me, and as bad as I wanted to check him for thinking that was all it took for him to calm that bitch in me, dude just didn't come off as the breed of man that would submit to a woman, no matter how dominant she might be. Though I was as hot as a tea kettle, I placed my hand in his and allowed him to lead. We wound up at the window that gave us a view of the murky swamp behind the house. The night seemed to move, and if it wasn't for the glow of the black panther's greenish-yellow eyes fixed on us, I'd thought that the sleek animal was merely a figment of my imagination.

It paused to study us, staring as if it could see us standing there. Ghetto stepped behind me and wrapped his arms around my waist. I could feel his *lower* strength *strong* against my back side, and as if the panther wanted to give us privacy, it seemed to growl with a menacing flash of sharp teeth before disappearing into the night.

"You see that, ma, the beauty of that panther is so raw because we're on the *safe* side of its ugliness. We both know it's not safe to get too close. Lions, tigers, wolves and bears are the same—each of these beautiful creatures is a wonder to *look* at, but that's as far as that beauty goes, because if you get too close, that same beauty will become an ugly truth. There's a monster lurking just beyond that shit. *Surface* beauty. The only thing that can make an animal wild is if they've never been taught to care. They don't understand the notion of love. All they know is how to protect and kill for their food." Ghetto rested his chin on my shoulder and gazed up at the full moon.

"*I'm* just like those animals, Heaven, that's all I've been taught. Your beauty could *never* be what *I* see as a trophy because a woman's ass, titties, or pussy is something that a man can never possess. He can never *own* a woman's beauty. Only that woman can lock that down for solely him, but what *I* want is your mind…that heart that's in your chest, that same heart you fear being broken. Those are the trophies I'm playin' for. A trophy is *earned*, mama, just as one's heart and mind." His clarification made me feel stupid for my earlier reaction. I allowed my fingers to glide over his arm.

"My fault, Ghetto, I feel soooo stupid, but—"

"Chill, ma, you don't owe me that." He sliced my apology in half before kissing the back of my neck. "My point is, the shit I'm searching for, you or no other woman can give or offer me, Queen, 'cause I'm searchin' for myself. The man *beyond* the gangsta... The nigga that I've spent my entire life hidin' from, *myself*!" He gave it to me before tapping my chest, right where my heart beat at. "I'm tryin' to dig up the man I buried underneath all these bricks of pride and misconceptions. I'm not who you think I am, Ms. Lady, and in the morning you'll get a glimpse of the typa shit that's deep enough to make a certified gangsta wanna become a Muslim, just so he can find peace within the thousands of pieces his heart cracks into while bravin' the black love of the streets."

***

-Stick Talk-

My flesh, Twitcha Lee, had jimmied the lock of the back door and let me in through the front. The house was dim and smelt like an old wooden cabin but was nicely furnished. My eyes went to the huge buck's head that hung above the fireplace. The antlers were wicked and sharp like old tree branches of a leafless, ancient tree, and as I studied the mantled deer's head, the old adage played in the walls of my mind: *You eat what you kill!* I smiled a crooked smile as the hushed pleas came from down the hallway.

"Please, don't kill us. Who are these-these *people*, Johnathan?" I'm assuming it was the Mrs. of the house that spoke, and I chuckled. She'd said *these people,* as if she meant, these niggers! I gave the end of the blunt mouth to mouth as I made my way through the Smith's home. I could feel the fear swelling in the air as I made it to the threshold of the bedroom door.

"What-what do you mean I have company? How'd you get in my house? Do you know who you're fucking with? I suggest you get the hell out my—" Officer Smith's declaration trailed off when his vision found me. My bloodshot eyes were glassy from the toonchie I'd been polluting my lungs with, and as I exhaled a long stream of smoke, I allowed my eyes to journey around the room before feasting on my prey.

"Who the hell are you people? I'm an officer of the law and—" Officer Smith tried his hand at intimidation, but my flesh, Daddyo, crashin' the butt of the choppa down on the side of his head closed the curtains on that tough boy shit and brought the bitch out the man. His wife surprised me. I saluted her for being a rida, but this wasn't a B-list movie where the killa had sympathy for the innocent.

"Please, take whatever you want, just don't hurt us!" she cried as she flung herself over her unconscious husband. Blood oozed from the crack in his skull and instantly soaked through her thin nightgown. I smiled before nodding at two of my youngins, and they wasted no time gettin' to the business.

"Noooo, don't do this, *please!*" the woman cried as two of the goons snatched her off the man and began to bound her wrist and ankles.

"Wha-what's going on?" The corrupt officer had regained his consciousness and had to bear witness to the desecration of the woman he loved. Twitcha Lee ripped Ms. Smith's nightgown down the middle, and though it was merely an accident due to the fight she was puttin' up, the sight of his wife's perky titties bursting free, sent the officer into an uproar.

"I'm gonna have you sons a bitches thrown in jail, I swear to God! The judge will fry your asses for this!" he raged as Twitcha Lee and my flesh Hurk snatched him up. He fought the good fight, but Hurk was a three-hunnid-pound bulldog of a man and wasn't too fond of white men. He clubbed the man over the head with his massive fist, and I witnessed Officer Smith's lights go out once more. His body crumbled to the floor and the squad immediately subdued him.

"Look what I found," a feminine voice spoke from behind me.

"Dad? Mom?" I spun in surprise at the sound of the second voice, a young boy.

"Fuck?" The question slipped from my lips unintentionally. My vision captured the redbone woman that stood behind him, holding a plastic Glock to the back of the boy's head. Red Diamond was a boss bitch and the head of RBO. She stood five-five, thick, and was as solid as any nigga I knew. It was said that her and Ghetto had a *special* thang goin' on, but neither of 'em ever admitted to it. My eyes drifted from the lady killa and found the frail kid she held at gunpoint. He appeared to be no more than twelve or thirteen years old. His strawberry-blond hair was matted to his head, and the goo in the corners of his eyes told me that she'd given him a rude awakening. My heart and mind were conflicted as I thought of what Ghetto would do in this situation. The boy wasn't a part of my plans, and I knew that Ghetto was the typa nigga that believed in innocence. *Ain't no innocence in war!* I thought before returning my gaze to my sista in arms.

"Bite for a bite, a life for a life, sis. I don't know how to turn the other cheek," I spat as I nodded toward the living room.

***

-Empress-

"Empress, why don't you just trust the girl? Heaven is all the way solid, sis. You know what though—"

Egypt thought she knew it all. I mean, I loved the girl with all of me, but she irked my last nerve with all the extras. The girl acted as if she could read a bitch's mind and shit. *Hated it!* I continued layering my feathered bob as she paused in her search for whatever it was she was looking for. I turned my head to the right so I could get a closer look at the back of my head, but something told me to look up, and that's where I found her reflection glaring at me suspiciously. I paused with my hot comb midway to my hair.

"What, bitch, spit it out already!" I spat with a roll of my eyes.

"Bitch, boo! The truth is, you're on some jealous shit. It ain't even about *the lick* anymore, you're more concerned wit' Heaven's *feelings* for that boy. Damn, Empress, you're actin' like you're tryin' to compare dicks wit' the man!" she spat. Untying the scarf from around her head, sis began to pat the back of her noggin as if it would stop the itch. I rolled my eyes at her before returning to my task. She could talk all that big girl shit she wanted, Heaven was fallin' for that nigga Ghetto, and I wasn't havin' it! *Period!* I thought as I caught Egypt's reflection as she turned her back to me and began opening all the drawers and cabinets in the bathroom.

"What the hell are you lookin' for?" I inquired, carefully working the hot comb through my hair. Egypt paused and placed her small hands on her small waist and gave me this peculiar expression.

"I can't find my comb."

***

-Stick Talk-

"Mmmmmah! Pweeeese!" Officer Smith attempted to plead, but the gag in his mouth prevented his words from being understood. We'd positioned him, his wife, and his son on the living room couch, side by side. I allowed my vision to capture the tear-streaked expression of his wife before I sat my gaze on the child. Fear was dominant in his stare, and as I looked from my left to my right, I knew that his fright was warranted. Me and the fam were lined up like a shooting squad as we stood over the bound and gagged family, and when my eyes finally found the petrified stare of the man of the house, I knew I was the scariest gorilla he'd ever set eyes on.

Blood from his wounds speckled his face as his eyes grew wide in fear. I'd raised the modified Louisville slugger and inspected it, the sharp razor wire that I'd had wrapped tight around it gleamed under the soft light in the room.

"You stole my youngin' from not only me, but now I gotta watch my grandmother cry for the spilt blood of an innocent child. My brother didn't deserve the hand you dealt him, homie, and now you gotta answer for the hate you served him." My words were ominous, and the fear in playboy's gaze transformed into suspicion as his gaze drifted to the baseball bat.

"Yu ont nooo fukit pwit!" His words were indecipherable as he rocked back and forth with the angry declaration. I assumed he was attempting to let me know that I didn't know who I was fuckin' wit', *but* my response proved that I clearly didn't give a fuck. *Whack!*

The bat knocked blood from the Mrs.' head, and when a splash of blood wet the side of his face, Officer Smith truly lost his marbles. A soft breath escaped the lady's lips, and I didn't know if her spirit had betrayed her body with that first swing, the second, the third, or one of the numerous other swings I'd taken. All I knew was that I'd slipped into a dark place, until—

"Stick, Flesh, calm the fuck down!" Red Diamond's voice penetrated the pools of blackness I'd fallen into. Subconsciously, I detected the frustration in her tone, but it was the underlying *fear* I detected that screwed my head back on straight. First thing I noticed was the blood. A red river of it ran deep, and splotches of it stained different places of the room. The substance dripped from the bat and when I looked to my people, I noticed they'd stepped away from me in alarm. My vision found Red Diamond, and to my surprise, her eyes were *suspicious* as she slick aimed the tool in *my* direction.

"The fuck is wrong wit' you, bruh, you good or what, my nigga?" Her question confused me until my gaze drifted to my artwork. My head slightly tilted to the left as I studied the blood bath. Mrs. Smith's head was twisted at a weird angle, and the slashes across her neck and chest told the tale of *my* hate, but it was the child's broken and mutilated body that caused the vomit to rush up my throat and slip from my lips. *Fuck!* was all my mental could think as the scene branded itself in the walls of my mind.

"Ooooo kodddd!" Officer Smith's muffled cries kidnapped my attention. Patches of his wife's blond hair and scalp rested on his shoulder as he squeezed his eyes shut and rocked in place. He seemed to be trying to mentally escape the madness that *he* created, but I knew there was a reality that followed you no matter how far one retreated into their mental, and I guess Red Diamond felt that hate had followed the officer far enough. She strolled over to dude, and as if he could sense the devil lurkin', Officer Smith's eyes drifted open. He looked up into the nubian's eyes that stared down at him from within the angry apes mask, and the man lost it.

"Arrrrrugh!" he screamed.

Boom! The Glock jumped in Red's hand.

Boom! Boom! Flames shot from it twice more as the slugs gave the corrupted officer deliverance from what we all knew he wouldn't be able to live with. Without takin' her eyes from me, Red Diamond gave my soul the peace it cried for.

"It's ova, Flesh, lil' bruh can rest well now. Let's get the fuck outta here."

Renta

Chapter 12
Die Real... Voodoo Too?

Day Two

-Heaven-

9:30 A.M.

Who goes to a prison for breakfast? my mind screamed as the correctional officers ushered us into a small room with a viewing window. As we took our seats, I got the shock of my life as I peeked through that glass and into an *execution room! Fuck?* My mind had been attempting to correlate the morning's events without me having to spazz on Ghetto's sneaky ass. I'd fallen asleep in his arms and awakened to him watching me. Under ordinary circumstances, the shit would've been some real creepy, some weirdo typa stuff to do, but Ghetto had this way of making me feel as if I was the most beautiful bitch he'd ever set eyes on.

He'd risen and gathered his things for a shower but paused to tell me we were going out for breakfast. The crazy part was, I'd *never* heard of the prison system having a restaurant or bed and breakfast. *Well, unless someone was housed there!* I thought as I set my glare on him, but Ghetto's attention was held captive. I followed his gaze until I found the sobbing white woman that was being comforted by a middle-aged man. He held her close to him as she dabbed at her eyes with a handkerchief. "I can't do this, Robert, I just can't," she cried.

"It'll be ok, Jenny, we're here to see Benedict's murderer brought to justice. He *deserves* this—*you* deserve this," the man whispered loud enough for all to hear, but gently enough to convince the woman that legalized murder was better than any other execution. I witnessed her resolve as she squared her shoulders and stared up into the window of that room that had robbed so many men and women of their second chance, and that woman spiritually died before my eyes. My eyes reverted to Ghetto, who gritted his

157

teeth so tightly that his jaw muscles imprinted his cheeks. I wondered so much, like, *what the hell are we doing here!* I wanted to ask him exactly that, but the sound of a door opening came over the sound system that was built into the small room.

All eyes diverted to a group of correctional guards, one chaplain, and the warden of the unit as they entered the death chamber. In their midst was a tall albino man with long dreads, and as soon as he entered the room, he paused to study the execution table. He smirked, and as if feeling his presence, as if he was certain that Ghetto had come and he knew exactly where the man sat, the condemned man looked up through the glass and right into the eyes of the man that had brought me to that evil place.

***

Genevieve rummaged through Heaven's overnight bag in search of something, *anything*, that would have a piece of the girl's DNA. The elder woman knew that the promise she'd made so long ago, the deal she'd made with the darkness, she knew it was a deal the gatekeeper would collect on if she didn't do something to prevent having to share Ghetto's love.

"De girl must not win my boy's heart, she's no good for him. She doesn't deserve his love—no one does," she mumbled to herself. Ghetto's grandmother searched through Heaven's things and just when she thought she'd have to resort to conniving means, she found the perfect object for the darkness she would call upon. She pulled the comb from the bag and held it up for a closer inspection. There was a small cluster of hair caught in the teeth of it, and as she freed the strands of hair, Genevieve smile wickedly at her dark intentions.

***

-Ghetto-

My heartbeat was a crooked melody that only a real nigga could get groovy to. I watched as they strapped my dude to that table and it took all I had to tame the devil in me. I couldn't understand how those people could murder a mu'fucka for the same shit they were doing—*murder!* It was as if since they were killing a man that had gotten caught doing wrong, that made the act of their murdering him noble. They brought in a man of the cloth to read verses from the same Bible that spoke against an eye for an eye, and that same man of God watched those people whack a mu'fucka. "Do you have any last words or requests?" the executioner asked, as if he gave a damn about if my family had something to get off his chest.

"What's blessins, Flesh, why you lookin' like it's the end of the world?" Kiest ignored the sucka and gave me a smile. He turned his attention to the ceiling, as if freedom would fall through the roof. He lay still as the executioner plunged the needle in his arm, and though I could tell that he tried to hide it, my brotha from anotha motha flinched.

"This that shit that only a nigga that's been in the field can feel, bruh. I know I'm 'pose to be strong, but it's fuckin' wit' me." I spoke my peace while poundin' my fist over my chest where my heart beat at. My vision blurred with the truth that slipped from my lips, and as the first drop of salty water fell from my right eye, Heaven reached over and attempted to wipe it. Without intending to, I grabbed her wrist and held it tight as I glared at her, but the look in her vision made me release her and intertwine my fingers with hers.

"Gangstas cry too, my nigga, we just do it in the dark—where nobody can see. I wanna say don't cry for me, but who else gone do it?" Kiest smiled a sad smile as the first injection entered his veins. "You gotta always see *beyond* the shit we as street niggas have used to protect our hearts, fam. Sometimes we build the wall to protect it from the shit that can hurt it but wind up trappin' it in a dark room." Kiest turned his head to look at me and a spider's web of dreadlocks fell across his face. He stared at me from between them and smiled as a lone tear fell from his eye.

"The point of life, Flesh, is to be able to die knowing you can rest well with the shit you did while you lived. A fuck nigga will never know peace 'cause there's too many snakes in his dreams.

Us?" he asked as a weird expression eased onto his features, almost as if he were fighting to see straight. "We-we die hard, my dude, the same-same way we liv-lived." His words slurred. I felt water leak from both of my eyes, and as the tears snaked down my face, Heaven squeezed my hand. I saw one last tear drop from bro's eye, and in that tear was a vision of his greatest sacrifice.

The investigation room was cold, they'd had him in that deep freezer of a room for hours before two officers stepped in and offered him refreshments. "Have you eaten, Mr. Osborne, want a drink? A cigarette perhaps?" A tall, lanky homicide detective offered. Kiest smirked and shook his head in amusement at the good cop attempt before fixing his gaze on the other detective who stood silently studying him from the door. He knew the man would play the bad cop sooner or later—he'd been through enough homicide investigations to now know they play. The lanky detective's name was Scott, and he'd worked the beat for years before being promoted. He and Kiest had had a few run-ins and each time, the sly crook had beaten him. He smiled while taking a seat and tossed a manila envelope onto the table. He knew he had the man by the balls.

"You know you've fucked up, right? We have you not only on armed robbery of that bank, but the murders of Chuck Spincer, Jerry Benedict, and Michael Spincer, an officer of the law. Your dumb ass added insult to injury by ramming that truck into a squad car and adding obstruction of justice to the bucket list." The man counted off the charges on his fingers. "The big boys will be taking over this case, but the higher ups have compassion, Kiest Osborne, more than your scum bag ass deserves," he spoke while opening the folder. Scott laid out seven photos of known Louisiana Stick-up kids, and as Kiest's eyes fell to the line-up of Ghetto, Thugga, Lil' Nukkey, and four other cats he'd never seen before, he was careful not to allow his facial to betray him. He looked up into the eyes of the detective and shrugged indifferently, and that's when the other man in the room decided to make his entrance.

"You arrogant prick!" he growled as he stormed over to Kiest. Cuffed and defenseless, Kiest was helpless when the man backhanded him. Blood filled his mouth as he glared up at the disrespectful detective, but the officer wasn't deterred. He reached down and roughly held the bound man by the jaw so tightly that his lips puckered. "Who are they, are these the other four scum that aided in the heist? Answer me, motherfucker!" Spittle flew from his mouth with the demand.

"Woah-woaaah, Partner, be easy. I'm sure Mr. Osborne will help us, especially with the sweet deal we're offering him." Detective Scott played his role to the tee. He pulled his partner's fingers from around Kiest's face and stepped between the two men. "Now, everyone just calm down, be cool," he spoke as his eyes bounced back and forth between the two. His partner seemed to relent before tossing his hands up in the air in surrender. He gave Kiest one last glare before making his way back to his post by the door. Scott clapped his hands together.

"That's better, everybody be cool." He acted as if he were soothing the tension. Kiest watched him lean over and take up two of the photos before holding them up to him, one of Ghetto and the other of Lil' Nukkey. "We know your little crew aided you in the heist, and the prosecutor is willing to cut you some slack. The guy really has a hard-on for this Devonte, Ghetto, *Bousard and is willing to bend the rules for your cooperation. I mean, come on, Kiest, you're guaranteed the needle for—"*

The man's words died in his throat when Kiest spat a thick glob of bloody spit in his face. "Tell dem hoes to get they needles ready. I wanna see if that shit strong enough for a real nigga's veins anyway. I don't know none of them niggas you talm 'bout. I plead the fifth, white boy, talk to my lawyer!" he spat.

"You dirty nigger!" the detective raged before punching Kiest in the face.

It seemed as if the punch was so powerful that it snapped me back to the present. The tear dripped from bruh's face, I watched it splash against the floor, and that's when a deep realization held my breath for ransom. All through the ages, people have made a spectacle of murder! The law permitted the taking of a life only if it was by the hand of those of authority, but if a nigga did it, it's viewed as heinous and his life is forfeited to a system that killed for killing. Murder was the greatest form of entertainment known to mankind! The coliseum in Rome, where people filled the rafters to *enjoy* watching gladiators fight till the death. Europe and the United States, where people gathered to see a mu'fucka be hung for crimes as petty as theft, and even present day, where people came to execution viewings that were meant to give them a view of *Justice*!

"I hate you! I hate you! Die, you piece of shit! You took my husband from me—from our children! Just die!" the white woman I'd noticed earlier shouted and caused my heart to bleed as my eyes shot back to my flesh.

"It's ok, Jenny, it's ok. Benedict can rest in peace now. His killer is where he belongs now." The cock sucker beside her consoled her, but it was *my* heart that turned upside down. Those people had released the third and final serving of poison into my nigga's veins, and Kiest's body shook violently as he gritted his teeth. Bro was at war with the reaper, but in the end, he died with his eyes open and a crooked smile on his face. A rainstorm clouded my vision, and the pain made me wanna blow my brains out.

***

Genevieve sat in her favorite rocking chair, humming an old slave hymn. She'd sown the last stitch into the rag doll she'd placed Heaven's hair into, and as the shadows played over her pretty features, Genevieve's hum transformed into a dark chant of old Latin. The faster she spoke, the tighter her grip became on the doll. Her eyes rolled to the back of her head so deeply that all one could see was the whites of her orbs, and as a soft wind blew through the halls of the small house, Ghetto's grandmother smiled a crooked smile.

"Yuh no worthy of his heart, yuh evil girl!" she hissed with slanted eyes, and as she allowed the words to slip from her lips, she bent the leg of the doll in an inhumane way. "Auuuha!" She exhaled as she pitched forward in her seat. Her eyes were white yolks as she pulled herself upright in her chair, but before she could get comfortable, her back arched at a wicked angle, as if some unforeseen force was attempting to snatch her heart out her chest. The old woman's mouth fell open in a silent *O* as she stared absently into nothing. "Save him!" she cried.

***

-Egypt-

I'd just taken a hot bath, and the Epsom salts I'd added to the water had my skin super soft. I had another date with Mr. Earl of East Arlington, and the boy truly had that bag! I made my way over to the mirror and cupped my mouthful of titties, my chocolate-hued nipples were taut and semi-long. I made a sad face and poked my bottom lip out. "Shame, you'll never get none of this pussy," I spoke to my reflection as I thought of him.

Absently, I ran my hands down my body, my stomach, and stopped as I gently massaged my thick thighs. Glancing down, I inspected my coochie. My cootie cat was pretty, but the light stubble that had grown had to go. I reached down and slid a manicured finger inside her before bringing it to my nose for the smell test—*water*. I smiled before turning for the cabinet above the toilet. I rolled my eyes. *I don't know why these hoes keep puttin' the razors up on the top shelf like everyone tall like they asses!* I thought, having to stand up on the toilet to reach the top shelf.

I found the electric razor and was stepping off the toilet when things went bad. "Oh my god!" I screamed as my foot slipped and I fell. I hit the ground hard, my right leg twisting inhumanely beneath me. It was strange, I couldn't understand *how* my leg had twisted so badly. "Help-help! *Please!*" my plea echoed throughout the house. "Please, Empress, I-need-*hellllp!*" I cried. Moments passed, but she burst into the bathroom with a baby Glock clutched in her hand. She pulled up short when she spotted me lying on the floor with my leg bent at an unnatural angle. Sis had a look of shock on her pretty face as she stared bewilderedly at my leg. I felt faint, but my anger was mounting. I couldn't understand why that bitch was just standing there, staring like I wasn't 'bout to die or some shit. "Empressss, please get me some helllp! It hurrrts!" I cried. Tears welled up in my eyes as I began to whimper.

"Oh, damn, sis, wait, umm…" She seemed flustered. Her eyes kept diverting from my face to my leg. I just couldn't understand why she was just staring!

"Bitch, I'm gonna fuck you up. Em, please call an ambulance! Nowww!" I was in tears as I gritted on her. I prayed I lived through the pain. I was gonna beat her ass!

***

-Heaven-

I could tell that someone had been in my things, and I had a good idea who that someone was. *Nosey bitch!* I thought as I did inventory to ensure that none of my things were missing, and that's when I found it. *Egypt's comb? How'd this get here?* I wondered as I pulled the comb from my bag and studied it. I sighed. *Maybe I accidently packed it in my haste to leave*, I thought before tossing it back in my bag. I knew if I didn't confront that lady about her disrespect, it would only get worse. First, it was the sneaking through my things, but next, it would be her poisoning Ghetto's mind about me. I didn't want to add more drama to the already somber mood, but a woman has to set boundaries that she won't allow anyone to cross.

I stormed through that small house and into the living room where I'd seen her last, but she wasn't there. Only after I'd searched every room did I try the kitchen, and even that was empty. I glanced out the window facing the back yard, and that's where I spotted the old hag, out back, in a beautiful garden. When I stepped out the back door and made my way over to her, Ms. Genevieve was bent over, planting a pretty flower into the soil, and without looking up or doing anything to show that she'd heard me behind her— "They call this flower de devil's trap. It's a root born from de honey suckle family and grows in the untamed forest of distant lands. My grandmother used to tell me it protects the house of those you love, and some people even prepare them with perfume before burying them in their yard. It's said to trap de devil before he enters de home," she spoke without looking up.

How the hell did she know I'm standing here? My mind was a room of curiosities. Genevieve finished her planting before climbing to her feet to face me, and when she turned to do just that, I was taken aback at how youthful her features were. When I saw her the day before, I could've sworn she had *a few* wrinkles, but under the kiss of the sun, they were gone. She studied me with her smoke-gray eyes. "So, maybe my grandmother was wrong about de flower, or just maybe, you're a different kind of devil entirely?" The old bitch shot a slug. She studied me with a peculiar expression on her face before reaching up and gently holding my chin between her thumb and pointer finger. "Yuh have de gift in your blood, and what you see in the cards of foresight scares you, hmmm?"

Her words sent chills down my spine. I wanted to slap her hand away, but I had manners, and on top of that, her revelation lifted a weight off my shoulders that I didn't know was there until that moment. Few people knew the burden of seeing the future, and for that woman to know what she knew, it gave us a common ground.

"Why'd you go through my things, that's disrespectful and—"

"And what you don't understand is that what you see in de cards is *your* doing! Devonte can't love you, chile, it's too dangerous... It's not in de cards for de union to be," Genevieve cut me off, her words almost urgent. My eyes dropped to slits as my blood pressure rose. She must've sensed that *other side* of me, 'cause her fingers fell away and she took a step back to put some space between us.

"And who the hell are you to tell me who my heart can call for? Ghetto, Devonte, or whatever the hell you call him, is a grown man, and he doesn't need you to hold his—"

"Y'all good or what?" The sound of his voice saved the old bitch from the checkin' she deserved. Both of us looked in the direction of the porch and we both smiled.

"Yea-yeah, we were just having a chat about de flowers, yuh know?" The bitch continued to smile as she lied to Ghetto's face, wiping her hands on her pant legs and making her way over to him. The smile slipped from my lips as she passed, and I had to fight the urge to call her on the secret, messy shit she was on. My eyes found Ghetto, and the look in his eyes told me that he wasn't fooled by all the fakin', but it was the primal pain in his gaze that allowed me to place my grievances to the side.

If only for the moment! Ghetto was a wounded animal, and as I glanced back at the garden, my vision found the place his grandmother had just buried the strange flower. *The devil's trap?* I thought before returning my gaze to where Ghetto stood, shirtless on the porch.

"Well, bitch, if the shit really works, why your evil ass gets past it? Yea, the devil's trap my ass!" I mumbled before making my way toward the dude that was playing for my heart.

Heaven Got a Ghetto

Chapter 13
Last Night to Win Your Heart... Poetry

"Catrina, where the little girls room at? I have to pee, baby," the pretty girl asked. She stood from the couch and was already heading down the hall before she received a response. Heaven's younger sister had become a butch and had begun to drink and party so often that she tended to forget the names of her many bed partners. At that moment, she was in the kitchen preparing drinks for them and praying she could slay the young tender before her moms came home on one of her heroine binges.

She'd moved her and Heaven's T-Jones in with her in an attempt to keep the lady off the streets, but those cold streets that had stolen her husband from her seemed more of a home to Ismerelda Domingo than the three-bedroom apartment that her younger daughter had provided. "It's down the hall, the second door on the right, and make sho you clean that thang good when you wipe," Catrina shouted in jest.

"Oh, don't worry about that, I'm a big girl, mami, I—Ahhhh! Oh my god, oh my god! What the fuck!" The pretty girl's panicked screams caught Catrina by surprise. With drinks in her hands, she rushed out the kitchen and down the hall where she found her date bent over and vomiting on her carpet.

"Bitch, are you crazy! What the—" she began, but when she stepped around the heaving girl, life became a little more jagged for her. The glasses fell from her hands, and the only thing that prevented them from shattering was the carpet. The amber liquid spiled and oozed out on the tiled floor of the bathroom where there, slouched on the toilet with a needle hanging from her arm, was Ismerelda Domingo. The glazed-over stare told the tale that no child should have to read, or in Catrina's case, *see*.

"Mama, Mama?" The shock was evident in her voice. She took one step into the room that she and Heaven's queen had taken her last breath in, and as if gravity demanded her attention, Catrina fell to her knees. Tears in her eyes, Hennessy soaking through the material of her pants, and a heart that was liquefying in her chest, the girl couldn't take her eyes off her mother's stiff form. She silently prayed for her queen to reverse her decision to leave, but death wasn't a door one could use to come and go as they pleased. "I—we need you, Mama." She cried a frivolous cry.

***

-Heaven-

The room was dim, but the mood was filled with power. In the height of police brutality, a businessman as the president, and a national emergency of killings, my people still found a way to enjoy themselves. Me and Ghetto sat at a candlelit table in the back, in tune with the sista that had just taken the stage.

"We're livin' in troubled times, ain't' we, brothas and sistas?" were her first words, and the crowd acknowledged her with raised glasses and a plenitude of, "Sho' ya rights, and sholl is!" I merely nodded my head in agreement. "For those of y'all that's new to this spot, my name is Asiatic and I come here every Saturday to get the heavy shit of the week off my chest." Her voice was thick, like warm, melted chocolate.

"Alright now, give it to us Asiatic, give it to us, baby!" someone from the crowd encouraged. Laughter resonated throughout the room. Asiatic smiled a seductive smile, her red lips bringing life to her high-yellow face. She was wrapped head to toe in African garb, her head in a multi-colored wrap, and the black, gold, and green dress rode her petite curves as she stared out at the crowd. "This piece I'm about to do was inspired by those we lost to the hate of the times. Y'all vibe with me now." Asiatic smiled as her eyes drifted closed as if she was transporting herself to another place. "I call this piece—

I watched as lady's lips parted and life poured out in a soft aggressiveness. "I wish I could revive Nat Turner...Malcolm...or maybe just show Martin how our people are dying for the color of their skin even after the dream he had way back when... How they've created the projects and call them government assistance, built a school not too far from them, placed a store across the streets, and then…" Queen paused as her eyes cracked open and she allowed her vision to capture her audience. "Then, built a gate around those projects to trap us in.

"My people's history has been gutted, then reconstructed by the same people that infiltrated our land, they spread us out and played on the psychology, made the black woman and black child watch the defamation of the black man. This one for Sandra Bland, Douglas Lewis, Tamar Rice, and George Floyd, the ones that were stolen from us too early and left empty spaces in history with no one to fill the void. We're battling with a moment of insanity, these words should be parental advised."

Asiatic stepped to the edge of the stage and gazed up at the ceiling as if she could see clear through it and up into heaven. "We must see beyond the disguise, the devil twist the truth like the rope made into a noose, so God must ordain over his earth, protect his galaxy and never let him through. Thou shall not eat on the sabbath, *Yet*, our people are famished, so I feed 'em the leavened bread but tell 'em to hide it so the pharisees don't catch it. We live with a borrowed identity, a stolen religion, and the last names of slaves masters.

"The doctrine of Willie Lynch's theory—*I'mma behave massa!*" She giggled as the room fed her energy. A dark-skinned man with long dreads stood up and toasted her.

"Ummhmm, tell it like it is, Black woman, tell it like it is." He cheered her on before downing his drink. Asiatic held up a fist of power before feeding us her power.

"That's what she screamed as he bombarded her with his filth, drove his nature inside her to the hilt until he infested her blood with his milk. A moment of genocide, can you imagine how many children have died in the wars of Chicago? Black woman can't let her cries go 'cause as she holds her slain seed in that sheet, the coroner tells her she gotta let the child go. There's power in the revolution if only we can see beyond the pollution, separate the knowledge from the confusion, and stop believing that forty acres and a mule is enough restitution!" She brought her words to an end with a raised fist to the loud applause in the room. I gave it up for Queen before glancing at my date. Ghetto's relaxed demeanor was perfect for the atmosphere, but just behind the swinging dreads, through the rose-tinted lenses of the gold-trimmed Cartier glasses that covered his eyes, I knew pain resided.

"I've never been to anything like this, it's nice," I offered. Ghetto nodded slightly, and though I couldn't see them, I knew his eyes were digesting my face, the style I wore my curly hair in, and though he professed to be this extraordinary kinda guy, I knew he couldn't resist a glance at all that cleavage I had on display.

"I've never been the kinda nigga to front, even though I wanna impress you and act as if I'm just this cultured kinda dude, but the realist shit I can tell you is shid, it's my first time rockin' like this too." His truths gave us the ease we needed. We shared a laugh, and never being the one to pass up on a perfect opportunity, I took advantage of the moment.

"That's what's up, Papi, but you don't have to impress me any further, I'm already open. I'm more curious about how you're feeling. That shit back at that prison was some fucked-up shit, and I could tell you and dude have a lot of history. You good?" I asked with a raised brow. Ghetto leaned forward and slipped the designers from his face, his dark eyes running so deep that I had to look away to keep from drowning in his stare.

"You ever heard the term pyrric victory, ma?" The question caused me to return my vision to his as I nodded my confirmation, wondering where the question would lead me. Ghetto's eyes traveled toward the stage before his words opened my mind. "That's what's up, but did you know that they coined that phrase from a cat named Pyrrus? He was the king of Epirus." I didn't know that, so as I leaned forward and picked up the tube of the hookah pipe, I allowed my eyes to tell him to continue. "Dude defeated the Romains at Heraclea and Asculum, but you wanna know why his victories were less of a celebration than the tears he'd shed by the pyres he'd set aflame after those wars, mama? You know how a victorious king's name became the description of *loss*?" he asked as he slid from his seat and stood, looking down at me. I put the hookah to my lips and sucked smoke from it before replying.

"No, Ghetto, I don't know. Tell me, Daddy." My eyes took in the cranberry-colored, silk button-down he wore with the cranberry-hued Dior pants. Dude's drip was always exclusive, and though I'd come to the conclusion that he was a hustla, I just couldn't see *D-boy* in his aura.

"It's 'cause, though he won the wars, he'd buried way more of the people he loved than the ones he celebrated with. Imagine goin' to battle with ten thousand of your closest family and friends by your side, ma, win that war, but have to bury nine thousand and eight hundred of those same people you'd shed blood wit'." We watched each other, getting lost within the moment as I exhaled a cloud of smoke. Ghetto left me in the wake of his Givenchy fragrance. Confused, I turned in my seat to see where he was headed and found him paused with his back to me.

"Truth is, my heart fucked up 'bout my nigga, but every real nigga I've ever known got a raw deal. I took you to see those crackas take my dude down to let you know that the life I live is filled wit' dirty hands dealt by a crooked dealer. I'mma either win big or take a big boy loss, but either or"—Ghetto turned to look at me before taking slow steps backward—"these past three days havin' you in my presence have been nice victories, but if by the end of all this shit, after our time is up, if you choose to walk away from the gamble of the hearts, then, just like Pyrrus, just like all the gambles me and my flesh Keist took in the name of livin' our dream, you'll just be anotha reason I sat at the table of life, wonderin' why the fuck I keep gamblin' somethin' so precious." His words penetrated me when he knocked his fist against his chest to indicate it was his heart he was casting to the gamble.

***

-Stick Talk-

"What, nigga, quit cappin', you ain't that freaked out, Stick!" My dude Daddyo had tears in his eyes from the power of his laughter. The park was lit that Saturday and it was a fashion show. Boys had brought their toys out to show the streets how they were livin', and me and the squad was out lurkin'. I laughed to myself at the arrogance of street niggas. It never failed! When a mu'fucka got 'em a nice lil' bag, it was like a disease, they had to show the world they were getting to it, but I assume that money blinds people. D-boys hustled for their shine and stick-up boys made their livin' off of takin' it from 'em. Predator and prey was a never-ending reality that would forever keep some niggas full and the next cat starting all ova.

"Naw, bruh, I was there. I saw the shit wit' my own two, fam," Twitcha Lee's hatin' ass added his input. My eyes studied the swagged up white boy and laughed. Dude was supa smart, but what had won him a spot in the circle was his loyalty to the flesh Nukkey. I pushed him playfully.

"Damn, my dude, this my movie. I ain't shame to be the star!" I jazzed. I looked back to my fam, Daddyo.

"Yea, that hoe a monsta, my G. I swear, bruh, that hoe was lickin' my ass so good that I pooted and damn near peeled shawty's skin off her face! When I looked down, the hoe's eyes were back and her hair was stickin' straight up on her head like she'd got electrocuted. I'm tellin' y'all, ain't nothin' like a nasty bitch. You need to get ya ass ate, bruh, ain't nothing like it!" I capped before reachin' down and grippin' my dick head. At just the thought of the freak bitch, Empress, my shit was comin' to life. I still hadn't gutted the bitch. She was on some *I ain't givin' up the pussy in the first month,* typa shit, but I was plottin' on it.

"Naw, fam, I'm good on all that, that's otha level shit! You bet not kiss the hoe, though. If the bitch lickin' yo' ass, how many otha nigga's ass she done sucked on?" Daddyo all of a sudden wanted to be a smart guy. I was just 'bout to check him 'bout the slick business he was kickin' 'bout the bitch *suckin'* on the kid like I was fag or summin, but—

"What's up Stick Talk, I see you on ya fashion." Her voice was high pitched, but lil' one was born for a playa. I knew Charmane from round the way, and I was up on the fact of how her bow-legged ass fucked wit' a dude from the otha side. I glanced down at the pale pink and baby blue Chanel shoes on my feet, they complemented the cotton candy pink and baby blue Chanel unit I wore. Though the sun had begun to duck behind the clouds, the jewels in my RNO choker were wet, and when my eyes lifted to find Ms. Lady watching the movie me and the gang were creating with the drip, I knew that between her legs was just as wet. *These hoes for everybody!* I thought with a crooked smirk.

I was leaning against my burnt orange Hell Cat wit' the Lambo doors lifted high like the wings of a bald eagle. As Lil' Baby's "Bigger Picture" shook the trunk, I made my way over to lil' baby to let her get an up close and personal view at how I was drippin'. She and two of her homegirls were on some real thotie shit, but I liked that slut look. All three girls wore a different shade of boy shorts that rode up in their ass crack, and as I set my stare on Charmane, I let her know it was all 'bout her lil' red ass.

"Yea, I hear that slick shit you spittin', ma, but what I'm tryin' to see is if you're just in the mood for giving out compliments or you gonna let me introduce you to some of this RNO shit," I jazzed before gettin' on my bold shit. I reached out and pulled lady to me before dropping my hands to that ass. I knew I was in violation 'cause her dude was the *op*, but if the hoe ain't have no respect for her own nigga, shid, why would I? I squeezed all that as she looked up at me.

"Boy, you RNO niggas somethin' else." She giggled before pulling herself free from my grasp. "You know I got a nigga though, and you know he ain't—"

"Mane, I ain't tryin' to discuss lil' buddy, *you* the only one owes him respect. You know I been tryin' to pipe that, so you knew the dog was gonna fetch the cat when you pulled up on ya teasin' business. Look, let's get on some exclusive shit. Lose ya company and meet by the restrooms ova there." I nodded my head toward the public restrooms at the edge of the park. The thick chocolate bitch beside her sucked her teeth and rolled her eyes, like she and her girls were beyond fuckin' or suckin' in a public environment. Charmane must've taken offense, because her face balled up.

"Damn, bitch, why you all in my situation? I don't be sayin' nothin' when *you* out doin' you!" she spazzed before cocking her left leg out and placing her hands on her hips real sassy-like. My eyes fell to the imprint of them pussy lips in those stretch shorts before traveling past the tattooed cherries on her thigh and landing on the crisp J's on her feet. I smirked. *Jordan's used to be exclusive, but now everybody has 'em!* My thoughts were comical but—

"Don't start, Charmane, don't even start. I'm sayin', you know how crazy YB and them BGM niggas is, *and* you know he'll be here. Get yo' ass whooped if you want to, bitch. When that nigga go upside ya head, don't be callin' me crying." Chocolate's voice was laced with *envy.* I could tell her words had gotten to lil' one as Charmane's eyes drifted from her homegirl to me, weighing her options. Bitch had the boy all wrong. I knew the nigga YB and his caliber, and if a hoe had to compare this RNO shit on any level, she was as lost as a car wit' no navigational system. I chuckled before adjusting the burna on my hip. I reached down into my pocket, freed a fifty-dollar bill from the bankroll I had on deck, and held it out to the chocolate girl with a playa's smirk to my lips.

"Here, lil' mama, go buy you some class. Real bitches don't turn they nose up at the same shit they do. Be for real, if it was *you* I was tryin' to run dick in, we wouldn't still be standin' here, huh?" I kept it gully wit' the cock-blocking thot, but instead of digesting it, she got straight on some bummy shit. The bitch should've become a sign language teacher for the mute with all the finger points and hand signals she was doing as she spoke.

"Fuck you, nigga, you ain't shit! I wouldn't fuck you if you had a million-dolla dick, and as a matter of a fact," she paused and turned her glare on Charmane, "let's go, Charmane. We got better shit to do." She shot her shot. I slipped the fifty back in my pocket and chuckled at the situation. I didn't have to waste time sweatin' no female, I was too lit.

"Look, you've been wit' enough stone-cold suckas to know when you in the presence of a real nigga. I'm *Real Niggas Only*, so that means I'm only rockin' wit' real bitches only! If you and ya girl on the middle school shit and she can pull you away from what we both want, tear yo' ass. I'mma be waitin', but not for long." I gave it up and nodded toward the restrooms. Without waiting for a response, I turned and allowed those Chanel kicks to carry me that way, and I was willing to bet the bankroll in my pocket I'd have that broad bent over one of dem stalls in a few minutes. I could sense a thirsty, nothin' typa bitch from a mile and lost in a crowd.

***

-Ghetto-

I use to write poetry, but neva really shared it wit' anyone, but as I stood up there on that stage with my heart upside down, all I could see was the warm spotlight. I knew I was being beheld by curious stares, but it was one I wanted to be captured by. "I really ain't no poet or the typa cat to let my heart speak, but shid, it's open mic *and*..." I emphasized the word as I gazed out where I knew Heaven was prolly lookin' at me as if I'd lost my marbles. I smiled as I stared out from the strands of dreads that had fallen over my face. The room had become as silent as a graveyard, but I had some shit to say. "Tonight is the last night I got to win a special lady's heart, so y'all forgive me if the shit I'm 'bout to kick sounds..."

I frowned as I searched for a word that was sufficient for my spiel, but just outside the glare of the spotlight, Heaven made her way down one of the aisles leading to the stage and paused midway. Our eyes wrestled, but as I took in the sleeveless, black catsuit she wore that night, I knew that sometimes a man had to piece his peace together, and that woman was the quiet I needed to hush the storm inside me. I stepped to the edge of that stage and took a seat, allowing my legs to dangle over the edge. The crowd's eyes left me and fixated on Heaven as the words I was seeking slipped from my lips.

"Different... This shit may be different, but I ain't ever believed in love, and now that I know that it *may* be real, I wanna talk to her so..." I paused to take a deep breath, and on my exhale, rode my convo with what I'd never believed in. "*Love*, there's so many things I gotta tell you, but I'm afraid I don't know how, 'cause there's that slight possibility that you may look at me differently. *Love*, so many times I wondered of your mysteries, even studied you down through the histories... Malcolm X and Betty... Martin and Coretta King... Nelson and Winnie Mandela, the most powerful chemistries.

"I come from the ghetto where we're fightin' for victories, and the crazy part is that all three of the women I named, outlived their men and held on to you even while embracing you through pain without remedies. But love?" I allowed my eyes to travel up and down lady's stature before pushing my dreads to the back.

"I once heard that when one finds you, *till death does us part*, truly exist, but honestly, I don't know if I've ever captured you because I can't remember a life other than this. The life of the ghetto where the black woman doesn't know loyalty and the black man fucks her mentally and physically without the thought of if she concieves...

"He leads her to believe that he'll never leave, and since she found love through her pussy, she actually believes that her beauty is enough to make him find you... In her... for real! The story of Adam and Eve, naw, I'm speakin' 'bout after that serpent conversed with Eve and told her the truth of the fruit that hung from those trees... and now Queen sees that what homie really felt for her was never...really love! Honestly, though, Love, I think I felt you somewhere. A one-night stand, slept wit' you somewhere... but damn, maybe I left you somewhere?

"Do you remember me, too? A moment of déjà vu, or maybe just a fantasy that I wished came true, 'cause, *love? Heyyyyy, you,* I remember you now! I remember feelin' like I could die from the thought of losin' you... But... But...I remember saying I'd never fall in you, so why am I choosin' you now?

"Hold up, wait-wait, please—am I losin' you now? *Love!* Look, let me explain... I'm scared 'cause everything I've ever allowed close to my heart walked away without thinkin' of it. Left me with broken pieces of it, and at times I felt like I had to think of somethin'...

"Tears created an ocean so deep in my eyes that I needed to blink or somethin'...

"A moment of insanity, standin' on the brink of somethin', 'cause love? I need you to give me faith, and if I died today, I don't want to be the man that didn't recognize you when you were standin' right in my face!

"*Love?* There's so many thangs I gotta tell you, but I'm afraid."

***

-Stick Talk-

"Get it, get that shit! Yea—Yassss!" she cried as I pounded that cat from the back. Charmane gripped the seat of the toilet, shorts around her ankles, and head thrust back in ecstasy as I searched for that nut.

"Take this dick, bitch, take that!" I growled as my strokes lifted lady up on her tip toes. I gripped her waist with my left hand and gripped the handle of the FN in my right. The devil had a way of showin' up in some of the most unlikely places, and I lived to show 'em that he wasn't the only mu'fucka 'bout that action. I felt that demon explode from my nut sack, and just like I expected—*The devil arrived!*

***

VROOOOOOM! The first Ducati zoomed into the park, followed by a trail of colorful bikes. The rider of the Ducati was a light-skinned character the streets knew as YB, and dude was whacko in every aspect of the word. He killed the growl of the fire-red bike and hopped off, his eyes already scanning the crowd of people for a threat. He'd pulled up next to a metallic blue box Caprice that was vibrating with bass. The driver was a true playa by the name Hurk and was a solid nigga from the RNO family. Their eyes locked as YB's hand eased down beside the pocket he had his tool stuffed down into, but Hurk already had his banga restin' in his lap.

178

"If I wanted to plug you, you'd be slumped already, my G. Let's not ruin the vibe!" he shouted over the music. YB studied him before his vision fell to the big calico laid across Hurk's lap. The extendo was what curbed his pride and caused him to turn his attention to the chocolate woman on the passenger side of the car.

"Sup, Binky, where Charmane at?" he asked her. The chocolate girl that had warned her friend earlier that this would happen could tell that YB wasn't feeling her rockin' wit' the *op*, so she did the only thing a woman of her caliber knew to do. Lady glanced over at Hurk, who was on his phone texting, before returning her gaze to the madman.

"Umm, I think she went to the restroom."

***

-Stick Talk-

The freak was pulling her panties and shorts up over all that ass when my phone vibrated on my hip. I freed it and checked the text message my mans Hurk sent. *Snake ass bitch just told that BGM nigga you got his bitch campin' in there, be on point*, the text read.

"Boy, you a fool. If I would've known that dick was that lit, I woulda been gave you the cookie!" She smiled with the compliment, but when her eyes fell to the burna in my grip, a look of confusion eased onto her features.

"Stick, why the hell you got that—"

"Bitch, fuck you doin' in here?" YB's voice sliced her question in half. I slipped back into the stall, but not before I saw the relieved expression on her face. I really wasn't in the mood to down that boy, so I chose to save me *and* the bitch a headache. I stepped up onto the toilet, grippin' the pole tight in my hands, if that boy got on some where's Waldo shit, I was gonna melt his face. *ON ME!*

"Heeeyyy, baby, thought you wouldn't be here till later tonight!" I heard Charmane gush with *false* excitement. I bit my tongue to keep from laughing as I heard the sounds of rustling followed by a surprised giggle. I knew he'd hugged her and maybe squeezed that ass in the process. I wondered if he could smell my dick work on her, and just when the thought entered my mind—

"Bitch, hol' up!" he spazzed on some policin' the pussy typa shit. The sounds of him sniffing on the lady let me know it was 'bout to be some smoke. That gangsta in me told me to just aim and give it to 'em from through the stall, but the shoota in me quieted the urge. If it was up, I wanted to get my mans and not have to guess about his fate. What's that smell, Charmane? I *know* you ain't been fuckin' no nigga up in here. Matter fact—"

He was on the move. I heard him fling open the door of the first stall. "Bitch, if I find out you got a nigga hidin' up in this mu'fucka, I'mma slump both of y'all!" he growled as he kicked open the second stall, the one next to the one I was camped out in. my adrenaline surged through my veins in anticipation of the showdown. *As soon as dude gets in front of this door, I'mma fire his ass up!* My mental was homicidal.

"Baby-baby, stop trippin', I ain't seen you all dayyyy!" Charmane whined and brought dude's death date to a hanging moment in time. It sounded as if she'd stepped up into his space, and from the sound of movement, wrapped her arms around his neck in a lovers embrace. "You think I'm a hoe or somethin', YB, huh? You think that low of me?" The pause after her play told me that she was giving him the puppy dog eyes and poking her bottom lip out. "It's hot out here, Daddy, what you think I'mma smell like? Stop playin' and give me kiss!" I heard her purr.

Muah! Muah! Their lips smacked as I slipped from the stool as silently as a cat burglar in a house of sleeping people. I snuck to the door and peeped out the small crack between the door and the wall of the stall. Charmane had dude's back against the stall with her tongue down his throat. As they smooched, the nasty bitch cracked her eyes open and saw me. Her eyes grew wide, and to her credit, the bitch knew how to put on a good show. She reached down and gripped the weenie ass nigga's dick print.

"Let me get some of this dick. That's why you trippin', you need some of this good," she seduced after breaking the kiss. Lady pulled bruh into the stall and kicked the door closed, and that was my cue to make my exit. *A bitch ain't shit*, I thought as I slipped from the stall and left a murda charge *and* their moans behind.

Chapter 14
Fentanyl

-Heaven-

A week later

Dead. Mama's dead, Heaven! She killed herself! I could still hear Catrina's voice in my head as I sat there staring at the floor. The gang was there. Catrina stood, leaning against the far wall, and I could tell that my sister was more woman at that moment than the boyish person she'd been projecting these past few years. She and my moms had grown closer while my own relationship with the woman had become distant, but that didn't take away from the way the loss touched my heart. Egypt sat next to me on the couch, her leg in a hard cast and propped up on a stack of fluffy pillows, and Empress's sour ass stood by the window, staring out at the morning's drizzle. The mood was solemn as we listened to the rainfall.

"I don't understand none of this. How'd so much happen in three days?" I was honestly talking more to myself than to any of them, but I should've known—

"Yea, if you was home, where you belong, instead of out playin' house wit' *our* food, maybe you'd understand a lot of the things that's been amiss under ya fuckin' nose!" Empress turned to glare at me.

"Shut the hell up, Empress, ain't none of this shit her fault, you always on the dumb shit. You make me sick, damn. Stop wit' all the dramatics!" Egypt spat with a roll of her eyes before wincing from the sudden movement. Though they'd prescribed her a variety of pain killers, my girl was still in pain. I met Empress's mug with a drama-filled expression of my own.

"Naw, Egypt, let this bitch speak, she seems to have *a lot* on her mind," I spoke low before easing from the couch and making my way over to my long-time friend. She turned to fully face me. "Talk that shit, what's up, Empress?" I wasn't in the mood for the extras, and if that broad was looking for some smoke, I was gonna give it to her.

"Y'all chill, man, it's too much going on for us to be beefing amongst ourselves." Catrina slipped between us.

"Oh, she mad 'cause I'm tellin' her the truth and y'all know it! Why don't y'all tell her the truth and stop all the fakin', huh? Tell her, tell her that while she's out fuckin' the op, our money done ran low waitin' on her ass! Tell her, Catrina, tell her that she's been havin' her head so far up her ass that she couldn't even see that she was leadin' her own mama to the—"

Bam! Before she could finish with the bullshit, I reached around my sista and knocked the rest of her words back down her throat.

"Heaven!" my sista shouted in surprise, but the shit was up.

"Bitch, you got me wrong!" Empress spat and pushed my sister out the way. The first punch dazed me, but the second one almost sat me on my ass. Out of pure instinct, I kicked out and up between her legs, and she folded over with her eyes bulged out. I hit her with a crisp three piece that knocked her lace front askew on her head, before turning and running to my room. When I returned, I had that steel clutched so tight in my grip that it hurt my palm.

"Heaven! Don't do it, we're sisters!" Egypt's cry was frantic as she attempted to rise from the couch. I aimed the pistol at my childhood friend's face with evil intent. I could feel the blood dripping from my nose and running over my lips as I glared at her. I used my free hand to wipe it away, but it merely smeared across my face.

"Bitch, you *know* you're out of line! I should knock yo' face all over that wall!" I gritted. Catrina jumped her *supa save a hoe* ass in between us again, but this time, I was ready to pop her ass too.

"Catrina, I swear to God, if you don't get the—"

"No! This ain't how it go, sis, we're family!" My sister's eyes were pleading.

"We all we got, Heaven, and she's right. It's *you* that's been on the other shit. You're choosin' that nothin' ass nigga over us and that ain't what's up. Now mama done killed herself because—"

"What! Are you serious, Catrina? Like, am I really hearing this from *you?*" My heart ached so bad I *had* to cut her off before she said something she couldn't take back. I dropped the gun down by my leg as my eyes found Egypt in a questioning gaze.

"I'm not in that shit, you're a grown woman, sis, but I won't lie, my pockets have been hurtin'." Her words were merely a camouflaged mirror of their feelings. Though it wasn't a damn thing funny, I laughed to keep from crying, because it never failed. It was *always* the ones you loved that robbed you of your happiness. Without another word, I turned for my room to get dressed. I needed to get away from them before I did something I'd regret.

***

-Ghetto-

I stared out at the vast expanse of green fields. The dreary sky caused it to look like a scene out of one of those scary movies where a car broke down on the side of the road, in the middle of nowhere, and the boogeyman was coming for 'em. Me and Stick Talk were camped out in a stolen Toyota, awaiting the green light on the bizness. I squinted to gaze out further into the distance, and there in shadows of the misty wet grass, sat a seemingly abandoned house. As I studied it, my mental was burglarized by a sexy intruder. It had been a week since me and Heaven had thugged down in the boot, and I wasn't sweatin' lil' baby, but she'd yet to get back at me. It fucked with me a little, but shid, I had to put my heart on silent for a moment. I was back in the field with my animals and we'd laid on that lick for weeks before we was ready to take it down. *I wonder what mama doin'. She ain't thinkin' 'bout a nigga?* I wondered.

"You feel me, Flesh?" Stick Talk's voice pulled me back from my thoughts. The windshield wipers glided across the windshield at a slow pace as I glanced down at the mac in my grip.

"Naw, I zoned out. What you say, fam?" I glanced over at bruh. He was checking his .223 when I knew my mind was astray, and Stick Talk chuckled before cutting his eyes at me.

"Damnm, Bro Bro, that pussy got you gone, mane!" he capped, but seeing the look I gave him, the smile slipped from fam's face as he leaned back in the seat and fixed his gaze out the wet window.

"I ain't talkin' 'bout shit, bro, I was just asking your thoughts on that boy Trump and the crazy shit he's been saying, but…" Bro left the rest of his thoughts hanging in the air as he massaged the side of his rifle as if it were his gal's sore feet. I leaned back in the driver's seat of the stolen car and glanced up in the rearview mirror. A black Denali was about twenty yards behind us and waiting for my signal. My eyes fell to the gorilla mask that laid beside the pole.

"Fam, Donald Trump was born not only into money, but also a racist perspective. Did you know that after he got his bachelor's degree in finance, he went to work in his old man's real estate enterprise and wound up controlling that mu'fucka? By 1973, the justice department sued the entire Trump gang for racial discrimination in housing! Bro, the man was obviously racist in *the seventies*, so what do you expect from him during a time our people winning?" I gave it to him. My phone vibrated on my hip and we both knew it was our inside man. I checked the text and smiled.

Ten minutes and it's a go, Flesh, Twitch Lee confirmed. Being a white man had its perks, especially when one had the brain to utilize his resources. I put the jack back on my hip. "Lil' bro, that white boy up there in that oval office has never given a fuck 'bout the United States of America. He's a capitalist, he ran for president for only two reasons. *One*," I counted off one finger, "he knew his bread was long enough to practically *buy* his way into that *white* house. It's nothin' that America loves more than a republican and a whole bunch of money, and Donald Trump has both characteristics." I help up two fingers. "*Two*, dude knew that if he got in that position, he'd have unlimited resources to tap into the countries that were once beyond *his* reach.

"It's always about clout, fam, position is *everythang* and that boy is a hustla before *everythang*! The shit he says should never surprise a conscious man because America has *never* been great! How can a land that's stained with so much blood, hate, and greed be great, fam? If you ask *me*, Trump is a good man." My words brought an instant frown to my flesh's face. He lifted his hands in the air as if to say, *Bruh, what the hell you talm 'bout?*

"Why would you say some crazy bidness like that!" he spat, confused. My phone vibrated on my hip and without having to read the message, I knew it was show time. I slipped the angry ape mask on over my head before lifting the mac .90 off my lap.

"Bro Bro, there's millions of prejudice mu'fuckas that hate the color of our skin, not just white people. The only difference between Donald Trump and a lot of people like him is the fact that that white man doesn't hide the fact that he doesn't like us." I pushed open the driver's side door before glancing back at him from the evil eyes of the gorilla mask.

"Bruh, I'd rather face off with the enemy that makes himself known than to be at war with a mu'fucka I can't see, and ole Donald Trump does a perfect job at making sure we see him tryin' to make America great again. It's more than color with him, family, dude sees the money." I laughed with the words before slipping out into the kiss of chilled rain. I glanced back at the black SUV and gave the signal. We'd move the rest of the way like Navy seals—silent and deadly.

***

The room was alive with the manufacture of illegal opioids, and in various corners, boxes stacked up as high as the ceiling. Each box had a label that gave reference to its contents. *Oxycodone, morphine, percocets, and methadone.* The pills' net worth on the streets was in the millions, and the ten chemists that were assigned to mix the compounds of each drug and place them into pill compressors worked diligently to ensure that the revenue continued to increase. There were four armed men that patrolled the illegal pill lab, and the sounds of the compressors were a hissing melody that promised a generous pay off when the pills were delivered to the streets of Dallas/Ft. Worth. Everyone in that room wore surgical masks over their mouths and noses to prevent exposure to the most potent drug being manufactured in the depths of that house.

In the next room over, the same metallic sounds of compression could be heard as two white men and one Hispanic woman worked in union. All three wore lab coats, gloves, eye protection, and face masks. Death could be immediate if not careful. One of the men cut a microgram of fentanyl with a dose of heroin, being careful not to overdo it. Though the drug fentanyl was created in 1959 by a doctor named Paul Jansen, its potency was so powerful that merely *touching* it unprotected could cause an overdose. The man passed it to the next man in their process, and he blended the mixture before handing it to the woman who carried it to one of the five compressors in the room.

She poured the powdered substance into a suction cup that distributed it to the left pill press, then watched as the machine compressed the powder's inner core into tablet form. The compressed tablets then moved through a short tunnel until they reached the die cavity, and as the machine worked its magic, a Hispanic man in an expensive suit entered the room. His eyes were studious as he observed the creation of his cartel's wares. Amingo Beltran had snuck into the U.S. merely to see the industry they'd created. Mexico was a poverty-stricken country that survived off its commerce between the United States and other nations, but its most profitable commodity was its perpetual drug market that was made lucrative by the many cartel syndicates.

The United States had been attempting to put a stop to the multi-billion-dollar market, but it had become a juggernaut. During the Mexican war, the United States had forced Mexico to surrender the lands of California, Arizona, New Mexico, Nevada, Utah, and Colorado, all six states becoming major points of entry for the import of *Narcotics*. What the DEA tended to forget was that all six states were owned by Mexico first, so those people knew the lands intimately, and that's exactly how a container truck had entered through Arizona under the guise of a transporter of fresh fruits. It passed through New Mexico and didn't stop until its destination was reached.

Amingo Beltran had snuck into the states and unloaded the false compartments of the truck right there in the crooked streets of Dallas/Ft. Forth, and that's how he found himself in that lone drug lab the cartel had created in the city of Denton, Texas. He observed as the small, bluish-green tablets fell out the machine with stamped bar numbers in the center of them, and curious, he reached down to obtain a pinch of the white powder the chemists were pouring into the compressors, but—

"Don't!" Her voice was muffled by the mask, but the man detected the urgency in it. His eyes found hers as she shook her head *no*. She knew his actions would be fatal and didn't want his blood on her or her associates' hands. The lady took Amingo by the arm and led him out the room and into the hallway. "Es no buena idea." She told him that what he was intending to do would kill more than merely his curiosity. She continued to pull him away from the noisy sounds of production until they exited the house and reached the front porch. The Hispanic woman closed the door behind them before pulling the mask from her face, and fixing her gaze on the polished man, she freed a pack of cigarettes from the pocket of her lab coat.

"What were you doing in there, trying to kill yourself?" she asked him in Spanish. Amingo Beltran pulled his mask down and fixed her with a frown.

"Gulia, don't ever put your hands on me in front of the workers. You're my older sister, but *I'm* going to be the head of our father's organization one day." He glared at her. The woman merely smiled as she lit her cancer stick. She hated her brother. She felt that the only reason he'd risen in the ranks so fast was because he was the only boy born from their father's loins. *Amingo is a puta, he doesn't have the balls to run the business!* she thought as she took a deep pull from the tobacco.

"Si, but dead men can't run an operation from the grave." She smiled over the smoke. "That stuff back there is fentanyl." She paused to nod back at the house. "It's a hundred times more potent than heroine, and with merely a *touch* of the narcotic you can overdose! Though a kilo of it can make anywhere from one *to* two million dollars street value, and even with those numbers being nine hundred thousand and two hundred dollars *more* than what one could make off a brick of heroine, the death toll of the drug makes it one of, if not the strongest drugs in rotation!" She flicked the ashes of her cigarette onto the porch while giving him a superior expression. Amingo watched as his older sister put the cigarette back to her lips and began to suck on it so powerfully that her jaws dented in.

His eyes fell to the red glow of the cancer stick before chuckling and running his hands down the coat of his tailored suit. His eyes fell to the shine of his freshly polished Italian loafers. *Jealous puta!* he thought. "You know, you've always been a spoiled b—" *Pijfff!* A suppressed gush of heat cut through the air and caused him to pause. Amingo Beltran gazed down at the tips of his shiny shoes in confusion. A thick spray of dark liquid had just splashed against them. His gaze slowly lifted and was just in time to see the fireworks. *Tu Tu! Tu Tu!*

A different caliber of assault violated the woman's body than the .223 bullet that had melted her face. Caught in a deadly trance, Amingo Beltran stared horrified as high-powered bullets pierced his sister's body in such a rapid succession that every time gravity attempted to pull her down to the ground, another ball of lead would hold her upright. Gulia's head snapped backward as her lifeless eyes stared pleadingly up at the heavens, but the reaper's heart was as black as his clothes as he snatched her soul from her body. Blood exploded from her and bathed her brother in its essence, and only when a thick splash of it wet his face did he snap out his moment of stupidity and attempt to cheat the hands of fate. Amingo turned to run, but it was too late.

Bttttah! Bttttah! Two bursts of black talons flipped him into the air as his back opened up like a watermelon dropped from a high place. He was a fighter, a man that wanted to live, but the road he'd chosen to travel was a gamble of life or death, and as the young man's lungs filled with blood, he knew the dice hadn't landed in his favor. He coughed a soft spray of blood as he attempted to crawl to safety.

"Hel-p, *ple-ase!*" he cried as he left a trail of blood behind. Blood spilled from his lips, but the help he needed would never come.

"Sup, Homie, you don't look too good." The devil had arrived. The killer used the toe of his shoe to kick the wounded man over onto his back and stood over him. Whatever Amingo was expecting to find, *surely* wasn't what he came face to face with.

"No! Nooo!" he whimpered as he stared up into the face of the most heinous gorilla he'd ever set eyes on.

"Tell my flesh, Kiest, we still at it." The gorilla chuckled.

TTTTTAH! The mac .90 cried as hollows exploded from its mouth and tore through Amingo's neck and face. Ghetto breathed slow behind the gorilla mask as his eyes lifted just in time to save his life. *Boom! Boom! Boom! Boom!* He dove off the side of the porch as a hail of bullets spat from the *op.* One of the four guards that manned the spot ran forward, firing a submachine gun relentlessly. He yelled in rapid Spanish as he fearlessly let that pipe speak, but as soon as he made it to the door—*Click! Click!* The clip ran empty. Without hesitation and still speaking blasphemies in his native tongue, he extracted the clip and replaced it with a fresh one.

"Yu no know who yo fucky with, el diablo, puta, el diablo!" The seasoned killer looked back up, and what he saw froze him. Spread out in the rain were ten gorillas. Each man glaring out from behind those ape masks clutched sticks with stocked banana clips. They moved like trained soldiers as some army crawled, whereas others stalked for their food, but no matter the men's style of hunt, one thing was for certain—*They were hungry!* Red dots appeared over their prey's chest and face.

"Pinchè madrè!" he roared as he aimed and planned to take a few of them with him, but his chest became a canvas of red and white meat as the barrage of slugs knocked him back through the threshold of the house. After his smoking body lay motionless in the front room, silence was born. The only disturbance of peace was the patter of the rain as it began to fall harder. A shrill whistle sliced through the silence and brought all eyes to Ghetto, who held up three fingers to warn the squad that there were three more hittas on the lurk.

During the slaughter, he'd made his way to the side of the house and peeped through a crack in the boards the people had used to board up the windows and spotted the three remaining killers. Ghetto used his fingers to draw a circle in the air, and the gang was on automatic when they spread out to surround the seemingly abandoned house. His gaze found Stick Talk before he nodded toward the front door, and without needing the verbal, the goon pulled the pin on a pressurized can of tear gas. He flung it into the doorway and as it rolled and tumbled, gunshots erupted from within the house.

Stick Talk dove to the ground and with the stick clutched in one hand, he scrambled to get out the way as a line of hot lead cut through the ground where he'd just lain. It sounded like a loud roll of thunder as his brothas returned fire. The power of the assault knocked chunks off the house, and neither man let up until the clips spent empty on the first five men's tools, and that's when the next three men stepped forward to put that work in while their people reloaded. Ghetto waved his gun in the air franticly. *Please don't fuck round and kill Twitcha Lee, mane. Fuck we gonna tell his people!* His thoughts were on their brethren inside the spot they were takin' down. The fire ceased and he didn't waste time being the one to show 'em how it goes. He crouched low and with that tool aimed, he ran toward the door and up on the porch.

Ghetto had no respect for the dead as he stepped on Amingo's stiffening form and kicked the slain guard that lay losing his bowels. The gas was still thick in the place, but not so thick that he didn't notice the many bullet holes that peppered the walls. He coughed from the strength of the powerful gas, and when he heard the distant coughs of the survivors of the fire his team had just laid down, his eyes followed the direction the sound came from. He stepped deeper into the house and without being told, the squad followed.

Chapter 15
Forty Acres and a Mule

-Ghetto-

Two days later

"And that's how many of you have been so privileged in this great country of ours. Now, who can tell me which president *besides* the great Abraham Lincoln, that's done more for African Americans than any other president?" Professor Kennedy proposed. His voice echoed throughout the vast lecture hall as he pointed his lectural stick out at the class as if it were a microphone.

"Don't kill yourselves to answer. I'm sure at least one of you good people are dying to outwit the rest!" His sarcasm broke the silence in the room as a trickle of laughter erupted from a few. I was slouched down in my seat, and truth was, I'd snuck so many glances at Heaven that I'd begun to feel like a stalker. I'd noticed the seat next to her where her ace usually sat had been empty the last few times we'd attended class. *I wonder if Stick Talk piped that yet. Lil' one is ready, ready!* I thought before—

"Yes, Mr. Thompson, who might you say?" the professor asked a slim white dude with spiky hair and a severe case of acne on his face. The cat leaned forward and even *I* was curious to who he'd say.

"Yeah, like, the dude Donald Trump has opened the economic door for the um, the um, the African people to live, work and run their businesses. He's the reason so many black people have jobs and—"

"Get the hell outta here, playa, Donald Trump ain't did shit for black people, but show us that America will *forever* be a confederate country! The only other president besides *Obama* that did anything for people of color is Andrew Johnson!" He was cut off by a light-skinned brotha that was sitting a couple rows down from me. The room exploded into open debate as I shook my head at those

192

clowns. Those people were lost in the sauce if they thought Abraham Lincoln or Andrew Johnson gave a damn about a nigga. Trump was a KKK member in an expensive suit, but the doors he'd opened for a *hustla* that could see beyond the man's prejudices were limitless. My eyes drifted to the professor.

"Excuse me, excuse me, everybody calm down!" he shouted as he patted the air in a calming manner. The room quieted, but tensions were evident. "Yes, Mr. Thompson, Andrew Johnson is correct! On the day of December sixth of 1865, the abolition of slavery was brought before the senate to be ratified," the old white man acknowledged, as if the seventeenth president was the negro's savior. My eyes scanned the crowd and just as I thought, the people were sopping that shit up like it was grandma's biscuits and syrup left over on a breakfast plate. There were nods throughout the classroom, even the eight other people of color were acting as if they'd just grown fond of ole Andrew Johnson, but the only thing *I* liked about the cracka was that though he was acquitted, the sucka was impeached for violating the Tenure of Office Act. I smiled as the teacher taught *half-truths*, but I couldn't help glancing down at lil' baby. Heaven seemed to be intentionally trying to not look my way and it had a nigga kinda warm.

"Mr. Johnson finished what Mr. Lincoln died attempting and—" My laughter didn't only cut his bullshit short, but it had finally gained me what I'd been craving since the last night we'd spent in the boot. Heaven, along with the rest of the class, turned to face me with curiosity in her gaze. "And what, Mr. Bousard, do you find so funny? *Please* share." Professor Kennedy put me on blast. My laughter simmered to a chuckle as I gathered my things. I was done with the higher learning shit. I'd learned more from the corners of the gutta than I could ever learn sitting there listening to those European people praise *their* ancestors for tryin' to keep a nigga controlled by the whip. I was done. The only major to me would be hustlenomics, but I had to mentally crush that white man before I pursued it.

"Professor, you're full of shit, my nigga." My acknowledgement rocked the room and caused a nervous stir around the class.

"Excuse me? I'm, I'm gonna have to—"

"Yea, yeah, playboy, you're gonna have to ask me to leave and report to the dean's office and all that shit, but dig," I cut his sucka as off. I slid from my seat as the man's face became as red as the blood I'd spilt a few days before. I could feel Heaven studying me as I gave it to 'em. "See, what you *not* telling these kind folks is the fuck shit Ole Andrew Johnson was on, like that forty acres and a mule he fucked my people out of. You do remember that four hundred thousand acres that the government took from confederate slave owners and was supposed to disburse to the freed slaves, right?" I asked and could tell that I had the attention of every mu'fucka in that classroom, but just like usual, someone wasn't feeling black oppression.

"Aww, here we go with this crap. You guys got freedom, man, what else ya want? Who came up with that forty acres and a—"

"Listen up, white boy, and I'll learn ya ignorant ass somethin'." I big chested the white man without waiting for a rebuttal. I made my way to the center aisle. "The forty acres and a mule policy was a *white man's* idea. You ever hear of William Tecumseh Sherman, Professor?" I asked midway down the aisle. Me and the older man's eyes locked as he nodded his confirmation of the knowledge.

"Well, if you're familiar with dude, surely you're up on the *special field order No. 15* he issued on January sixteenth back in 1865?" I raised a brow with the question. Though dude hid it well, I was a predator and sensed his uncertainty.

"The-the um, no, I'm not sure, but I'm sure the-the *policy*, as you call it, was a handsome idea. I'm highly educated in the subjects of—"

"Bullshit, *half*-truths!" I crushed his explanation. "That's what you're *highly* educated in. So, dig this, William T. Sherman's policy spoke of the forty acres, but *not* the mule part. That wouldn't come until later. See, that four hundred thousand acres of land was the coastline that ran from Charleston, South Carolina, St. Johns in Florida, to Georgia's Sea Islands, *and* a few miles in from the coast." I'd made it to the front and paused at the professor's desk. There was a shiny apple on it and I picked it up to inspect it. "That was to be given to my ancestors, but the truth of it all is, that idea came from a convo between Sherman and a secretary of war named Edwin M. Stanton. They'd gathered twenty leaders of the black community in Savannah, Georgia to solve the problem. The people of color chose a reverend named Garrison Frazier to speak for 'em, and he told those white boys *the people* wanted land. He told them that was the best way Black folk would be able to take care of themselves," I educated as I buffed the apple on my Balenciaga sweater.

"I think you need to leave, Mr. Bousard, or I will be forced to have you removed," Professor Kennedy threatened and began to make his way toward the phone for good measure. I laughed. I'd paid my own tuition and hadn't broken any law outside of aggravated *verbally* whoopin' his ass. I could hear him speaking to security on the phone, so I turned to the stunned class. I bet they'd never witnessed no boss shit like that. I retrieved the lecture stick the snitchin' professor had discarded in his haste in getting to the phone and pointed it out at the crowd.

"Reverend Garrison Frazier told those Caucasian folk that the best way those freed slaves could take care of themselves was to be given land they could cultivate by their own labor. The man said he and the people of color wanted land they could maintain themselves, a land that they could work until it produced the means they could use to *buy* it! See, William T. Sherman and Mr. Stanton wanted to know if those freed slaves wanted to be scattered out amongst those white folk or in colonies by themselves, and that old reverend said..."

I paused to slap the stick against the oakwood desk before using a southern drawl to mimic that old reverend. "We would prefer to live by ourselves 'cause there is a prejudice against us in the south that will take years to get over!" I mimicked. I smiled before tossing the apple in the air and catching it. "In the end, President Lincoln approved special field order No. 15, and it was Ole William T. Sherman that ordered *the army* to lend the black folks mules. *That's* where the mule part came into effect," I spoke with finality. I was moving so much that my pants had inched down low on my waist, and just as I pulled them up, the door to the classroom burst open.

195

Two campus officers along with the dean of the school came up in that bitch like I'd been holding that classroom hostage and had just laid my weapons down to surrender.

The two guards headed in my direction with evident intent in their eyes, but before they killed my vibe, I had a little more to say. *Just a little.* "That forty acres and a mule shit was a cool play, but just like every other righteous act has been tainted by power hungry mu'fuckas, guess what? This is the part about Andrew Johnson that this cock sucka of a professor didn't mention." I paused to toss the lecture stick to the floor. Though I could tell I still held the attention of the class, my vision found the Caucasian cat that had earlier tested my third eye and acted as if freedom was the only thing my people deserved after four hundred years of servitude. Though his lips never parted, it was the slight nod of his head that gave me the satisfaction of knowing when I left that room, the sucka would never again test the superiority of a god's mental.

"Come on, Buddy, let's not cause a scene." The first security guard was a burly white cat, but he paused a few feet away. I chuckled. *Damn, I'm glad I didn't bring my burna in this bitch!* I thought before turning and heading for the door. Professor Kennedy's scary ass was just a big ole pussy cat. He hid behind the second security cat that had shown up to *escort* me from the premises. My eyes found the dean and just as I was 'bout to inquire about the loot I'd paid to attend the school.

"Say, Homes, what were you saying about the vato Andrew Johnson?" an ese cat in the first row of the class asked. All eyes drifted to the Hispanic man before all our vision found the administrative man of UTA. I could see the confusion intermingle with curiosity in his stare as his eyes found me in a questioning gaze. Dean Shaw shrugged his thin shoulders as if to say, *What the hell, go for it!* I chuckled gently, and when I turned back to the class, my gaze lifted a few rows up into the aisle and into the dimness where Heaven sat with her leg crossed over her knee, real bossy like.

"In 1865, Ole Andrew Johnson did the unthinkable! He finished what Abraham had started and made the abolition of slavery a reality. *But*"—I smiled before glancing around at the assembly—"the man was a confederate sympathizer that owned his own slaves! Though he advocated for the thirteenth amendment, he did it merely to *save* the lives of certain confederates." I smiled as my eyes drifted to Professor Kennedy, who looked as if he'd have a heart attack at any moment. I tossed the apple into the air and watched as it soared until it descended and he clumsily caught it.

"The man was smart. Andrew Johnson knew that to give the freed slaves that forty acres and that mule, to give us our own land, he knew it would've changed the legacy of American history. So, though Lincoln had approved it, Andrew Johnson overturned the order of special field order No.15 and returned the land to those same *confederates* that spilled America's blood to keep people of color controlled under the crack of that bitch ass whip!"

***

-Heaven-

"Hey, Ghetto, wait up. Damn!" I called to him as he made his way to a cranberry-red, '82 Fleetwood Cadillac I'd never seen him in before. As I power walked toward him, my eyes fell in love with the beauty of the old school car. The twenty-eights it squatted on were the same color as the deep-colored paint, and by the time I'd made it to him, Ghetto had pulled the door open and I caught a peek of the white interior. I smirked at the bright-red lip-stick kisses. Hundreds of the lip prints were strategically placed all over the co-caine-white seats. *Cute!* I thought as he slipped behind the wheel and the engine came to life with a smooth purr.

Let's get a bag, bae/we get money we ain't trippin' 'bout what the tag say/Went got the Rolls truck, you got the matchin' Wraith/you ain't wanna have a threesome, you wanna play it safe/now you a big ole big ole freak, you comin' out ya body/ long as I got you and you got me, we don't need nobody. Yo Gotti's "Like That" came blasting out the speakers as he closed the door without acknowledging me. *Fuck?* I wondered, and just when I thought he'd pull off and leave me standing there like I was one of those bird ass bitches he was used to messing with, the window came down and the music muted.

"Sup, Ms. Lady?" He nodded at me as if I was one of his home-boys. I allowed my vision to see beyond the Cartier lenses. *Are you serious, God? Out of all this time, why are you allowing my heart to melt now?* I silently argued with God. As me and Ghetto studied each other, I hated him, I wanted him, I was so confused!

"I've been busy, but I was gonna get up with you. I never got the chance to thank you." My words were sincere as my eyes drifted around the parking lot. It was more out of searching for an escape from his stare than the curiosity of what was going on around us. Ghetto's eyes were like TV screens, and one could watch his thoughts playing out in his pupils. He'd gambled for my heart, and I could see that he felt as if he'd crapped out.

"Thank me? For what, ma? Dig, you don't owe me none of what my intent wasn't meant for. My heart just called for your presence during a time I felt like Atlas, and had to hold my world on my shoulders, but that's all. I *used* you for a few days and now I don't need you. So, naw, *I* should be thankin' you." His words were like a powerful punch to the heart.

"Wha-what!" The word slipped from my lips in disbelief, but Ghetto's only response was the sound of the window rolling up before the music vibrated the car.

I would take you to Chanel if you want me to, was all I could hear as the old school slid out the parking space and out the parking lot entirely. I stood there with my arms crossed over my breasts, bouncing my left foot. I rolled my eyes before turning to head for my car. *You'll be ok, girl, you have to put on ya big girl panties now. He's just like every other nigga!* I mentally gave myself a pep talk. My eyes drifted to the rented Kia that passed by at a moderate pace. I knew that it was Empress behind the wheel, because I'd texted her and informed her that Ghetto had left class early and to follow him. The boy Stick Talk was just like every other lame, street nigga that finally hits that one lick they'd been waiting on, and as soon as he got a few coins in his pockets, he told the bitch he'd been gutting all the tea she needed to serve his ass a cold deal. In his case, the boy spilled his guts to a snake in heels, and Empress was a poisonous species. I rolled my eyes again, but this time, it was more of me fighting my tears. I honestly didn't wanna kill Ghetto.

Chapter 16
Treachery

Two nights later

"Are you sure this is the place, Empress?" Catrina asked for the third time. We were three deep in the rented Kia, her and Empress in the front, and I sat dolo in the backseat. It was our first time hitting a lick without our girl, Egypt, and the shit didn't feel right.

"Chill, bitch, I know what I'm doin', damn! I just talked to Stick not even an hour ago, and he said he and that nigga Ghetto was at the spot gettin' to it." Empress's words were sharp as she glanced up in the rearview at me, no doubt checking to see how her words had affected me. I watched her place a cherry Blow Pop between her lips before rolling my eyes and diverted my attention out the window. It was two in the A.M. and we were sitting three houses down from the house we were stalking. Every house within that subdivision was a two-story luxury home that was equipped with a two-car garage. I remembered thinking, *It ain't no way a man runnin' a trap or a bando way out in west Aggtown like these white folks don't notice.* My eyes fell to the pink and white baby nine that rested in my lap. It had colorful Louie V designs all over its frame, causing it to resemble a child's toy, but all the heads I'd busted with it was a testament of its reliability.

As I studied it, something happened between me and that cold metal that not even *I* could explain. *I'm done! After this, I ain't fuckin' with Empress no more. This hoe always on her shit!* As soon as the thought hit me, my eyes felt as if they were being led by an internal navigational system as they found Empress's studious gaze fixated on me *still!* The car was dark, the only light being the glow of the distant streetlights. The only parts of her shadowed face I could see were the shine of her lips as they slid back over the red sucker and the whites of her eyes. I saw her eyes flicker and that slick smile she was known for curve her lips before she slipped the pink mask on her face that we'd made our thing.

I was confused until the headlights of a smoke-gray Chevy SS illuminated the inside of our car before it pulled into the driveway of the beautiful home we were about to take down. I shook my head in disgust. *Traitor ass nigga!* I thought as I sucked my teeth and slipped my own mask on over my face. Niggas wasn't shit! The driver of the SS sat inside the car for a moment longer, probably trying to build his nuts up to do the unthinkable. *Somehow*, Empress had gotten to the dude, Hurk, and just like so many other men that had more dick than they did brains, the snake ass dude traded his loyalty for the pleasure of getting his dick wet. I watched the huge man slip from the driver's seat before glancing back at us and inconspicuously nodding before heading for the house. It was one thing for a bitch that a man barely knew to do some hoe shit, but for a nigga that he came from the trenches with to violate, there could be no forgiveness!

Snake ass dude! I thought as Empress and Catrina slid from the car, hunched over with their pistols in their hands, and ran toward the front door where dude was waiting. Empress slid to the side of the door and Catrina to the other before *glaring* back at me and frantically waving for me to catch up. *Snake?* I thought as I slid out the car and into the kiss of the night. It was crazy because that's exactly how *I* felt, like a dangerous ass serpent!

***

-Ghetto-

"The virus is highly contagious and has reached the United States. Texas's first case of COVID19 was reported on February thirteenth, and it's due to an infected person that was evacuated from Wuhan, China to Lackland Air Force base in San Antonio. The coronavirus is said to be a mild case of influenza, and even our great president has dubbed it a 'hoax' that China..."

The news anchor reported the outbreak of some shit called the coronavirus. My eyes drifted from the plasma TV that was mounted on the wall of the dining room and found the long, marble counter in the kitchen where we had *at least* three thousand *K* packs of different kinds of pills stacked in rows.

I had separated the oxies and fentanyl from the other shit because I had other plans for the heavy narcotics. I knew that those drugs would draw a lot of attention, so I planned to fence them to my outta town connects. My eyes took inventory of the roxies, perks, codones, and the many other opiate tabs we had on deck, and the only thing my mental kept replaying was, *We made it nigga!* With the pills, we were looking at a cool few mill, and the fentanyl was a ticket by itself.

"What you think 'bout this COVID bidness, Flesh?" Stick Talk's question brought my gaze to him. He was sealing another package of pills and studying me with a sly smirk on his face. I was assuming he'd figured the same thing I did about our status in the streets. I chuckled before making my way to the refrigerator and taking two bottles of Vitamin Water out. I tossed him one before cracking the seal on mine and taking a deep gulp from it.

"Bruh, I take *all* pandemics serious, especially when China is involved. Bruh, China is big on population control and even limits the amount of children each family in that communist country can have. China and America have *always* had a strange relationship, but the one thing that keeps 'em bonded is the same motive that both countries will kill for." I gave it to him before picking up one of the packages of pills and looking over at him, and in union, we both answered.

"Money!" Me and bro laughed. "So, I don't see China *purposely* releasing that virus into the air. It stops production! Nigga, damn near every household appliance or device a nigga owns comes from China! I can't see those chinks fuckin' up commerce over no war shit. Bruh, this shit may change the world as we know it. Think about it, Stick, we're in a fucked-up time already wit' the polar caps melting and pushin' us into global warming!" I held up one finger. "Then, these fag ass laws killin' us and gettin' away wit' it. Flesh, the riots, the deaths, a *businessman* for a president. All that shit is—"

The sound of the doorbell cut me off. My eyes diverted in the direction of the front door before curiously returning to my dude. He noticed my hand paused by the burna on my waist and chuckled before freeing his own tool and tossing it to me. "That's Hurk, fam, he called and told me he was comin' to get this shit and distribute it to the circle." Stick Talk eased my apprehension.

"No doubt, havin' all this bidness up in this bitch got a nigga noid." I chuckled as bro headed toward the door. Only if we would've known how thin the line between loyalty and a nigga's weakness when it came to a wet set of pussy lips was, maybe I could've prevented him from lettin' the devil in.

***

-Heaven-

"Who dat on the lurk, know that ain't my nigga Hurk!" the boy Stick Talk capped from the other side of the door. The man Hurk was a boulder of a man, and as I studied him, I couldn't detect an iota of shame 'bout him betraying his mans. He smiled real big.

"What's the bidness, Flesh, you gone let me in or what, family?" His voice was as calm as a slow breeze on a warm day. I wouldn't lie, I was praying that Stick Talk somehow sensed something, *anything*, out of place and didn't open that door. I hated the position my girls had put me in, and when I heard the locks being disengaged, I knew that there was no turning back.

"Flesh, you're thirty minutes late, and I can bet my last cent you was somewhere laid up with one of those funky pussy hoes you be finding at the butt naked." Stick Talk chuckled as the door swung open, and in that moment, things took on a slow-motion effect. Light spilled out from the open door as the two men gave each other a pound.

"Say, Flesh, I got someone I want you to meet," Hurk's deep voice rumbled as he stepped back. Even without being a witness to it, I knew a look of confusion fell over Stick Talk's face, and Empress didn't waste time capitalizing on the moment. She spun around from the side of the threshold and—

"Oh shit!" Stick Talk shouted in surprise while trying to slam the door shut on her arm. *Boom!* The tool jumped in her hand and I spun toward the door in time to see Stick Talk's body jerk as his side exploded in a bloody mess.

"Fuck! Fuck!" he cried while clutching his side and attempting to turn and run. "It's a hit, bruh, set-up!" he shouted to whomever else was in the house. My heart pounded against my chest as—

"Naw, naw, nigga, bring yo' ass here!" Hurk growled while rushing the smaller man and placing him in a chokehold. *Boca! Boca! Boca!* Someone fired from around the corner. Empress dove to the ground as I took cover behind the couch. I couldn't see Catrina, but the nigga Hurk held Stick Talk upright, using him as a human shield. I didn't know where the gun came in.

"Watch out, Ghetto, dead all that reckless shootin', my nigga. If you want this nigga back in one piece, chill out and let's talk like men, bruh!" he shouted. The silence was thick, and just when I was anticipating more lead being sent our way, my heart coiled in my chest when the dread head cautiously stepped from around the corner aiming *two* burnas at us.

***

-Ghetto-

Come on, fam, not Hurk, not one of our own! I remembered thinking as I rounded that corner with those tools ready to spit. My heart cracked at what I saw. Hurk held my family in a chokehold and held a burna to his noggin'. I could tell that Stick was in pain as he clutched at his bloodied side. His eyes were evil slits as he stared back at me.

"Put the gun down, playboy, let's not shed any more blood. We ain't here to kill nobody, bro, just here to get that work up out ya," Hurk spoke, but a movement to my left caught my attention. A nigga with a *pink* ski mask rose from behind my suede sectional couch and trained his banga on me. It was something off about the way he moved, and as the figure made its way toward me, it hit me—a female! It hit me hard.

"If you want this boy alive, Ghetto, drop the burnas, mane. We ain't here for blood shed, we just want the shit, you got my word," Hurk bargained while diggin' the barrel of the pistol into Stick Talk's head.

"Bruh, fuck this nigga, you bet not surrender those straps or we both gone. Shoot it out in this mu—" Stick Talk began before Hurk's massive muscle flexed as he squeezed it tight against bro's throat. My brotha's blood-soaked hands shot up to the bigger man's forearm, clawing at the man's arm in a desperate fight for air. My mind raced as my vision fell to the bloodied hole the bullet had torn through fam's side.

"You gonna let him die, huh! We gonna kill both you niggas and still get—"

"Aiiiight!" I relented and cut Hurk's spiel off. At that moment, I saw a third figure move to my right. *Pink ski mask, fuck goin' on?* My mental was rattled as I did something I'd never done before. I laid my guns down and faced off with a man I once considered my brother, my flesh!

"Naw, naw, bruh, I know you fooly wit' the toolie, don't try and play me up in here. Kick them hoes over here." Hurk nodded toward the two burnas.

"Nigga, fuck you doing, you-you lost ya mind, fam!" Stick Talk rasped while fighting to stay conscious. Nonetheless, I never took my eyes off the big man as I kicked the two bangas and watched them slide across the marble floor. Hurk chuckled before releasing his captive, and as soon as he did, my dude fell to his knees, no more energy left to stand on his own. *Bruh needs a doctor. I'm 'bout to give these boys what they came for, and if they let us make it, we'll find 'em and deal them a closed casket affair!* My thoughts were homicidal when Hurk's deep chuckle summoned my attention. Before he did the unthinkable, I registered it and was already in motion. I dove toward Stick Talk to shield him. Hurk's trigger rose, leveling the pistol with bro's dome. The dazed look on Stick Talk's face was filled with a mixture of confusion and fear as he studied me sluggishly.

Boca! The gun burped as the bullet knocked my flesh's body forward. Stick Talk fell face forward and into my arms before we crashed to the floor. My boy's blood soaked through my clothes and before I knew it, I'd blacked out. I didn't know when I'd scrambled to my knees and lunged for the burnas, but they were snatched up before I could get to 'em. "Nigga, why the fuck you do that!" a voice I never thought I'd hear coming from the other side of a gun shouted. The world seemed to freeze in time as my eyes shot to the fourth figure I'd just noticed. Her eyes were slits as her glare slid from Hurk and captured mine.

"Well, guess the hoax is up, now." The figure that had popped up from behind the couch smiled before reaching up and pulling the pink ski mask off her head. "Where the mula at, playboy? And as you can see"—Empress smiled a wicked smile—"we ain't got no problem dirting somethin'." She nodded down at Stick Talk. My eyes never left the fourth figure, and even when she peeled the mask off and all that curly hair tumbled down over her face, I still shook my head in disbelief. *Now, why would a pretty woman that's going to school for criminal justice need a tool?* I remembered thinking that day at the lake. Heaven rolled her eyes as if *I* was the one violating.

"Ghetto, don't make this any harder than it already is, just chill, nobody else has to die," she pleaded as the only figure that hadn't revealed their identity strode past and made their way to the kitchen.

"Bingo!" she shouted as soon as she spotted our ticket out the hood. My eyes fell to Stick Talk's still form, and my heart cracked. My dawg had taken one to the head, and just as my eyes blurred, something strange happened. Though his head was soaked in blood, Stick's eyes popped open and fixed on me before closing shut. He was alive! My eyes lifted to reclaim Heaven, and there was a moment before—

"I'mma need some help wit' all this shit!" the girl shouted from the kitchen. Hurk's fag ass wasted no time lending a hand. He shoulder bumped me on his way into the kitchen, and after a brief assessment, Empress followed in his wake.

"I'll give you love birds a moment." She giggled as she passed. Heaven held the burna steady, trained on me as her eyes fell to Stick Talk. She smiled a small smile before her vision returned to me. "He's still alive. It wasn't 'pose to go this way," were the only words the punk bitch could offer a nigga as I sat there on my knees, my family's blood staining my shirt, and my heart twisted in a knot.

"So, this what you do for a livin', huh, you're a stick-up kid?" I chuckled at the irony. *You live by the bullet; you'll die by the bullet!* I reflected on the words Kiest had once told me. The crooked bitch just shrugged indifferently as if it was just another day in the neighborhood for her, and as my eyes took in the pink Dickies one piece she wore, it hit me. *This bitch been squatting on me this entire time! They were just waiting to catch us slippin', but how they know 'bout this spot?* I wondered until my eyes fell to Stick Talk. I shook my head in shame. Just 'cause a nigga was a gangsta didn't make him intelligent. If a mu'fucka didn't give a damn who they gave their pussy or dick to, it was a clear indication that they held their life in that same regard.

Boca! Boca! Two explosions followed by the sound of something heavy crumbling to the floor told me that Hurk had outlived his usefulness. Moments later, Empress and the bitch that still wore the ski mask entered the room with two trash bags stuffed wit' me and my peoples hard-earned wares. Empress carried her bag to the door and sat it down before turning back and making her way back over to us.

"Y'all hurry up and let's get out of here before we all get a life sentence!" the masked girl encouraged before rushing out the house. Even before she lifted the burna and aimed at my thinking cap, I knew the girl Empress had ill intent for me, but—

"Wait, naw, Em, this is personal! *I* gotta do it, *me,* Empress!" Heaven grabbed the lady's arm and held tight. Empress's tool never moved away from me as her eyes flickered toward her sister in arms. Her stare was uncertain as they studied each other, but after a few moments of deliberation, something passed between the two women that only the two of them could attest to. Empress exhaled a long whoosh of breath.

"Aiiight, look, you got five minutes, Heaven, five, and we're leavin' ya ass. Kill the nigga and let's go, sis!" she spoke over her shoulder as she made her way to retrieve the bag. We watched her make a hasty retreat before my and Heaven's eyes connected.

"I'm-I'm sorry, I wasn't gonna go through with this. I mean…" Her words were unsure as her eyes pleaded for me to understand. "Just know that I-I—"

Spissh! The thick glob of saliva I spat at her hit her in the center of her chest and caused her to swallow whatever the hell it was that she'd been fighting to get out.

"Bitch, fuck you and yo' explanation," I spat as I spread my arms out wide. "Let's get it ova wit'. Do it, bitch!" I shouted with that gangsta shit staring out from my eyes. Heaven's eyes leaked a slow trail of salty water.

"Im-Im sorry, Ghetto."

"Fuck you, you treacherous bi—"

BOOM!

Heaven Got a Ghetto

Chapter 17
A Casket... Not an Uber

-Heaven-

A month later

You know, today, as I thought about you, I wondered what life would be like if we'd met under other circumstances. What if my soul wasn't so dark... your heart so untrusting? I wonder if love would be sufficient enough to allow us to find forever within maybe...the possibilities? I'm smiling because I keep a picture of you hanging up on the walls of my mind. Every time my head feels the coolness of my pillow and I stare out my window, I stare at the stars for a sign. I never got the chance to ask you, do you believe in shooting stars? Maybe I'm just this foolish woman that believes in wishes, but it just feels so real to me. That "one day"... That one day that we meet again...under different circumstances. Maybe in another life... A different place...another time. Until then? I'll continue to fantasize...of you...

Your fingertips grazing my skin...your eyes...drowning me within, that look you'll give me that silently tells me that you want me. Just me! I wish for you. Not the gangsta, but the man in you that I envision our son admiring. But maybe I'm getting ahead of myself. Smiles! For some reason, I'm thinking of a black rose blooming underneath the kiss of the sun. I wonder if it knows that it's different than the many red ones that bloom around it? Unique. I'm speaking of you, King. Your thorns make it hard for one to hold onto you, but only one that understands that it's the spaces between the thorns that speak of your strength will be able to appreciate what you truly are. An anomaly!

I miss what we never had the chance to create. I detest the fork in the road that keeps us moving in opposite directions, because now that my heart has become an empty room, I wish that I can change the cards. Please turn around and meet me where the fork in the road begins. I'll wait for you! My face is on my pillow, I'm staring at the stars for a sign. Just saw a shooting star, sun, guess what my wish was?

"Damn, bitch, you still writing in that journal!" Empress's voice caused me to look up from my writing. I closed my journal and rose from my seat. We hadn't really talked in the month that had passed. Shit just wasn't the same. We'd moved out our old house and into a five-bedroom spot on the southwest side of Fort Worth. Though Catrina, Empress, and Egypt were under the same roof as me, we'd become a million miles apart. Whereas me and Egypt seemed to grow closer, the death of our mother had caused Catrina to become distant, and Empress had become even more of a pill head. The pill game was a sweet lick, and being dancers allowed us to corner the market, but I was just tired of the life. I'd transferred to TCU and only had a semester to obtain my associates in business management. I wanted to get out the life while I was ahead and off of the law's radar. I turned to Empress.

"Yea, just a lot on my mind. What has you up so early, all chipper and shit?" I stretched as my eyes went to the opened window. The sun had just risen and still had shades of pale gray, light pink, and a beautiful red splashed against the horizon. Birds flew by in a flock of black silhouettes, and the soft breeze spoke of a nice day. My vision returned to Empress and I caught her sneaking a peek at my breasts. I was braless underneath the muscle shirt, and my hardened nipples tented the material. I crossed my arms over my chest and gave her *that* look to let her know I wasn't for the bullshit. Empress asked before placing her manicured hands on her shapely hips.

"Don't tell me you've forgotten?" she asked wit' a raised brow. "The operation?" she reminded me.

"Ohhh, snap, I forgot all about it!" I answered before giving her a fallacious smile. "You go gurrrl, ain't nobody gonna be able to tell yo' fast ass nothin' now! You getting the *entire* package?" I was more than curious. Empress made her way over to my dresser and picked up a bottle of my too-expensive perfume. She sprayed a nice squirt onto her wrist before bringing it to her nose.

"Girl, yasss!" she squealed before returning the bottle to its rightful place and turning to face me. Sista girl smacked her ass.

"Girl, I'm about to fatten this ass up a little more and get these titties a cup or two bigger." She glanced down at her small breasts before cupping them and poking her bottom lip out in a cute little pout. I giggled.

"And what about the—" I began but paused when my phone rang. I held up a finger to tell her to wait as I answered. "Sup, sis?"

"You comin' in tonight or what? I heard that cute one you're so into is supposed to be up in the spot with them eastside stop six niggas," Egypt gushed. I could hear the clinking of bottles and I knew she was hard at work. Ever since her accident, my girl had gone from booty shaker to a sexy ass bottle girl. "What you drinking, cutie? I know you're the bottle type." She giggled at whomever she was serving at the club. "Oh, yea, well, I'm an expensive bitch, lil' daddy. You sure you can handle all this?" The loud smacking noise told me that she'd teased him with a slap of all that ass she carried. I heard her giggle before I left her to it.

"I'll be there sis, don't kill 'em all until I get there and we can stop the show together." I wasn't sure she could hear me over the music in the background coupled with her flirtatious innuendo, but before I hung up, I made sure to let her know that I loved her. Since we'd taken down those RNO niggas, we'd heard of how their squad had been on some real cowboy shit throughout the metroplex. Obviously, they didn't know who the culprits were, because they'd been at war wit' another faction that repped the *BGM* moniker.

I'd heard that the *Been Getting Money* boys were wit' it, but those RNO cats were savages! So, just to keep them boys off our trail, we'd relocated *and* switched clubs to dance at. V-Live was turnt, and only boss bitches got chose. Not only had my tips gone up, but it seemed like everybody and their mamas were on the perks and roxies. The pill game was lit, and me and my sisters were who fed the epidemic.

"Heaven! Damn, bitch, where'd you go?" Empress's voice held a tinge of frustration as she snapped her fingers in front of my face.

"My fault, I was just thinking. What were you saying, Em?" Empress playfully rolled her eyes before turning to make her exit.

"Girl, whateva! Just know that when you see me again, I'm gonna be all woman! A badder bitch!" she sang over her shoulder. I giggled. Empress was living her dream. Though I really wasn't fuckin' with her, I was happy for my sister. I began to get ready for work and in the midst of doing me, my journal fell off the bed and opened to my last entry. I smiled when I picked it up and tossed it onto the bed.

"Guess what my wish was, Ghetto, hmm? Take a wild guess," I whispered.

***

-Ghetto-
4:00pm

Stiletto's was poppin' even at that early hour. I was learning that there wasn't any particular time that lust woke up or went to sleep. It all depended on the person and what he or she chose to invest their time into. I sat at a back table, nursing a bottle of Cîroc as I observed the call of seduction as D-boys and nine-to-fivers alike paid to see women create just the illusion of what *could* be for the right price. I'd turned down numerous dances. I was on the lurk for a particular freak, and though I wasn't into the trickin' bidness, I planned to make it rain on lady. I took the bottle by the neck and turnt it up, and as if the game God deemed me worthy—

"Heyyyy, you! Didn't think I'd see yo' sexy ass round here again." A feminine song touched my ears. I placed the bottle on the table and allowed my eyes to drown her in my stare. Chocolate-hued, chubby thick with a nice set of titties, Queen was the true definition of ratchet! She batted her two-inch eyelashes as she admired the drip. The black-on-black Versace unit I wore was highlighted by a big bird yellow Ermenegildo Zegna jacket and a bright yellow pair of Ferragamo loafers. She slick took notice of the white and chocolate VVS stones on my wrist and neck, and I acknowledged her with a gold-fanged smirk.

"And why's that, *baby*, you don't think the show you put on for me the first time we met was memorable?" I was on my bullshit. She smirked back before pushing a lock of blond hair out her face.

"I'm sayin' though, last time you were here you sidelined me and my girl Plush for that mix-breed bitch, Heavenly. I didn't think I'd see you again now that her and her lil' crew are banned from the club." Her words stirred the waters of confusion within me, and I allowed my facial expression to tell the tale. Just as I anticipated, she got on some gossip shit.

"Oh, you must ain't heard, huh?" She giggled. I shook my head to let her know I wasn't up on the rumor mill, and she did the rest. "Yea, word on the street is her and her lil' crew got tickets on their head for stickin' niggas up. They say they was luring them from here and having their niggas at the room waiting in the bathroom for the play!" Shawty added her own twist to the truth. "You gonna let me dance for you or what, Daddy? I've been *dreamin'* about grindin' against that monster you teased me with last time," she baited me, not knowing that I was a shark that would swallow the bait, hook, *and* the mu'fucka that was attempting to entice me.

Lady made her way into my booth and straddled me without my consent. Up close and personal, she was more attractive than she was from afar, and I wondered why so many women stole their own beauty with all the extra additives. I slapped that ass to encourage mama, and she began to grind that pussy against me in an attempt to rise the dragon. "Damn, Daddy, I see you already saluting a bitch." Ms. Lady's choice of words caused me to chuckle, and I bit my tongue from the urge to give in to full-fledged laughter.

The rigidness she was feelin' was my burna that she kept grinding up against, but I was assuming she took my smile as confirmation, because she turnt and began making that ass clap as if she was applauding my erection. I took that as my cue to go in for the kill. I took the bankroll out my pocket and hid it beside me. When lil' one felt I had enough of the back view, she reclaimed her seat in my lap.

"I never got a name, handsome. I'm Coco, and you are?" She smiled down at me as she wrapped her arms around my neck and grinded against my *tool*. I wrapped my arm around her waist in a loose grip before staring up at her.

"Dig, my name is meaningless when business is concerned," I began before licking my lips and glancing around before recapturing her gaze. "You seem to be a bread winner, Coco, and I'm tryin' to put a bankroll in ya purse. You wit' it or what?" I showed my teeth. Coco's dance came to an instant halt as she studied me. The reflection of my diamonds danced across her cleavage and the lower part of her face as she gave me a suspicious glint.

"What you mean? I'm lost. I'll do *private* dances and even do house visits, but that shit gone run you a check, *and* I'm bringin' my homegirl wit' me." She was as a matter of fact as she began to move again. *Thirsty bitch!* I thought as I chuckled.

"Naw, mama, I ain't on all the extras, I just need a lil' info." I dangled the meat before the lioness. Her grind was slow.

"Info? What kinda info you talking about, you a cop or something?" Her dance paused again as we studied each other. *I hope I ain't gotta catch this bitch after work and torture what I want from her!* My mental was dark as I reached around Queen and squeezed those ass cheeks.

"The girl, Heavenly, where she at, ma? I'm tryin' to see 'bout her." The prelude was over. Lady's lids dropped low until she was glaring at me from between slits for eyes. She quickly climbed out my lap and put some space between us.

"Uh, uh, nigga, you up in here on some private eye shit. I'm 'bout to let the bouncers know 'bout yo' snooping ass, and I bet you won't be 'round here no more!" she spazzed and attempted to make good on her threat until I reached out and took hold of her wrist. I could tell she was 'bout to scream on me, so I made sure to get her attention.

"Coco!" I shouted loud enough to capture her *and* a few other's attention. She had something slick on her tongue until she saw the roll of big faces I held up to her. The punk bitch's entire attitude did a 180-degree turn. She sucked her teeth.

"What the hell y'all lookin' at, mind ya business!" She went left on the onlookers that *she'd* made privy of our dealings. Coco climbed her chubby ass back into my lap and smiled a thirsty smile. "Now, what was you sayin' 'bout Heavenly? I think you have the wrong club, Daddy. I think her and her girls work at *V-live* in the *D*." She opened her hand and held her palm out to be paid. I peeled three hundred from the knot and paid the snake bitch for being who she was. She took that lil' bit of bread and slipped out my orbit as quickly as she'd come. I couldn't help but laugh as I took the bottle to the head for the second time that night.

V-live, huh? Bet they ain't know the devil likes to see that ass clap too! I chuckled at my own thoughts before standing to leave. Revenge was at the tip of my tongue, and I wouldn't be satisfied until it filled my entire being with its sweet nectar.

***

-Empress-

"I must ask you, Ms. Lockhart, are you sure you want to go through with this procedure? This will change the direction—"

"Doc, save the speech for another bitch. I know the risks of this operation, and there's nobody that can stop me from going through with it." I cut the physician off midsentence. I was sitting on the edge of a hospital bed preparing to get my titties filled with silicone. I was set for two weeks of surgery and healing, and even was taking the fat from my stomach and arms and getting it in my ass and thighs. I had always been thick, but not fully proportioned. Every girl had an insecurity no matter how bad she was, but not every girl had the money to fix what she saw wrong about herself.

So, I was on my YOLO shit. I was even going as far as getting lip fillers. Those Kardashian bitches wasn't gonna have shit on me! "Well, you just sit tight, Ms. Lockhart, things will go pretty fast." The old white man smiled a wide smile that was more suggestive than assuring. I could tell that he wanted some of what only a bad bitch could offer, and I returned that cheesy ass smile. *Who knows, old man, I may suck ya dick if you do a good job. I swear, I got the sloppiest head you've ever had!* I thought with a giggle as Dr. Bergeron patted my leg as if he could read my dirty little mind!

216

***

-Heaven-

3 A.M.

"Now, you sure you don't want me to walk you to the car, Heavenly? You know these weirdos out lurkin'. At least let me walk you halfway," Bone, one of the club's muscle-bound bouncers, offered. I gave him a genuine smile. He'd been so protective since I'd been dancing at V-live.

"Boy, I'm good, stop being so extra!" I laughed before holding up my iPhone. "Plus, my boyfriend on the phone. If anything happens, I'll scream loud enough for you *and* him to come runnin'!" I smiled to ease his apprehension. "Bye, Bone, you be careful. See you later, handsome." I waved before putting the phone back up to my ear. "I'm here, what were you saying, Pap?"

"Oh, so now I'm yo' boyfriend, huh? Just a few minutes ago I was put in the friend zone. You a trip, Heaven, but who was that nigga anyway? I know you ain't still strippin' and shit?" I rolled my eyes at my *ex*. He was always on the extras and shit. I glanced down at the pink mini-skirt I wore and smiled; it was cute with the matching jacket. I was on chill that night and wasn't for Pap's jealousies, that's why we weren't together now. I pulled at the bottom of my mini-skirt.

"Pap, *you* know you're not my man, boy bye!" I giggled while making my way to my car.

"I take that as a yes, that's why dude callin' you *Heavenly* instead of Heaven. You know I ain't feelin' that shit, mane. Matter fact, why you ain't came through to fuck wit' ya boy?" Pap got on my nerves with his twenty-one questions, and on top of that, the man just didn't seem to get it. We could never be an item. The attraction was pure but love had nothing to do with the physical. A woman that gives herself to a man based off of attraction opens the door for bullshit because there's nothin' to build on. Pap was a handsome man that my heart refused to love. I opened my mini-purse and reached in for my keys while attempting to balance the phone between my head and shoulder.

"Boy, get out my business! So, what if I still strip, what, you look down on strippers now? Let me guess, I'm a hoe now 'cause I shake my ass for my chips? Pap, get off this phone before I have to cuss yo' *frontin'* ass out! Nigga, I met *you* in the club," I spat before sucking my teeth. Niggas got on my nerves with the double standards! I hit the alarm and watched my car come to life. "You over there talking about *come through* like you gone get you some, boy, you know—"

"Hang up the phone." I froze at the sound of his voice.

"Hello, Heaven, who dat?" Pap had heard him too. "Bitch, I know you ain't had no nigga wit' you this whole time and been frontin on—" he was saying when the devil snatched the phone out my hand and added fuel to the fire.

"Say, she'll fuck wit' you in traffic, Daddyo, she busy right now," Ghetto spoke into the phone before disconnecting the call. The feel of the cold steel against the back of my head prevented me from going for the gun I had in my clutch purse. It was a small twenty-five, but anything was plenty when a bitch was caught with her panties down. I stood as still as a statue, *waiting* for the bullet. "The thing 'bout karma is, she's the type of bitch that never forgets what a mu'fucka invests in her. She reflects her lover, so if you livin' foul, when she returns, that's the sort of gift she'll come bearing." His voice was steady, lethal.

Ghetto dug the barrel into the back of my skull. "Give me the purse, Heaven. *Please* don't make me paint this pretty car with your noodles," he asked as if he was speaking in the love language. I was hesitant. If I gave up my only weapon, I'd be as naked as a newborn, but if I tested his "G," it was a good possibility that it would cost me my life. I didn't know Ghetto's get down. I'd never witnessed him squeeze a trigger nor was I sure that he would squeeze one, but I knew one thing and two things for sure.

His potna ain't got the lethal injection for no reason. I know a killa when I see 'em! Common sense clouded my mental as I handed him my purse. I wanted to scream, but if I was gonna die, I didn't want my death to come from being gunned down from the back.

"I let you live, Ghetto, not for you to come find me and gun me down for the favor." I wagered for my life, but Ghetto merely laughed.

"Bitch, walk, and if you scream, cry, or try any funny business, I'm gone separate your spirit from ya physical," he gritted. "Walk, bitch!" he growled, and though I couldn't see him do it, I swear to God I could feel his finger tighten around that trigger.

***

-Ghetto-

I'd led her to my whip I'd parked a few cars down from hers, an all-black CTS I never drove. Pulling my keys from my pocket, I hit the button to unlock the trunk, and as soon as it opened, I could feel the lady stiffen in fear.

"Get in!" was my only demand.

"Look, if you're gonna kill me, do it. I ain't —"

"Bitch, you gonna either get in that trunk or after I slump yo' snake ass, I'mma pull up on ya sisters and smash they punk asses too!" I offered. I was ready to rock her to sleep, and just when my patience had run thin and my finger tightened around the trigga—

"Fuck you, Ghetto, I wish I woulda killed yo' ass when I had you down bad!" she hissed as she climbed her thick ass into that trunk. She was still attempting to get comfortable when I smashed the trunk down on her head. "Ouch! Damn, Ghetto, you could've let me get in all the way before you did that shit!" Her muffled words were comical. I glanced around to ensure I didn't have to do the extra work of whackin' a nosy mu'fucka before making my way to the driver's side of the whip.

"Yea, whateva, bitch, this is your hearse, not no mu'fuckin' Uber ride," I spoke more to myself than to the condemned woman. "A casket!"

Chapter 18
Rated R

I'd allowed the CTS to crawl slow down through the long, snaking road that led to the circular, Mexican-tiled driveway in front of my lion's den. I glanced up at my house before pushing the door open on the Cadillac, and before I could fully slip out the seat, my two bitches were silently at my side. Dre Dre and Kiesha held the fort down during my absences, and as the two massive K9s sniffed and licked at me, I could tell they missed a real nigga. I scratched and tickled behind Dre Dre's ears until Kiesha bullied herself into my embrace on her jealousy shit.

Bam! Bam! Bam! Bam! "Let me out of here, Ghetto, I can't breathe!" Heaven cried as she beat on the trunk. I chuckled. I'd cut the emergency release in the trunk and ensured the seats didn't let down in the back seat. Her pleas were like blood to a vampire to my queens. Both dogs growled deep, menacingly, but it was Dre Dre's overprotective ass that scrambled to the backseat and began to nip and sniff at the black leather as if she knew dinner was just beyond the soft material.

"Dre Dre, out, girl!" I demanded, and though I could see the reluctance in her posture, the K9 was bred to heed my command. She gave one last snap of the teeth before she turned and exited the car. I closed the door before making my way to the back of the whip. I hit the release on the remote and watched as the trunk rose. As soon as it lifted—*grurrrr!* Both dogs began to growl and got low to the ground as if they were preparing to pounce on their prey. I chuckled when Heaven sat up with hate in her stare, her eyes automatically falling to my hands.

When she registered the absence of the burna, confusion bled into her gaze and I could tell that she hadn't noticed the two wolflike German Shepherds.

"You can try and scream or even run, but both will be detrimental to your well-being, mama. We're deep in the country with a mile or so between me and my neighbors, plus…" I paused to nod behind me. Heaven's eyes grew wild in fear as the deadly, guttural sounds of Dre Dre and Kiesha's growls reached her ears. Both animals were as black as the reaper's clothes, but even with them being mere silhouettes against the blackness of the night, the evil slant of their golden eyes coupled with the razor-sharp glow of their canines, my babies told the tale of a bloodied conclusion. "I don't think my two ladies would respect you disrespecting our peace in this beautiful little piece of country of ours. Get out and be easy, ma, they won't feast unless you pose a threat or I tell 'em to," I instructed.

Heaven's glance trailed from the dogs to the darkness of my crib, and finally, her wide eyes settled on me. She seemed more comfortable in the trunk. "Get the fuck out, mane. I ain't gonna ask again." I kept my tone placid, but it was Kiesha inching toward the trunk on her haunches that created the threat. "Kiesha, Dre Dre, here girls, sit!" I commanded, and though both dogs showed their teeth, they made their way beside me and sat. Only then did Heaven hesitantly climb out the small compartment and face off with her fate.

My eyes instantly fell to her bare thighs. The skirt had ridden up, and though she hurriedly pulled the material down to a safe length, I'd already captured a heaven that had nothin' to do with her name.

"Welcome to Ranch El Diablo." I smiled before turning and heading for the house. Dre Dre nor Kiesha followed. The only parts of their body that moved were their necks and eyes as they hungrily watched Heaven scamper behind me.

***

-Stick Talk-

As I sat with my back to the cold slab of my brother's tombstone, the brain freeze-filled K2 blunt had my entire body numb. I continued to suck the soul from it as the moon shone a pale gray against the night's sky. A flock of dark crows flew low before one of them settled on a tombstone just in front of me. It squawked a long sound and set its predatorial glare at me. I wore all black, *a black Champion hoodie with the hood up over my bandaged head.

Two straps rested in my lap as my dome throbbed with a distant ache from where that hot lead had entered it, and that shit was a constant reminder of the betrayal of my own nigga.

Instinctively, I brought my hand to my head. My shit was wrapped in a million dollars' worth of gauze and masking tape to keep the wound from getting infected. The slug had entered underneath my scalp, over my skull, and out the side of my dome at a crooked angle. Some would consider me lucky to have dodged the hands of the reaper, and I was grateful that the lead hadn't penetrated my thinking cap and cut my lights out, but the near-death introduction had me on some other shit.

My trust was on zero, and though he acted as if he had his ear to the asphalt, my gut told me that Ghetto knew the mu'fuckas that had aided that sucka, Hurk, in takin' us down, but for some *strange* reason, he was protecting them! As I put the blunt to my lips and inhaled, my mental ricocheted me back to the night my life flashed before my eyes.

"Say, Flesh, I got someone I want you to meet!" Hurk's voice was as real now as it was the night he committed treason. I remembered him stepping back and allowing his shoota point-blank action at me. I could hear the treachery in his tone. I remembered turning to take cover, but that boy was 'bout his business when he squeezed that trigger. Boom! I could still hear the echo, the burp of the burna right before the hot lead folded me. I thought it was over for the kid when Hurk snatched me up, but that wasn't what got me. The strangest part to me was the lack of verbal from the other three killahs. Why the fuck these niggas so quiet? My thoughts were on fire, but my main thought, the one that bothered me most, was the last one I had before that pussy boy Hurk tried to snatch my soul from my body! Why the fuck these boys wearin' pink masks?

***

-Heaven-

Thank God he'd left those demons outside! I thought as I stood in the middle of his gorgeous family room. The entire interior of the house had a medieval feel. Black and white marble beams and fixtures, the floor was black and white checkered marble, with a huge portrait of a massive, growling gorilla created into its surface, all of the room's amenities were breathtaking. My eyes drifted to a beautiful, off-white grand piano that he'd had placed in front of three huge windows that rose all the way to the ceiling and overlooked a glowing, indoor swimming pool.

This boy got that bag! I thought as I made my way to the far wall where he had a strange collection of portraits and paintings. I'd never seen anything like it, they were beautiful, *powerful!* My eyes were drawn to a painting depicting a group of white men pointing down at the slain bodies of a young boy and girl, both were only children. I frowned at the viciousness of it. In the portrait, an angry African American woman glared evilly out at the stunned group of white people as her remaining two children seemed to cling to her in a plea for their own lives.

"It's called, *The Modern Medea.*" His voice surprised me, I hadn't heard him enter the room. "It's not the original, but it still ran me a check." I turned to face the man who'd kidnapped me and my breath became trapped somewhere in my chest. Ghetto must've taken a quick shower and changed into his—well, the *lack* of his night clothes. Shirtless, his long dreads hung loose over his muscular shoulders and chest. I'd never seen him without clothes, so my eyes took upon a beautiful exploration of his masculine anatomy. Tattoos ran intricately over his dark skin and covered every inch of his chest, arms, and stomach, but the most intriguing piece was a huge gorilla that sat in the center of his stomach.

The animal held a pistol to its own head, roaring with a menacing growl. Around the piece were the words, *Before I sell my soul, I'll lose everything! RNO shit!* The last two words dipped low on his stomach and were partially hidden beneath the waist band of the silk, black, Armani pajama pants he wore. Before I could tame the urge, my vision had paused at the thick imprint of his—

"It's a piece by an artist named Thomas Satterwhite Noble." He snapped me back from my...my *tour.*

"Huh-oh, the painting! Yes, it's-it's, ummm…"

"Fucked up?" He attempted to help, but only succeeded in heightening my embarrassment. I glanced up at his face and for the first time since he'd entered the room, I noticed the two champagne glasses in his left hand and chilled bottle of some type of liquor in the other. I shook my head in confusion. The man was a sexy ass paradox. I watched as Ghetto sat the glasses down on a very expensive looking coffee table before twisting the cap off the bottle and pouring *too much* liquor into each cup. He handed me one before taking a nice drink from his own. Skeptical, my eyes found the bottle he'd placed on the table. *Hennessy White!* I'd never heard of it, but for some reason, Dej Loaf and Lil' Wayne's "Me, You and Hennessy" played in my head as I accepted the drink.

"Yes, fucked up," I finally responded as my stare captured him and I brought the glass to my nose. "What, you're trying to poison me now, Ghetto, is that how my story ends? Girl kidnapped, found dead by poison?" I giggled, yet the man's sense of humor was on zero. Ghetto took another drink from his glass before—

"You being disrespectful, ma?" was his only question. Our eyes danced, and for some reason, I relaxed. Bringing the glass to my lips, I took an unladylike drink. The smooth liquor had a slight burn, but I liked it. Ghetto made his way around me and stood before his collection of art. "The lady slave in this picture is a woman named Margaret Garner. She was a runaway slave that fled Kentucky back in 1856. She escaped from a plantation with her four children and chose Cincinnati as her duck off.

"Her owner tracked her and her seeds, and when he and mounted men were about to snatch them up and return them to bondage, Margaret cut her daughter's throat, killin' her on the spot..." His words trailed off as he ran his fingers over the oiled painting. "She tried to do her three sons, but they stopped her. This lady would rather slay her offspring than to have them returned to slavery." Ghetto sounded as if he felt the woman's pain.

I took another drink of my glass before stepping over to a crazy picture that I wasn't sure if it was the liquor or if my eyes were really seeing what I thought they were. "And this one?" I was curious. Ghetto's eyes followed mine, seemingly lost in deep thought.

The man downed the rest of his cup as if it were water, and not to be upstaged, I followed suit. I frowned and began to cough. I'd finally gotten a laugh out the man! He studied me as I sat my glass down, and that's when shit took a drastic turn.

***

-Ghetto-

"You know, I should blow yo' brains all over this floor," I spoke my soul. I could tell that the liquor was on lady's ass and she was attempting to understand the twists and turns I was taking her through that night.

"Wha-what?" was her only response. My eyes took in the soft pink Balenciaga jacket and skirt that molested lady's curves, and though I didn't know what caused me to do it, I snapped and got on some real animalistic shit. Without warning, I spat in shawty's face. It caught her off guard when the speckles splashed against her right eye, and not knowing what else to do, she rose both hands as if the police were telling her to freeze.

"Nigga, are you *crazy*!" Heaven stressed the last word before she began to tremble in rage. There seemed to be a pause in time— the calm before the storm before the woman got to the business. Though I recognized the assault before it came, my reaction wasn't as quick as I intended it to be. Heaven's fist connected with my nose and before I could react, the mad woman had a handful of my dreads in her grasp.

I had never been the breed of nigga to physically take it there with a woman, but as blood trickled out my nose and the lady's nails raked across my exposed chest, I had to make an exception. In seconds, I had her by the throat, squeezing so tightly that I thought her neck would snap at any moment. Heaven released my hair and scratched at my arms, my face, anything that was exposed to her wrath.

"I-can't-bre-breath!" she cried, and the tears that clouded her vision did something strange to the vessel in my chest that beat and distributed my blood throughout my body. I lifted her by her throat until she was barely balanced on her tip toes, before pushing with every ounce of strength I had. Heaven's body fell backwards with the force, and as I watched her crash to the floor, I rushed to the piano and snatched the Glock .17 I kept stashed inside it, and with it in my grip, I stalked over to the crying woman.

She was a fighter. As soon as I was close enough, Heaven kicked out at me, but I sidestepped her attempt. "Come here, bitch!" I growled before reaching down and snatching her by a handful of her curly hair.

"Fuck you, let me gooooo!" she cried as she repelled me, but the grip I had on all that thick ass hair was like a vice grip. She scrambled to her feet as I drug her to the piano bench and forced her down onto it. *I'm 'bout to dome this hoe!* I thought while regretting not finishing her back at the club.

"I hate you. I hate you, bitch ass nigga!" she cried when I released her and put that banga underneath her chin. Heaven glared at me as a fast river of salty tears cascaded down her pretty face, and just before I pulled the trigger and sent her brains flying toward the ceiling, something in her stare fucked wit' me. *Resolution!* She was ready to die.

"Do it, bitch, do it!" she hissed, her stare fearless. I gritted my teeth as my finger tightened around the trigger. *Fuck it!* I thought as I pulled the trigger.

Click! The empty gun sounded off. Heaven attempted to suppress it, but I saw when she jumped, and before she could bounce back from the surprise of still breathing, I did the unthinkable.

"You stupid, son of a—" Heaven began until I leaned forward and ran my tongue from her chin to the bottom of her eyelid. Her tears tasted like a bitter candy in my mouth, and as I repeated the process to the other side of her face, Heaven froze in confusion. I kissed her eyelids, her forehead, the tip of her nose, and *finally*, her lips. The woman tensed as her eyes bore into mine, never reciprocating my gesture, but her lips were so soft, I lost myself within stolen kisses trapped within a moment of insanity. I kissed lady and kissed lady, and finally, Heaven reached up and held my face still and opened her mouth to accept me.

Our tongues danced as we explored each other, our hands wickedly trespassing barriers of privacy. Before I knew it, she had my masculinity free from the silk pajama pants and was gripping me so tightly that it seemed as if she was cutting off my circulation. It was painful pleasure as I used my hands to push the skirt up until it bunched around her waist, and just as I'd assumed, she went pantyless.

I broke our tongue wrestle and fell to my knees before her. Pushing her legs open, my vision fell to the masterpiece that made her a woman. That pussy was as pretty as the woman that possessed it, and as my eyes captured her slightly damp lower lips, I wondered what the hell I was about to do. I'd never eaten pussy before and had vowed to never place my lips where a woman bled every month, but as my eyes lifted to find Heaven's eyes still leaking as she stared down at me uncertainly, I understood the power of curiosity was sometimes more powerful than one's willpower, and as I placed both of Queen's legs on my shoulders, I pulled her to the edge of that bench so that her ass cheeks slightly spilled over its edge.

My eyes fell back to her paradise and a thin, trimmed line of hair was the only trail I needed to follow to the path to her ecstasy. I didn't know what the hell I was doing as I flattened my tongue against her kitty and ran it from the bottom to the top and back again.

"Oh, my." The words slipped from her lips and brought my eyes up to feast upon the pleasure my licks were causing. Her eyes were half-mast and her mouth was open in a slight *o* as she stared down at me. She had the type of pussy lips that folded inward and as I used my finger to spread her open, I used my tongue to glide over her pinkness until I felt that small button at the entry of her. I began to make slow, tight circles around her clit until lady reached down and grabbed a fistful of my dreads. "Ghet-Ghettoooo! Baby, wait, I've never—we can't—babyyyy!" she cried as I captured her flesh between my lips. I didn't know if my spit was supposed to be oozing out the sides of my mouth.

I didn't know if it was her, my mouth, or a little bit of both, but things got real slippery as I bathed her with my tongue. Heaven's legs tightened around my head, and the shit excited me. I wrapped my arms around her thighs and forced her open.

"Unnn-fuck-fuuuck-fuck!" she cried as I placed my mouth to her clam and began to tongue kiss that pussy as if it were her mouth. *I wonder if I put my finger in her ass will it make her bust? I'm trying to do it to her!* My mental was grasping for innovative ways to make her cum, so I tried it.

"Nooooo, that's-that's, hissss, that's my-my ass, papi!" she cried as I eased my thumb inside her exit wound. Queen's body vibrated in my grasp. I could feel her fighting to close her legs while attempting not to fall at the same time.

"Let me taste that cum, ma, you gone let me or what?" I mumbled over a mouthful of her clit.

"Uh huh, uh huhhh, yasss!" she moaned as she lost the war. Heaven smashed my face down into that pussy as her juices flooded my mouth, and not knowing what else to do, I swallowed her until the last drop. With a final kiss to her oasis, I released her and climbed to my feet. Shawty damned near melted off the bench but caught herself before crashing to the floor. I chuckled as I slid the sleeping pants the rest of the way off.

I stood before lady as bare as a child fresh out the womb as Heaven's eyes transcended from my face to my *thick* seven and a half inches that saluted her. A look of uncertainty fell over her face. I was uncircumcised and wondered if she was about to get on some little girl shit, but there wasn't a speck of disgust in her gaze. She was *curious*! Or maybe it was fear? I didn't know, and as I pulled her to her feet and replaced her on the bench, the only thing on my mental was burying my nature inside her.

"Come here," I demanded while spreading my feet apart stroking myself.

***

-Heaven-

The demand turned me on, but I was as scared of the unknown, as a child walking into a haunted house on Halloween. Ghetto sat there stroking himself in a sensual motion. He seemed confident and unabashed with his uncircumcision, and as I admired dude, I wondered how I'd let things go that far. *What the hell am I doing?* I wondered, but even as the thought blew through my mind, I was slipping out the skirt. It fell to the floor in a puddle of soft pink as he observed me. I could feel my juices running down the inside of my thigh as the jacket joined the skirt on the floor, followed by my shirt. My nipples were taut as I allowed Ghetto's vision to behold what no other man had before.

"You like what you see, Ghetto?" The words came from the lips of a grown woman, but internally, my stomach felt as if it were the net that had captured a thousand colorful butterflies. Pre-cum coated the head of his power, and with the foreskin pulled back, the mushroomed head seemed as fat as a baby's fist. *Pretty!* was the only word that came to mind as I studied his dick, my juices around his mouth.

"Come here!" There was that demand again. I glanced down at the heels I'd worn. The straps ran up and around my calves, too much to undo, so I did as I was told. The few steps it took me to get to him seemed like a journey, but as soon as I was in arm's reach, Ghetto reached out and pulled me into his lap. His throbbing manhood was pressed against his stomach as I straddled him, and when he reached up to massage my breasts, I could feel his pulse within it. I watched as my right nipple disappeared inside his mouth as he rolled my left one between his thumb and pointer finger. The shit felt so good that I held his face against me. "Hissss!" I sucked air through my teeth.

"Ghetto, I've-I've never—" I tried, but before I could reveal my secret, he had his tongue in my mouth, kissing me so deeply that I didn't know whose breath I was breathing. "But, I've never—" I tried.

"Huuuuuah!" I inhaled a sharp intake of breath as he bit down on my bottom lip so hard I thought he'd drawn blood. My mind was a maze of thoughts that I became lost within. I barely felt when he'd lifted me enough to position himself to enter me. Our eyes met in a collision, his hunger, my vulnerability. The two crashed head on as the head of his lower self-kissed my pussy lips, and the contact seemed to bring me to a fork in the road that could either lead me to a place in life I'd never ventured, or far away from what could've been.

I stood frozen in time, only an inch away from being stripped away from what I'd held onto for so long, and I studied him. "This time, you gambled and won." Tears filled my eyes as visions of the past few months flooded my mind. The expression on Ghetto's face let me know that he understood me. On our last night in Louisiana, he'd said he was gambling with his heart, and though I tried to change the cards, he was relentless in his bid. My mother, my father, the distance that had formed between me and my sisters, all of it, it took ahold of me and wouldn't let go.

The tears slid down my face and I watched as Ghetto caught them with his tongue. I felt his hands slide beneath me and cup my butt. "We can chill if—" I silenced him with soft kisses. I *needed* him... I wanted to feel something, *anything* other than what my heart had been feeling. I wrapped my arms around his neck and with my eyes on his, I impaled myself onto him.

"Ahhhhhh!" I cried as he opened me up. My eyes opened wide in pain as I froze midway and burying my face in the crook of his neck, I sunk my teeth into his flesh.

"Damn, ma, what the fuck?" he growled as my tightness hugged the upper portion of his nature like a python does its prey.

"Hissss, it hurrrtts, Ghetto!" I moaned as he spread my ass cheeks and gently bounced me from the tip of his dick and back to that midway point. Though I was as wet as the ocean, I felt as if he was tearing me in half. My teeth broke the skin on his neck and drew blood, but I think the vice grip my pussy lips had on his strength held his attention captive. As he bounced me in a beautiful motion, pleasure began to march its army toward the formation of pain. My mind was the battlefield that the loser would become the casualty upon, and as all that I'd lost in my life began to play its trumpet, pleasure was the first to react to its war cry. My pussy was a sticky puddle beneath me.

"How—why the fuck you so-so tight, lady?" Ghetto's words were forced as he leaned forward and sank his teeth into my collar bone. The sting of the bite was kissed away as he left wet kisses down my chest until my nipple was immersed back in his warm mouth. My body was a burning flame as he guided me back up that trail of his sword, and as I wrapped my arms around his head and took ahold of a mass of his dreadlocks, I knew that pain had lost the war. I yanked his head back, his lips making a wet popping sound as they released my nipple. I forced his head back until he was staring up at me. I stared down at that warrior, eye to eye before *forcing* myself down onto his blade.

"Ohhhh, shiiiitt!" I cried as he split me open. Pleasure and pain became the same as I rose and fell back down onto him. "You win, pa, youuu win!" I cried as my face contorted into a mask of erotic pain. I felt my hymen tear, the blood of my cherry oozing out of me with my nectar as I leaned down and nibbled his ear. "I'm giving it all to you, everythang! My tru-trust, my Goddddd, my heart, and-and…" I fought to speak, but that dick? That first-time dick had me calling on Jesus, Muhammad, Jehovah, and "*Ghetto!*" I cried as he held me around the waist and grinded beneath me. "*My virginity, baby,* I'm—Yasss, I'm giving you-you *all* of me!" My body shook as my love came down for the second time that night.

Chapter 19
Love Wins... Love Steals

-Empress-
Next morning

I stood with my back to the full-length mirror, smiling back at my reflection as I attempted to make my new, forty-nine-inch fatty clap, but going from a thirty-nine to ten more pounds of thickness took some getting used to. I was impressed with the ass job. "Ouuuu, bitch, they ain't gone be able to tell you nothin'!" I whispered to myself. I turned and cupped my new set of thirty-six double D's, *so firm, I know Heaven's hatin' ass ain't gonna like this!* I giggled at the thought.

"Soooo, you like?" Doctor Bergeron's question caused me to jump. I'd forgotten he was in the room. With a smirk on my face, my eyes found him. The doctor's eyes were glued to the job he'd done, and when he finally lifted his vision to mine, the elder white man's face became flushed with red. He was embarrassed at being caught within the thralls of *lust*. I snickered while facing him fully before placing my hands on my slim waist.

"You created a masterpiece, Doc, now for the finale," I spoke in glee.

***

-Ghetto-

The absence of her body heat made me feel empty inside. My eyes cracked open to a ray of sunlight seeping through windows surrounding the living room. I sat up on my elbows, attempting to recall the events of the night before. That Henny was fooly!

"Good morning, sleepy head, how'd you rest?" Her voice was the energy I needed to think clearly. The images flooded my mental like water through a snapped dam. The poetry of our love making, the pallet I'd made on the marble floor for us to sleep on, the early morning conversations, all of it. I smiled as I glanced at her. Lady was standing over by my painting collections again. Heaven had a sheet wrapped around her, hair tousled, as she ran her fingertips over the oiled canvas. "Who is this woman?" she asked in a curious whisper. I smiled as I slid from the pallet, tossing the thin sheet that covered me.

Dick semi-hard, I made my way over to Queen and wrapped my arms around her waist, and as soon as the softness of all that booty rested against my midsection, my nature swelled in acknowledgement. "This is a woman that made it possible for all this business right here." I chuckled as I pulled her hair.

"What you mean, boy, I know you ain't sayin' what I think you are?" She glanced at me over her shoulder and it was automatic, I kissed the side of her face.

"This is Madam C.J. Walker, formally known as Sarah Breedlove. She changed her name after marrying a salesman by the name of Charles Joseph Walker. Long story short, Mrs. Walker is the first African American woman to become a self-made millionaire. With a dollar and twenty-five cents, she invested in a dream where she claimed a big black man came to her and told her what to mix up for her hair, and the shit worked!" I smiled while running my fingers through Ms. Lady's curly hair. I loved bringing my people out of the triple stages of darkness. Being deaf, dumb, or blind was a sin to a people that had spent so much time deprived of the right to learn. "I fucks wit' Mrs. Walker because even with critics like the great Booker T. Washington not feeling her vision because he thought that hair straighteners and skin bleaching creams would lead to our people adapting white folks' concepts of beauty, the lady went door to door pushing her product. Hence, how black folk started fuckin' with the perm." My words caused Heaven to touch her hand to her silky hair with a giggle.

"Boy, ain't no chemicals in my hair, all this is official!" She wasn't having it. "My mama was black and my dad..." Her words seemed to trail off at the mention of her folks. After our journey of passion, the night before, she'd opened her heart to me and told me of the many losses she'd had to take in life. My heart went out to Baby. A black woman's strength would always be the power of the people. I tightened my embrace around her to let her know she no longer had to carry the pain alone. "And that one?" she asked while pointing at an enlarged photo I'd had encased within a golden-edged picture frame. I studied it for a few seconds before speaking. The picture depicted a man aflame with a fire gallon jug beside his burning body.

"That's a Buddhist monk named Thich Quang Duc. There was a president in Vietnam that wanted to convert the country's religion to Catholicism, and the man went so far as passing a law that made flying the Buddhist flag illegal there. He tried this shit in a nation where Buddhists held the majority." I paused to kiss Queen's shoulder where the sheet had fallen away.

"Yes, but why is this man on *fire*? Is this real? Why do *you* care of this, are *you* Buddhist?" Heaven's curiosity flowed out in a river of questions. I chuckled before kissing her bare neck. I reached around her and pulled the sheet loose from her hands, and it fluttered to the ground in a pool of black silk. Flesh to flesh, I held lil' mama.

"Naw, mama, I'm far from Buddhist, and fuckin' right this is as real as it gets. Long stories are boring, so dig..." My right hand made a slow trail down her body. My fingertips were as light as a feather as they traveled over her hardened nipples, down her flat stomach, and paused at their final destination. I ran them over her clit, down her pussy lips, and back to that pearl before I began making small, gentle circles. Heaven's lips parted slightly in pleasure.

"At ten A.M., Thich Quang Dur sat down on a crowded street. That day, bruh would give a protest that would go down as one of the world's most *stand-up* demonstrations of standing for what one believes. As he sat, he began to recite a mantra over and over."

"Damn, Pa-pi, you—ummm!" Heaven's cries had my dick at full stance.

"As he sits there, a brother of his cloth begins to pour five gallons of gasoline onto him. His people gather around him to prevent the police from stopping their demonstration as Duc lights the match and immolates himself!" I whisper urgently. Heaven had leaned forward and placed both hands against the portrait. I used my leg to push hers apart until her feet spread out enough for me to do me. I pushed down on the lower part of her back as I used my dick head as a tease and ran it between her ass crack, between the lips of her garden, back up, and finally—

"Unnnnn!" she cried as I slid inside her with a crooked angle.

"Fam, fam set himself on fire for the shit he believed in, ma. Every time I look at-this-shit-shit—"

That pussy had me gone. With each stroke, I thought my soul would escape from my nut sack. "Every time I look at this picture, I remind myself that when a person stands for somethin', they gotta be willin'-willin', baby, to die for it!" I spoke as my strokes became feverish. Queen's waterfall leaked around me until her waters saturated my pubic hair, my nuts, and ran down her leg. I reached down and gripped her by the waist before my entire body became a powerful dance as I stroked lady from the back. I watched her ass cheeks jiggle as she lifted onto the tops of her toes before reaching back and gripping my right wrist.

She dug her nails into my flesh as she glanced back at me. "I-baby-I think-think-I love-love, youuuu!" she moaned. The words caught me off guard and did something to my crooked heart that I couldn't explain. My strokes were at top speed as I pumped, my sweat glistening on my body. The explosion was internal before external as my protein surged from my faucet.

"Ohhhhh, shit!" Baby cried as she busted back. It was a shootout, but as hers coated me, mine penetrated her.

"I love you too, ma, even though you gonna have to teach me how to love. Will you?" I gritted the question as I pumped every drop of my seed into her.

"Yes-yessss, Pa, I'll teach you!" Her words brought my vision back to the portrait of Quang Duc. Though Heaven's handprints stained the glass, I saluted the man in the picture. The flames covered his body from head to toe as his face squinted in agony, but legend has it, fam didn't make a sound as he burned. He burned for ten minutes straight before death welcomed him, and as my vision fell to Heaven's quaking body, I knew that the things I wanted to build wit' mama were worth dying for.

"I love you, I love you, I love you." She was on repeat as I slipped from within her ocean and pulled her into my arms. She turned and wrapped me in a tight embrace before I kissed her forehead.

"Teach me how to love, Heaven. Fix my heart, ma."

***

Back in the swamps of Louisiana, sitting in her rocking chair, Genevieve rocked back and forth, humming an old slave hymn. The day had been good to her until something strange happened. The sunny sky dimmed as clouds rolled in front of the sun. The old house she'd called home for so long began to fill with dancing shadows. The old woman's eyes trailed to the bay window as the wind blew through the trees of the swamp. Suspiciously, she allowed her eyes to roll over the living room. For some reason, it seemed to be getting darker. Genevieve began to rock a bit fast as a barely audible whisper was birthed from the shadows.

"The debt must be paid, your soul!" it chanted repeatedly. Genevieve's eyes widened in fear as she began to rise from her seat, but—*Blam!* The front door blew open with a force that almost snatched it off its hinges. A strong gust of wind invaded the house as its frame began to vibrate as if it were fighting against the strength of the wind.

"No, I'm not ready, not yet!" she cried as she fell back into the chair as a dark shadow appeared on the wall. Featureless, besides the wicked horns that seemed to form from its head, the shadow was exactly that—a spot of moving darkness. At the sight of it, Genevieve's chest tightened in pain as if her heart was attempting to escape from her chest. "No, I—wait!" she cried as her back arched. The old woman's head jerked backwards until she was forced to stare up at the stained ceiling.

"The debt must be paid! With your soul! The debt must be paid! The debt must be paid!" The chant's whisper became a decimal louder, more urgent. Suddenly, her breath became a fight. Gene-

vieve's hand went to her chest, clutching, scratching, the pain un-
bearable. Within her last moment of life, an ocean of hate drowned
her as she realized why she was about to die. The girl, Heaven! The
prayer for Ghetto's love. The sacrifice! "I hate you!" she cried at
the thought of Heaven as her last breath was snatched from her
body. At the height of her last breath, the clouds rolled away from
the sun and the shadows faded away. Ghetto's grandmother passed
with her eyes open. A cool breeze blew over the putrid waters of the
swamp, soft, but strong enough to cause the rocking chair to rock
her dead body back and forth, allowing her one last rock of her favorite chair.

Chapter 20
Bitch, What?

-Empress-

Two weeks later

The house was empty as I made my way down the hall that morning. Egypt and Heaven were out grocery shopping and Catrina had spent the night with some girl she'd met at the club, so I had the spot all to my lonesome. I made it to the living room just as my phone began ringing. *Ugh, why mu'fuckas always gotta choose the wrong time to bother a bitch?* I thought as I made my way back to the room where my phone rested in the center of my queen-sized bed. I crawled onto the bed and laid down on my stomach, my thong resting high between my plump ass cheeks as I glanced down at the screen. *Fuck?* I thought as the phone fell from my grasp in surprise.

"What the hell?" The words slipped from my lips as I stared down at a dead man's number flashing across the screen. My heart pounded in my chest as I contemplated whether I should answer or not. *How the hell is he calling me? This nigga is supposed to be six feet underneath the earth along with his other two potnas we left slumped that night!* My mind was a battlefield of questions and before I knew it, I'd swiped the accept button. "Hel-hello?" I whispered.

"Damn, bitch, fuck takin' you so long to answer the phone, you duckin' me or what?" Stick Talk's voice was agitated.

"Oh my god, bae, where you been? Word on the street is that something bad happened to you. I've been soooo worried! I wanted to call, but my old phone with your number in it got stolen and I couldn't transfer it. Where you at, Pa, what took so long for you to call!" I fished. Something just didn't feel right, and he was supposed to be DOA, but there he was, sounding as healthy as a man being accepted into the Navy.

"Yea, some lames tried to take me and my bro out. One of our own set us up for the take down, but they wasn't wit' the shit like

238

that. I played dead on 'em and my dude Ghetto got me to the hospital in time to save my life. Shit crazy, love, but I'm tryin' to see you." The man's revelation stole my breath away. *Ghetto!* That nigga was 'pose to be as dead as Stick Talk!

"Oh, that's so fucked up, is Ghetto good? I mean, he didn't get hurt, did he?" My heart began to fill with murderous intent.

"Yea, bruh coolin', but I think *he* had somethin' to do with us gettin' hit. I don't know if it was on some snake shit or he just knows the shootas, but sommin' fishy, homie." Stick Talk's assumption let me know that Ghetto had kept our identity secret, but why? I wondered before dude put the pieces together for me.

"You ain't seen him or sommin'? Him and ya girl Heaven been on some real heavy shit lately." He did it to me. My eyes dropped to slits as my mind traveled back to that night. *"Wait, naw, Em, this is personal! I gotta do it, me, Empress!"* I could hear her voice as clear as day.

"Empress, can you hear me, mane? I'm tryin' to see you." Stick Talk's voice snatched me back to the present.

"Yeah, ok, give me a lil' bit and I'll hit you later. We can hook up, cool, bae?" I attempted to mask the betrayal I felt.

"That's a bet, huh, just be ready 'cause I ain't fucked nun in weeks and I'm tryin' to crash sommin'." I hung up without a response. My mind was upside down as I scrambled from the bed and stalked toward the bitch's room. Heaven must've let Ghetto live after I'd left her to end him.

"I knew I should've put a bullet in his head. I knew this bitch was too weak to do it. I knew it!" I hissed as I entered her room. I didn't know what I was looking for, I was just heated! I went directly over to her dresser and began tossing the drawers, and only after I'd gotten to the third one did it register to me that something was terribly wrong. *Empty!* The word echoed through my mind. Each drawer I'd opened was empty! I rushed to the closet, and though a few boxes of shoes lined the floor and a few articles of clothes hung from hangers, I knew that was merely a figment of Heaven's wardrobe. The girl was secretly moving her things. *But why?* I wondered. She was a grown woman and could do as she pleased, so I didn't understand why she'd be on some slick shit.

"Where the hell is her shit?" I asked no one in particular. I found myself looking beneath her bed before pushing her mattress away from the box spring, and that's where I found Heaven's journal. It rested on the white surface. I stared down at it as if it was the Holy grail before calming myself enough to take a seat and open it. I flipped through the entries until I found...

Last night...

Last night was majestic, something abnormally beautiful. You asked me to teach you how to love, and I told you that I would while lost within our passion, searching for a hidden treasure in the distant lands of possibilities. I've searched for a you my entire life. I used to sneak out the windows of my thoughts just to meet you underneath the streetlights... At times, it was hard for me to sleep nights, because I feared falling asleep, only to have to abandon you in my dreams. You wanna know something special? Loving the right person can change your heart, and the word love spelled backwards with the letters "Ve" added to the end creates the word evolve! Change! Maybe the process of evolution isn't so crazy when one knows that before a flower can become a rose, it had to be a seed first.

Last night, I felt when you penetrated my hymen and took me on a roller coaster ride that defied gravity. You explored my anatomy for moments of forgotten curiosity. Curiosities? I've always been curious of what Heaven would be like from down under. Always wondered what it would be like to be touched by gentle caresses, soft kisses, and fed the fruit from the devil's hand. Maybe it was the devil's plan for us to fall so deeply off the cliff of the forbidden? I lose my mind when I reflect on the night that I almost did the unthinkable, spilt your blood upon the petals of the white rose. Unforgivable! Unthinkable! I love you! You're a secret that I fear revealing to my sisters, for the revelation wouldn't allow them to see our chemistry, but more of a betrayal of our sisterhood.

Yet, I want to share with them of my happiness, gossip with them about how you deflowered the black rose of my essence. I giggle at how tough I've always been, but in the moments of shallow breaths, stolen chastity made me so-so, woman! Thank you! Giggles! Just thinking about last night.

"What the fuck are you doing in my room!" Heaven's shrill voice snatched my eyes from the journal. She stood in the doorway to her room, and from the look in her eyes, I knew she wanted to get on her bullshit. *Good, that makes two of us!* I thought as I stood and returned her glare.

"Oh, bitch, you in violation now, and I swear to you, this time, we're gonna tear this bitch up!" she vowed as she kicked her heels off and took a step toward me.

"What's up, why y'all yellin' and—" Egypt was steps behind her but paused when she noticed the disarray of the room. "Fuck? Empress, what kinda bullshit you on now?" Her eyes squinted at me suspiciously. My eyes never left Heaven, even when I snickered at the sneaky bitch.

"You wanna tell her, or do you need me to? 'Cause I'll be happy to," I spat.

"I don't know what you're talking about, but, bitch—"

"Save it, Heaven!" I cut her off with a raised palm before tossing the journal at her feet. Heaven's eyes dropped to the leather-bound book of secrets before returning to me. Her eyes softened and I watched as she deflated. The girl bent and retrieved the journal before uprighting herself.

"See, this is exactly why I don't fuck with you, Empress, you love the messy shit and always on some competitive stuff." She smiled as she turned to the closet and made her way inside it. Her words had been sharp and hurtful, but it was what it was. I stood there and crossed my arms over my breasts, shaking my head sadly as Heaven came out the closet with a duffle bag she was stuffing the rest of her belongings into.

"I'll be back for the rest of my shit some other time."

"Where you going, Heaven, what the hell is going on, Empress?" Egypt was already blaming me. *Fuck it!* I thought with a roll of my eyes.

"Oh, you ain't know? Ms. Thang is leaving us for the same nigga she was supposed to had killed!" I spat. Egypt's mouth fell open in surprise as her eyes drifted to Heaven.

"What's up, sis, what she talking about?"

"Have you ever been in love, Egypt, like, real love?" Heaven's question almost made me gag. I mean, how was this bitch talkin' about loving a man that we'd robbed! The look on Egypt's face was priceless as she studied our sister. I guess she couldn't digest the bullshit the girl was kicking either. She shrugged her shoulders indifferently.

"Yea, I mean, no, I've never loved someone on an intimate level, Heaven, but what does love have to do with you *leaving*? I mean, yea, the idea of you falling for a man that we took down sounds crazy but can't nobody speak on what you do with your heart. Shid, if you accept dude, so do we." Egypt sounded just as crazy as Heaven.

"Speak for yourself, Egypt, that nigga 'pose to be *dead*, dead, Egypt! What's gonna happen when he wants his shit back, or better yet, when he wants revenge?" I brought rationality to the situation. Heaven gave me a bitter laugh as she shook her head, as if I was the most pitiful thing on the universe. I returned her sneer. "This shit ain't got nothin' to do with no love, it's pure selfishness, it's so Heaven!" I pointed my finger at her.

"Well, I guess that's all that needs to be said. I'll always love y'all, y'all my sisters, but this is something I just have to do. I have to give my heart a chance. Can't y'all understand that?" she asked as her eyes bounced back and forth between me and Egypt. I rolled my eyes at her. Heaven always thought she was our leader, Heaven always wanted her way, Heaven, Heaven, Heaven!

"Come here, girl," Egypt beckoned while spreading her arms out wide. Heaven walked into her embrace as if there was no other place she'd rather be. "Awww, my girl done went and fell in love! You bet not be a stranger, Heaven, don't forget about ya sisters," Egypt's friendly ass gushed as if that shit was acceptable. Heaven turned to face me as if she was expecting the same acceptance, but I wasn't havin' it.

242

"So, what about us, ya sisters, Heaven? Ya know, the bitches you came from the dollhouse with?" I reminded her. Heaven seemed to think about it for a quick moment before reaching down into her bag and pulling her favorite pistol free. Our eyes met as she tossed it onto the exposed box spring.

"What about y'all? You, Catrina, and Egypt are grown women, and with the pills we took from Ghetto, we don't have to ever look back or go back to stickin' niggas up. Either way, I'm done, Empress, I'm out, ma." The tramp had the gall to shrug her shoulders as if her answer justified her betrayal.

"And what if that nigga comes for us, what, you're gonna gun us down with him, huh? You think that fool is just gonna chalk the loss up and let bygones be bygones? Bitch, please!" I knew I was being petty, but the hoe deserved it. Heaven sucked her teeth at me before turning to Egypt. She air kissed both sides of her face before speaking over her shoulder.

"Just consider it a gift, E, no harm, no foul." She surely left a bad taste in my mouth and just as she turned to leave, I reached down and snatched up the discarded baby nine she'd tossed onto the bed. Without a moment's hesitation, I stepped forward as I aimed and pulled the trigger.

Boca!

"Empress! Em, can you hear me?" Egypt's irritated voice snapped me back out my fatal fantasy. My eyes fell to the pistol that still laid on the box spring as the sound of the front door closing told me Heaven had made her exit. "Damn, bitch, it ain't that bad. You standin' here looking at that tool as if you wanted to do the unthinkable!" Egypt laughed as she reached down and scooped up the gun. I headed for the door.

"Almost, sis, almost."

Chapter 21
Poisonous SEEDS
Stick Talk

"Yeaaa-yea, fuck that ass, Stick Talk, doooo it!" Empress cried as I pumped in and out of her back side. I could feel her body trembling beneath me at the same time I erupted inside her. I roared like a victorious lion as my kids shot from me. I pulled out and shot my milk onto all that ass she had back there before collapsing beside her. She snuggled up to me and pulled my arm around her waist. For the past eight months, we'd been rocking real tough, and though she'd only let a nigga cut a few times, it had become more than a sex hype with me. I kissed the side of her sweaty face at the same time my phone began vibrating on the nightstand beside the bed.

"Let it ring, baby, you said it was just us tonight," Empress whined. It was sexy. I chuckled before reaching over and retrieving my phone. Glancing down at the screen, I smiled. It had been weeks since I'd heard from my guy. Ever since he'd locked all the way in wit' Heaven, Ghetto had distanced himself from the streets. I respected it, even more so that he'd planted his seed in lady.

"Chill," I warned Empress. For some strange reason, she and Ghetto wasn't feelin' each other, and I couldn't put my finger on it. "Sup, stranger, I ain't think you fucked with the lil' people no more!" I laughed.

"What's blessings, Flesh, two twenty-one, you know it ain't nothin' like that. Just been thuggin' with my nubian and makin' sure her and the new world she carryin' in her stomach straight. Dig, though, that's why I'm gettin' at you, fam. One of my potnas out there in East Texas hosting a dog fight and it's gonna be some big money out there. You tryin' to slide with me or what?" bruh proposed. I glanced down at Empress. She was acting as if she was drifting off, but I knew she was all ears.

"That's a bet, just let me know the bidness and I'll meet you there," I accepted. Me and fam spoke the specifics before ending the call, and as soon as I placed the phone back on the nightstand, Empress got on some real live bullshit!

"So, what, you really doin' this?" she spat before removing my arm.

"Huh?" I was lost. "What you talking about, fam?"

"Like, can't you see how that nigga using you? You're like his bitch, nigga. *You* and all these other dudes puttin' in all the work while this nigga and his bitch laid up in the country, getting full off y'all's labor. Are you blind or just like being sonned?" Her words were hurtful, but most of all, poisonous. She'd been on that exact trip since the day we'd linked back up, and I didn't know if she was on some divide and conquer shit or if there was some truth to her spiel.

"Man, gone head with all that shit, Empress, you being disrespectful." I turned on my back as she slid out the bed on her pouting business. I watched as she slid her panties on and headed for the bathroom. Though I didn't want to admit it, but every time the lady spoke her blasphemies, it fucked with me. It did seem like every time someone needed to come up missin', Ghetto sent me or one of the other bros. *Nah, bitch playin' a dangerous game, bruh solid*, I thought as the sound of the toilet flushing caused me to look up at Empress as she came back in and climbed back in the bed.

"I'm sorry, Daddy, it's just..." Her words trailed off as her facial expression gave away her frustration. I pulled her close to me and kissed her forehead. I was weak for the lady.

"Sup, spit that shit out," I encouraged her. Empress's eyes swallowed me before she released a long breath. She smiled up at me before pushing me back onto my back and slipping her head underneath the covers. I watched the form of her head slide down until I felt her hands fondling my nuts. Her soft lips left a wet trail all over my johnson as she spoke over licks of my nature.

"Baby"—*Muah!* "I think Ghetto"—*Muah! Muah!* "Set you up to get robbed that night and made it look like something else. Why else would they kill Hurk if he's the one turned 'em on to the lick?" The feeling of my lil' man disappearing in her warm mouth, coupled with the seed she'd just planted tore my mind and body apart.

"Never, bro official!" I managed to get out before placing my hand on top of her bobbing head. *Smop!* Her lips popped when she came up off that dick.

"All the work you said they took y'all for, I wouldn't put it past my own mama to take me down for. Think about this," she paused to take me back in her mouth as she began to suck and stroke me at the same time, and the bomb she dropped on me was enough to turn a devout Christian against Jesus Christ himself. "Why were you and Hurk the only two shot? Why they didn't try to take him out too?" *Muah!* She signed the question with a wet kiss to my nature.

Heaven Got a Ghetto

Chapter 22
Just Us

-Heaven-

The garden was beautiful, and as I watched a gold butterfly with white and black spots gracing its wings, I couldn't remember a time I'd been happier. The day was hot, global warming was real! Ghetto and I had decided to have a picnic out by the pond and I'd let his crazy ass choose the food for the occasion. As I studied the finger foods he'd chosen, I tried my best not to laugh. I placed my hand over my mouth to stifle my laughter, but like always, Ghetto ain't miss a thing.

"What's so funny, ma?" He rose from his spot where he rested between my legs. His eyes followed mine and confusion could be seen all over his handsome face. "What? You ain't feelin' my spread!" He feigned surprise. "Come on now, stop frontin', lady, you know this fancy!" He chuckled before pointing at a bowl that was filled to the brim with hot Cheetos.

"Who don't rock with hot Cheetos, ma, where you say you from again?" He made a goofy face before pointing out sliced apples with caramel drizzled all over them. "Apples? Caramel? Huh, yea, you gotta feel that! What 'bout this?" He picked up a Styrofoam cup filled with sour apple stringed candy. He pulled one of the long candies free and held it in front of my face. "So you don't remember these, mane? I know you ain't too bougie for these boys!" He laughed at the face I made. "Hold up!" he shouted before using his free hand to scroll through his phone until he found what he was looking for. Aaliyah's "Missing You" began to play. I didn't know why, but he always played it when we were alone.

"Now, where were we?" He smiled before placing one end of the stringed candy into his mouth and—

"Hmmm!" He encouraged me to do the same with the other end. I giggled as I humored him, and there, as that golden butterfly fluttered around our heads, we raced to see who'd make it to the middle of that candy first. I couldn't tell who won, but the moment our lips

248

met in the middle, the child in my stomach must've known it. The kick made Ghetto jump in surprise. I laughed while he rubbed my belly. Who would've ever thought a gangsta like him could be so loving?

***

"Black Lives!"
"Matter!"
"Black Lives!"
"Matter!"
"Black Lives!" a strong, light-skinned sister shouted to the hyped crowd.

"Matter!" they responded to her power. The cities of Dallas and Fort Worth were on fire and filled with a cry for justice. There'd been another police killing. A man by the name of George Floyd had been murdered by a Minneapolis police officer, and the people were in an unrest. "Justice for Brella Tyson, we—want justice!" someone shouted from the crowd. Though the city was outraged behind the most recent murder of a man of color, the no-knock warrant that had stolen the woman's life was a fuel that would push the flames across the state. Stores were being plundered and other places of business were being set ablaze in an attempt to make their voices be heard, but for all the protests in the world, Donald Trump seemed to only understand more violence.

"You won't keep killing our people and we just stand by and watch! Today, we take a stand for Breonna Taylor, for Tamir Rice, we stand for Freddie Gray, Sandra Bland, Eric Garner! Today, we fight for Trayvon, Douglas Luis, and Breonna!" the light-skinned sista shouted as she pumped a clenched fist in the air. The group of twenty protesters was gathered outside of a Dallas courthouse and was surrounded by a platoon of fully suited task force officers. The protesters held up painted signs with words like *I can't breathe*, *Black lives matter*, and *Stop police brutality!* Catrina, Heaven's only sibling, was right there in the thick of things. Life had taken its toll on her and Queen just wanted to fight for something, *anything!*

"Our people matter! We won't bend to your Jim Crow laws; the times of Bull Connor is over! Power to—"

Pow! The crack of a rifle echoed through the air and cut the woman's plight short. At first, all was still as the confusion set in, but the cries and agony of the fallen woman brought all eyes to her fallen body. She'd hit the ground hard before balling up in the fetal position. The rubber bullet that had struck her rested a foot away from her weeping body. The eyes of the officers shifted to their comrade that had fired the shot, and the tension rose in the air as they battled with their loyalty to the force and humane principality. Catrina's blood began to boil, and before she could stop herself, she'd reached down and took her bottled water off the ground. Without a second thought, she hurled it at the closest officer she could find, and that set off a trickle of violence that would end with blood shed.

"Fuck the police! Black lives matter!" she shouted as if the mantra was her war cry.

***

"Aye, partner, I think we've got something here," the detective spoke before taking a sip from his coffee cup. The feds were in alliance with the BRPD in accordance of the state's bank robberies, and Detective Scott and his partner were front and center. The cluttered office was filled with overdue files and a collage of pinned photos. Scott sat behind the desk and didn't even give his partner the decency of looking up as he read over paperwork his chief had requested earlier that morning.

"Not right now, Bud, I'm trying to finish up the report on the search and seizure ordeal we conducted on the Rivera guy last week. The cock sucker was busted red handed with a hundred and thirty pounds of smoke, and now his lawyer is screaming foul for the S and S. Geez!" he huffed. His partner, Mallory, smiled before tossing a stack of papers on the desk, directly on top of the report he was so bent on finishing.

"What the hell, Mallory, didn't I just—"

"I think that'll put a fire under your ass," his partner cut him off before taking another sip from his coffee. Scott studied him for a brief moment before his eyes fell to the paper.

"This better be good, man, the chief is…" His words trailed off again as he read the bold print. A slight frown eased onto his face the more he read. *Could it be?* he thought as the taste for the hunt made his mouth water.

A string of deadly heists in the Dallas/Ft. Worth area leaves a trail through the metroplex. The culprits are calculating and deadly and have… He stopped reading as his eyes shot up to find the triumphant smirk on his partner's face. Everyone knew how bad Detective Scott wanted to nail the evasive Devonte Bousard, AKA, Ghetto, but the man had always been one step ahead of him. He thought he'd caught a break with the bank robbery, but not only did the man have loyal friends that were willing to take the needle for him, but the entire RNO family seemed to have up and disappeared into thin air. He returned his partner's smile.

"You don't think this is who I think it is, do you?"

251

Chapter 23
The Cards Don't Lie

-Heaven-
Sat. Night 8 P.M.

For some reason, my spirit was troubled, and the baby just wouldn't be still in my stomach. I rubbed my hand in a circular motion to soothe him. "Be still, Kalief, what's wrong with you boy?" I asked as if he could answer me. I sat Indian style on our big suede couch as I shuffled the cards of fate. Ever since I was younger, whenever something troubled me, I dealt the cards, searching for answers that they may or may not have to offer. Ghetto was in the shower, preparing to go to some sort of dog fight, and Egypt was on her way to keep me company.

I finished the shuffle and peeled the first card from the deck. *The card of love!* The depiction of a clear stream flowing through a sacred heart caused me to smile. I'd surely found the notion. The next card was a strange depiction of an old castle door being unlocked, and I knew it was the card of endless possibilities. I smiled as I flipped the next card, and as soon as my eyes captured the image of the weeping woman, clutching a soggy handkerchief to her bosom, my heart began to gallop in my chest. *The card of powerful loss?*

It had never been in my reading before, and as I wondered its implications, Ghetto strutted into the room as if he were a key model for Gucci. The tree-bark brown Gucci pants were ideal with the forest-green Gucci shirt and loafers. His dreads were twisted back into two thick braids and he complemented the look with his famous Cartier lenses. The golden frames glistened as his eyes fell to the cards laid out before me. *Aww shit!* his gaze seemed to say when his eyes lifted to meet my worried one.

"Why can't you just stay at home tonight, baby? It'll be other dog fights." My thoughts slipped from my lips in a whiny plea. Ghetto's chuckle pissed me off even after he made his way over to me and planted a soft kiss against my forehead. It was just like a man to not heed the power of a woman's intuition.

"Stop worrying so much, Queen. I'll be back before you even notice I'm gone. I'm just gone thug wit' the guys and I'll be right back in your arms, I promise, Lady," he promised before kissing my lips and attempting to pull away. But I wasn't trying to hear it. I wrapped my arms around his neck and held tight.

"Papi, something just don't feel right. Just stay, Pa, *please*," I begged. I held him loosely while gazing up into his dark eyes, and as I willed my vision to reveal to him what I didn't know how to verbalize, Kalief began going crazy in my womb. He must have felt it, because Ghetto's eyes fell to my stomach before returning to me questioningly.

"See, even your son feels it. Baby, listen to me, if you go out there tonight, somethin' bad is gonna happen. Ghetto, just listen to me, Pa, *pleeease!* I can't explain it, but—" The sound of the door cut me off as my and Ghetto's eyes danced.

"You gonna get that or what's up?" The man's smile irked me to my core, and I had the mind to just let the bell ring as I held him. "You're too spoiled." He chuckled, and before I realized it, the man was tickling me in the spots only he knew the tenderness of.

"Stop, boy, you wrong, you so evil!" I giggled as I surrendered to his slick tactics. "Stooooop, you're gonna make me pee, baby!" I cried, and before I knew it, he'd kissed my stomach and headed to answer the door. Moments later, I heard the door open and—

"Heeeey, bro, where my girl at?" Egypt's cheerful voice filled the room. I didn't know what his response was, but when my girl found her way into the living room, Ghetto wasn't with her.

"Heeyyy, Ms. Thang, how's my favorite girl and my godson?" She hugged me before air kissing both sides of my face. I smiled, always happy to see one of my girls. Though I'd left the life and squared up, I could tell that the hustle didn't stop.

"Hey, girl, you lookin' good," I gushed as she stepped back and spun slow on her six-inch heels.

"You liiiiike, you like?" she sang as I admired the one-piece Moschino suit she wore. It was multi-colored with the Hello Kitty

253

image plastered in numerous places all over it. My eyes fell to the pink, peep-toe Tims on her feet, the six-inch heel was more of a golden spike, and when my eyes lifted to find hers, the crooked smile alone told me all I needed to know. *Lick money!* We shared a sisterly laugh as I looked toward the front door. "Where'd Ghetto go, I know he ain't leave?" My heart began to pound in my chest as I fixed my gaze on her. Egypt rolled her eyes before slipping her heels off and plopping down beside me on the imported couch.

"Damn, bitch, let that man breathe. You done had 'em cooped up in this big ass house playin' house for months." She didn't understand that my worry was on one hundred until she looked at me. "Heaven, why are you lookin' at me like that?" My girl stared at me with the *Bitch, what's wrong with you!* face. Kalief began moving in my stomach as I climbed to my feet and began rubbing my belly.

"Something bad is gonna happen, Egypt, I feel it! I need to stop him, Ghetto is in trouble!"

Heaven Got a Ghetto

Chapter 24
Cold World

The pit was deep out in the country of East Texas, and the old cat that sponsored the dog fights had become like an uncle to me. Clifton Shorter was an old OG that had been in the game since the late seventies, and only the old heads that he dealt with knew the man was movin' more dope throughout the states than Frank Lucas and Bumpy Johnson were back in the gap. He usually didn't rock with anyone under the age of forty, but the man had a soft spot for a real nigga and knew I was beyond my years. I'd parked the whip out in the large field he'd reserved for parking, and for as far as the eye could see, candy-painted foreign cars sat side by side out on the sundried grass.

Rolls, a few Continentals, Lams, and even a Bugatti Chiron was on deck, and as I stepped to the entrance of the converted warehouse the man had transformed into a sizable gentlemen's club, I wondered how he also was creative enough to have a lower level installed. *That's* where he hosted his famous dog fights, and as I knocked on the steel-enforced door, I laughed to myself. "Ole Clifton is as noid as a dopefiend in a crack house that's been up too long," I whispered as the door slid open to reveal a Wrestlemania-built cat I knew as Brick, and as I reached my hand out to greet fam, I almost lost it.

Snap! A drooling mouth of razor-sharp teeth snapped at me as a monstrous bridled pit bull lunged at my neck. "Woah, Boy, easy, easy." Brick yanked back on the thick chain he had attached to the spiked collar around the dog's neck. I jumped back, my hand inching toward the strap on my waist. If that boy hadn't calmed that beast down, I planned to knock its brains all over that floor.

"What's good, Ghetto, long time no see, Homie. The ole man's missed you." Brick smiled real big and my eyes fell down to the monster he had on that leash. It had simmered down and sat back on its hunches as the man stroked it behind its ears. I nodded after the dog licked its chops and gazed up at me curiously. We'd recognized the predator in each other, and only then did I acknowledge the big man.

"No doubt, Brick, shit been crazy in my world, my dude, but ain't nothin' to a boss." I gave him a genuine smile before extending him the forty-dollar cover charge, and an extra fifty to let me slide through with my burna. I laughed as he pocketed the loot before he and his dog stepped to the side to allow my entry. As soon as I entered the spot, the smells of the nightlife hit me head on. I knew that if I continued to go straight, I'd find myself standing in the center of butt naked extravaganza, where naked women danced in cages. I took a left toward the restrooms and entered the coed room. To the unwelcomed, the place was merely a spot to relieve themselves, but for the VIPs, we knew the business.

I made my way to the last stall and paused as I smirked up at the camera lens that was positioned directly on that stall. My eyes fell to the out of order sign on the door until I heard the automatic lock click and the stall door pop open. I stepped in before resecuring the door and fixing my eyes on the spot where the toilet was supposed to be. The steel door had a sizable slit for a peephole and after I knocked, the slider slid back to reveal a dark pair of eyes.

"What!" a gruff voice demanded. I held up my fist so he could see the ring I wore with the dog fights crest on it, and after a quick inspection, the hatch was closed and the bolts that held the door shut were loosened. The steel door swung open to reveal another muscled cat, but unlike Brick, my boy Zeus was a true playa. My eyes swept over the Balmain shirt, and his slacks were crisp and accessorized by a playa's pair of Giorgio Brutini loafers.

"What ya know good, young blood, they said you'd shown up," he greeted as we embraced. I saluted the love as I stepped through the door and into another world. The door led back outside, but to the back of the establishment. The area was fenced off and made into a sizable octagon. At least two hundred people crowded the pit below where I found the man of the hour standing over a bloodied and mangled dog. The animal laid on its side, staring absently into the hyped crowd, and as I watched, ole man Clifton Shorter reached

Renta

inside his Armani suit coat and slipped a snubbed-nose pistol into his grasp. He aimed at the barely breathing dog, and as he used his free hand to place a wet, half-smoked cigar between his teeth— "Well, ole boy, you've outlived ya glory days, get ya some rest," he spoke before—*Boca!*

He pulled the trigger and put the poor creature out of its misery. Zeus shook his head while making a cross over his chest as if he were a Catholic. The man dropped his head and said a silent prayer, and I followed suit. Everyone knew that Clifton Shorter loved that dog and it had won him a lot of money. Zeus slapped me on the shoulder before turning to re-bolt the door.

"Gone on over there, you know the ole man will be glad to see ya." He nodded once he was finished. I saluted fam before making my way through the hyped crowd. I could tell there was big money in the spot as familiar faces came into view, and as I made it to the front of the action, I felt lucky.

"God damn, foreign mutt done made me kill my damn dog!" Clifton spat as I made my way beside him. Two young cats that worked for the old man removed the dead dog as another youngin' began to use a rake to go over the coursed dirt to cover up the puddles of blood that stained the ground.

"What's the bidness, OG, ruff night, huh?" I shouted over the ear-splitting noise. Clifton glanced over his shoulder at me as he counted out thirty crisp one-hundred-dollar bills from a thick stack he held. The old man merely shook his head in frustration before handing the three bands to another man about his age who I could tell was happy to accept his winnings.

"I told ya that my ole chow dog was a monster, Clifton Shorter. Maybe next time you'll bring out somethin' more elite, eh." The man seemed humbled, but the jab was noticed. Clifton pulled the cigar from between his teeth and spat on the ground. His glare spoke volumes as he sent a silent message to the other OG. If it was any other dog, he may not have been so tender, but the man had had a special love for ole Spike. The other man held his hands up in surrender before disappearing into the crowd, and only then did Clifton return his attention to me.

"Mu'fuckas don't got no respect these days." He shook his head. I allowed my eyes to be blessed by the old head's attire, and I was able to appreciate the quiet boss shit he oozed. The olive-green Kangol matched the linen shirt, and the mint-green Ferragamo slacks sat perfectly atop the olive-green Ferragamo boots. I nodded my appreciation as the older man's vision ran from my head to my Gucci kicks. "And where's your slick ass been for these past few months, G? I've been hearin' some things in the streets, and they've not been too appealing to the ears, I tell ya that!" His words were more of a probing inquisition than an accusation, and I nodded my agreement as my eyes found the pit.

On the left-hand side, one of the young cats that had carried the slain dog out the arena held the leash of a massive, grayish-blue furred pit bull. The animal bared its sharp teeth as drool dripped from both sides of its powerful jaws as it stretched the thick chain in an attempt to get at its opponent. My eyes flickered to the far-right corner of the pit where a black and white-spotted mutt of a dog sat back on its haunches, his furry tail lazily slapping against the dirty ground as it watched the other dog. I frowned. *What the fuck kinda dog is this? It looks like they found a dog and just tossed him in the pit!* My thoughts were comical.

"Yea, things have been crazy, OG, but the entire year of 2020 has been ugly, huh. You hear 'bout that Covid shit they sayin' has hit us?" I asked him. He nodded before—

"Hey, Cliff, what ya say, I got twenty-five on the pit?" someone shouted from the crowd. The old man's eyes traveled toward the pit and fell upon the aggressive pit bull before drifting to the docile mutt. He studied it for a mere few seconds before nodding with a crooked smirk.

"I'll take the bet and put an extra five to make the gamblin' live!" he shouted, and at the mention of his foolish bet, it seemed as if everyone in that vicinity began shouting in an attempt to get in on the bet. I gave the OG a strange expression before my vision drifted to the spotted dog. It still sat, wagging its tail, tongue hanging out of its mouth like the growls and antics of the other dog meant nothing.

"What you gonna do, Young blood, you gonna get in on some of this good money or continue to stare upside my head?" Ole Clifton proposed as my eyes returned to him as a pitch-black brotha I knew as Clark came over and began marking the bets down on a small spiral notebook while collecting all the wagers for the OG. He was Clifton's bookie and a vicious henchman that had stood beside the old man for years. After a brief moment of silently cursing him and shaking my head in frustration, I dug in my pocket and freed a roll of six grand. I peeled three from the stack and grudgingly held it out to Clark.

"I'm in wit' this ole nut case." I placed my bet. The OG had never led me astray, and I knew he hadn't survived a dirty game with millions of illegal dollars by being foolish, so three bands wasn't shit to give to the gamble.

"I see ya boy has been having a good night," he spoke with a nod toward the other side of the pit. My eyes followed his indication, and that's where I found my boy Stick Talk. He had a winner's stack of money in his hand as he took a deep pull from a blunt he held between his lips. As if he could feel my eyes on him, Stick's eyes found me from across the smokey pit at the same time the dogs were let loose.

Grrrrr! Growls could be heard over the loud ruckus of the crowd, and to mine, and I'm sure, the rest of the crowd's, amazement, the spotted mutt took off running toward the menacing dog with the same hunger for beef as its opponent showed only moments ago. The two dogs crashed into each other in a clash of snapping teeth and sharp claws, but my eyes were fixated on the woman beside Stick Talk. I hadn't set eyes on the punk bitch since the night she and Heaven stuck us for our business, and truth be told, on the strength of Heaven, I had put the loss behind me. Empress's eyes found mine as she pulled a cherry Blow Pop from her lips, and as Stick Talk turned to take another bet, the snake bitch blew me a wet kiss. I gritted my teeth against the urge to rush over and put one in her dome.

"What's all that about, youngsta, why would ya man's lady friend be blowin' you sweet kisses? The look in ya eyes tells me that it's more out of a taunt than it is flirtation," Clifton leaned over and shouted in my ear. At that moment, the vicious pit bull's teeth sunk into the neck of the dog I'd placed my bet on and began to shake it viciously.

"It ain't shit, OG, I just ain't feelin' the broad, and she knows it," I replied, but knew my excuse sounded lame. A quick glance at the ole man let me know it hadn't fooled him either, yet he merely placed the wet cigar back between his teeth and nodded. He watched as the pit bull threatened the six grand we'd put up as our dog whined, scratching at the other dog's face as if that would help.

"See, young buck, the thang about these dog fights is, you never know which beast will prevail. Both dogs go in, not knowing why they're fighting, just knowing that death is the only conclusion. See, people are just like that. We fight for a chance to live and really don't know what we want to live for. So, we do what's natural to us, we fight! We fight to live and sometimes life kicks us in the ass over and over again until we're broke with no purpose, but..." he paused as the spotted dog's sharp nails dug into the bigger dog's left eye. The pit bull shook a few more times before releasing the smaller dog with a yelp, and before it could recover, the smaller dog's teeth sunk into its snout. The pit shook loose before lunging for another death grip, but the smaller dog dodged and went for the bigger dog's hind leg. The snap of the bone as the spotted mutt's jaws clenched tight around the leg could be heard throughout the assembly.

"Aw, hell naw, come on, man!"

"Boooo!" the crowd shouted as the pit fell back in pain, but the smaller dog was relentless in its attack. It shook its head as it gnawed on the other dog's leg. Clifton Shorter had a crooked grin on his face as he spoke to me.

"We still fight, Young Blood, we fight because that's all we know. One never knows their purpose until they've either won or lost the fight, because it's only in the value of what one has fought to lose or win that they realize the worth of the fight as a whole," he was saying as I put a hand to his arm and turned to disappear into the crowd. The OG gave me a questioning look, but all I could tell him was to gather my bread as the owner of the pit bull began screaming for the dog fight to be brought to a stop. Clifton Shorter chuckled before glancing back at me. "Wha-what's goin' on, Ghetto? You—" he was saying, but I was on a mission. Empress had just received a call and had excused herself for privacy. *I got ya ass now!* My mental was dark waters, though I didn't know what I was gonna do when I caught lady one on one.

***

-Heaven-

"You said you wanted to learn how to suck dick, right?" Egypt asked with a smirk and a raised brow. I rolled my eyes at the girl. We'd been in the kitchen, practicing how to please a man with a banana. I'd thrown up three times already, my gag reflexes just weren't on my side. I'd called Ghetto over and over again, only to get the same result, the voicemail, and he knew how much the shit irked my last nerve!

"Noooo, bitch, not like that. Look, let me see." Egypt took the large banana from me and carried it over to the sink to wash it off. "See, it takes a big girl to properly suck a nice dick, sis. Most bitches think they know what they're doin' just 'cause they get the nut they'd worked so hard for, but no, Heaven, sucking dick takes *skill*, baby. A man will nut if you blindfold him and place his pipe in *anything* warm with a little movement, but only a boss bitch knows how to truly please her man and make that mu'fucka *explode!* See, imagine this is his dick and here's his nuts." She held the curved fruit by its end and pointed at the end tip to indicate where the man's testicles would be.

Egypt ran a finger along the inside of the banana. "Every man's cock has a thick vein running underneath it. It controls the blood that circulates through it that brings it to life. See, if you grip the dick right here, it slows the blood flow and creates a pleasurable pain for his ass, so while you hurt him, you have to make that pain the *best* pain he's ever felt," she spoke as if she was teaching me dick 101. I watched my sis place about two inches of the fruit in her mouth before bobbing her head in a circular motion. I made a face with a scrunch of my nose.

"Unnnn, girl, you so nasty!" I sang as Egypt's freak ass began to make wet sounds with her mouth. I suppressed a giggle because the woman was oh so serious about her business.

"You have to pay special attention to the head, kiss that mu'fucka!" she spoke over a mouthful of the banana. *Smop!* She made a popping noise as she pulled away, and I didn't know if she was playing, but Queen extended the bruised piece of fruit to me as if I was gonna place my mouth back on it. Again, I scrunched my nose and lips before pushing her hand away.

"*Ugh.*" I made my way over to the fruit basket I kept on the counter before choosing another banana and turning to face her.

"Ugh, bougie much!" She rolled her eyes before tossing the first banana in the trash. "Really, bish, don't be actin' like my mouth nasty. We've eaten off the same forks most our lives and—"

"And you wasn't giving those forks sloppy head either," I cut her off before she could remind me of some of the stupid things we'd done while growing up fast.

"Well, you're right about that, but don't be acting like just because I've tasted more *exotic*"—Egypt used her fingers to form quotation marks—"parts of a man's anatomy than just his lips and tongue, that my mouth is unsanitary. Bish, ain't nothin' wrong with tastin' a little protein. It keeps the skin smooth!" My nasty ass homegirl ran her manicured hands down the sides of her pretty face like she wanted me to see how milky her flawless, mocha skin was. I laughed as she began to make her tongue dart in and out of her mouth like a snake before becoming serious.

"Ok, now you try it. The tip of the dick is the most sensitive part of the male organ, Heaven, and—"

"What about his balls?" I cut her off again. I was curious of every way to pleasure my man. Though I was a master of seduction, I was as clueless as Stacy Dash in the movie when it came to sex. Egypt repaid me in kind as she scrunched her nose and gave me that

Bitch, you so nasty! face. I blushed but wasn't ashamed of my curiosity. If I didn't do it, some other bitch would surely be glad to do it for my man.

"The nuts are a weird thing, sis. Some men like them sucked, some enjoy them licked, and many find it painful. My specialty is *all* tongue, baby. You can never go wrong with your tongue!" She began flickering her tongue again as I placed the banana to my lips. I planned to suck Ghetto's dick so good his dreads would stand up on his head and dance like the snakes on Medusa's head.

***

-Ghetto-

I found the treacherous woman weaving in and out from between cars, I assumed she was heading for her own. I stalked at a safe distance, blending in with the night as pieces of lady's phone convo carried on the wind.

"What you mean the nigga on to you?" She sounded frustrated. I shook my head in amazement. *This hoe stay on the extracurricular!* I thought as she stopped at a soft pink Shelby super snake Mustang, that had two white racing stripes running down the middle of it. The white twenty-twos that bitch squatted on made the car's sex appeal stand out in the lot of exotic whips. I eased the tool off my waist as I crept up behind lady.

"Well, don't even sweat it, I'm on my way and…" Her words trailed off as the steel kissed the back of her head and for a moment, my mind carried me back to the night I'd caught Heaven down bad in that same fashion.

"All it will take is the slightest addition of pressure and your noodles will add another color to this pretty paint job you have on this car. Give me the phone," I whispered between clenched teeth. I could hear whoever was on the other line asking who I was, and Empress's silence only made their inquisition more urgent. Lady was a killa, but a smart one. She moved slow as she handed me the iPhone that I dropped to the dry ground.

"Empress? What's up, sis, are you ok?" the caller was asking before I stamped down onto the phone's face. Twice-three times until the screen shattered and there was no more life in that bitch, and to my surprise, Empress's body trembled as she broke down into sobs. My heart was crooked. I didn't give a fuck 'bout all that. My eyes scanned the lot for witnesses, I was gonna do lady that night.

"Turn around and face me, but move slow, huh. This bitch stays horny and I love to finger fuck her." I wanted her to look me in the eyes the way she did the night she stood over me with evil intent. The bitch did as she was told, and that's when I got the second surprise of that night. Where I'd mistaken her tremble as sobbing, the bitch was actually laughing uncontrollably. I frowned at the realization as I kept the banga aimed at her noggin.

Oh, this bitch think I'm pussy, huh? My grip tightened around that steel as her mockery fed the urge I had to do her.

"Nigga, you thought you were smarter than *me*, huh?" she shouted as she stood up straight and faced off with me.

"Just like every other nigga, but I'm—" she was saying before my hand found its way around her neck. I squeezed the rest of her disrespect down her throat as my finger tightened around the trigger.

"I-hate-you!" she rasped, sensing what was coming next.

"Yea, tell me about it when we meet again in hell. Tell Hurk I send my love," I growled and squeezed the trigger. *Boom!*

Confusion and pain surged through me as I released the bitch and spun in the opposite direction. My side was on fire as blood poured out of me, and as Empress climbed back up from where she'd fallen, I knew it wasn't my gun that had gone off.

"Nigga, fuck, what you doin', Stick?" I growled as I clutched my side to slow the flow of blood. Stick Talk stood there, eyes wide, as he aimed his tool at *me*!

"What the fuck is up, Flesh, you-you was 'bout to dome my gal?" he asked as his eyes drifted to Empress, who was attempting to catch her breath.

"Nigga, you shot *me*? Bruh, *this* hoe is the one that stuck us that night, she—"

"Don't believe him, Bae, the nigga followed me out here and tried to push up on me. I told him I got a man and even asked him why he'd had you set up. He was tryin' to kill me 'cause—"

"Shut the fuck up!" Stick shouted as he swung the pistol back and forth between me and that snake hoe. I could see it in Bro's eyes, he didn't know who to trust. I knew the shit looked suspect finding me hemming his thot up, but I couldn't understand why he'd shot *me!* Sometime in between him popping me and me turning to face off with him, Empress had gotten her car door open and I noticed how the punk bitch was half in and half out the car.

"Fam, this shit not how it 'pose to go. Somebody lyin', mane, and—"

"You just gonna believe this nigga ova me, huh? Nigga, this bitch ass nigga has you so brainwashed that you don't even see the betrayal! Why ain't he tell you this shit before *now* instead of followin' me out here on some sneaky shit! Huh?" Her words did it to him, and at that moment, I realized that in a lot of instances, a man could love the wrong bitch for the right reasons. *Fuck it!* I thought as I used every ounce of strength I could muster to turn and lift the tool to finish what I'd intended to do out the gate.

Empress attempted to dive into the car as the tool burped in my hand. *Boca! Boca!* I fired, but—*Boom!* Another hot ball of fire knocked me against the car, splashing a slash of my blood against its feminine paint. *Boom! Boom!* I fell to my knees when the other two slugs lit my back up. The tool fell from my hand, and while taking some of the hottest, hardest, and most painful breaths I'd ever taken, I left a bloody handprint against the side of the car as I used it as support to turn around to face my killa.

As soon as I faced him, I fell back against the car, sliding and leaving a dark smear of blood down its side as I fell to the ground, back against the earth, and only my head resting against the bottom of the car. I stared up at the nigga I'd brought into the fold and began to love like a brother. Our eyes met in the midst of tainted love. My vision blurred as water filled them before sliding down the sides of my face. The pain of his betrayal hurt more than the slugs he'd filled me with, and as Empress climbed from the car and rushed over to him, I spoke the only word that came to mind.

"Heaven!" I rasped as I gazed up at the stars.

"Baby, I love you, I love you!" Empress cried as she clung to dude. I smiled my last smile as my breath disappeared and I faded to black. *Punk bitch played a nice game!* was my last thought.

***

-Heaven-
Three hours later

The people of Minneapolis are in an outrage over another senseless murder. An African American man by the name of George Floyd was murdered by a white Minneapolis police officer and...

"What's going on with you, child?" I asked in irritation. Kalief was going crazy in my womb and had snatched my attention away from the ten o'clock news. I sat with my feet pulled up underneath me, curled up on one corner of the couch as Egypt sat on the other side, shaking her head in disbelief at the TV.

"This shit is becoming outrageous. I mean, these dirty ass pigs are just killing us and—"she was saying before her phone cut her off. As if he could hear the phone, the child I carried in my womb began kicking like he knew karate. I rubbed my stomach, attempting to sooth him. "What's up, sissy?" Egypt answered her phone as I slid from the couch and headed for the kitchen. I had to find something to snack on, maybe that was the boy's problem.

"Yeah, I'm here with her right now, why, what's up?" I heard Egypt speak into the phone as I made my way to the freezer. I opened the steel door and pulled out a tub of vanilla ice cream, before reaching into the fridge and grabbing a bottle of ketchup. I made me a nice bowl of the frozen cream before squirting a few splashes of the red condiment on top. At that moment, Egypt came in being nosey.

"Don't judge me!" I laughed without looking up. "Blame it on the baby, sis, I just—" I was saying as I dipped my spoon into the cream and lifting it to my lips. I glanced up before taking a taste, and that's when things turned strange. Egypt stood there gazing down at the tiled floor and when her eyes lifted, Kalief gave me a sharp kick that caused me to drop the bowl. It seemed as if everything took on a slow-motion effect as I watched the porcelain dish tilt as it fell, and shatter against the floor. Red and white splashed everywhere as my eyes made a slow return to Egypt, tears dripping from her eyes as she shrugged her shoulders as if to say *I don't know what I'm supposed to do!*

"Egypt," I began as my eyes seemed to find interest in everything around me, but her. "Why are you crying?" I asked as my vision recaptured her. Egypt reached out for me, but my glare made her fingertips fall short.

"I'm-I'm sorry, Heaven, I'm so-so sorryyy!" she began to cry so hard that she trembled. Her bloodshot eyes were red in agony.

"Bitch, if you don't tell me what's..." my words died in my throat as a world of craziness began to steal my sanity.

"Ma, you're live at this shit. I mean, where'd you learn the theatrics, the monotone, the serious look?" He laughed the first time I'd first read him what the cards of providence foretold. The night of the Omega party that seemed so long ago, I could see the card, the hands of death, as clear as I could that night. We sat at that table. My mind a tornado as I reflected on the last words he'd spoken before he left. "Stop worrying so much, Queen, I'll be back before you even know I'm gone. I'm just gone thug with the guys and I'll be right back in your arms, I promise, lady." The words were now a taunt of his love, his broken promises.

His love that I could *feel* was about to be snatched from me. My hands clenched into tight fists as I began to shake my head *No!*

"Egypt?" I began while attempting to see beyond the river in my eyes. "Where's, Ghetto?" The words slipped from my lips as I watched one of the toughest women I'd ever met, shatter into a thousand pieces. Egypt's hands cupped her pretty lips as if she could hold her pain in.

"He's gone, baby. Ghetto, he-he's dead, sis."

Heaven Got a Ghetto

Part 3

I wonder if Heaven gotta Ghetto?

When I die? Bury me a real nigga ...

Know that though I was imperfect, my love was boundless and I've always kept it real with cha, and ...

I wonder if Heaven gotta Ghetto?

For my niggas, my brothas? I want y'all to murder the nigga that murdered me... Toss an ounce of exotic in my casket, my FN, and an extra clip just in case I wake up to meet the devil that was waitin' for me to fall asleep.

I wonder if Heaven gotta Ghetto?

Baby? I don't want you to give my pussy to another nigga, but life is life, so all I ask is that you never fuck anotha nigga in my clique ...

Never forget how we thugged, and always keep it one hunnid... the stance of a real bitch.

There's always been a thin line between fuck shit and morality...

A big difference between a nigga that's just livin' to die in comparison to a man seeking immortality.

Damn... I wonder if Heaven gotta Ghetto?

I've always had a problem with believing in God 'cause I can't see the nigga sitting amongst the sun, moon, and stars...

Having the power to change the cards but allowing a solid man to have a play a crooked hand.

Heart black from loss... Black man crucified to the cross... rollin' the dice with fate, damn, my nigga, I just wanted to ball and fuck off a couple hunnid bands.

Maybe travel to distant lands...sit down with Jesus, Muhammad, whoever can make me understand.

I wonder if Heaven gotta Ghetto.

If it does? I hope I can meet Biggie and Pac, listen to Aaliyah, the song of her choosing...

Heaven Got a Ghetto

I'd get Trayvon, Sandra Bland, George Floyd, Breonna Taylor, and the rest of our people and tell 'em how their lives created a beautiful movement. But?

That's only if Heaven gotta Ghetto.

Renta

Chapter 25
Heaven Gotta Ghetto

-Ghetto-

A place to spend my quiet nights/Time to rewind, so much pressure in this life of mine/Quiet times I once contemplated suicide, and would've tried, but I held that iron, all I could see was my mother's eyes/No one knows my struggle, they only see the trouble, not knowing it's hard to carry on when no one loves you/Imagine me inside misery and poverty, no other man has ever witnessed struggles I've survived.

I could hear the sounds of Tupac's "Thug Mansion" in the distance, and it caused my eyes to fly open in alarm.

"Hey, Mr., you gonna stay sleep all day or get up and do something! My mama said-my mama said, if you sleep all day, you can't get no work done!" A child's voice caused me to blink and attempt to focus. The sun was bright as I blinked against it and tried to gather my wits. The last thing I remembered was— "Well?" The little boy was persistent and didn't seem to care about the last thing I remembered.

"I'm up, lil' one, I'm up." I sat up in confusion as I glanced around. To my surprise, I was on a long white bench, and as my mind cleared, I realized that it was a bus stop! I'd somehow fallen asleep at a bus stop? There was a long street a few feet away, but it was empty, and as my eyes fell to the little dude, I wondered who he was and where the hell we were.

"Where am I?" I asked curiously. The boy couldn't be any more than seven, eight at the most. He wore a red and blue Polo, short set, with his hat turned backwards on his head.

"You in Heben, fool, duh!" He hit his forehead with the palm of his small hand, and I chuckled at his silliness. *Heben?* I thought as my eyes were drawn to the brightness of my clothes. *Fuck is Heben at?* My mental was a raging river of questions as I took in the Heaven-white dress shirt and silk vest I wore over a pair of soft linen Armani slacks. The soft-toed, ostrich-skinned quarter boots on

273

my feet were freaky, freaky, but the problem with it all was, I knew I didn't have either article in my closet.

"Come on, Mr., we're gonna be late!" the little boy shouted before taking off running down the street. I was too shocked to follow, but I watched as he ran, and he ran until he'd gone too far for me to see him. A soft breeze blew as I returned my gaze to my attire, even the jewels I wore were lit.

"Heben?" I whispered, trying to remember if it was the name of a street I'd visited at one point in my life.

"Heaven, I think that was what Tamir was trying to say." His voice was deep and came out of nowhere and caused me to jump in surprise. My mouth fell open at the sight of dude. It wasn't the fact of me feeling the pure white Canali tux with the matching Berluti loafers that adorned his feet, and shid, it wasn't even the fact that the man had just materialized beside me out of thin air. Yet, the thing that stole my breath and convinced me that I was lost in some sort of dream was the fact that I was staring at a replica of myself! My reflection's dreads were as white as snow and hung loose, down past his shoulders.

As I studied him, I noticed the only difference between our physical was in age. My reflection was merely an older version of myself with a pencil-thin goatee. Dude appeared beside me as a gentleman. He sat with his right ankle crossed over his left knee as he read a *newspaper!* My eyes flickered to the heading and I almost laughed. *The world's prayers!* it read.

"Heaven? Mane, I ain't ever heard of no Heaven Street and, Bruh, this business is getting freakier by the second. Who are you, fam?" I was ready to get back to *my* Heaven, and away from all the unfamiliar, but playboy merely chuckled and continued to read his paper.

"Ok, let's see, Tonya says that she just got laid off and she and her kids may be put out their apartment." Dude shook his head with a look of irritation on his face. "I *just* gave you that job after you quit the last one I gave you 'cause you didn't like the pay!" He seemed to be speaking to the paper. "Jason just got shot two seconds ago? Well, I sent him warning after warning about the life he chose to live. I'll allow him to live and send him a wife to see if she can straighten him out. Ok, Alexandria wants her husband free from prison, Tay still asking for me to aid him in getting a couple of bricks, huh? Ole Steve just had another car accident and will be paralyzed, and *ahhh...*" The man snapped his fingers as if he'd just figured out the answer to a problem. "Heaven Domingo, there she is!" He smiled before glancing at me with a sly smirk on his face.

"Say, my nigga, how the fuck you know my gal? Man, fuck all that, who the fuck are you, dude?" My temperature was up, and that itch in my palm had me ready to go for that tool. My reflection, the older version of me, smiled as if that gangsta bidness he saw in my pupils was nothing more than a harmless expression rather than a threat. He studied me for merely seconds before lifting his arm and glancing at his wrist. The *AP* was plain Jane, but even the lamest man knows that Audemars Piguets costs a check.

"Well, I have a little free time to answer your questions, I suppose, but know I'm a busy man, Mr. Devonte? Ghetto? Whichever name you're going by these days." *Fuck this boy know my name, fam?* I wondered, but I held my tongue. Dude was stalling and I was tempted to flip out on him.

"I created you, Ghetto. I'm the man, the deity, that you've been doubting your entire life!" Homie seemed to have read my mental. He extended the paper to me, our eyes battled as I attempted to figure out his play, but even when my intent was to leave his gesture unanswered, it was as if some unforeseen force made me accept it. I shook my head slightly, not understanding how he'd just done that, but decided it was all a part of the weird dream I was having.

Dude climbed to his feet as I opened the strange paper and allowed my vision to search for the only thang I was curious about. I scanned until—*Heaven Domingo!* Her name was written in bold red letters with the word *prayer* in parentheses and inscribed with a small cursive script beside it. *Heaven Domingo : A prayer for another chance at loving Ghetto*, it read. I glanced up for clarity and to my surprise, tears were racing down dude's face. Uncertainly, I made it to my feet at the same time my mental exploded in a collage of visions. *"What's the b-I, Blow, you know you can ask me whateva,"* I remembered telling Stick Talk the day at the park while Jamal ran the court. I could feel the sun as if I was back there that day.

"You believe in God, Ghetto?" he'd asked.

"My nigga, if there is a God, He don't give a fuck 'bout niggas like us." I'd spoken my heart.

"So, you don't believe in Heaven or hell?" Stick Talk questioned.

"Flesh, when we die, ain't no movin' on to no mansion in the sky wit' golden streets! Ain't no big ass fire waitin' for the big bad wolf, Stick Talk, when you dead, it's ova! Closed curtains!" I gave him my truths and before my eyes, an entirely different scene formed.

I was much younger, maybe nine years old, and Memaw Genevieve had sat me down on our old rickety porch, and as she sat down beside me, I knew she had some heavy shit on her mind. "Devonte, who were you talkin' to last night? I heard ya whispering and carrying on when I passed ya door, chile," she asked as I sat and ate the Fruit Roll-up she'd given me to snack on. I glanced up at her before shrugging.

"I don't know, Memaw, Mrs. Jackson told me that when I go to sleep, I 'pose to pray to God and He will give me a wish." I chewed the soft candy slowly as my eyes drifted out toward the still waters of the swamp that surrounded our spot. *"But, Him ain't give me nothin' yet, Granny."* My words were indifferent, but my grandmother had a point to prove. Genevieve popped me in the back of the head.

"Ouch, Memaw, why'd you do that!" I was confused as to why the hell I was getting hit for asking for a simple wish. My G-lady reached over and roughly took my chin between her thumb and pointer finger and forced me to look at her. My mouth and lips were sticky with the candy as I stared wide eyed at her.

"Boy, I bet not eva hear ya talking to ya self again! Ya hear me!" she spat, her gray eyes turned to slits. I nodded feverishly, even though I'd just told her I wasn't talking to myself! I was asking

God to grant my wish of blessing me with a lot of money so I could *move her out the slums. My eyes watered. At that age, a child's in-* *tent was somehow connected to his emotions, and he'd never un-* *derstand why he could be disciplined for something he didn't mean* *any harm in doing.* "The black man is God, Chile. You *are God,* *and don't ya let anyone tell ya different, ya hear me?"* I continued to nod, even though the vision had vanished, and I was back in the present, face to face with a crying, older version of myself.

"I am, son, I just am," he spoke, and in that instant, my mind decided to remind me of the betrayal of my nigga. My hands in-stinctively went to my side. I remembered the first slug Stick Talk had fired into me. My eyes grew wide as I recalled falling, dying! "Hell naw. Fuck naw!" I spat, and that's when shit got real. "Nigga, if you're sayin' you're *God*, you a hoe ass nigga!" I gritted as we faced off. Dude's eyes didn't change, but out of nowhere, the sun dimmed, and the wind became an angry hiss.

"Be conscious, Ghetto, of your words, son. Disrespect won't be tolerated here." God's voice was even, but firm. His white dreads began to sway in the wind, and right before my very eyes, the day became a dreary gray. The bench, the street, the *peace*, it all melted away, and to my astonishment, clouds formed around us. The clouds were dark pillows against the gray sky, and directly in be-tween me and the man, a streak of lightning struck and caused me to jump.

"Mannn," I drug the word out as I began slapping the sides of my face in an attempt at waking myself from the strange dream I seemed stuck within. My mouth was agape as the man that called himself God, cried, and as his tears fell from his face, my eyes fol-lowed their descent.

"Ahhhh! Ahhhhh, mane, wait, hold up, fam, wait!" I was last in my hysterics as I jumped from one foot to the other as if I was bare-foot, standing on hot coals. Glancing down, I realized that me and God were standing in mid-air, and his tears had created a storm be-neath our feet. There was a city below us and his tears, his tears became the rain that bathed it.

"I've given you chance after chance, Ghetto. I've watched as you killed, I let you steal, I allowed you to *live!*" His words calmed me. I studied dude for a moment, and as if the shit he'd just spoken had given me some sort of peace, I frowned. *Fuck it! If I can't wake up, I may as well play this shit out. It's just a dream!* I mentally told myself.

"Nigga, *what!*" I spat vehemently. "Chance?" I raised a brow in question. "Bruh, fuck *you* been my entire life, huh? While me and my fam was down there starvin', having to kill for a chance, that same chance you talm 'bout? Huh, my nigga? How you lettin' niggas get whacked by the niggas they love? Huh? Huh!" I was as hot as a tea kettle, and as the OG's eyes suddenly dried, something strange happened.

"Life is all about choices, Ghetto. Take a walk with me, young man, and I'll show you," God spoke, and before I could wrap my mind around what he was saying, I began to tumble through the sky.

***

-Ghetto-

"Ahhhhhh, come on, mane, come onnnn!" I cried as I fell and fell. The wind flying past my ears told me that I was falling at a devastating speed, and if I wasn't dead, I knew I would be soon. "Ahhhhhhh!" I shouted and—

"Ghetto! Ghetto?" I heard his voice nearby, and when I cracked my eyes open, I felt like a lil' bitch. God stood before me, watching me as if I hadn't just fallin' out the sky.

"Sayyy, dude, don't do that shit again, that ain't cool," I admonished. I began dusting myself off as if I hadn't just been screamin' like—

"God, I know I've done a lot of wrong, and, Heavenly Father, I don't deserve your love, but I feel like I'm dyinnnn', God! Please? *Please*, God, bring him back to me." I'd know her voice anywhere, anytime. I froze in mid-movement and glanced at God before allowing my eyes to take in the room. The grand piano, the gorilla trapped in the marble of the floor, and the imported furniture were all just as I'd left it. *My crib!* The reality of my situation was sinking in, and as soon as my eyes captured her, it was as if someone had doused a cold bucket of ice water in my face. *I'm dead? Like, I'm a ghost?* My mental was lost in a maze of roads like I couldn't seem to choose my route home from.

The only light source in the room was the four candles she'd lit. "Ghetto, you told me you'd never leave, *baby,* you-you said you love me, Pa, so why you leave me like this, huh?" Heaven cried as she hugged one of the soft pillows she'd used to decorate the couch. She sat with her legs pulled up underneath her as she rocked back and forth to the melody of her own cries. My heart cracked in my chest as I rushed over to her and fell to my knees in front of her.

"Heaven, chill, ma, chill, baby, I'm here. I'm right here," I soothed her, but the strangest thing happened when I reached forward to hug her. My arms passed *through* her, and I gasped as the feeling of air swam through my being.

"She can't hear you, youngin', she can't feel you, nor you her," God spoke. On my knees, my eyes becoming baptized in my own tears, I looked at him. The man didn't blink or look concerned with the pain a nigga was feeling. I turned back to my Queen, leaned forward, and brought my face inches from hers. I attempted to kiss her tears away, her pain was drowning a nigga.

"I'm here, bae, I swear—" I tried as my lips sunk into the side of her face. She merely continued to rock back and forth, hugging the pillow as if it was her last grip on sanity.

"Huh, Pa? Huh? Why though? Why you leave us-us, baby! I hate youuuu!" my earth shouted suddenly. I stared at her, perplexed. *Hate you, I hate you!* The words seemed to echo throughout the house.

"Naw, Heaven, don't say that, bae, I-I—"

"You said you were coming right back, Ghetto, you-you said you'd make it back home, baby, to me. You lied—You broke my heart." Heaven's pain pushed the river over my eyelids until the tears leaked down my face. Suddenly, I lost control and rushed to my feet. Without warning, I rushed Him, and as soon as I got close enough, I began to swing as hard as I could. I was so in tune with trying to knock His ass out, that I didn't notice that God had disappeared.

"Why? You didn't-have-to-fuck over-me like-this!" I growled as I swung. His silence was what allowed me to see beyond the wetness in my eyes. He wasn't there.

"*You* did this, bruh, *you* did this to the woman you love, the woman that loves you." His words came from behind me. I spun toward His voice, and as soon as I spotted His ass standing beside the piano, I lunged for Him. He disappeared once again as I crashed to the floor in a heap. I rushed back to my feet and knew that He was back in the spot I stood only moments ago, even without turning to look. My eyes fell back to the first and only woman I'd ever loved. Heaven rested her chin on the pillow as she cried.

"It ain't 'pose to end like this, fam, naw, not like this," I whispered as I glanced around at all the shit I'd acquired along my way of thuggin', the marbled floors, the floating staircase that led to the second floor, the cars, the loot? All that shit seemed so meaningless at that moment. I'd have traded it all for just one more shot at loving Queen. "Why you take me *now*, just when I found love, my dude? My child—My entire life you've done fucked-up shit, or at least watched it happen. Why? You know everythang before it happens, right? So why you let shit like this happen? Kids gettin' whacked, crooked ass police killin' my people, stillborn babies? Why, my nigga?" My words were low, but sincere. I glanced up at the man that called himself *God* and let Him see the pain drip from my eyelids. God studied me, His eyes too deep for me to understand its depths.

"Maybe you've been looking at things wrong, son. See, *everything* in this thing we call life has an ending. Stillborn babies you ask?" I watched the man pause and put His hands together to form a cupping motion as if He were about to cup water in His hands. Before my eyes, I watched a mirage of a miniature ocean form. God blew softly on the still water until it began to spin and spin until it became a twirling hurricane right in the palm of His hands.

"They'll call this hurricane Laura." He glanced up at me. The miniature storm had his face aglow with a grayish-blue hue. "Sometimes, Ghetto, the beginning of a life *is* the ending of that life. It's not always *I* that takes the life, nor *I* that creates the storm. People search for reasons in all things, Ghetto, but reasons have nothing to do with the cycle of life, but everything to do with one's need to understand," He spoke as He closed his hand over the miniature storm and glanced over at Heaven.

"See, Ghetto, you *chose* the streets over her, over your child." God shrugged as his eyes drifted to the four candles she had placed sparsely out on the table. "Many men do, and when it comes time to accept what comes with their *choice*, who do you think they blame?" He asked with a smirk on his face. The flames on the candles danced, their shadows playing in the darkness of his pupils. God blew a soft breath and a flame died on one of the candles. A black swirl of smoke snaked from it, and Heaven's wet eyes drifted to it.

"If a child is born stillborn, it's automatically assumed that *I'm* cruel, that life is evil. If a child is killed by a stray bullet, *I'm* blamed rather than the shooter. Yet, why can't the baby have been born stillborn merely because it wasn't meant for *that* child to come at that moment? Why couldn't that child's murder had been exactly what it was? The choice of a people." He gave it to me before blowing another soft breath and extinguishing the flame of another candle. Heaven frowned as she studied it.

"Yes, I could change the result of self-choice, son, but where's the lesson in that? If I intervene every time an evil happens in this world, evil would have a *good* result. Death, pain, loss," he paused to look at me, "are the mothers of life, love, and gain. It's all about the perspective, Ghetto, and I wanna show you what the life you lived has done to your culture of people." A soft breeze blew through the room, and without Him saying so, I knew the scene was about to change.

"Wait!" The word burst from my lips in an urgent plea. God glanced at me curiously as I made my way over to where my queen sat. "I just wanna let her know that I'm sorry, that I'm here for her, mane, I fucked up, my "G"—" I paused as I reluctantly looked away from her and glanced at the older me. "At least give me that much," I pleaded. God nodded His consent, and to my surprise, He kept it playa with a gangsta.

***

-Heaven-

My heart felt like someone had taken it out and smashed it with a sledgehammer. *He's dead, Heaven, someone shot him. Ghetto is dead, sis!* Egypt's words were a stabbing mantra that seemed to be on repeat within the walls of my mind. I felt numb, empty. I just couldn't believe that he was gone. As I sat there, staring absently at the dancing flame of the candles, I frowned as another flame died. It was the second one that had extinguished on its own. The snake of black smoke that emitted from it dissipated into the air as my vision blurred behind a fresh lake of tears.

"You promised me, baby," I whispered softly, and in the midst of the pieces of my heart sliding out my chest, the strangest thing happened. *I miss you/It's been too long and I'm lost without you/ what am I gonna do, I've been needing, wanting you, Baby/wondering if you're the same and who's been with you/is your heart still mine?/I wanna cry sometimes/I miss you.* Aaliyah's "Missing You" played softly from the speakers. I shot to my feet, the pillow still clutched to my chest, my eyes fell to the two extinguished candles. *Could it be?* I wondered.

I'd read the future for years, but I'd never had any experience with paranormal situations. Egypt was upstairs asleep, and no one else was there, so *how, who'd* turned on *that* song? Who'd turned on the radio? My mind was a highway that led so many places. My eyes canvased the room. There was a thin line between sanity and the insane, and though I delved within the studies of the supernatural, I didn't know if I truly believed in ghosts, but I was learning that when love was pure, real, the heart would give into the possibility of anything that meant more time with who it craved for. "Ghetto?" I whispered as Aaliyah's song drove me to the edge of madness. "Ghetto, baby, I-I miss you, Pa. I don't know how to breathe without you. I don't *want* to breathe without you. Please, baby, give me just one more chance to love you, Pa, *please*? Please? Huh?"

Tears dripped from my face as I look up toward the ceiling. I hugged the pillow as if it were him. My soul was on fire for love. When I didn't get an answer, the room seemed to become claustrophobic, the smell of his Givenchy cologne seemed too powerful. I slowly made my way over to the mantle above the huge fireplace where I'd placed a digital picture frame. I picked it up and began to flip through photos of us. There were too many memories captured within still life that I just couldn't keep tormenting myself like that. I stopped at a picture of us at the state fair, and my eyes fell to the three-carat diamond ring on my finger. Ghetto'd proposed that night, and there were strangers that sat above us and underneath us. As that Ferris wheel paused our cart at the point of its highest peak, I'd accepted.

My eyes drifted shut on the memory as tears leaked down my face. "I hate you! I hate loving you!" Something snapped inside of me and without much thought, I flung the picture frame. *Pishhhh!* It shattered into a thousand pieces when it made contact with the wall. "Ah." My mouth fell open in a silent *O*. The pillow slipped from my hands as I glanced down at the water wetting my shorts as it ran down my left leg. A sharp pain exploded in my stomach and caused me to cradle the slight baby bump.

"Egypt! Egypt!" I cried as I found my way to the couch. Moments later, Egypt groggily made her way down the stairs.

"You alright, sis?" she asked. I could barely speak, but when I finally did, my words snapped the girl all the way into consciousness.

"Call Aunt Helen—no-no, just call an ambulance. My water just broke," I moaned.

Renta

Chapter 26
Red Diamond

-Red Diamond-

"That ole boy, Joe Biden, is good for that old oval office. I'm telling y'all, the man is the change we need! He brings some flavor to that *White* House," Mr. Brown, one of the four barbers in Big Walter's barber shop, acknowledged. The buzz of multiple sets of clippers filled the room, and it seemed as if half the metroplex had shown up to Big Walter's that Saturday morning. The spot had always been lit, and it was said that even some big celebrities traveled from all over just to get a line-up there.

"Man, get the hell outta here with all that riff raff, Mr. Brown. That white man is just riding the wave of our struggle right now, and as soon as he gets in that office, he gonna fuck over the ghetto. See, that shit these presidential candidates be talking about in terms of bringing about a change is for the old folk," Big Walter spoke while stepping back to study the edge-up he was adding to Stick Talk's head. He stepped back to study the edge-up he applied to the right point before making his way to the back to tighten up dude's shag style cut.

"People don't understand that each new president comes with their own vision of change, but it's the vision of those past forty-five presidents that ole Biden has to contend with before he can bring about even a semblance of evolution," he added while leaning back to get a closer look at the high taper fade he'd applied to the cut.

"Yea, and I think the man can get it done. All these police killings, this Covid shit, I'm telling you, man, one more *day* of Trump will cause the next Civil War!" Mr. Brown was adamant as he dusted off his customer. The entire room seemed in agreement as heads nodded their sentiments, but Big Walter sucked his teeth with a slight shake of his head.

"You fools don't know shit 'bout no politics, it takes more than racial consciousness to run a part of the world. Joe Biden did some major shit with selecting Kamala Harris, but that was all for the times. He sees the pigs whacking us, he sees the 1960s repeating and dude is seizing the moment, but see," he paused while blending the taper in a little more, "Donald Trump understands an international language that not only the United States of Amerikka speaks, but Europe, South America, Asia, Africa, and Australia has a bilingual education of: *money!* The man specializes in economic relief, fam, and—"

"Naw, Big Walter, I won't let you praise a mu'fucka that's out here legalizing the genocide of Black folk!" Raheem, another barber, cut him off as he oiled his clippers. "The man is a rapist! All these women coming forward with these allegations, dude is sick. He's unapologetically racist, and even his own Republicans have had enough of dude's bullshit, ock."

Big Walter poured barber powder onto a dusting brush before using it to dust the excess hair off of Stick Talk. The man merely chuckled as he glanced around at the men in the room. "See, *that's* the same shit that fucks up ole Joe Biden's campaign! Those rich mu'fuckas that we've never even heard of those billionaire sons a bitches that *live* for investing and making money don't give a damn 'bout no damn racial discrimination or that that man touches women inappropriately! The shit he's done for the economy is all they see, and the moves he's making with foreign affairs is meant for a businessman!" He nodded to Stick Talk to let him know he was finished before pulling the clothes shield off of him.

"Come on, man, if Joe Biden gets up in that White House and doesn't know shit about *business*, economic stability, or even mere economy of scale in an international viewpoint, it's gonna be the great depression all over again! We're all gonna be out of a job. See, mu'fuckas can't see beyond the color barrier to see the future, but I can! Think about it," he paused to hand Stick Talk a handheld mirror. He smiled as the boy admired the TLC he'd put into the haircut.

"Big Walter, I don't know shit 'bout no ecosystem or whatever the fuck you talm 'bout, but I know you're fooly with the clippers, my mans." Stick Talk brought some ease to the tension when he confused the ecosystem with the economic system.

"Sho you right, youngin', and if these brainless friends of mine would let me prove to 'em that *they* don't know shit either, we'd be better off!" He cracked a smile as Stick Talk overpaid him for a job well done.

"You the crazy one, Big Walter. You actually think Trump gonna get a second term after all the—"

"Yea, nigga!" Big Walter cut Raheem off in mid-sentence. "Think of the past, Grover Cleveland is considered the twenty-second *and* the twenty-fourth president because his two terms weren't consecutive. Back in 1892, due to the Sherman Act, dude had money problems and that shit caused an economic depression!" He counted off one finger. "He didn't get reelected! In 1929, Herbert Hoover stood as the thirty-first president when the stock market crashed and the economy collapsed. The great depression is what got his ass replaced by Franklin Roosevelt." Big Walter counted off a second finger. "George H. Bush had the highest presidential ratings in history, but due to the economy slipping into recession, his ass was defeated by Bill Clinton! Guess what?" he asked just as Stick Talk nodded to the few he fucked with and made his way toward the door.

"That boy Clinton won his reelection in 1996 because the economy was strong! *Nobody* likes to lose money. When the economy is fucked up, taxes go up, gas goes up, and dope prices rise. *That's* my point!" he was saying when I pushed the door open and almost bumped right into the man of the hour. Stick Talk took a step back with something slick on his tongue before he realized it was a real bitch in his presence.

"What's blessins, Flesh, what's the fruit?" I acknowledged him like family. Stick Talk smiled before relaxing, but I could tell he wondered the business.

"The blessings are righteous, Nubian, and the fruit is ripe. What you doing at the barber shop, you tired of all that hair?" he asked with a light chuckle. I smiled, showing him the golden fangs on my teeth. They were sharp and complemented by a red ruby in the center of the two teeth.

"That's what's up, 'cause there's a few heads of the table that wants to taste the fruits with you." I caught him off guard, and though he held his calm demeanor, I was a lioness and hunted for my food. I sensed his disease.

"Huh, why, what's up?" he asked. I'd known dude since Ghetto and I used to be one, and though he'd grown on me, I'd always sensed the snake in Stick Talk. The *reckless* ambition. As soon as I heard the news of my baby getting *stepped on*, I felt it in my soul that this nigga had dealt Ghetto a bad hand. I shrugged my shoulders and his eyes fell to my titties. *Snake ass nigga!* I thought. I rolled my eyes before glancing over at Big Walter.

"You know I respect you, OG, but we need to borrow ya spot for a few seconds." I glanced around at the frowns forming on those boys' faces and knew that my request wouldn't be respected because I didn't have a dick swinging from between my legs. "Ya'll mu'fuckas mash out, shop closed," I demanded anyway, and just as I thought, no one budged.

Someone even snickered, and that's when I got on my stupid shit. *Damn, why niggas think they're the only ones that deserve respect!* I thought, but even as I reached down into my Birkin bag and made my way over to the one that found my demand so funny, the answer came to me. *Men only respect bloodshed!*

***

-Stick Talk-

"Girl, you better gone head with all that shit. You ain't running shit up in here!" Raheem considered himself checking her, but me and Big Walter were the only two in the room that knew how much Red Diamond enjoyed to give it up.

"Shut up, Raheem!" Big Walter demanded with a stern look. Raheem frowned, but only if he knew how much his life depended on his silence, he'd have cut out his own tongue! Most niggas saw the short, thick red bone and allowed her beauty to rock 'em to sleep, but Red Diamond was as certified as a mail package. The blood-red hair, the matching contacts in her eyes, and the hue of her skin was devilish, but the black one-piece Valentino Haute Couture short suit she wore rode her curves like a car speeding around a road that led up a mountain. The front of the Spandex material was unzipped down to her navel and gave a teasing view of the blood-red, Vickie's Secret bra that hid all them titties she had. I watched her slowly make her way over to a hustla I knew from 'round the way and stand before him.

"Sup, playboy, you find something funny?" she asked with a seductive smirk before fixing him with a bloodied gaze. Red Diamond ran the tip over her tongue, alluring her prey.

"Red, ain't no need for all that, this ain't the place." Big Walter attempted to ease the tension, but dude didn't understand that bravado wasn't a part of the inscription of one's tombstone. "Bitch, you better get the fuck—"

Boca! The side of the big purse tore to shreds when the bullet made its exit and found home in dude's leg.

"Arrrrugh! Shit-you-you shot me!" he cried as his hands flew to the volcano the slug created in his flesh. Blood shot up and soaked his skinny jeans. Red Diamond ignored him as her eyes fell to the Fendi kicks on her feet. Blood had sprayed them and she seemed fucked up about it.

"I said, get the fuck out!" she shouted. I almost burst into laughter as niggas created a stampeded to get far away from lady, but it was Raheem's fronting ass that had me beside myself in laughter.

"Oh shit!" he shouted as his eyes grew as big as an owl's at the sight of the blood.

"Ouch, nigga, hol' up!" the dude in his chair shouted as the clippers bit into the back of his neck. It was a useless plea, and he understood it only after the clippers fell, still buzzing into his lap. Raheem was already making his exit by the time kid realized what had happened. He followed suit shortly after, and it only left me, Big Walter, Red Diamond, and the crying man in the building.

"Don't kill me, fam, please don't kill me, I just wanted a haircut, man!" the bloody man cried as he rocked back and gripped his leg. At that moment, the chime over the door sounded, and an air of arrogance pervaded the air   after the sense of danger settled. The first man was a six-foot-four block of all muscle. As he entered the shop, his long, blond-tipped dreads swung about his shoulders like the snakes that writhed in all directions on Medusa's head. Wearing a black muscle shirt and black joggers, dude was a walking billboard for hood nigga, but it was the Draco with the money nuts drum attached to it that had all eyes on him. One by one, at least ten more killahs brandishing .223's and AR's entered the spot and fanned out.

My eyes touched each of them before the fragrance of Ralph Lauren's Polo Red wafted through the room. Two men in Italian suits entered the room, one dark and the other one a lighter shade of black. *Lil' Nukkey and Thugga!* The names of the two heads of RNO blew through my mind like a soft wind down a closed-in alleyway. Though I'd never met Lil' Nukkey outside of the few times Ghetto's bitch ass FaceTimed him, I'd kicked it with Thugga down in H Town, and the vibe I got from dude was homicidal.

"What's the blessings, Flesh, what's the fruits?" Lil' Nukkey asked with a crooked grin that made him like more like the Chucky doll than a family member greeting a brother in arms. Thugga made his way over to one of the barber chairs and took a seat without acknowledging me. That should've alerted me, but I rationalized that it was no way they could know I was the one that had stepped on Ghetto.

"The table gucci, Blow, and I ain't partook of the fruits this morning. Shit been dumb busy, fam. What's the fruits on y'all's plates? I see introductions come in a show of force." I nodded at the henchmen they'd brought along for our first face to face. The sound of sniveling caused all eyes to focus on the leaking man. I saw Nukkey's eyes bounce to Red Diamond before recapturing the weeping dude. Thugga's deep chuckle caused her to shrugged her shoulders in indifference.

"Nigga thought shit was sweet," she spat before glancing down at her Birkin. "Wack ass dude made me ruin my brand-new purse! Matter fact, why yo' bitch ass still up in this bitch, nigga? You better leave with your life while you still got it!" she gritted as she pulled the tool fully out the holey purse and aimed it at playboy's top. His eyes grew wide as he attempted to get to his feet, but his leg wouldn't support his weight. He fell back down into his seat, but Red Diamond wasn't in tune with her heart. "Bitch, you can walk, you can crawl, or you can hop your way up out of here, but you better choose fast!" she was saying when Nukkey took his seat in one of the many chairs.

He faced me and forever seemed to pass before he spoke. His eyes were dark, studious. "The fruits of the day are power and respect, Flesh, see," he paused before unbuttoning his suit jacket and peeling it off. I watched him rest it neatly across his lap before leaning back in his seat and resting his elbows on the armrests of the chair. "The allure of power can drive some of the stiffest niggas to violate the code. See, Bruh, I learned a lot 'bout niggas from that movie, *Paid in Full,* and ever since Ghetto brought you to the table, I saw Alpo in your eyes."

"Alpo? Nigga, what the fuck you—" I began, but—

"Hold up, Bro Bro, I'll nourish you after I feed you the fruits. We're men, we ain't gotta be disrespectful to see eye to eye." Lil' Nukkey was as calm as the moment before a dangerous storm, but the look in his eyes told the story of that gangsta shit. My eyes fell to the two P.89's he had holstered underneath each of his arms, and I could feel beads of sweat form on the bridge of my nose. Shit was 'bout to get stupid!

"See, fam, just like Alpo, you just wanna ball till you fall, but forget that even the least important part of a team can do that. Niggas always wanna be the chief, but most niggas don't know how to lead a tribe to a good water supply. My question is, what *boss* nigga would *want* to ball till he *falls!*" Dude seemed to spit the last word. I glanced over at the boy Thugga. His dark eyes devoured me, and though his demeanor was relaxed, he'd slipped his burna free and had it resting in his lap.

For easy access! I realized as my fingers tingled. I wanted to up my own pistol, but I was out gunned, out manned, *and* out of pocket. Those boys would've slayed me. I lifted my hands like, *So what you sayin'?*

"Flesh, I ain't feeling how you comin', and Alpo was a snake *and* a rat. If that's what you consider me, then, we might as well smoke it out in this bitch." That *G* shit pumped through my veins. Lil' Nukkey nodded in acknowledgement of my gangsterisms. Big Walter began sweeping up the hair from the floor as he pretended not to be listening, and though it was against RNO's laws to speak table business in the presence of a civilian, Lil' Nukkey leaned forward and rested his elbows on his knees.

"It's gonna be plenty time for all that when we find out who was crazy enough to spill my nigga's blood. Stick Talk, Scarface fucked the game up when he convinced mu'fuckas that money brought power, and power brought respect, Homie. J.F. Kennedy, Malcolm X, Pop Smoke, Tupac, Biggie, El Chappo, and even Escabar are prime examples. The money brought power, but the power didn't bring the respect!" He gave it to me before standing and making his way over to a big poster of Malcom X that someone had stuck to the wall.

Nukkey pointed up at the image of the ex-Nation of Islam activist. "Money and power got fam whacked at the height of his game. The power of his position made him forget that a nigga can't speak the sins of a respected man in public, whether the accusation is true or not. Who took fam down?" he asked.

"Bruh, I don't give a fuck 'bout no Malcom X or none of that shit. I'm tryin' to see what the bidness is!" I cut the extra shit in half. My fingers itched to go for the pole on my hip, but—

"Right, right." Lil' Nukkey chuckled as he turned to face me. "I'm sayin', though, Flesh, how you and Ghetto was in the same spot, same time, and he gets slumped, and he's the *only one* getting buried?" Dude looked me up and down as if I was busted and couldn't be trusted.

"How you leave that bitch without blood on *your* hands or without *your* life being took? You and Ghetto was one, and if anything, if it was *me*, I'd have whacked *you* first and then ran down on the head of the table. I'm sayin', my dude, shit looking *suspect*."

The nigga finally got to why he'd pulled up to my section of the state, squadded up. I chuckled, Lord knew I wanted to up that pistol and put his brains all over that poster. "So, what you boys saying is y'all think I, what, whacked my main man? The same nigga that I shed blood with *and* for?" I asked, and though I was as guilty as charged, my pride was my Achilles heel. The sucka's face transformed into a mask of that *on go* shit as he stepped up into my face and allowed me to see the blood in his eyes behind our fallen brother.

"Naw, fam, that's what *you* just said. I asked *exactly* what the fuck I asked," he spat. My eyes watered, and I won't lie, the thoughts in my mind fucked with me.

"Nigga, you shot me? Bruh, this hoe is the one that stuck us that night, she—" Ghetto cried, in shock.

"Don't believe him, bae, the nigga followed me out here and tried to push up on me. I told him I got a man and even asked him why he'd had you set up. He was tryin' to kill me 'cause—"

"Somebody gotta pay for this. The streets will flood with blood until my nigga's soul ain't tossin' and turning in his grave, seeking revenge." Lil' Nukkey's voice brought me out the reflection I'd become lost within. Shit was crazy, I'd murked my main man and I truthfully didn't know if I'd done it over the pussy, or because I thought ill of bruh. *Is Empress the snake?* I wondered.

"We through here, homie? I got shit to do," I asked. Lil' Nukkey glanced over at Thugga, who studied me with a crooked smile on his face.

"You good, my 'G,' but take dude with you." He nodded at dude Red Diamond had plugged. Homie was crawling toward the door, leaving a red trail in his wake.

"Man, hell naw, I ain't fuckin' with that. He better get the—"

"Yea, you're gonna help 'em or *you* gonna need help." Thugga's deep voice finally joined the convo. I started to check that shit, but unlike the boy Nukkey, Thugga was ready for action. In the blink of an eye, the gun was in his hand and showing me I was now an outcast of the fam. *Not good!* My mind screamed as my eyes drifted from the burna being aimed at me and fell to the wounded man that had climbed halfway to his feet. *Shid, at least I'll be able to use the boy as a shield if shit gets ugly!* I thought as I silenced my pride, and with a grit on my face, I made my way over to dude.

My thoughts were everywhere. I wanted to go for my tool and fire at least one of those fools up but knew that would be suicide. *Man, I gotta get to Empress and get us the hell out of Aggtown before we both end up floating face down in the Trinity River!* I thought as I put playboy's arm over my shoulder and allowed him to use me as a crutch.

"Fam, don't be bleeding all over me. As soon as we make it outside, you on your own." I drew the line.

"Stick Talk," Lil' Nukkey called. I glanced over my shoulder at him. "Keep yo' ear to the street, Bro Bro, we're trying to see Ghetto's killah buried before we lower him into the ground. And," he paused as he made his way to Big Walter's barber chair and took a seat. The OG accepted the fifty from dude's hand and placed the black smock over the tailored clothes he wore. "Don't leave the city, playboy, you don't want shit to look any more suspicious." Lil' Nukkey covered all bases.

I didn't respond, I just headed for the door with a wounded man leaning against me. My heart pounded as I made my way. I could feel their eyes on me and wondered if a bullet would enter the back of my head. We made it to the door safely, and I smiled. I knew as soon as I made it out that door I would be a hunted man. I planned to dip out the city and catch each one of those boys at a later time. One of us *had* to die or—*Boca!* The gunshot made me tense.

"Fuck! Arrrrugh!" Dude I was helping wailed as he collapsed. I quickly spun while thrusting my hands out forward as if I could block a flying bullet.

"Wha-what the fuck?" I shouted as the scar tissue from my head wound began to itch. Red Diamond stood aiming a smoking gun at us. "My ass, dog, they shot me in the assssss!" homie below me was crying, but my vision never left that She Devil. She smirked at me as she aimed the burna at me.

"Tell Empress we send our love." She smiled as I turned and hurriedly made my exit. I left dude in my haste. *Fuck 'em.*

***
-Red Diamond-

"Pleeeease, don't kill me, mane. I got six kids, three baby mamas, man, pleeease!" homeboy was whining.

"What you think, Nubian? You know the nigga better than we do," Lil' Nukkey inquired. I glanced around at the room of killahs before spitting on the ground. My eyes fell to the crying man as he crawled out the door.

"That nigga lyin'. Stick Talk knows *something*," I spoke my heart. My eyes watered at the thought of blasphemy. I could never understand what made a man or woman do the unthinkable to the ones that loved them. I'd watched Ghetto thug with Stick Talk like a brother, loved him when we warned him to study dude a little more. Lil' Nukkey was right when he compared him to Alpo. It was as if Stick Talk had taken the man's character right out that movie, *Paid in Full.*

Thugga rose to leave but paused beside me. "It don't matter what he knows. As soon as the streets confirm what I think *we all* know, I'mma crucify that boy. Real niggas only, sis, on me," he vowed. I nodded before locking eyes with bro.

"Real bitches only, bro, but if it gets certified that one of our own is responsible for shedding the blood of my baby, your crucifixion will have to wait," I told him as I headed for the door. I didn't have to tell him the rest. We both knew that Ghetto was my heart, and if Stick Talk killed him, I'd take his heart out to replace the one he took from me. *Literally!*

Renta

Chapter 27
A Crooked Twist

-Heaven-

"Push, girl, I see his head. Pushhh, Heaven!" Catrina's excitement only served to piss me off. I wanted to kill her!

"Ahhhh, God!" I cried as I held tight to the guard rails of the hospital bed with all my might. Sweat covered my entire body, and I could feel my might slipping as I huffed and puffed. My hair stuck to my face like a wet spider's web. I'd gone into labor half a month early and it was kicking my ass.

"Just give me one more good push, Ms. Domingo, and that should do it!" Dr. Morris encouraged me, but he could save the lies.

"I'm pushinggggg!" I cried as my head thrust back in agony, causing me to stare up at the ceiling as I pushed with all I had. "Ghettooooo, I hate youuuuuu!" I cried as I pushed with all I could muster. A long drip of salty water eased out my left eye and slid down the side of my face. Even in the midst of that crazy pain, I missed him.

"Whoaaaoo!" Catrina shouted gleefully, and even when I felt the small life slip from my womb, even when the umbilical cord was cut and the sounds of my baby boy filled the room? I just couldn't seem to find my way out of the dark spot in my heart I'd suddenly retreated to. *You're supposed to be here, bae, your son will need you to show him the way. "I" need you to show "us" the way, Pa.* I fell back against the pillow, spent! All the energy seeped out of me as my eyes dropped low with the thought. *God, I'll do anything! Just-just give him one more chance. Give us one more try, please?* I gave a silent prayer in my mind.

I'd thought that same prayer I'd been praying since the day I'd gotten the news. Catrina made her way beside me with a tentative smile on her pretty face. "They took Kalief to be cleaned up," she whispered as she pushed the moist tendrils of hair away from my face. When I didn't answer, my sister knew. "You miss him, don't you, ma?" she asked before exhaling an exaggerated breath and kneeling beside my bed. My baby sis wiped a fleeing tear away from the side of my face as I fought exhaustion.

"Sometimes, I wonder if there's really a God, you know? Like, if there is, why he's letting shit go so bad? What we do to Him to make Him shit on us so much?" I wondered out loud. Catrina studied me for mere seconds before her eyes fell to the floor. I was the eldest and I'd always been the glue, that bitch that had no emotions by appearance, but now the mask was off. I was revealing that I was more woman than animal, and my sister didn't know how to take it.

"There she is, your mother wants to have her time with you!" a nurse cooed to my child when she entered the room with Kalief wrapped inside a soft blue cloth. She made her way over to me and handed my child over. As soon as that life was cradled in my arms, my heart clenched. His skin was a *pale* caramel, and the soft curls on his head were an inheritance of *my* gene pool. *Your daddy would love you, little man*, I thought as I smiled down at him.

"What will you name him?" Dr. Morris smiled with the question.

"Kalief, Kalief *Ghetto* Bousard," I whispered. I never looked up to gauge his reaction, but I'm sure the middle name was something that raised their eyebrows.

"Bousard? That's-that's not such a common name these days. Where'd you come up with the Bousard name, are you related?" The doctor asked. I glanced up at him curiously, and the look he was giving me unnerved me.

"No, it's my child's father's last name. He was murdered a few weeks ago." Just the reminder made my eyes water. I glanced down at my sleeping son, but the doctor's next words snatched my attention back to him.

"I don't mean to pry, Ms. Domingo, but you wouldn't happen to know a Devonte Bousard, would you?" he asked. Me and Catrina's eyed connected before I allowed my stare to fix on the older white man. That must've been all the confirmation he needed. Doctor Morris excused the nurse, and though he tried to do the same with my sister, the girl wasn't trying to hear it. I'd reluctantly allowed the nurse to take my child, and as soon as the door closed behind her, Dr. Morris reinvented my hope in God.

"If you know him or anyone in his family, that would be a great help to us. He was brought here a few weeks ago, riddled with bullets. We tried to find his family, but the man has no emergency contacts and everywhere we turned wound up being a dead end." The man's words were leading, a tease of the things my heart craved. Yet, I was afraid to believe. If what I assumed he was saying, wasn't what he was saying, the fall from hope would shatter me.

"Look, dude, what are you saying? Stop talking in circles!" Catrina lost her patience. Doctor Morris's eyes flickered to her in fear before returning to me in question. My body trembled in anticipation as I studied him, but my tongue didn't seem to work, so I merely nodded my confirmation. The man nodded slightly before his words overpowered the exhaustion my body had begun to surrender to.

"Well, we've had the man here on life support and have been unable to pull the plug without a family member's consent. We've tried to..." His words died in his throat as I bolted upright in that bed before ripping the IV from my arm. The pain was unspeakable, but I needed to know that I was hearing correctly. I needed to know I wasn't hallucinating! I almost collapsed from the pain, my weakness, but Catrina caught me and led my hands to the guard rails.

"Ms. Domingo!" The doctor finally found his voice. He rushed over to me and attempted to help me back into the bed. "You're in no condition to—"

"Where is he! Are you sure that it's *him*? *Please*!" I pleaded as I cut him off and balled a fistful of his doctor's coat in my hand. At that moment, nurses rushed into the room, but my vision never left him. Doctor Morris raised a palm to assure his staff that all was well, but his words stole more energy from me than giving birth to a child ever could.

"Yes, Ms. Domingo, Devonte Bousard is here. He's brain dead and the only way he's still breathing is through a ventilator, but we're fighting for him."

"Take me to him!" I urged with a tighter grip on the man's coat. Suddenly, I began to see spots, and the only thing I remembered before fading to black were the only words that allowed me to succumb to the overbearing call to unconsciousness.

"We will, but first, you must rest. You must heal."

***

-Stick Talk-

I rushed into the one-bedroom apartment me and Empress had copped on the south side of Aggtown. We were renting until our spot was finished being built out in Cleburne, Texas, but shit had just gotten funky. We needed to ghost the city before the city made us ghosts. "Empress, we gotta mash, ma, they on to us!" I shouted as I rushed into the room, but my words were useless. The place was as empty as a drunk's bottle of cheap wine.

Damn! I thought as I pulled out my phone and sent the bitch a quick message. I didn't have time to waste. Though I didn't truly know the heads of the body, I knew the squad of RNO was made up of young savages that thrived, that lived to spin on something.

I made my way to the closet and found my duffle and began throwing shit in it. I only needed a few changes of clothes, so I quickly made my way to the safe we kept at the back of the room. I emptied all I had into the bag before snatching up a few things Empress would need. The bitch had boxes of shoes stacked so high that they damn near came up to my nose. The first five boxes were expensive heels, Manolo, Jimmy, Valentino, Schiaparelli, and many other designer names. By the eighth box, I still hadn't found a normal pair of tennis shoes, but the ninth box concealed something that gave me pause. *Fuck? Why would this be in here?* I wondered as I lifted the envelope from underneath a golden, spiked pair of Dior heels. I tossed the shoes to the side as I stared down at the thick envelope that had a big *certified* stamp on the front. My eyes fell to who it was addressed to, and a frown of confusion contorted my face.

***

-Ghetto-

It was that time of the day when the sun seemed more orangish-red than yellow, where it was so low to the earth that it looked as if one could jump up and touch it. Two young boys, neither a day older than nine or ten years old, dribbled a basketball in the front yard of a nice four-bedroom house. The lowered basketball goal was low enough that either boy could fulfill their dreams of being LeBron.

"On BGM, I'm gonna shake you, fool, bet you can't get the ball, ah-ah-ah!" the boy with the ball mocked as he dribbled the ball between his legs. He was excited when he noticed the look of frustration on his friend's face, and just when he had victory in his hands and was driving to the goal, the defending boy swiped the ball out of his hand. Victory had betrayed him and shined its pretty face upon the boy's friend. He watched as the boy he'd grown up with captured the ball, and right as the front door of the house swung open, *swoosh!* The ball soared through the net.

"Aight, boo, I'll catch up with you later. I left you a lil' dough on the dresser, that should hold y'all till I get back." YB told his queen as he embraced her. Being the second in command of the BGM gang made him and his family a target, so just like any other smart man of the streets would do, he moved his peeps out to the suburbs. He kept the streets and home separate, but the catch 22 of the streets was found in the fact that no matter how far a nigga runs from the game, as long as he continues to play, the score would eventually show up at his safe haven.

"Thank you, baby, when will you be back?" his baby moms inquired with a quick kiss to his lips.

"Yea, Dad, when will you be back?" his son seconded. YB gave his lady another kiss before turning and making his way over to his son. He squatted down until they were eye level and he smiled at his mini me.

"Sup, lil' nigga, what you got going on?" he asked as his eyes flickered to the other child. "What's up, Jay, I see you got handles with the rock!" he acknowledged as the boy dribbled the ball between his legs and gave his best version of a young AI.

"Yea, I'm gonna be like Kobe when I grow up. I'mma go to the NBA and dunk on all them fools!" The boy's excitement got a chuckle out of YB. Though the kid was his best friend's son, he loved him like his own.

"That's what's up lil' man." He nodded his acknowledgement before returning his attention to his son. "What 'bout you, lil' daddy, what you gonna be when you grow up?" he asked curiously. The little dude twisted his fingers up into an intricate sign before giving his father a big smile.

"I'mma be BGM, just like you, Dad!" he proclaimed with true passion. YB laughed at that, but his lady didn't find the humor.

"Oh, no you not, you're gonna do something good with your…" Her words trailed off as her eyes drifted down the street. I didn't know why He'd brought me here, but God stood silently beside me and allowed His eyes to follow the lady's. Curious, so did mine, and that's when my eyes fell to slits of suspicion. A black van was easing down the street, and though it seemed harmless enough, the vehicle just seemed out of bounds on the quiet street of that subdivision.

"Ya mama's right, lil' one, you should be a—"

"YB, baby, I think something is wrong," Lady cut the spiel he was giving his son off. I noticed the frown ease onto YB's face as he looked up at the mother of his child in confusion.

"What you mean, Tiff, what's…" His words trailed off as his vision followed hers. By then, the van was almost upon us. Me and YB had been enemies since I'd made the move from Louisiana to Texas. RNO and BGM niggas could only coexist on two different sides of world, and we did what we needed to do as gangstas, but we also kept it grown up. I watched as he erected himself and pushed his son towards his lady. "Camron, Jay, y'all get in the house. NOW!" he demanded, but the hands of fate waged war against his late reaction.

Scurrrt! The van sped up, and just as it was close enough to do what it do, the side door slid open and four masked gunmen jumped out on their monkey business. "Get the fuck in the house, GO!" YB's panic was evident as he pushed his family toward the door.

My eyes were locked in on the four shootas, each one brandished a fully stocked stick with big drums attached to them, but it was the masks they wore that held me captive. *Angry gorilla masks!*

"Ghetto sends his love, my nigga, a hundred rounds of it!" the lead ape growled right before that pipe began vibrating in his hands. Life took on a slow-motion effect as fire began to fly from the barrels of all four guns. Out of instinct, I dove for the two boys at the same time that a spray of blood burst into the air. *Bttting! Bttting!* The sounds of shells fell to the street. *TuTuTuTu! TTTTah! TuTu-TuTu!* The different caliber of assault rifles sang a deadly tune as the killahs satiated their taste for blood. I landed dead on my face, but looked up just in time to see YB's baby moms dance her last dance.

Her arms were outstretched as if she were crucified to mid-air as her body shook with every chunk the high-powered bullets knocked from her body. I glanced down, and somehow, the young boy, Jay, had fallen beneath me, but with my translucent state, kid seemed to have been resting *inside* my spiritual form. He had his small hands over his ears as tears ran down his face. I rose to my knees and—

TuTuTuTu! Bullets ripped, and before I could get out the way, I watched them tear through my chest and torso. It was strange to watch the bullets penetrate me without blood being spilt. It was like dropping rocks into a water well and watching the water leap up from the impact.

Scurrrr. The sound of tires snapped me out of the intrigue, and only then did I notice the silence. I saw the van disappear off the street right as— "Come on, Tiffany, don't do a nigga like this, ma, wake up," YB cried. He'd survived the arrival of the reaper, but the collateral damage would make him wish his soul was snatched along with his lady's. Blood speckled his face as he pushed a piece of hair out of her face. The lady's eyes were vacant as she stared up at him, and as my enemy closed her lifeless eyes, the strangest shit happened. Tiffany's spirit lifted as it separated from her physical. She glanced around until her eyes settled on something that caused her hands to go to her mouth as if to muffle a scream.

My vision followed hers, and that's how my heart split from the vision. Camron, her and YB's son, lay splayed across the green grass, blood leaking from the corners of his mouth. *Dead, senseless. Dead!* My mind was a tornado as YB glanced up, maybe just realizing that the silence wasn't such a good thing. "Cam? Jay?" he called. The young boy that wasn't his son cried beneath me, and as YB's eyes drifted from him to the still form of his seed, insanity overpowered his "G."

"Naw, no, hell nooooo!" he roared as he hurriedly crawled toward his fallen boy. As life did what only life could do, my eyes found the ghost of the slain woman. She was shaking her head at the scene before us, and as soon as her eyes found me, then God, the only word she could utter is—

"Why?" At that moment, she began to disperse, but her question was the same one I craved the answer to. I glared at God, who stood to the side, staring expressionless at YB. "Why the fuck you let this shit happen, my dude? This child didn't have shit to do with this. You could've stopped this," I gritted. God's eyes slowly found me in a studious gaze.

"You know what I've always found to be crazy, Ghetto?" He asked as He nodded toward YB shedding tears over his dead son. The sight fucked with me because the boy's spirit rose just as his mother's had, but the boy had something he wanted to do before he passed on. He stood, and as YB allowed his tears to speak the condition of his heart, his son reached up and wrapped his arms around his neck for their last hug.

"I never understood how people *choose* to live a particular way, how you brothers enjoy the lifestyle of the streets, but when the choice made comes with an adverse consequence, you ask *why?* What is beyond me, Ghetto, is how you or any other man could look down upon or fault another man for continuing the exact cycle of life that *you* promote." His words frustrated me. I gritted my teeth against my rebuttal. I wanted to spazz on fam, but lady truth could never be two faced. I turned and walked away. I was fucked up because all the *whys* I had for God, He gave to me, and truth was, I didn't have an answer.

***

-Stick Talk-

The first document was a notary, a legal name change. *On this day, it is hereby noted that Preston Lockhart has changed his name to Empress Lockhart.* My heart pounded against my chest as I read. I didn't understand, I didn't *want* to understand! I shuffled through the papers until the evidence of the greatest cross stared me in the face. *Surgery? Genitalia mutilation?* I read and re-read the process of Empress's sex change, and before I could stop it, vomit rushed up my throat. I threw up all over the papers that had just changed my life, and just as I tamed the dry heaves I had—

"Where you at? Why'd you leave the front door open?" Her voice drifted from the front room. My eyes were slits when I slipped the tool off my waist.

Baby, fuck me in the ass, I like it in the ass! The bitch nigga's voice played in my mental as I turned and headed for the living room. Empress was a dead bitch, man, whatever the fuck he was. I couldn't believe it. This entire time, this hoe was a *man!*

To Be Continued ...

Coming to a hood near you, *Heaven Gotta Ghetto 2: Me, Myself, and the Devil*

Submission Guideline

Submit the first three chapters of your completed manuscript to ldpsubmissions@gmail.com, subject line: Your book's title. The manuscript must be in a .doc file and sent as an attachment. Document should be in Times New Roman, double spaced and in size 12 font. Also, provide your synopsis and full contact information. If sending multiple submissions, they must each be in a separate email.

Have a story but no way to send it electronically? You can still submit to LDP/Ca$h Presents. Send in the first three chapters, written or typed, of your completed manuscript to:

LDP: Submissions Dept
Po Box 944
Stockbridge, Ga 30281

DO NOT send original manuscript. Must be a duplicate.

Provide your synopsis and a cover letter containing your full contact information.

Thanks for considering LDP and Ca$h Presents.

Coming Soon from Lock Down Publications/Ca$h Presents

BOW DOWN TO MY GANGSTA

By **Ca$h**

TORN BETWEEN TWO

By **Coffee**

THE STREETS STAINED MY SOUL **II**

By **Marcellus Allen**

BLOOD OF A BOSS **VI**

SHADOWS OF THE GAME II

TRAP BASTARD II

By **Askari**

LOYAL TO THE GAME **IV**

By **T.J. & Jelissa**

IF LOVING YOU IS WRONG... **III**

By **Jelissa**

TRUE SAVAGE **VIII**

MIDNIGHT CARTEL IV

DOPE BOY MAGIC IV

CITY OF KINGZ III

By **Chris Green**

BLAST FOR ME **III**

A SAVAGE DOPEBOY III

CUTTHROAT MAFIA III

DUFFLE BAG CARTEL VI

HEARTLESS GOON VI

By **Ghost**

A HUSTLER'S DECEIT III

KILL ZONE **II**

BAE BELONGS TO ME III

A DOPE BOY'S QUEEN III

By **Aryanna**

COKE KINGS V

KING OF THE TRAP III

By **T.J. Edwards**

GORILLAZ IN THE BAY V

3X KRAZY III

De'Kari

THE STREETS ARE CALLING II

Duquie Wilson

KINGPIN KILLAZ IV

STREET KINGS III

PAID IN BLOOD III

CARTEL KILLAZ IV

DOPE GODS III

Hood Rich

SINS OF A HUSTLA II

ASAD

KINGZ OF THE GAME VI

Playa Ray

SLAUGHTER GANG IV

RUTHLESS HEART IV

By Willie Slaughter

FUK SHYT II

By Blakk Diamond

TRAP QUEEN

By Troublesome

YAYO V

GHOST MOB II

Stilloan Robinson

KINGPIN DREAMS III

By Paper Boi Rari

CREAM II

By Yolanda Moore

SON OF A DOPE FIEND III

HEAVEN GOT A GHETTO II

By Renta

FOREVER GANGSTA II

GLOCKS ON SATIN SHEETS III

By Adrian Dulan

LOYALTY AIN'T PROMISED III

By Keith Williams

THE PRICE YOU PAY FOR LOVE III

By Destiny Skai

I'M NOTHING WITHOUT HIS LOVE II

SINS OF A THUG II

By Monet Dragun

LIFE OF A SAVAGE IV

MURDA SEASON IV

GANGLAND CARTEL IV

CHI'RAQ GANGSTAS IV

KILLERS ON ELM STREET II

JACK BOYZ N DA BRONX II

By **Romell Tukes**

QUIET MONEY IV

EXTENDED CLIP III

THUG LIFE IV

By **Trai'Quan**

THE STREETS MADE ME III

By **Larry D. Wright**

IF YOU CROSS ME ONCE II

ANGEL III

By **Anthony Fields**

FRIEND OR FOE III

By **Mimi**

SAVAGE STORMS III

By **Meesha**

BLOOD ON THE MONEY III

By J-Blunt

THE STREETS WILL NEVER CLOSE II

By K'ajji

NIGHTMARES OF A HUSTLA III

By King Dream

IN THE ARM OF HIS BOSS

By Jamila

MONEY, MURDER & MEMORIES III

Malik D. Rice

CONCRETE KILLAZ II

Heaven Got a Ghetto

By Kingpen
HARD AND RUTHLESS II
By Von Wiley Hall
LEVELS TO THIS SHYT II
By Ah'Million
MOB TIES II
By SayNoMore
BODYMORE MURDERLAND II
By Delmont Player
THE LAST OF THE OGS II
Tranay Adams
FOR THE LOVE OF A BOSS II
By C. D. Blue

Available Now

RESTRAINING ORDER **I & II**
By **CA$H & Coffee**
LOVE KNOWS NO BOUNDARIES **I II & III**
By **Coffee**
RAISED AS A GOON I, II, III & IV
BRED BY THE SLUMS I, II, III
BLAST FOR ME I & II
ROTTEN TO THE CORE I II III
A BRONX TALE I, II, III

DUFFLE BAG CARTEL I II III IV V

HEARTLESS GOON I II III IV V

A SAVAGE DOPEBOY I II

DRUG LORDS I II III

CUTTHROAT MAFIA I II

By **Ghost**

LAY IT DOWN **I & II**

LAST OF A DYING BREED I II

BLOOD STAINS OF A SHOTTA I & II III

By **Jamaica**

LOYAL TO THE GAME I II III

LIFE OF SIN I, II III

By **TJ & Jelissa**

BLOODY COMMAS I & II

SKI MASK CARTEL I II & III

KING OF NEW YORK I II,III IV V

RISE TO POWER I II III

COKE KINGS I II III IV

BORN HEARTLESS I II III IV

KING OF THE TRAP I II

By **T.J. Edwards**

IF LOVING HIM IS WRONG…I & II

LOVE ME EVEN WHEN IT HURTS I II III

By **Jelissa**

WHEN THE STREETS CLAP BACK I & II III

THE HEART OF A SAVAGE I II III

By **Jibril Williams**

A DISTINGUISHED THUG STOLE MY HEART I II & III

LOVE SHOULDN'T HURT I II III IV

RENEGADE BOYS I II III IV

PAID IN KARMA I II III

SAVAGE STORMS I II

By **Meesha**

A GANGSTER'S CODE I &, II III

A GANGSTER'S SYN I II III

THE SAVAGE LIFE I II III

CHAINED TO THE STREETS I II III

BLOOD ON THE MONEY I II

By J-Blunt

PUSH IT TO THE LIMIT

By **Bre' Hayes**

BLOOD OF A BOSS **I, II, III, IV, V**

SHADOWS OF THE GAME

TRAP BASTARD

By **Askari**

THE STREETS BLEED MURDER **I, II & III**

THE HEART OF A GANGSTA I II& III

By **Jerry Jackson**

CUM FOR ME I II III IV V VI

An **LDP Erotica Collaboration**

BRIDE OF A HUSTLA **I II & II**

THE FETTI GIRLS **I, II& III**

CORRUPTED BY A GANGSTA I, II III, IV

BLINDED BY HIS LOVE

THE PRICE YOU PAY FOR LOVE I II

DOPE GIRL MAGIC I II III

By **Destiny Skai**

WHEN A GOOD GIRL GOES BAD

By **Adrienne**

THE COST OF LOYALTY I II III

By Kweli

A GANGSTER'S REVENGE **I II III & IV**

THE BOSS MAN'S DAUGHTERS I II III IV V

A SAVAGE LOVE **I & II**

BAE BELONGS TO ME I II

A HUSTLER'S DECEIT I, II, III

WHAT BAD BITCHES DO I, II, III

SOUL OF A MONSTER I II III

KILL ZONE

A DOPE BOY'S QUEEN I II

By **Aryanna**

A KINGPIN'S AMBITON

A KINGPIN'S AMBITION **II**

I MURDER FOR THE DOUGH

By **Ambitious**

TRUE SAVAGE I II III IV V VI VII

DOPE BOY MAGIC I, II, III

MIDNIGHT CARTEL I II III

CITY OF KINGZ I II

By **Chris Green**

A DOPEBOY'S PRAYER

Heaven Got a Ghetto

By **Eddie "Wolf" Lee**

THE KING CARTEL **I, II & III**

By **Frank Gresham**

THESE NIGGAS AIN'T LOYAL **I, II & III**

By **Nikki Tee**

GANGSTA SHYT **I II &III**

By **CATO**

THE ULTIMATE BETRAYAL

By **Phoenix**

BOSS'N UP **I , II & III**

By **Royal Nicole**

I LOVE YOU TO DEATH

By Destiny J

I RIDE FOR MY HITTA

I STILL RIDE FOR MY HITTA

By **Misty Holt**

LOVE & CHASIN' PAPER

By **Qay Crockett**

TO DIE IN VAIN

SINS OF A HUSTLA

By **ASAD**

BROOKLYN HUSTLAZ

By **Boogsy Morina**

BROOKLYN ON LOCK I & II

By **Sonovia**

GANGSTA CITY

By **Teddy Duke**

A DRUG KING AND HIS DIAMOND I & II III

A DOPEMAN'S RICHES

HER MAN, MINE'S TOO I, II

CASH MONEY HO'S

THE WIFEY I USED TO BE I II

By Nicole Goosby

TRAPHOUSE KING **I II & III**

KINGPIN KILLAZ I II III

STREET KINGS I II

PAID IN BLOOD **I II**

CARTEL KILLAZ I II III

DOPE GODS I II

By **Hood Rich**

LIPSTICK KILLAH **I, II, III**

CRIME OF PASSION I II & III

FRIEND OR FOE I II

By **Mimi**

STEADY MOBBN' **I, II, III**

THE STREETS STAINED MY SOUL

By **Marcellus Allen**

WHO SHOT YA **I, II, III**

SON OF A DOPE FIEND I II

HEAVEN GOT A GHETTO

Renta

GORILLAZ IN THE BAY **I II III IV**

TEARS OF A GANGSTA I II

3X KRAZY I II

DE'KARI

TRIGGADALE I II III

Elijah R. Freeman

GOD BLESS THE TRAPPERS I, II, III

THESE SCANDALOUS STREETS I, II, III

FEAR MY GANGSTA I, II, III IV, V

THESE STREETS DON'T LOVE NOBODY I, II

BURY ME A G I, II, III, IV, V

A GANGSTA'S EMPIRE I, II, III, IV

THE DOPEMAN'S BODYGAURD I II

THE REALEST KILLAZ I II III

THE LAST OF THE OGS

Tranay Adams

THE STREETS ARE CALLING

Duquie Wilson

MARRIED TO A BOSS... I II III

By Destiny Skai & Chris Green

KINGZ OF THE GAME I II III IV V

Playa Ray

SLAUGHTER GANG I II III

RUTHLESS HEART I II III

By Willie Slaughter

FUK SHYT

By Blakk Diamond

DON'T F#CK WITH MY HEART I II

By Linnea

ADDICTED TO THE DRAMA I II III

IN THE ARM OF HIS BOSS II

By Jamila

YAYO I II III IV

A SHOOTER'S AMBITION I II

By S. Allen

TRAP GOD I II III

By Troublesome

FOREVER GANGSTA

GLOCKS ON SATIN SHEETS I II

By Adrian Dulan

TOE TAGZ I II III

LEVELS TO THIS SHYT

By Ah'Million

KINGPIN DREAMS I II

By Paper Boi Rari

CONFESSIONS OF A GANGSTA I II III

By Nicholas Lock

I'M NOTHING WITHOUT HIS LOVE

SINS OF A THUG

By Monet Dragun

CAUGHT UP IN THE LIFE I II III

By Robert Baptiste

NEW TO THE GAME I II III

MONEY, MURDER & MEMORIES I II

By **Malik D. Rice**

LIFE OF A SAVAGE I II III

A GANGSTA'S QUR'AN I II III

MURDA SEASON I II III

GANGLAND CARTEL I II III

CHI'RAQ GANGSTAS I II III

KILLERS ON ELM STREET

JACK BOYZ N DA BRONX

By **Romell Tukes**

LOYALTY AIN'T PROMISED I II

By Keith Williams

QUIET MONEY I II III

THUG LIFE I II III

EXTENDED CLIP I II

By **Trai'Quan**

THE STREETS MADE ME I II

By **Larry D. Wright**

THE ULTIMATE SACRIFICE I, II, III, IV, V, VI

KHADIFI

IF YOU CROSS ME ONCE

ANGEL I II

By **Anthony Fields**

THE LIFE OF A HOOD STAR

By Ca$h & Rashia Wilson

THE STREETS WILL NEVER CLOSE

By K'ajji

CREAM

By Yolanda Moore

NIGHTMARES OF A HUSTLA I II

By King Dream
CONCRETE KILLAZ
By Kingpen
HARD AND RUTHLESS
By Von Wiley Hall
GHOST MOB II
Stilloan Robinson
MOB TIES
By SayNoMore
BODYMORE MURDERLAND
By Delmont Player
FOR THE LOVE OF A BOSS
By C. D. Blue

BOOKS BY LDP'S CEO, CA$H

TRUST IN NO MAN

TRUST IN NO MAN 2

TRUST IN NO MAN 3

BONDED BY BLOOD

SHORTY GOT A THUG

THUGS CRY

THUGS CRY 2

THUGS CRY 3

TRUST NO BITCH

TRUST NO BITCH 2

TRUST NO BITCH 3

TIL MY CASKET DROPS

RESTRAINING ORDER

RESTRAINING ORDER 2

IN LOVE WITH A CONVICT

LIFE OF A HOOD STAR

Renta